What Others Say . . .

Deepak Raja's work is surely the most important contribution to literature on *khayāla* vocal styles to come out in recent times. His minute and colourful analysis is astounding testimony to decades of deep aesthetic and intellectual engagement. His parsing of the formidable variables of *khayāla* style here is a real gift to those of us who have puzzled over the elusive qualities of this beautiful music. His essays on selected musicians are both enlightening and entertaining. I recommend this book to anyone who listens thoughtfully to India's classical music.

Prof. Allyn Miner
Department of South Asian Studies
University of Pennsylvania, Philadelphia, USA

Deepak Raja has adopted a unique kind of systematic analytical approach to the study of Hindustani music, which yields original and intriguing insights. Students and lovers of Indian music will find much that is compelling and thought-provoking in this book.

Prof. Peter Manuel
Professor of Music, John Jay College, New York, USA

This book is a pioneering effort in the study of Hindustani Music. I know of no previous work that pays as much attention to detailed analysis of the individual stylistic characteristics of the great vocalists of the past. Moreover, the analysis is firmly grounded in an extensive study of a large array of recordings. This feature by itself is a huge departure from the established norms in past writing on this subject, in which the treatment has been with a broad brush, thereby often leading to generalities that are not objectively sustainable. Here an attempt is made to impose some rigour in this process, by relying on material that is available for detailed analysis — such as recordings, interviews, and so on.

Here, Deepak Raja applies to stylistic analysis a metaphor he previously originated, applying ideas from the plastic arts to the study of *khayāla* styles. This metaphor involves looking at the total phenomenon of creativity in *khayāla* styles as a meld of three facets: an architectural facet, a sculptural facet, and an ornamental facet. This point of view is original, stimulating and effective, and provides a conceptual and analytical framework for understanding *khayāla* stylistics. The reader will find much here that is of interest historically as well as musically. This book should be required reading for every serious student of music whose vision goes beyond performance alone. We are in Deepak Raja's debt for an outstanding book.

Prof. Ramesh Gangolli
University of Washington, Seattle, USA

Basing the findings and conclusions on pointed instances from audio-recordings, using physical parameters for analysis and yet treating the art as an organic form, keeping the discussion restricted to the musician's music alone, the felicity in the use of language — all these impart objectivity, dignity and intimacy to Deepak Raja's writings on music. His deep knowledge of the music of the stalwarts and his eagerness to recognize and understand the music of the most recently risen artiste have carried this book ahead of and beyond the earlier writings on the *khayāla* music.

Prof. N. Ramanathan
Professor of Music (Retd.), University of Madras
Currently, Adjunct Professor of Music,
Chennai Mathematical Institute

Deepak Raja has achieved a unique synthesis of articulate musical description and thoughtful cultural background. He supports and respects the traditions of Hindustani classical music; but manages to achieve the personal distance necessary to avoid the emotional and analytic excesses of many volumes in this field. *Khayāla Vocalism* offers scholars an important alternative perspective on Indian musical priorities and thinking; it is essential for the interested listener (Indian or foreigner) who wishes to reach a better understanding of the most important vocal form in the classical music of 20th-century India.

Prof. Gregory Booth
Department of Ethnomusicology,
University of Auckland, New Zealand

I am not an authority on Indian Classical music to ably judge the scholastic quality of *Khayāla Vocalism*. But I know Deepak Raja and the dedication with which he works on a chosen project. Going through *Khayāla Vocalism* I was highly impressed by Shri Raja's expertise and deep passion for the subject. I am confident that readers will find his analysis of great value.

Mrs. Vijaya Mehta
Executive Director,
National Centre for the Performing Arts, Mumbai

Scholarly and meticulously researched, this is an extremely valuable book on Indian classical music.

Namita Devidayal
Author of ***The Music Room*** *(Random House, 2008)*

Like all Deepak Raja's writings on Hindustani music, including his earlier work, *Hindustani Music: A Tradition in Transition*, the present work too impresses with the knowledge, information, candour, analytical acuity and felicity of expression that he has brought to it. Art music is rarely written about in such a clear, readable manner.

Shanta Gokhale
Culture columnist and theatre personality

Assimilate like a student, analyse like a master, express like an artiste. This has been the hallmark of scholar-musician Deepak Raja's approach, making this wonderful book a seeker's destination and a reader's odyssey.

Ashok Roy
Author of ***Music Makers*** *(Rupa, 2004)*

To me Deepak Raja, or Deepakbhai as I call him, is a senior disciple, a talented musician, a respected journalist, a critical analyst of Indian music and a close family friend.

As an author, his first book *Hindustani Music: A Tradition in Transition*, written in lucid and scholarly language, is much in demand. His second book — *Khayāla Vocalism: Continuity Within Change* — projects profound analysis of the vocal form of *khayāla*. His conclusion which maintains "Continuity within Change" is indeed thought provoking. I am sure it will be extremely useful to academically interested musicians as well as aspiring students.

Pandit Arvind Parikh
Eminent Sitarist and President,
Indian Musicological Society

I have known Deepak Bhai for a long time. I have seen his association with my Ustād and father, Ustad Vilayat Khan and we have spent some wonderful times discussing music. His thoughts on our music and tradition I have always found to be very refreshing and I feel that he expresses them with a great amount of clarity. I always look forward to our meetings and our long chats.

Ustad Shujaat Khan, *Sitarist*

As in his earlier book — *Hindustani Music: A Tradition in Transition* — Deepak Raja continues to provide a fresher and analytic evaluation of the changing profile of the *khayāla* style in this book, covering all the major *khayāla gharānās* of Hindustani music. Continuity and change is profoundly explained by the author. Scholar, performer and connoisseur — all will benefit from the reading of this valuable book.

Prof. RC Mehta
Prof. of Music (Retd), M.S. Univ. of Baroda,
Founder-Editor, ***Journal of the Indian Musicological Society***

Deepak Raja's book on *khayāla* vocalism is a remarkable output of research done over the years. He is one of the most outstanding musicologists I have ever come across, not only because of the depth of his scholarship in the field, but also because of his ability to think like a very sensitive performer. I am definite there will be wide appreciation of this masterly work.

Prof. Sugata Marjit
North Indian Classical Vocalist and
Director, Centre For Studies in Social Sciences, Kolkata

During my work in the Musicology department of the National College of Arts, Lahore and in the Sanjan Nagar Institute I have found Deepak Raja's commitment to our classical music and his painstaking scholarship to be a very valuable asset. We have benefited greatly from his past writings and looking at his latest work I find it an even more valuable link in our fund of serious writings. We extend our gratitude and look forward to a further continuation of his important work in the realm of Indian Classical Music.

Raza Kazim
Director, Sanjan Nagar Institute of Musicology,
Lahore, Pakistan

Deepak Raja's contributions to *Śruti* magazine have been weighty in substance but also very readable, addressed to the serious music lover, not the scholar. He is an editor's delight; his copy needs no editing, and he has perfect understanding of the ideal length for the extremely readable profiles of *khayāla* musicians, which we serialized in *Śruti*, and appear in this book. Here's a role model for all aspiring writers on the arts — analytical and completely focused on the art and the process, not anecdotal like much writing we see in this genre.

V Ramnarayan
Editor, **ŚRUTI** *Magazine, Chennai*

KHAYĀLA VOCALISM

Continuity within Change

New Vistas in Indian Performing Arts

1. **Hindustānī Music and the Aesthetic Concept of Form**; by Anjali Mittal (ISBN 81-246-0134-8)
2. **Hindustani Sangeet and a Philosopher of Art** — Music, Rhythm and Kathak Dance *vis-à-vis* Aesthetics of Susanne K. Langer; by S.K. Saxena (ISBN 81-246-0180-1)
3. **Speaking of Dance** — The Indian Critique; by Mandakranta Bose (ISBN 81-246-0172-0)
4. **Performing Artistes in Ancient India**; by Iravati (ISBN 81-246-0207-7)
5. **Ritual as Ideology** : Text and Context in Teyyam; by T.V. Chandran (ISBN 81-246-0275-1)
6. **Tantra-Mantra-Yantra in Dance** : An Exposition of Kathaka; by Ranjana Srivastava (ISBN 81-246-0268-9)
7. **Hindustani Music** : A Tradition in Transition; by Deepak Raja (ISBN 81-246-0320-0)
8. **The Art of Tabalā Rhythm** — Essential, Tradition and Creativity; by Sudhir Kumar Saxena (ISBN 81-246-0368-5)
9. **Kathaka, The Tradition**— Fusion and Diffusion; by Ranjana Srivastava (ISBN 81-246-0473-8)
10. **Exuberance of Indian Dance** — Performer and Performance; by Utpal K. Banerjee (ISBN 81-246-0444-4)
11. **Khayāla Vocalism**: Continuity within Change; by Deepak Raja (ISBN 81-246-0481-9)

KHAYĀLA VOCALISM
Continuity within Change

by
Deepak Raja

Foreword by
Ulhas Kashalkar

Introduction by
Lyle Wachovsky

D.K. Printworld (P) Ltd.
New Delhi

Cataloging in Publication Data — DK
[Courtesy: D.K. Agencies (P) Ltd. <docinfo@dkagencies.com>]

Raja, Deepak, 1948-
Khayāla vocalism : continuity within change / Deepak Raja.
p. cm. (New vistas in Indian performing arts ; no. 11)
Includes bibliographical references.
Includes index.
ISBN 13: 978-81-246-0481-6 (HB)
ISBN 10: 81-246-0481-9 (HB)
ISBN 13: 978-81-246-0482-3 (PB)
SBN 10: 81-246-0482-7 (PB)

1. Khayāl – History and criticism. 2. Vocal music – India. 3. Musicians – India. 4. Hindustani music – History and criticism. I. Title. II. Series: New vistas in Indian performing arts ; no. 11.

DDC 782.009 54 22

First published in India, 2009

ISBN 13: 978-81-246-0481-6 (HB) ISBN 10: 81-246-0481-9
ISBN 13: 978-81-246-0482-3 (PB) ISBN 10: 81-246-0482-7

Published and printed by:
D.K. Printworld (P) Ltd.
Regd. office : *'Srikunj'*, F-52, Bali Nagar
Ramesh Nagar Metro Station
New Delhi – 110 015
Phones : (011) 2545 3975; 2546 6019; *Fax* : (011) 2546 5926
E-mail: dkprintworld@vsnl.net
Web: www.dkprintworld.com

To my mother
Smt. Kamlini Raja
who gave me my love of music
and of literature
and so much else!

Foreword

OVER the last 50 years scholars and critics of various backgrounds have interpreted the *khayāla* scene from different angles and enjoyed a wide readership amongst connoisseurs. Because the *khayāla* is the dominant genre of vocal music, and is evolving continuously, it is important that every generation of commentators contribute to the understanding of its basic features and contemporary trends. I am therefore happy to associate myself with the work of Deepak Raja and welcome this opportunity to share with his readers my views on the genre.

Definition

I believe the author is right in defining the *khayāla* genre relying largely on aspects of architecture, structure, and presentation protocol. I also endorse the manner in which he has dealt with issues of stance or demeanour — aloofness versus intimacy — pertaining to the definition of the genre.

Historically, the progression from *dhrupada* to *khayāla*, and *khayāla* to *ṭhumarī*, itself represents a steady relaxation of the atmosphere in classical music. Within *khayāla* itself, aloofness appears to have been the dominant feature of the traditional *khayāla* up to the first quarter of the twentieth century. Thereafter, there has been a drift towards informality. Today, aloofness cannot be considered fundamental to the *khayāla* genre. In fact, vocalists who have introduced emotionally explicit (or lively) elements of *ṭhumarī*, *ṭappā*, *bhajanas*, and folk music, into the genre have enriched it greatly, and sustained the interest of succeeding generations of audiences. The integrity of the *khayāla* is not threatened by the mere loss of aloofness. Its strength lies in its architecture.

Having said this, we must, of course, accept that genres of vocal music also differ in other respects. Technically, *khayāla* is like a median between *dhrupada* and *ṭhumarī*. It maintains the depth and rigidity of structure as in *dhrupada*, albeit to a far lesser degree. At the same time, it enjoys flexibility and allows for emotional appeal that *ṭhumarī* demonstrates, again in a far lesser degree.

While *dhrupada* emphasizes the *tāla* (the rhythmic cycle) and its *mātrā*s (beats and cadences), *khayāla* is more closely knit with the *ṭhekā* (the rhythmic cycle without reference to cadences) than the *tāla*. *Ṭhumarī* is *śabda-pradhāna* (poetry-dominant). In the *ṭhumarī*, the lyrics and their treatment are of utmost importance, while the poetry is given a secondary status in *khayāla*. Though there is considerable emphasis on the poetry in *khayāla*, *ālāpa* or *tāna*s in *ākāra* (non-poetic articulatory devices) too are common.

In *dhrupada* the *rāga vistāra* (elaboration) is done through Nom-Tom *ālāpa*. *Khayāla* (with the exception of Agra *gāyakī*) has more of *ākāra* based *ālāpa* or uses the words of the *bandiśe*s. This is perhaps related to the tradition of vocal music being accompanied by *bīna* or *Rudra vīṇā*. The *dhrupada ālāpa* is said to be of the *bīna aṅga*. The use of Nom-Tom *ālāpa* is a reproduction of this. And since *khayāla* vocalism was not bound by the *bīna* legacy, and the human voice has a longer breath span, *khayāla* musicians did away with the use of the Nom-Tom syllables and moved to clear open *ākāra*. Although the *laya* (tempo and progression) was maintained, it was not emphatically shown with Nom-Tom syllables. *Dhrupada* does not allow the use of *murkī*s, *khaṭkā*s, *tāna*s, etc. and these are features which *khayāla* has. The *saragama* is one articulatory device which is a recent addition to *khayāla*, but is not permitted in either *dhrupada* or *ṭhumarī*. *Khayāla* also allows use of a variety of *tānas*, *tihāīs*, *bola-bāṇṭa*, and other melodic forms and embellishments, which *ṭhumarī* cannot accommodate, because it has to stick to the poetry and cannot drift too far from its theme and emotional content.

Khayāla in Performance

Conceptual issues apart, a musical genre lives and evolves in, and through, its interaction with its audiences. A majority of audiences are not musically literate, and therefore, may not appreciate all the nuances of vocalism. But, one thing any musically sensitive person can receive is the emotional content of a raga. As long as a *khayāla* singer can use the available structure to communicate this content to his audiences, he does justice to his task.

In addition to the mastery over *svara*, *tāla*, and the architecture of the genre — which are basic — a vocalist succeeds by understanding the personality of the *rāga*, and the range of emotional statements it can make. Every facet of his rendition needs to reflect this understanding. Some *rāga*s provide a choice between various melodic facets and moods within the same basic grammar, while other *rāga*s have uni-dimensional personalities. The key to musicianship lies in knowing the difference between uni-dimensional and multi-faceted *rāga*s, and making a conscious choice where it is available. Once the choice has been made, it has to guide the choice of *bandiśe*s, the choice of *laya* and *tāla*, the approach to the unfolding of the *rāga*, and the overall tenor of presentation.

The melodic contours of *rāga*s and our ideas about their emotional possibilities have evolved over centuries in the Hindustani tradition. This is why I am often intrigued by the trend towards importing *rāga*s from the Carnatic tradition into Hindustani repertoire. In addition to differences in scales and intonation practices, the very notion of *rāga*-ness is very different in the two traditions. Admittedly, a few Carnatic *rāgas* like Ābhogī and Haṁsadhvani have been absorbed successfully into Hindustani system. But, as a general trend, I see severe limitations because there is no yardstick for validating the *rāga-svarūpa* (melodic personality) of Carnatic *rāgas* in Hindustani transformations. Without a yardstick, they may pass off as *dhunas* (*rāga*-neutral melodic entities), but are not likely to mature as Hindustani *rāgas*.

I can appreciate the attraction of Carnatic *rāgas* as a means of making our music more accessible to south Indian audiences. My experience, however, suggests this logic may not be particularly sound. When I perform in the south, concert hosts generally plead with me not to perform Carnatic *rāgas*. They want me to sing the mature Hindustani *rāgas* which they do not have in their tradition. It seems to me that, irrespective of the audience profile, the maturity with which we handle *rāgas* is far more important than either their novelty or familiarity.

Maturity and the Tradition

When we speak of maturity in handling a *rāga*, we have to acknowledge the role of *khayāla gharānās* in evolving different approaches to communicating the raga experience. Traditionally *khayāla* is described as *aṣṭa-āṅga* (having eight facets). But contemporary *khayāla* does not necessarily include these eight facets. Each *gharānā* has taken a few of these facets and invested several generations of musical energy in integrating them into a distinctive and coherent style. Along with this coherence and distinctiveness — and indeed consistent with these — each *gharānā* also specialised in certain *rāgas* and developed a distinctive approach to treating them.

The *gharānā* legacies allow each *khayāla* vocalist to shape his music with inputs from as many sources as he is exposed to, and evolve a new *śailī* (idiom) or sometimes even a new *gāyakī* (style). The beauty of *khayāla* lies in the fact that despite this individual freedom, the basic tenets of the *gharānā*'s musical philosophy remain intact. The evolution of a musician's vocalism also depends a lot on the individual's personality, and strength or weaknesses in certain departments of the craft or art. A direct result of this is evident in the fact that various disciples of the same *guru* have different, distinct styles.

A *gharānā* has therefore to be understood as the accumulation of musical wisdom, rather than a xeroxing machine. It is intended to liberate an individual's creativity without allowing it to drift towards disjointedness. A disciple who follows a *gharānā* has the liberty to express himself better with the principles and spirit of the *gāyakī* (style) ingrained in him. Even the deviations he makes will be within the periphery.

As opposed to this, a student who follows only an individual stylistic model — rather than the *gharānā*'s ideology— is limited by the role model's strengths and weaknesses. Such a vocalist is more likely to emerge as a clone. His music might represent maturity of a kind; but, perhaps not the kind that our tradition values.

While *gharānā*s are designed to ensure a degree of continuity, they are certainly not resistant to change. In the last 25 years musicians from all major *gharānā*-s have broken the shackles and have enlarged the aesthetic scope of their music. In other words several limitations of each *gāyakī* were overcome. For instance, Agra *gāyakī* underwent some change owing to musicians like Jagannath Buwa Purohit and, after him, Sharafat and Yunus Hussain. Contemporary Jaipur *gāyakī* too is different from the Jaipur *gāyakī* of Kesarbai Kerkar and Lakshmi Bai Jadhav. Gwalior too saw a change with the overall tempo of the music having slowed down. Even trail-blazing innovators like Kishori Amonkar and Kumar Gandharva have emerged from thoroughbred *gharānā* training.

Considering the strengths of the *gharānā* institution, no one can argue that it has no relevance today. Though the major *gharānā*s stand considerably weakened in recent years, their wisdom is not totally lost yet. The urgent need is to ensure the transmission of this wisdom from one generation to another.

How Khayāla Vocalism has Changed

With the weakening influence of *gharānā* stylistics over the concert platform, some of the specialist facets of repertoire also appear to be going out of circulation. For instance, Gwalior vocalists no longer perform sub-genres like *ṭappā-khayāla*s, *khayāla-numā*s, *aṣṭapadī*s and *caturaṅga*s, which were once the hallmark of the *gharānā*'s repertoire. Likewise, Agra vocalists no longer perform good *ālāpa* in Nom-Tom, or perform rare *rāga*s like Dhanāśrī, Barwā and Gara, which were once the pride of the legacy.

Today's performers are focused on technical finesse. Very few musicians do justice to the *ālāpa* of the *vilambita khayāla* which is the lifeblood of *rāga*-based music. They seem to be in a hurry to get to the second half of the rendition and shoot off *tāna*s at dazzling speeds. Though musicians of yesteryears also had amazing technical command in the *tāna*s department, they did not neglect the *ālāpa*. Their *tāna*s were rich in imagination and the melodic features of the *rāga* they were performing. Sadly enough, in the totality of today's *khayāla* vocalism, the spirit of the *rāga* is receding into the background.

This is why it is common experience that concerts of yesteryears have remained with listeners for ever. Today's music rarely leaves such a mark. Today's concerts charm listeners with their eclecticism and dazzling craftsmanship. They are unable to achieve the soulful quality of maestros such as Abdul Karim Khan. Today's musicians elicit thunderous applause from a naive audience and feel good about it. It worries me that today's youngsters are so easily carried away by such shallow attractions.

Another loss I lament is the replacement of the *sāraṅgī* accompaniment with the harmonium. The harmonium is unsuitable for accompanying vocal music; and its limitations are well known. We work with it because there are just not enough *sāraṅgī* players qualified to accompany mature vocalists. Quality musicianship is, of course, available amongst harmonium players. The younger amongst them are also getting around the limitations of the instrument. Some of their solutions are working pretty well. The present situation is not exactly unbearable. But, nothing can replace a good *sāraṅgī* accompanist as a partner in a *khayāla* performance.

I am also nostalgic about the quality of sound that the earlier generation of electronic equipment used to produce. I yearn for the warmth and depth of the sound we enjoyed when just one large rectangular microphone was considered sufficient to capture the singing, the *sāraṅgī* or harmonium, and the *tabalā*, and music was delivered through valve-type amplifiers. I am sure modern electronics can deliver equally good, or even superior, results. But, systematic research is needed on sound engineering for Hindustani vocalism, and an army of engineers needs to be trained to deliver better results. The need is urgent because a lot of discerning listeners are not happy with what they are getting today.

While the *khayāla* seems to be losing some of its valuable qualities, it has certainly also gained value in some respects.

When we listen to the musicians of yesteryears, we observe a certain indifference towards the application of technique and voice. While there was no compromise on the content, their relatively unrefined presentation and technique would perhaps face rejection in today's times. Today's musicians are, by comparison, more aware of the subtleties of presentation and have paid great attention to finesse. They have achieved improved voice production, a clean command of *svara* and *tāla* and adopt a gripping presentation format that appeals to audiences at different awareness levels.

Technology has simplified the lives of vocalists, even beyond the obvious. For instance, electronic *tānapūrā*s are today almost as authentic as acoustic *tānapūrā*s. And, they are getting better everyday. We no longer need to travel with our *tānapūrā*s and fear damage in transit, or worry about the availability of good *tānapūrā*s or *tānapūrā* players in different parts of the world. Two electronic *tānapūrā*s, embedded with sampler technology, work almost as well as acoustic *tānapūrā*s.

Today's musicians are as talented and hard working as serious musicians have always been. In terms of general exposure, education and awareness, they are way ahead of earlier generations of musicians. Their only weak point is that they lack the patience, composure and tenacity that classical music requires.

Grooming Khayāla Vocalists

The biggest threat to the future of *khayāla gāyakī*, and particularly to the continuity of *gharānā*-based training, is the shortage of competent *guru*s. Moreover, after Independence, cultural activity shifted to the metropolitan cities. In the cities, the *gurukula* institution (the traditional system of personalized training requiring the co-habitation of *guru*s and their disciples) could not survive. Even the *guru-śiṣya paramparā* (the sanctity and the intensity of the relationship between the teacher and the taught) is struggling. As a result, today, we have a surfeit of vocalists without a sense of direction, depth in communication of musical ideas and discipline in presentation.

The university system has proven itself incapable of producing quality musicians. A replica of the European conservatory may, or may not, work. In India, the closest we have to a successful nursery for *khayāla* vocalists is the Sangeet Research Academy (SRA), supported by ITC Ltd. In its 30 years, the institution has produced a few star performers, many A-grade radio artistes, and several very competent teachers.

Fortunately, quality music education has not yet become totally dependent upon corporate support. Though on a smaller scale than before, the *guru-śiṣya paramparā* still functions as an informal institution in the big city environment, and continues to produce good vocalists. We can only hope that this institution will survive.

Good Musicians and Successful Musicians

As a teacher, I am interested in the process by which we turn out good musicians, and how good musicians become successful musicians. After launching their careers, what musicians do with their training is partly a matter of destiny and partly of the kind of relationship they build with audiences.

There is no sure-fire formula for success. Many musicians believe that they have to make compromises with classicism, or deviate blatantly from the tradition, to achieve success. I am not sure if populism works as a strategy, considering that the audience for classical music is small. In a small market, the rewards of enlarging the appeal of your music can only be marginal. On the other hand, excellence pays off generously. When you sing to please yourself, and invite the audience to rise to your level of aesthetic sensibility, you are rewarded not only with artistic satisfaction, but also in terms of opportunities to perform, remunerations, social status, and quality of life.

I do not suggest that making a career in vocal music is a cakewalk. The path is strewn with frustrations and the temptation to explore short-cuts or even to abandon music in favour of safer careers. It takes a long time for a musician to turn into a mature artiste and convert it all into fame or financial success. The success that singers can achieve in popular music by the age of 25 or 30 is very rare in classical music. Even at the peak of their professions, which will usually come after 40, classical vocalists cannot expect to match the lifestyles of their peers in the popular music industry. Even with the utmost dedication to the cultivation of the art, the rewards may not be commensurate with the effort, because success depends a lot on public acceptance. And, as always, stardom will be achieved only by a handful.

While the struggle is cruel, the environment is broadly more supportive today than has ever been. Hindustani music has a bright future, with awareness of its richness growing all over the world. In recent years, international audiences, already enthusiastic about instrumental music and *dhrupada*, have also become receptive to *khayāla* vocalism. The corporate sector is maturing as a patron of the classical arts. There exists a demand today for every level of musicianship, albeit at its appropriate level of remuneration. Even struggling classical vocalists now have a variety of avenues available in the popular media to make a decent living — if they have the temperament for it.

In my view, the musician's inner struggle to achieve a maturity in the communication of musical ideas is far more important than his struggle to secure a place in the music market. Once the inner battle has been won, the market is more easily conquered. But, musicians are easily distracted from this truth, and audiences can easily become unsympathetic to musicians, while they are waging their inner struggles.

The Role of Scholars and Critics

The musicians' struggles — inner or outer — cannot be alleviated. But, they can be made more rewarding for those who strengthen the tradition. With this objective, we should value literature which helps musicians understand their struggles, makes audiences sensitive to the struggles of musicians, and holds both parties responsible for preserving and strengthening the tradition.

The media can do for classical music — though on a much

smaller scale — what they have done for cricket and the stock market. With the growth of intelligent analysis, and informed opinion expressed through the media, any field of activity can expect to enlarge its following, while also cultivating a small group of connoisseurs who bring maturity to its appreciation. Classical music cannot compare with cricket and the stock market for appeal to the mass media. But, good books can certainly reach out effectively to the classical music community in India and abroad.

Deepak Raja's present work is valuable in this context. He is thorough in his research, and writes with sympathy and insight on musicians of diverse backgrounds and levels of musicianship. This kind of analysis of *gāyakī* (vocal styles) and musicians may have appeared in academic literature. But, to the best of my knowledge, it has never been presented to the general public. The richness of his language and clarity in articulation will make this book widely accessible to readers all over the world. I hope that an enlarged edition of this work will follow soon, and cover many landmark musicians of the 20th century who do not find a place here.

I do not necessarily agree with Deepak Raja's views on the individual musicians covered in this book. But, it is not important that I should do so. He has a point of view, which is well argued and, therefore, deserves to be considered. I compliment the author on his achievement, and recommend his work to all music lovers and musicians interested in *khayāla* vocalism.

Pune, 30 January 2008 **Ulhas Kashalkar**

Preface

THIS book presents stylistic perspectives on the music of nineteen contemporary and modern *khayāla* vocalists representing some of the major stylistic traditions, and covers almost a hundred years of vocalism. These perspectives have emerged from my work as Repertoire Analyst for India Archive Music Ltd. [IAM], New York, between the years 1996 and 2005.

The literary product of this association appeared to possess value independently of the recordings it was originally intended to accompany. Some facets of this work have been published in *Śruti*, the performing arts monthly published from Chennai, and elicited an appreciative response. It seemed a worthwhile effort, thereafter, to conceptualize, recast, and rewrite all available writings on *khayāla* vocalism in the form of a book for reaching a wider audience.

In some respects, this book is a companion to my earlier book: *Hindustani Music: A Tradition in Transition*. The earlier book contains detailed backgrounders on the four major genres of Hindustani vocalism — *dhrupada, khayāla, ṭhumarī*, and *ṭappā*. For the reader's convenience, the chapter on *khayāla* from my earlier book is reproduced here as an annexure. However, this book also deals with the stylistics of *gharānās*, and with individual musicianship. This required a sharper conceptual-analytical approach to the genre. I have, therefore, written here a fresh chapter titled "Defining the *Khayāla* Genre". This chapter functions as a summary introduction to the *khayāla*, and aims at sharing with readers the conceptual tools directly relevant to appreciating the book.

Many readers will look askance at the selection of vocalists covered here. The selection was determined by the publishing arrangements contracted by IAM and assigned to me for documentation. It cannot, therefore, be subjected to a test of historical significance. The selection does, however, reflect a substantial degree of discernment, and spans a wider cross-section of musicianship than commonly covered by authors on Hindustani music. As a result, it delivers valuable insights into the recent interplay between continuity and change in *khayāla* vocalism. The big picture emerging from this selection defies easy conceptualization. But it is, I submit, more faithful to the socio-cultural reality than one that a purposive study of only landmark vocalists might have delivered.

The original purpose of interpreting the music of vocalists covered here was ostensibly "promotional." You are, therefore, permitted to suspect that the essays on individual musicians are essentially laudatory and uncritical. If, however, you permit the book to reveal its honesty, which may often surface between the lines, you will encounter writing that is sympathetic, descriptive, analytical, and without the remotest resemblance to advertising.

Either because of this, or despite this, it is expected that many readers will disagree with my interpretation of the stylistic tendencies of the vocalists covered. Several musicians — or their admirers — will also be displeased with what I have said about their music. This won't be the first time, or the last time, that critical writing will have met with such a response. It is a risk I accept without harbouring any delusion that my share of disagreements and annoyance will be smaller than that of others in my profession.

An important caveat to the observations in this book relates to the stage of life and performing career at which each of the vocalists has been studied. Each essay in this book has been documented for when it was written. Wherever possible, I have also documented the approximate period from which the sample recordings were drawn for study. In writing the essays, I have also been particular about pointing out the stage of life-cycle issues relevant to the understanding of the music. These aspects require your special attention, so that neither you, nor I, may be held guilty of misinterpreting a vocalist's musical personality.

The book, like all other works of this nature, is vulnerable to the bias of the author's stylistic preferences. Your only protection against this is the author's disclosure. Through the choices I have made as a student of music, and those made by members of my family, I have developed a special relationship with the music of the Kairana and Jaipur–Atrauli traditions. You may use this knowledge to judge the reasonableness of my observations.

This book is, essentially, neither about individual vocalists, nor about *gharānās* of *khayāla* vocalism. It is about continuity and change in *khayāla* vocalism. This focus appeared to warrant the grouping of vocalists into appropriate stylistic legacies. I have done so, knowing that a few classifications are debatable. The necessity of classification, and its controversy potential are, both, reflections of the contemporary socio-cultural reality.

The stylistic hallmarks of the *gharānās* have largely lost their grip over contemporary *khayāla* music. Despite this, contemporary vocalism has identifiable antecedents, and the link with the past — however tenuous and diffused — needs to be acknowledged. I have dealt with the *gharānā* phenomenon in elaborate detail in my earlier book. In this book, I have tried to explain my point of view, in brief, with a chapter titled "Stylistic Legacies in Khayāla Vocalism".

While the legacies provide a backdrop to the understanding of the general stylistic tendencies of vocalists, the analysis of musicianship must reckon with several dimensions which are individualistic. The framework for this appreciation is provided in a chapter titled: "Stylistic Perspectives on Individual Musicianship".

For understanding *khayāla* stylistics, I have drawn generously upon significant recent literature on musical aesthetics, and Hindustani vocalism. In accordance with publishing protocol, every idea or perspective attributable to a known source has been referenced. In order to keep the book reader-friendly, I have appended the numbered list of references to the introductory section of the book, while the body of the text merely carries the number of the reference cited.

Conforming to publishing conventions, all non-English words and terms have been italicized. The glossary at the end of the book attempts to explain all words in italics, especially to the reader unlettered in the Indian languages.

This book makes no claim to scholarship. In fact, I do not know if it belongs to any known genre of literature. It represents my way of interpreting what I have heard, and my way of sharing what I have understood. I place it in your hands in the hope that it will prove itself worthy of your time and attention.

Mumbai, 1 September 2008 **Deepak S. Raja**

Contents

Foreword — Ulhas Kashalkar xi

Preface xxiii

Acknowledgements xxix

Key to Transliteration xxxiii

Introduction — *Lyle Wachovsky* 1

SECTION 1: INTRODUCTION

1.1 Defining *Khayāla* Vocalism 3

1.2 Stylistic Legacies in Khayāla Vocalism 15

1.3 Stylistic Perspectives on Individual Vocalism 22

SECTION 2: THE AGRA LEGACY

2.1 Perspectives on the Agra legacy 28

2.2 Ustad Faiyyaz Khan 34

2.3 Sharafat Hussain Khan 44

2.4 Purnima Sen 52

2.5 Sugata Marjit 60

SECTION 3: THE GWALIOR–AGRA LEGACY

3.1 Perspectives on the Gwalior–Agra legacy 70

3.2 Yashwant Buwa Joshi 82

3.3 Ulhas Kashalkar 93

SECTION 4: THE JAIPUR–ATRAULI LEGACY

4.1 Perspectives on the Jaipur–Atrauli legacy 101

4.2 Surashri Kesarbai Kerkar 113

4.3 Dhondutai Kulkarni 128

4.4 Vijaya Jadhav-Gatlewar 137

4.5 Ashwini Bhide-Deshpande 146

4.6 Arti Anklikar-Tikekar 157

4.7 Manjiri Asnare-Kelkar 166

SECTION 5: THE KAIRANA LEGACY

5.1 Perspectives on the Kairana legacy 178

5.2 Sumitra Guha 193

5.3 Somnath Mardur 199

5.4 Mashkoor Ali Khan 206

5.5 Kaivalya Kumar 212

5.6 Rashid Khan 219

SECTION 6: THE PATIALA LEGACY

6.1 Perspectives on the Patiala legacy 230

6.2 Ustad Bade Ghulam Ali Khan 233

6.3 Bade Fateh Ali Khan 246

Annexure : An introduction to Khayāla 259

Glossary 281

Index 311

Acknowledgments

I ACKNOWLEDGE the blessings of Śrī Vighneśvara, who permits this endeavour to reach fruition and Śrī Naṭarāja and Mātā Sarasvatī who allow me access to knowledge of music.

My lifelong quest for knowledge of music has been guided by outstanding *gurus*, to all of whom I express my deepest gratitude (in chronological order): Shri Chandrakant Pandit (Gandharva), Shri Usman Khan Abdul Kareem Khan, late Shri Pulin Behari Deb Burman, Pandit Arvind Parikh, and Vidushi Dhondutai Kulkarni.

In the early-1960s, my Professor of Philosophy at Hindu College, Delhi, Dr Sushil Kumar Saxena, offered to oversee my grooming as an aesthetician. His aspirations for me remained unfulfilled. He gracefully pardoned my diversions and introduced me to his publisher, D.K. Printworld, as an ally for my work on music. I cannot thank Dr Saxena enough for his inspiration, kindness and affection.

In the 1970s, well before I became a professional journalist, three friends invited me to test my abilities as a writer on music: Vinod Mehta as Editor of *Debonair* magazine, Umaima Mulla-Phiroze as Managing Editor of the *Taj* Magazine, and M.J. Akbar as Editor of *Sunday* magazine. I seek the compassion of the abovenamed for the juvenility of my responses at a time when they were giving me a glimpse of destiny.

That I became a writer and, that too, a writer on music, owes a lot to departed friends, and mentors who had no idea of how they were contributing to this evolution. For their contributions, I gratefully salute the memory of Rev. Fr. Oesch, S.J., Chandrakant (Chandu) Kapadia, Narain Sadhvani (Sadi), and Patanjalee Amin.

For launching me as a writer on music with negligible proof of competence, I acknowledge my debt to Lyle Wachovsky, Managing Director of India Archive Music Ltd., New York. Since March 1996, he has kept me fully involved in his missionary task with rewarding work, unmatched friendship, and great depth of understanding. He has also given me a *carte blanche* for including any part of my work done for him in this book, and waived all copyright claims in my favour. For all his support, I remain most grateful.

My intensive and extensive exposure to recordings of India Archive Music Ltd. triggered off perspectives on several aspects of modern and contemporary music. In converting these into readable text, I have received invaluable encouragement from Kishor Merchant, Publisher of the *Mumbai Rasika*, and the late Dr. N Pattabhiraman, Founder-Editor of *Śruti*. After Dr Pattabhiraman's departure, his successors have continued to encourage my efforts. They deserve my sincere gratitude for the access they permit me to their esteemed columns.

My evolution as a writer has benefited greatly from the active involvement of a few friends, whom I have never met and may, perhaps, never meet. Because of their friendship, I have the satisfaction of having real people to address when I write. Else, I could have been vulnerable to the risk of addressing an assumed audience, the like of which may not exist anywhere on earth. Amongst these, I owe a special debt of gratitude to Ailsa Mathiesen in Canberra (Australia), Alessandro Dozio of Lausanne (Switzerland) and Eric Landen of Lake Forests (Michigan, USA), for their involvement in my work, and their willingness to find the time to scrutinize it before publication.

As a writer on music, my search for superior wisdom has led me repeatedly, and always fruitfully, to the doorsteps of three mentors (in order of seniority): my Guru, Pandit Arvind Parikh, the renowned musicologist, Prof. Ashok Ranade, and my learned friend, Dr Suvarnalata Rao. For their magnanimity and affection, I am deeply indebted to them.

In interpreting the styles of some of the vocalists covered in this book, I have been guided by the veteran musicologist, Prof. R.C. Mehta (b. 1918). This work would have been poorer without his affection and support.

Readers of this book will be staggered by the massive volume of recordings that has been studied in order to arrive at the perspectives presented in this book. All the recordings I needed for my research were generously loaned to me by three friends, who are substantial collectors of Hindustani music (in random order) — Mr Kishor Merchant of Bombay, Prof. Rohit Desai of Nadiad and Mr Bharat Jani of Ahmedabad. This book owes a great deal to their friendship and magnanimity.

The illustrations featured in this book have been made available to me from the archives of *Śruti* magazine/Samudri Archives, Prof. Rohit Desai of Nadiad, Shri Bharat Jani of Ahmedabad, and Mr Lyle Wachovsky of India Archive Music. Even if the illustrations play a relatively minor role in delivering the value of this work, their presence is important, and their donors are entitled to my appreciation. .

A majority of the contemporary musicians covered in this book willingly gave me interviews, and shared with me their perspectives on their music and their lives in music. Individually, they have contributed to more insightful essays on their own music. But, collectively, they have enriched my understanding of musicianship itself, and thereby rewarded my readers. I remain most grateful to them for their co-operation.

I owe a special debt of gratitude to my friend and graphic designer, Prof. Malti Gaekwad of the Faculty of Fine and Applied Arts, MS University of Baroda. Her professional competence and support have paid me rich dividends in the past and continue to do so.

The most direct contribution to this book has been that of my publisher, Shri Susheel Mittal of D.K. Printworld Pvt. Ltd., New Delhi. I am deeply obligated to him and his colleagues, for making my work acceptable to a discerning readership.

I admit, without hesitation, that without Pandit Ulhas Kashalkar's Foreword to this book and the Introduction contributed by Lyle Wachovsky, this book could have gathered dust on the shelves of many a bookstore. I express my deepest gratitude to them, and to the many well-wishers amongst authors, scholars, and musicians, who have previewed sample chapters of this book, and endorsed this work publicly.

My journey to this point would have been inconceivable without the support of my wife, Meena. She married a business executive, but ended up with a writer on music for a husband. For accepting the unpleasant surprises of life most gracefully, I remain indebted to her.

For all those — named or otherwise — who have made this book possible, I wish the satisfaction of having supported a worthy beneficiary.

Deepak S. Raja

Key to Transliteration

VOWELS

अ *a*	आ *ā*	इ *i*	ई *ī*	उ *u*	ऊ *ū*	ऋ *ṛ*	ॠ *ṝ*[1]
(Roman)	(palm)	(it)	(police)	(put)	(rule)	(rig)	
ऌ *ḷ*	ॡ *ḹ*[1]	ए *e*	ऐ *ai*	ओ *o*	औ *au*		
(able)		(there)	(aisle)	(no)	(loud)		

CONSONANTS

Guttural	क *ka* (skate)	ख *kha*[2] (blockhead)	ग *ga* (gate)	घ *gha*[2] (ghost)	ङ *ṅa* (sing)
Palatal	च *ca* (chunk)	छ *cha*[2] (catch him)	ज *ja* (john)	झ *jha*[2] (hedgehog)	ञ *ña* (bunch)
Cerebral	ट *ṭa* (start)	ठ *ṭha*[2] (anthill)	ड *ḍa* (dart)	ढ *ḍha*[2] (godhead)	ण *ṇa* (under)
Dental	त *ta* (path)	थ *tha*[2] (thunder)	द *da* (that)	ध *dha*[2] (this)	न *na* (numb)
Labial	प *pa* (spin)	फ *pha*[2] (philosophy)	ब *ba* (bin)	भ *bha*[2] (abhor)	म *ma* (much)
Semi-vowels	य *ya* (young)	र *ra* (drama)	ल *la*[3] (luck)	व *va*[4] (vile)	
Sibilants	श *śa*[5] (shove)	ष *ṣa*[5] (bushel)	स *sa* (so)	ह *ha* (hum)	
Others	क्ष *kṣa* (*kṣatriya*)	त्र *tra* (*triśūla*)	ज्ञ *jña* (*jñānī*)		

अं (ं) *ṁ anusvāra* is a nasal off-glide that immediately follows the pronunciation of a vowel as in *saṁskṛti*.

अः *visarga* = *ḥ* consists in abrupt release of breath after a vowel as in *prātaḥ*.

ऽ *Avagraha* shows non-pronunciation, that is, deletion of "a" after "e" or "o" as in *ime 'vasthitāḥ*. In Vedic ṣanskrit, it can also show word division.

HINDI LETTERS (extras)

ँ = *m̐*	ं = ṅ	ड़ = *ṛa* ढ़ = *ṛha*
(*candrabindu*)	(*anusvāra*)	

1 Longer form of the preceding vowel.

2 Aspirated forms of the preceding consonants. The compound words given as examples should be pronounced without a syllabic break at the underlined places. "tha" and "pha" should not be pronounced as fricatives.

3 retroflexed and written as "L *la*" in certain phonetic contexts.

4 Pronounced like "w," without aspiration.

5 "śa" is palatal; "ṣa" cerebral or retroflex.

Introduction

DEEPAK Raja's second book is a comprehensive study of *khayāla* vocalism through the stylistic analysis of nineteen contemporary vocalists. It is informed by the concept of "continuity within change," an approach which embraces "style" as the confluence of traditional *gharānā* stylistics, contemporary non-*gharānā*-based stylistics and each artiste's individual stylistic contribution. "Continuity within Change" is thus seen as an essential underpinning and strength of all Hindustani classical music, not just vocal music, and to a great extent responsible for its vitality and continued enjoyment by successive generations.

The expansiveness and thoroughness of Deepak Raja's investigations are immediately apparent as he lays out the parameters of *khayāla* vocalism drawing on notable scholarly sources to further document his analysis and make the case for his view of the elements that constitute *khayāla* vocal style. With similar attention to detail, Deepak Raja provides an overview of the stylistics of each *gharānā* intimately tied in with the crystallization of each *gharānā*'s style by the music of the seminal artiste of each *gharānā*, before delving into the analysis of individual contemporary artistes.

Seriousness of intent and comprehensiveness are to be expected, and as noted above, Deepak Raja has more than fulfilled expectations. But, the presentation of an incisive method of analysis coupled with clarity of vision in its use, is rare. Deepak Raja has always had a special interest in the presentation structure of *khayāla* vocalism. He has developed and expounds a critical approach based on the metaphor of architecture and uses it to great effect in his analyses, first identifying and delineating the basic *khayāla* structures in use and then, after distinguishing sculpture (the shape of a phrase) from its ornamentation, goes on to make a critical assessment of their usage. Writing on vocalists from both unique and varied stylistic backgrounds, Deepak Raja shows his method to be a valuable analytical tool applicable to all of them as a means of identification and comparison. This is a concise, well-considered methodology of comparative analysis, the brilliance of which is that its simplicity of application generates extensive results.

Equally valuable and fascinating are Deepak Raja's interviews with the artistes: he has a facility for extracting from each artiste an intimate and revealing portrait in words. These interviews together with the stylistic/structural analyses provide an unparalleled and integrated overview of each artiste's life and musical life as a *khayāla* vocalist, and of the state of contemporary *khayāla*.

It is personally gratifying to me that I was in the position to nurture the development of Deepak Raja's thoughts on the various aspects of *khayāla* music into a cohesive and integrated critical assessment of *khayāla* vocalism and *khayāla* vocalists. I am particularly pleased that Deepak Raja has been able to extrapolate so much from the diverse group of vocalists that I have chosen to record, a group that does not include many of the most famous names, but does include a fair share of less-known and virtually unknown artistes. Artistry of a high order and thoughtful individuality mark both the artistes examined and the resulting examination.

There is nothing quite like this wonderful book in my experience of Indian classical music analysis.

New York **Lyle Wachovsky**
07 August 2008

Section 1
Introduction

1.1

Defining the Khayāla Genre

In an oft-quoted description, Prof. Bonnie Wade[11] has described the *khayāla* genre of vocal music in the following words:

> *Among all Hindustani vocal genres, the khayāla provides its performers the greatest opportunity and challenge to display the depth and breadth of musical knowledge and skills. Its essence lies in the manner in which artistes take* ***the characteristics that distinguish khayāla as a genre****, make the choices that lie within their group traditions, summon their own creative individuality, and create a unique khayāla at each performace.* (Emphasis mine)

Interestingly, Prof. Wade has left the the distinguishing characteristics of the various genres for other authors to enumerate. I have attempted a definition of the *khayāla* genre in the backgrounder on *khayāla* published in my earlier book,[8] which is reproduced in this book as an Annexure. I wish now to rephrase the earlier definition, and welcome an opportunity of doing so.

> The *khayāla* genre is characterised by a linear (progressive) intensification of melodic and rhythmic densities and complexities, and a cyclical treatment of melodic elements within the central linearity of rendition. The manner in which the *khayāla* genre handles the relationship between its melodic and rhythmic facets distinguishes it most categorically from the two other mainstream genres of vocal music — *dhrupada* and *ṭhumarī*.

This formulation would have been obvious, if musicians

typically held conferences and passed resolutions to adopt norms for their art. Since such is not their style, the defining characteristics of the *khayāla* have to be inferred. The above definition commends itself as an inference based on the study of a wide stylistic spectrum of musicianship, spread over a period of almost a century.

Non-architectural facets (sculpture and ornamentation) have occasionally been suggested as additional defining characteristics of the *khayāla* genre. The practice of these facets, however, varies far too widely between stylistic traditions and individual musicians to justify inclusion in a definition. At least for the present, architecture appears to be the only feature that establishes the identity of the genre beyond reasonable doubt.

Sufficient evidence is available in archival recordings to suggest that the *khayāla* has drifted steadily towards linearity of architecture, thus conceding to it the status of a consensus. This is not surprising because, structure (architecture) and function (delivery of specific categories of aesthetic satisfaction) are inseparably related. There exists a variety of genres in Hindustani music because society requires them to deliver different categories of aesthetic satisfaction.

It is widely believed — perhaps correctly but without conclusive evidence — that linearity of architecture is the gift of the Kairana Gharānā to *khayāla* vocalism. Between the 1940s and the mid-1970s, however, this became, progressively, standard presentation protocol in all the major stylistic traditions of *khayāla* vocalism. Even Gwalior, Agra, and Jaipur–Atrauli traditions, which followed a less formalistic linearity till the middle of the 20th century, have thereafter drifted towards a more transparent linearity. This architectural feature can now be acknowledged as the direction which all *khayāla gharānās*/stylistic traditions have progressively, collectively and cumulatively given to it. It is therefore reasonable to assume that the practitioners of the art have considered its architectural linearity as the feature that delivers the desired category of aesthetic satisfactions, and sought to reinforce this feature in order to impart to the genre a distinctive identity.

It is fair to admit that, even today, the adherence to architectural linearity varies substantially between musicians. This divergence of practice does not appear to invalidate the definition I have proposed. The defining characteristic of the *khayāla*, or of any other genre, does not need to be mechanistically observed by every musician of every stylistic lineage in every rendition. Like any defining characteristic, linearity is a yardstick by which the concerned community identifies levels of compliance or deviance. The yardstick stands validated by the fact that all *khayāla* vocalists preserve even a semblance of linearity. The yardstick is also validated by the fact that the "establishment" frowns upon wilful and habitual breaches of linearity.

Since I have chosen to deploy a metaphor from the plastic arts to define the *khayāla* genre, the metaphor itself deserves some discussion.

The Plastic Arts Metaphor

I have discussed the use of the plastic arts metaphor in the context of Hindustani music in a paper titled "Architecture in Modern Hindustani Music" published in *Sangeet Natak* (Journal of the Sangeet Natak Akademi, New Delhi, vol. XXXVI, 1 November 2001). It will suffice here to reiterate the salient features of the analogy, as it affects the *khayāla* genre.

Every artefact can be seen to have an architectural facet, a sculptural facet, and an ornamental facet. The architectural facet relates to the structural and functional relationship between the components. The sculptural facet deals with the contours it defines. The ornamental facet concerns itself with features that aim explicitly to endear the artefact to the viewer. Stated differently, architecture deals with the manner in which the artefact functions, sculpture with the way it looks, and ornamentation with the way it seeks to please.

For interpreting artistic endeavour, metaphors are inadequate, but also unavoidable. It is observed that, traditionally, the visual and plastic arts appear to have provided the largest number of words and concepts for dealing with music. If a metaphor is the only way to handle art through language, and if the concepts and terminology of the plastic arts make the most sense to most people, it becomes advisable to systematize the metaphor and deploy it as a conceptual framework for the study of music.

The plastic arts metaphor is not only useful for interpreting the different facets of a piece of music, but also for classifying the aesthetic intent of different genres of music, different stylistic legacies in music, and even different musicians. It is possible, for instance, to describe genres of music as architecture-dominant, or sculpture-dominant, or ornamentation-dominant. Likewise, it is possible to classify individual musicians, or stylistic lineages (*gharānā*s) as being architecture-oriented, sculpture-oriented, or ornamentation-oriented.

Though not exclusively, this conceptual framework guides a great deal of the discussion on *khayāla* vocalism presented in this book.

The Terminology of Khayāla Architecture

In addition to graphic and plastic arts terminology, a discussion on the architecture of the genre needs to rely on words like "sub-genre," "movement," and "section" in a manner that makes their connotations contextually transparent, even when they are not categorically explained. These connotations may or may not correspond with the connotations the words carry in Western classical music. Of the words available to me for describing a particular architectural element, I have used the most appropriate word from the English language, and not from Western musicology. I make this observation in order to minimize the risk of confusion, especially amongst those who are well versed in the terminology of Western music.

The Linearity in Khayāla Architecture

The linear architecture of the modern *khayāla* is based on the assumption that the comprehension of an idea is best achieved when the stimuli are arranged in ascending sequence of density and complexity. By implication, therefore, any regression on either dimension is seen as dysfunctional to the communication of the idea.

The *khayāla* genre, as predominantly performed today, consists of two sub-genres, performed sequentially.

1. The *vilambita* (*baḍā*) *khayāla* performed at a slow tempo, with percussion accompaniment ranging from approximately 12 beats per minute (bpm) at the lower end to approximately 40 bpm at the upper.
2. The *druta* (*choṭā*) *khayāla* performed at a brisk tempo, with percussion accompaniment ranging from about 160 bpm at the lower end to approximately 240 bpm at the upper.

This structure establishes the first level of linearity in *khayāla* architecture.

There exists, in some stylistic lineages, an alternative practice of singing a *madhya-laya* (medium tempo) *khayāla*, with percussion accompaniment ranging from about 30/40 bpm at the lower end to about 50/60 bpm at the upper. In such cases, the vocalist may, or may not, append a *druta* (*choṭā*/fast tempo) *khayāla* as the concluding piece. The internal architecture of a *madhya-laya khayāla* rendition is, generally, akin to that of the *vilambita* (*baḍā*) *khayāla*.

The second level of linearity is established by the internal architecture of each *khayāla*.

In most cases, the *baḍā/vilambita* (slow tempo) *khayāla* consists of three distinct improvisatory movements. These movements are arranged in sequence for progressive intensification of melodic density (explicit intonations per minute). Though it is neither mandatory, nor universal practice, a majority of contemporary vocalists also choose to perform these movements with percussion accompaniment at progressively accelerated beat densities. The *baḍā/vilambita* (slow tempo) *khayāla* movements are:

1. *Ālāpa*: Low density melody, mostly anarhythmic, with improvised melody exhibiting only negligible, if any, correspondence with the beats of the rhythmic cycle.
2. *Bola-Laya*: Medium-density melody with a pulsation, and exhibiting a moderate-to-high correspondence with the beats of the rhythmic cycle.
3. *Tāna*s: High-density melody exhibiting one-to-one correspondence of melody with beats of the rhythmic cycle.

Though receding in recent years, there still is a practice, in some *gharānā*s, of doing away with the medium-density *Bola-laya* movement, and performing the *baḍā/vilambita khayāla* with only two improvisatory movements — low density and high density. Even with the omission of the intermediate medium density movement, the linearity of progression is preserved.

The *choṭā* (fast tempo) *khayāla* can have either only one or two distinct improvisatory movements:

1. Optionally, it could have an *ālāpa* as the opening movement. The *ālāpa* would be similar to the *ālāpa* of the *baḍā/vilambita* (slow tempo) *khayāla*.

2. *Tānas*: Similar to the *tāna*s movement in the *baḍā/vilambita* (slow tempo) *khayāla*.

As in the case of the *baḍā/vilambita* (slow tempo) *khayāla*, vocalists often choose an escalation of the accompanying percussion tempo during the course of the performance.

Cyclicity of Melodic Treatment

Since the primary focus of a *khayāla* is the unfolding of the *rāga*, the rendition follows well-established conventions for handling the melodic development. These conventions are more widely followed in low-density movements, wherein rhythm interferes the least with the melodic communication. The more fastidious structuralists amongst singers, however, also follow these conventions in medium-density melodic movements.

From this point of view, the most important movement is the *ālāpa* of the *baḍā/vilambita* (slow-tempo) *khayāla*. Mirroring the melodic protocol of the mediaeval *dhrupada* genre — the protocol itself probably predates *dhrupada* — the *ālāpa* of the slow-tempo *khayāla* is prescribed in four sections.

1. *Sthāyī*: This section undertakes melodic explorations in the lower half of the melodic canvas with the mid-point of the middle octave acting as the outer limit. The *sthāyī* always begins at the scale-base in the middle octave, travels downwards in steps into the lower octave, then travels upwards in steps, to the permissible limit, and returns to the scale-base of the middle octave.
2. *Antarā*: This section undertakes melodic explorations in the upper half of the melodic canvas with the mid-point of the middle octave acting as the separator. The *antarā* always starts at the mid-point of the middle octave, travels upwards, in steps, going as deep into the higher octave as the *rāga* permits, and then returns to the scale-base of the middle octave.

3. *Sañcārī*: This section covers the entire melodic canvas to summarize or highlight the salient melodic features of the *rāga*. The melodic structure of the *sañcārī* is left to the musician's imagination, and varies a great deal from one vocalist to another.

4. *Ābhoga*: This section wraps up the *ālāpa*, and finally folds up the canvas systematically unfolded in the earlier sections. The melodic structure of the *Ābhoga* is also left to the musician's imagination, and varies a great deal from one vocalist to another.

This four-section *ālāpa* is still evident in the *baḍā/vilambita khayāla* renditions of structurally fastidious *khayāla* vocalists like Kishori Amonkar. A significant number of vocalists today perform a three-section *ālāpa*, with a *sthāyī*, *antarā*, and a *sañcārī*. A vast majority, however, now perform a two-section *ālāpa* with only a *sthāyī* and an *antarā*. Despite the truncation of the presentation protocol in the *ālāpa*, the cyclicity of melodic progression is preserved. In contemporary vocalism, the elaborateness of the *ālāpa* appears to be determined by individual predilections more than a *gharānā*-based bias.

The medium-density *bola-laya* movement also generally follows an ascending-descending progression protocol, corresponding informally to the *sthāyī* and *antarā* sections described above.

Because of the variety of patterning options available, and the accent on the display of virtuosity in the *Tāna*s, the progression protocol in the high-density segment becomes more informal than it is in the medium-density *bola-laya* section. However, once again, structurally meticulous vocalists attempt to explore the melodic canvas with an approximation of the *sthāyī-anatarā* logic in the *tāna*s section, too. In such an approach, the *Tāna*s will start with melodic runs in the lower one-third of the melodic canvas, proceed thereafter to melodic runs centred in the mid-octave region of the middle octave, and culminate in *tāna*s concentrated in the upper one-third of the melodic canvas, to finally return to the scale-base in the middle octave.

In the music of disciplined musicians, the progression protocol for the *tāna*s section will be evident not only in the rendition of the *baḍā/vilambita* (slow tempo) *khayāla*, but also the *choṭā/druta* (fast tempo) *khayāla*.

Deployment of Musical Energies

While every major genre is distinguished categorically from others by its architecture, the major genres also differ from each other in terms of the deployment of musical energies in performance between the different facets.

The mediaeval *dhrupada* genre requires musical energies to be deployed primarily towards preservation of its architectural integrity.[7] The modern *khayāla*, on the other hand, demands the sculptural facet of performance to be the primary focus of musical energies. The *ṭhumarī* (the *bola-banāva* variety) differs from *dhrupada* as well as *khayāla* by demanding musical energies to be concentrated on the ornamental facets.

Allied to this is the relative importance of the elements that constitute vocal music — poetry, rhythm, and melody. In this respect, the *dhrupada* genre accords the highest sanctity to its poetic element, followed by its melodic element. The *khayāla* genre accords great importance to the melodic element, followed by the rhythmic element. The *ṭhumarī* genre (the *bola-banāva* variety) is once again a poetry dominant genre, though with melody almost competing with poetry for importance.

Manipulation of Musical Variables

Every genre of vocal music requires the manipulation of three musical variables — poetry, rhythm, and melody, but not in the same manner.

Dhrupada requires the isolated manipulation of melody in the *ālāpa*, which constitutes the durational bulk of the performance, and is performed generally without percussion accompaniment.[7] There is, indeed, a pulsation/beat involved in the second and third stages of *ālāpa* rendition, but mere pulsation does not constitute rhythm. In the rendition of the *pada*, the relatively shorter part of *dhrupada* rendition which is accompanied by percussion, the musician undertakes the simultaneous manipulation of poetry, melody, and rhythm.

Khayāla begins with a very short *ālāpa* (called an *Auchara*) which is pure melody, and is unaccompanied by percussion. Thereafter, *khayāla* rendition is accompanied by percussion throughout. From the beginning of the *baḍā/vilambita khayāla*, to the end of the *choṭā/druta khayāla*, the *khayāla* genre requires the simultaneous manipulation of poetic, melodic, and rhythmic variables.

The *ṭhumarī* genre (the *bola-banāva* variety) demands the simultaneous manipulation of poetic and melodic variables, with only negligible manipulation — if at all — of the rhythmic variable.

Demeanour

The veteran music critic, Mohan Nadkarni[6] has referred, with grudging acceptance, to recent deviations from the "formal aloofness" of the *khayāla* genre. Since aloofness belongs to the territory of demeanour, it presumably refers to the non-architectural predilections encountered in the *khayāla* genre. Nadkarni's suggestion that the *khayāla* could be defined by its demeanour in addition to its architecture (formalism), deserves discussion in the context of suggestions by some scholars, notably Prof. Peter Manuel, relating the rise and decline of genres in Hindustani music to socio-economic change.

The mediaeval *dhrupada* genre, which achieved its highest stature and excellence between the 15th and 18th centuries, has been interpreted as reflecting the authority and majesty of the Mughal Empire at its zenith. The ascendancy of the modern *khayāla*, as well as the *ṭhumarī* (both varieties), is synchronous with the decline of feudalism and the rise of bourgeois capitalism, which sought more effective vehicles for sentimental musical ideas. Manuel equates *dhrupada* with the feudal values of heroism and the *khayāla* and *ṭhumarī* with the relaxed mores of bourgeois society.

If the *khayāla* and the *ṭhumarī* are products of the same socio-cultural process, we cannot rule out the possibility that — at some stage of socio-cultural evolution — the two genres, interacting as contemporaries, would create a blurring of the distinctions between them.

Glimpses of this tendency were observed early in the 20th century. It may have begun as an attempt by the *khayāla* to invade, and annexe, the aesthetic space being gradually vacated by the *ṭhumarī*. By the third quarter of the 20th century, the *khayāla*'s encroachment over *ṭhumarī* territory had taken the form of a romanticist movement, spearheaded by Kumar Gandharva, Jasraj, and Kishori Amonkar.

Although this movement is, in parts, also revolting against formalism, it has been, primarily, a revolt against aloofness. The breach of formalism (architectural values) has not attained any substantial degree of acceptability within the establishment. But, the breach of aloofness has been fully accepted. Romanticism is now on the march, virtually threatening the survival of classicism.

On these considerations, it appears more than reasonable to exclude issues of demeanour from a definition of the *khayāla* genre, and restrict the definition to architectural linearity. But if, and when, the establishment is forced to reckon with the post-structuralist/post-modernist revolt against architecture, the present approach to defining the genre will require a review.

1.2

Stylistic Legacies in Khayāla Vocalism

THE essence of music making in the *khayāla* genre, as described by Prof. Wade (cited earlier), refers to three components of a *khayāla* rendition: (a) managing the characteristics that distinguish the genre from others, (b) making the choices that lie within the artiste's group traditions, and (c) harnessing the artiste's own creative individuality.

In the earlier chapter, we have considered the characteristics that distinguish the *khayāla* genre from its major contemporaries. In this chapter, I deal with the "group traditions" which constitute the choices available to the vocalist in the process of harnessing his/her creative individuality.

The notion of group traditions is better appreciated as the second tier of the tradition operating below the top tier, which we may call the "Grand Tradition". At both levels, the notion of a tradition remains valid because (a) being transmitted aurally from one generation to another, it remains unwritten, (b) it has a binding force legitimized by society, and (c) it allows for individuality and diversity, and therefore constant change.

Using an analogy from the world of information technology, the Grand Tradition (higher level) may be broadly described as the "Operating System" of Hindustani vocalism, while the group traditions may be broadly described as the "Applications Software." As in the case of computer software, the two tiers of tradition interact with each other over time, allowing widespread and major routines/features emerging in the group traditions (application software) to get incorporated into, or reflected in, or added to, the Grand Tradition (operating system).

The Grand Tradition

The first tier (higher level) Grand Tradition governs the "matter" of the music and the architecture of the genre performed. In this context, the matter consists of the universe of *rāga*s which constitutes the melodic raw material for Hindustani music, the universe of *tāla*s, which constitutes the rhythmic raw material, and the universe of *bandiśe*s which constitutes pre-composed poetic-melodic-rhythmic entities which function as the nucleus of *khayāla* presentation. The architecture of the genre, which we have discussed as the primary — if not the sole — differentiator between the major genres, provides the structure for the improvisatory effort involved in *khayāla* presentation.

Just as a large number of application packages draw upon a group of utilities and capabilities of an operating system, several group traditions function as distinctive and, in many ways, specialist interpreters of the Grand Tradition. Like any computer user, the *khayāla* vocalist deploys one of these group traditions (application packages) to create a unique piece of music at each rendition.

A *khayāla* vocalist thus makes stylistic choices at two levels, though these choices need not always be conscious or well-considered decisions. The first choice is made in terms of following one of the several group traditions (or sometimes a combination of them) for interpreting the Grand Tradition. The second level of choice is made in terms of the extent to which, and the manner in which, the group tradition will influence his/her *khayāla* renditions.

The question then arises: Why does the cultural process involve a group tradition as an intermediate interpreter of the

Grand Tradition when individual musicians could well handle the entire task themselves ?

The Answer is Simple

The Grand Tradition is too vast for an individual musician to absorb and process into something brilliant as well as original. But, once in a while, a genius comes along, who selects a segment of the Grand Tradition, and interprets it in an irresistibly innovative fashion. Each time the work of such a genius emerges on the scene, it acquires a following, and a new group tradition gets launched. Several successive generations of its followers work on the musical vision in order to progressively enhance its aesthetic coherence and its distinctiveness. With several such products of distilled musical wisdom (Group Traditions) available to choose from, the task of the individual vocalist becomes more manageable. He/she has only to adopt the prototype that corresponds best with his/her temperament, and determine his/her individuation effort in terms of the degree and manner of compliance with it.

Group traditions are thus, collectively, a phenomenon which gives every musician a wide choice of highly developed stylistic directions, and gives audiences a variety of mature stylistic prototypes interpreting different parts of the Grand Tradition.

Group Traditions as Stylistic Legacies

These Group Traditions, known as *gharānā*s, are major stylistic legacies, which have ruled *khayāla* vocalism for almost two centuries, and continue to be a force today, despite socio-cultural forces militating against their relevance. A *gharānā* means, literally, a household or a clan. The term was appropriate for defining a stylistic legacy in the era of hereditary musicianship, when everything conspired to make each musician a near-clone of the earlier generation. After the hold of kinship over musicianship loosened, tutelage links were still able to sustain the concept of a *gharānā*, though only as a stylistic lineage. In the contemporary context, with the grip of both kinship and tutelage over performance having been eroded, even the notion of a stylistic lineage is frequently questioned.

Despite this, the music of contemporary vocalists has a reference point in the past, and its antecedents are discernible to the cultivated listener. Though the *gharānā* terminology may have lost its relevance, my enquiries reveal that the stylistic prototypes — by whatever means assimilated — evolved by the major *gharānā*s have neither lost their usefulness to vocalists, nor their relevance to critical literature.

An elaborate discussion of the *gharānā*s is included in my earlier book[8] and does not warrant repetition. In this book, I recognize the contemporary reality by describing the group traditions as "stylistic legacies" rather than *gharānā*s. But, in deference to the requirements of familiarity, I have retained the names of the *gharānā*s, as commonly reported in recent literature on *khayāla* vocalism.

The Major Stylistic Legacies

In the third quarter of the 20th century, when the *gharānā*s were beginning to lose their grip over *khayāla* vocalism, considerable scholarly attention was accorded to the contribution they have made to the evolution and perpetuation of distinctive styles within the genre. The first major work on this subject was that of Vamanrao Deshpande[1], followed thereafter by Prof. Bonnie Wade.[1]

Deshpande[1] recognizes six major *gharānā*s as distinctive stylistic lineages: Agra, Gwalior, Jaipur–Atrauli, Patiala, Indore and Kairana. Wade also recognizes six major *gharānā*s, though her listing differs from Deshpande's. She lists Agra, Gwalior, Rampur-Sahaswan, Jaipur–Atrauli, Kairana and Patiala. In her opinion, the Indore/Bhendi Bazaar Gharānā is too close to Kairana to qualify for independent status. She acknowledges, however, the status of Ameer Khan, the principal exponent of the *gharānā*, amongst the towering originals of *khayāla* vocalism.

Deshpande[1] offers a conceptual framework for the aesthetic classification of the *khayāla gharānās*. He classifies their styles on a continuum defined by rhythmic orientation and melodic orientation as the two polarities. With reference to the two extremities, Deshpande observes that rhythm is the principle of motion, while melody is the principle of repose. The bias towards rhythm end indicates animation, playfulness, and dynamism, while a bias towards the melody end is soothing, tranquillizing, and even depressing.

Amongst the *gharānās* listed by him, Deshpande[1] places Agra at the rhythmic orientation polarity, and Kairana at the melody orientation polarity, with all the other *gharānās* falling somewhere in between on this scale.

He places Jaipur–Atrauli and Gwalior at the exact midpoint, but making a conceptual distinction between the two. He describes Gwalior as a simple fusion of melodic and rhythmic elements, while regarding Jaipur–Atrauli as a complex fusion. Patiala is placed towards the melodic orientation pole, though considerably short of Kairana. The Indore/Bhendi Bazar Gharānā of Ameer Khan falls between Patiala and Kairana towards the melody-oriented half of the spectrum.

Wade adopts a more elaborate framework for comparing *gharānā* stylistics. The important dimensions she lists are:

(a) Voice, vocal technique, voice quality, range, ornamentation.

(b) Preferences with respect to *rāga*s.

(c) Preferences with respect to *tāla*s.

(d) Preferences with respect to compositions.

(e) Preferences with respect to performance tempo and its acceleration during rendition.

(f) Balance between melodic and rhythmic elements.

(g) Structure (architecture) of the *baḍā/vilambita* (slow tempo) *khayāla* rendition.

(h) Preferences with respect to improvisatory movements and types of articulation.

By adopting different approaches to interpreting the Grand Tradition, the major *gharānā*s/group traditions/stylistic legacies have provided the *khayāla* genre with a rich variety of highly evolved stylistic tendencies and shaped the Golden Age of Hindustani music.

While this is, indeed, so, it is necessary to recall Deshpande's valid observation that the greatest vocalists of the Golden Age have been, almost without exception, products of multiple *gharānā*s. To this extent, it is necessary to recognize the individualistic character of *khayāla* vocalism, and to understand the stylistic legacies merely as a bank of stylistic resources on which the individual vocalist draws in order achieve a combination of aesthetic coherence and individual creativity.

Profiling of Gharānās/Stylistic Legacies

The essays on individual musicians covered in this book have been organized into separate sections, each covering a different stylistic legacy of *khayāla* vocalism. The legacies covered are (in alphabetical order):

(i) The Agra legacy
(ii) The Gwalior–Agra legacy
(iii) The Jaipur–Atrauli legacy

(iv) The Kairana legacy
(v) The Patiala legacy

Each section begins with a brief history of the *gharānā*, and a discussion on its stylistic legacy. These backgrounders also include notes on the different streams of the legacies and the music of some of the landmark musicians of each stream wherever archival recordings were available for study.

Classification of Vocalists by Legacy

In the backgrounders on each stylistic legacy, I have listed the musicians I have classified under the legacy, and attempted to explain the logic for the classification. In most cases, the justification arises from a combination of tutelage history and the stylistic tendencies evident in the music. However, where the history of tutelage is either ambiguous or diffused, I have relied on the stylistic tendencies alone to classify the vocalist. It is my hope that readers will agree with my classification of vocalists in most, if not all, cases.

1.3

Stylistic Perspectives on Individual Vocalism

IN the earlier chapter, I have dealt with the role of group traditions/stylistic legacies as banks of mature prototypes, drawing upon which the individual *khayāla* vocalist attempts to express his/her own individual creativity. In this chapter, I attempt to outline the methodology and the conceptual framework employed in the process of analysing individual musicianship, and communicating a sense of it in this book.

The Brief

My brief for myself was to answer three basic questions about each musician covered in this book: What is the music? How did it come to be what it is? What is the significance of this musician, or his/her music, within the stylistic legacy, or the Hindustani tradition, and perhaps, even in the totality of the cultural process? As a brief, this was admittedly over-ambitious in the specific context. However, as a direction for the enquiry, it was valuable.

The Methodology

The study of each vocalist began, typically, with one recording intended for release, and a biographical note on the artiste. With this as the starting point, the enquiry has generally taken the following steps:

(a) One recording, made on one day, is not sufficient for making even reasonably reliable observations on the musical inclinations of the vocalist. The study had to be based on a much larger sample of the musician's recordings. So, a larger sample was acquired from co-operative sources, whom I have named and thanked in the acknowledgements.

(b) On a preliminary auditioning of the sample, and from the biographical information available, it was possible to identify the stylistic legacy, or a combination of legacies, to which the musician subscribed. Once this was done, it became necessary to acquire sample recordings of the artiste's *gurus* and/or seniors within the legacy to serve as a reference point for elements of continuity/change, and conformity/deviance.

(c) The next step was to do a comparative analysis of the sample recordings of the musicians, with their *gurus*/seniors on all facets of the music. This was the most time-consuming stage of the research.

(d) Once this had been completed, the stage was appropriate to start relating the art to the artiste in terms of musical as well as non-musical facets of his/her personality. The biographical information provided by the artiste was the starting point. Referencing of published information was done for additional facts and insights. In a majority of cases, contemporary musicians also willingly gave interviews providing further biographical information and a perspective on their art, and sometimes, on life itself. All interviews were tape-recorded in order to avoid the risk of misrepresentation.

(e) Once these procedures were completed, the study of each vocalist was ready for reporting. In no case was the draft of the report submitted to the musician for either comments or approval. If any of the essays in this book has been read by the musicians covered, it could only have been read in print. In fact, many of the essays have undergone substantial change of perspective even after they appeared in print.

Conceptual Framework

The conceptual framework for interpreting individual vocalism necessarily derives from that considered appropriate for the *gharānās*/stylistic legacies. It must, however, obviously include several concepts that are uniquely appropriate for understanding individual vocalism. I list below the various dimensions of musicianship I have attempted to tackle in this book.

1. ***The voice***: Pitch, timbre, range, and cultivation.
2. ***The repertoire***: Biases in terms of genres of music, *rāgas*.
3. Approach to the handling/exploration/treatment of *rāgas*.
4. The approach to architecture, sculpture and ornamentation.
5. The approach towards poetic, melodic, rhythmic and dynamic (volume and timbre) aspects of the music.
6. The approach towards the pre-composed element and its relationship with the improvisatory facets of rendition.
7. The approach to the deployment of articulatory devices through the different movements.
8. ***Temperament and demeanor***: This refers to the seriousness or otherwise of the approach to music, introversion/extroversion of the music, and aloofness

or otherwise of the relationship the vocalist attempts to establish with the listener.

9. ***Assessment of the music*** against the backdrop of the stylistic legacy to which the vocalist belongs/appears to belong and, where relevant, the Grand Tradition. Degrees and areas of conformity and deviance.

10. ***Stage of life cycle***: This refers to the stage of life cycle/performing career at which the music and the musician have been studied. Every observation on either must be read with the caveat that musicians evolve, and even posthumous perceptions of musicians can change over time.

11. ***Stature, popularity, and significance***: This refers to the achievements of the vocalist at the stage of his/her career at which he/she is being written about.

12. ***Background factors***: This refers to all the factors that go into the making of a musician, relating to family history, socio-economic background, grooming in music, formal education in music and/or other disciplines, experience as a performing musician, and the relationship with the art, including engagement in musical activities other than performing.

While all the above facets were considered for the study, individual essays report facets only to the extent that they may appear significant in the particular case. In a few cases, the scope of the enquiry may have been limited by the non-availability of inputs from musicians.

Sequencing of Essays

This book was not conceived as a historical or evolutionary study, either of *khayāla* vocalism, or of the *gharānā*s/stylistic legacies. Despite this, the essays on individual vocalists have been sequenced chronologically by the date of birth of the musician — within each section covering a stylistic legacy. In addition to being non-controversial, this mode of sequencing was adopted because it appears to allow more than a suggestion of continuity within change.

References

1 Vamanrao H. Deshpande, 1973, *Indian Musical Traditions — An Aesthetic Study of Gharānās in Hindustani Music*, Bombay: Popular Prakashan, 2nd edn., 1987.

2 Vamanrao H. Deshpande, 1989, *Between two Tānapūrās*, Bombay: Popular Prakashan.

3 B.R. Deodhar, 1993, *Pillars of Hindustani Music*, Bombay: Popular Prakashan.

4 Peter Manuel, 1989, *Thumaree in Historical and Stylistic Perspectives*, Delhi: Motilal Banarsidass.

5 Ramanlal Mehta, 1993, *Agra Gharānā — Paramparā, Gāyakī, aur Ceeẓ*. Hindi. 2nd edn., Faculty of Performing Arts, MS University of Baroda.

6 Mohan Nadkarni, 1999, *The Great Masters — Profiles in Hindustani Classical Vocal Music*, Delhi: Harper Collins.

7 Deepak Raja and Suvarna Rao (ed.), 1999, *Perspectives on Dhrupad*, Baroda: Indian Musicological Society.

8 Deepak Raja, 2005, *Hindustani Music — A Tradition in Transition*, New Delhi: DK Printworld.

9 Ashok D. Ranade, 1984, *On the Music and Musicians of Hindoostan*, Delhi: Promilla & Co.

10 Carl Seashore, 1967, *Psychology of Music*, Minneola, NY: Dover Publications.

11 Bonnie C. Wade, 1984, *Khayāla — Creativity Within North India's Classical Music Traditions*, London, New York: Cambridge University Press.

Section 2
The Agra Legacy

2.1

Perspectives on the Agra Legacy

THIS chapter deals with those aspects of the Agra legacy which are immediately relevant to appreciating the stylistic tendencies of musicians covered in this book.

In recent times, the stylistic legacy, known as the Agra Gharānā, has been virtually defined by the music of Ustad Faiyyaz Khan (1886–1950). Faiyyaz Khan's music represented a convergence of two traditions founded in the 18th century — the Agra Gharānā, traced to Ghaghe Khudabaksh (1790–1880) and his brother Janggu Khan (1791–1852), and the Rangeele Gharānā, traced back to Ramzan Khan "Rangeele" (1759–1806). Agra vocalism is also closely associated with the Atrauli Gharānā, represented by Inayet Hussain Khan (1845–1936), mentioned in recent literature as the founder of the *gharānā*. By the time of Faiyyaz Khan's arrival, these lineages had forged strong matrimonial links and institutionalized the training of each other's progeny, thus effectively merging into what is now known as the Agra Gharānā.

Like a majority of *khayāla gharānā*s, the Agra, Rangeele and Atrauli Gharānās were founded by erstwhile exponents of the medieval *dhrupada* genre. What is significant, however, is that Agra vocalism retained *dhrupada*, not only as a pedagogical discipline, but also as a part of its repertoire. While Faiyyaz Khan enlarged the repertoire of the lineage further by excelling in the semi-classical genres, *dhrupada* itself, along with the *dhrupada*-inspired *khayāla*, remained the mainstay of Agra vocalism.

Veteran musicologist, R.C. Mehta[5] attributes the dominant aspects of Agra's post-*dhrupada* stylistics largely to its retention of *dhrupada* as a performing tradition, and the *gharānā*'s continued adherence to the *dhrupada* philosophy as the foundation of *khayāla* vocalism. I rely substantially on his work for this discussion.

Agra Stylistics

The Agra Gharānā is known for its full-throated and aggressive vocalization, inspired by some streams of *dhrupada* vocalism. This approach to voice production and delivery gives it a bias towards staccato intonation, and a marked angularity of melodic contours. Consistent with this bias, Agra vocalists tend to deploy the bolder forms of melodic execution from the *dhrupada* genre, such as *gītkīrī, khaṭkā* and *gamaka* to the near-exclusion of delicate ornamentations such as *murkī* and *kan*, more frequently found in *khayāla* vocalism of other lineages. The bias towards staccato intonation suppresses the role of *mīṇḍa* in Agra vocalism. In recognition of these features, Agra vocalism has been described as masculine. After Faiyyaz Khan, however, a progressive softening has been observed in the Agra Gharānā's approach to vocalization and the handling of intervallic transitions. This is a response to the growing sophistication of the acoustic environment, and to the challenge from melody-oriented rival styles.

The Agra tradition treats the *bandiśa* as the principal vehicle of the *rāga* in rendition. This, too, is a carry-over from the philosophy of the *dhrupada* genre. Not surprisingly, therefore, the *gharānā* has been a prolific composer of *bandiśes*, which have become immensely popular. The *bandiśes* of the Agra maestros have, indeed, even contributed to the preservation of some of the rare *rāgas*.

Teaching several *bandiśe*s in each *rāga* has been the *gharānā*'s means of imparting knowledge of *rāga*s to its members. The centrality of the *bandiśa* to the *gharānā*'s ideology is extended to the treatment of the *rāga* in performance. The poetic-melodic-rhythmic frame of the *bandiśa* provides the building blocks for the *ālāpa*, *bola-bāṇṭa*, and the *tāna*s movements. This differs substantially from some *gharānā*s (e.g. Kairana), which treat the *rāga* as an abstract melodic entity in the improvisational movements.

Although the *gharānā* tends to do the *ālāpa* in *bola-ālāpa* as well as *ākāra* articulation, the bias is clearly in favour of the *bola-ālāpa*, with the *bandiśa* itself providing the nucleus of phonetic and melodic material for the improvisation. The predominant use of poetry provides vowels, consonants, and potential for emphasis, required of the phrasing strategy, which relies on melodic angularities. The same approach is evident in the *gharānā*'s handling of medium-density *bola-bāṇṭa* improvisations, which Mehta[5] argues, are inspired by the *layakārī* (playful engagement of poetry and melody with rhythm) in the *dhamāra* sub-genre of *dhrupada*, associated with the spring festival of Holī.

The same inspiration explains the practice of rendering phrases and lines of the *bandiśa* in multiples of its pre-composed tempo (*dogunā/tigunā/caugunā*) in the *bola-bāṇṭa* section. The treatment of *tāna*s — primarily *bola-tāna*s — in the Agra tradition is consistent with this bias towards an explicit rhythmicality. This tradition is perhaps unique in its strong inclination towards multiple intonations per *svara*, with its 3-stroke and 4-stroke *tāna*s, akin to the last stage of the *druta ālāpa* in *dhrupada*, or the pattern of *tāna*s on the plucked instruments in the early 20th century. Irrespective of their melodic patterning, the *tāna*s of Agra vocalists always keep one eye on the rhythmic cycle, and its metric subdivisions.

The use of the *bandiśa* as the primary vehicle of *rāga*

presentation has given rise to an interesting practice, called *Mukhaḍā-bandī*, in Agra vocalism. The practice involves taking up a phrase from the pre-composed *bandiśa*, and converting it into a pseudo-mukhaḍā for improvisations around it. This creates an illusion of the musician having drifted virtually into a different *bandiśa*, until he returns to the main *bandiśa* to restore the aesthetic equilibrium of the rendition. This practice has been inspired by the *ṭhumarī* genre and greatly enhances the colourful quality of *khayāla* renditions.

In his book on Agra stylistics, Mehta presents a plausible, and elaborate, case for treating Agra vocalism predominantly as a transposition of *dhrupada* ideology to *khayāla* vocalism. This transposition, he points out, imparted a lively quality to *khayāla* vocalism, which was unique, and also immensely popular in its heyday. He also observes that, in the process of "*dhrupad*-izing" the *khayāla*, Agra vocalists also ended up "*khayāl*-izing" *dhrupada*. As a result, he avers, their *dhrupada* renditions ceased to pass muster as orthodox *dhrupada*.

A transposition of *dhrupada* ideologies into *khayāla* has inevitably taken place in other *gharānā*s too. But, in none of these cases have the vestiges of *dhrupada* stylistics remained as transparent as in the Agra Gharānā.

Faiyyaz Khan was the great integrator of Agra/Rangeele and Atrauli styles. But, even amongst his disciples and close associates, there were descendants of the Atrauli clan, whose stylistic inclinations were different from his. Even if the differences were minor, they were attributable to the residue of Atrauli stylistics, which had resisted the assimilative genius of Faiyyaz Khan. In a personal discussion on 24 January 2003, Prof. Mehta gave me a few insights into the differences. Agra was much more firmly entrenched in the poetic element of the *bandiśa* and its musical potential than Atrauli. The latter, by comparison, was more involved with melody and rhythm independently of poetry. As a result, Atrauli tended to be more expansive in its treatment of the *baḍā khayāla ālāpa* portions, and took longer to introduce the rhyhmicality of *bola-bāṇṭa* into the rendition than Agra does. The Agra *ālāpa* is, by comparison, more compact. Mehta also believes that, in all the movements, Atrauli music relied more on the element of surprise than Agra music did.

This view is broadly supported by the recordings of Ata Hussain and Sharafat Hussain, both of Atrauli stock, made available to me by Purnima Sen, who studied with both of them. The recordings I studied were of Ata Hussain's *ālāpa* and *dhamāra* in Darbārī, and a *choṭā khayāla* in Rāmakalī. On both these recordings, he is accompanied by his nephew, Sharafat Hussain, also of Atrauli stock. In addition, she provided a recording of Faiyyaz Khan accompanied by Ata Hussain. Ata Hussain's music displays a remarkably subdued rhythmicality in his vocalization, and a greater concern for melodic niceties than Faiyyaz Khan. The staccato intonations and sharp melodic angularities of Faiyyaz Khan's music are greatly subdued in Ata Hussain's music. This small sample — far from being conclusive evidence — suggests that Atrauli stream probably did represent the softer side of Agra vocalism.

Coverage of Vocalists

In this section, I include essays on the music of Ustad Faiyyaz Khan, Sharafat Hussain Khan, Purnima Sen, and Sugata Marjit. The classification of the first three within the Agra legacy poses no problems because of their pedigree by tutelage and the quality of their music. The last, Sugata Marjit, may be debated.

I place him in the Agra legacy on the basis of two factors. Firstly, despite the multiplicity of *guru*s he has had, his most substantive training has been under a disciple of the Rangeele Gharānā, which is now a part of the Agra legacy. Secondly, although his music is unorthodox, and has little in common with others discussed in this book, his cheerful approach to music making — wanting to make people dance — is consistent with the lively philosophy of the Agra lineage. On this evidence, the classification appears defensible.

2.2

Ustad Faiyyaz Khan
The Radiant Sun of Music

If any musician in living memory enjoys as fanatical a following as the football clubs of Calcutta, it is Ustad Faiyyaz Khan. His fans, though mostly above 80 now, will even come to blows to have him acknowledged as The Musician of the 20th century. Faiyyaz Khan (1886-1950) was, without doubt, the most versatile, popular and influential musician all through the second quarter of the 20th century. This was formidable stature in an era endowed with giants in every *gharānā* of *khayāla* vocalism.

He shot into prominence at the age of 20 with a brilliant performance at the Mysore court. When Faiyyaz Khan was 25, the Maharaja of Mysore granted him patronage, and later conferred on him the title of *Aftab-e-mausheequi* (the radiant sun of music). At the age of 32, he was appointed to the Baroda court. Over the next 30 years, he built up a towering national presence with Baroda as his base. He regaled three generations of audiences with *dhrupada, dhamāra, khayāla, ṭhumarī, ṭappā, dādarā, ghazala,* and *bhajan.*

He brought his Agra Gharānā to the forefront of modern vocalism, and even won the pioneering musicologist, V.N. Bhatkhande's admiration. With his command over Braj Bhāṣā (his mother-tongue) and *rāga* grammar, he composed many *bandiśes* in popular and rare *rāga*s under the pen-name "Prem Piyā." In the sunset years of feudal patronage, he contributed immensely to popularising classical music. Several of his songs entered films through the voices of K.L. Saigal, Lata Mangeshkar and Manna Dey, and remain a part of our heritage of popular music.

Faiyyaz Khan was described as the "Emperor of the concert platform." No vocalist after him, except possibly Bade Ghulam Ali Khan, has held his audiences captive in abject surrender like he did. According to Ranade, he was not satisfied with aesthetic realization of a musical idea. His music was driven by the passion for the conquest of audiences. To achieve this purpose, he freely used devices from *dhrupada, khayāla,* and semi-classical genres in any of the genres, supported by the unique acoustic potential of his booming, gruff, low-pitched, voice. His music was not only for the ears, but also for the eyes. He sang with his body as well as his voice. It was cheerful, extroverted music, involving, and dominating at the same time.[9]

Faiyyaz Khan in Classical Music

In classical music, Faiyyaz Khan is considered the tallest exponent of the Agra Gharānā in recent history. His father, a descendant of the Rangeele Gharānā (Ramzan Khan Rangeele 1759-1806) died before Faiyyaz Khan's birth. Faiyyaz was brought up and trained by his maternal grandfather Ghulam Abbas Khan and grand-uncle, Kallan Khan of the Agra Gharānā. According to some accounts, his paternal uncle, Fida Hussain Khan of the Rangeele Gharānā, also trained him. However, there is unanimity over Ghulam Abbas, who reportedly lived to be 110, having been his principal mentor. In addition to training young Faiyyaz in *dhrupada*, and *khayāla* for 20 years, Ghualm Abbas took him along on his concert tours of six to eight months a year, and enabled the budding phenomenon to hear the greatest vocalists of the time.

Faiyyaz Khan's music was rooted in the robust expression and ponderous movement inherited from the *dhrupada-dhamāra* genre. The "Nom-Tom" *ālāpa* became a mainstay of his repertoire, not only for *dhrupada*, but often also *khayāla*. In fact, he found this form so attractive for an unfettered exposition of the *rāga*, that he often deployed it for stand-alone concert presentation. With his fine sense of poetics, he developed a "conversational" technique of articulating selected words from the song-text, and allowed his *khayāla*s to communicate a modicum of literary value. He combined this with the exploitation of volume and timbre variations to achieve an incredibly powerful delivery of musical meaning.[9]

Despite a vast inventory of rare *rāga*s, Faiyyaz Khan restricted his concert repertoire largely to common and popular *rāga*s. He wanted to bring music closer to his audiences, and protect its enjoyment against bewilderment. He sang *vilambita khayāla*s a little quicker than they are sung today, but *druta khayāla*s a little slower. His *tāna*s never attempted the *svara*-density of present-day vocalists. In his music, *svara* and *laya* were both handled within the bounds of intelligibility, liveliness, and musicality.

Faiyyaz Khan in Semi-Classical Music

In the lighter genres, Faiyyaz Khan was largely self-taught.

He travelled frequently to Lucknow and Benares to study the *ṭhumarī* and allied genres as practised by the leading courtesans of the era. He acquired a vast collection of songs in the semi-classical genres — some of them erotic, and even downright obscene. He often rendered them with the seductive mannerisms typical of courtesans.[4] In its totality, his semi-classical repertoire probably added a lot to his popularity without, surprisingly, diminishing his stature.

The Music of Ustad Faiyyaz Khan

No concert recordings of his are known to exist. For understanding his music, we must rely either on 78 RPM discs, or largely unpublished radio broadcasts. In either case, we are looking at a poor representation of the original. The 78 RPM tracks have been digitally re-mastered by HMV, while private collections of radio broadcasts are often mutilated, and in terrible acoustic condition. Despite the aural discomfort, I chose to study a sample of radio broadcasts because of their longer durations (15-20 minutes).

The sample for this survey consists of 31 pieces of music, of which 11 are only partially recorded. The repertoire in the sample recordings is as follows: Only *ālāpa*: (five), *ālāpa* + *vilambita khayāla*: (two), *vilambita khayāla* only: (one), *ālāpa* + *druta khayāla*: (four), *druta khayāla* only: (eight), *vilambita khayāla* + *druta khayāla*: (one), *dhamāra* + *druta khayāla*: (one), *bola banāva ṭhumarī* (four), *dādarā* (two), *Ghazala* (two), *ālāpa* + *dhamāra* (one). Except for a few rare *rāga*s like Lacarī Toḍī, Kapar Gaurī, Nāta Bihāga, Paraj and Bhairava Bahāra, the melodic spectrum is dominated by *rāga*s considered popular and common even today. While this sample covers almost all the genres Faiyyaz Khan is known to have performed, we have no way of determining how representative this sample is — either of his radio broadcasts, or of his concert music.

Totally, we have 12 *ālāpa*s in this sample. Faiyyaz Khan's

*ālāpa*s deploy the Nom-Tom articulation borrowed from the *dhrupada* genre. However, the presentation format diverges from the *dhrupada* protocol. The anarythmic *vilambita ālāpa* of *dhrupada* is largely omitted in the sample recordings. Typically, they begin directly with pulsating *madhya-laya ālāpa,* and progress to the *druta ālāpa.* A *vilambita ālāpa,* as understood today, is evident in only two of the *ālāpa*s surveyed. Here too, staccato intonation restricts the aural experience of pure melody unhindered by pulsation. In the *ālāpa*s, Faiyyaz Khan feels free to use *saragama* articulation, a feature not heard in later Agra vocalism.

The sample provides four *vilambita khayāla*s. In almost all cases, the *ālāpa* movement is either missing, or has only a negligible presence. The movement, when included, mostly hovers around the melodic contours of the *bandiśa*. Since the *bola-ālāpa* is known to have been an important element of Faiyyaz Khan's music, it would appear that the *ālāpa* truncation was a concession to the limitations of the duration of a radio broadcast. The *vilambita khayāla*s in the sample concentrate a good deal on *bandiśa* rendition, and tend to move directly into the pulsating *bola-bāṇṭa* movement. The medium density *bola-bāṇṭa* and the high-density *tāna* movements are not consistently treated as distinct and sequential movements. It is not unusual for *tāna*s to be sandwiched between rounds of *bola-bāṇṭa,* or even punctuate the easy flow of *bola-ālāpa* passages. There are also instances of *tāna*s being followed by prolonged *bola-bāṇṭa* or even *ālāpa*-like improvizations.

Interestingly, only a generation after Faiyyaz Khan, when Bade Ghulam Ali Khan exhibited a similar casualness about the *khayāla*'s linear architecture, he was accused of jeopardising the future of Hindustani music. This raises the possibility that, in Faiyyaz Khan's era, the distinctive architecture of the *khayāla* was still in a state of evolution. Not having made a clean break from the *dhrupada* legacy, Agra was slower than others in aligning itself with the emerging architecture of the *khayāla*. This view is supported by the more compliant formalism of later, but otherwise orthodox, Agra vocalists such as Khadim Hussain and Latafat Hussain.

Faiyyaz Khan exhibits, and perhaps inspired, another feature of Bade Ghulam Ali's *vilambita khayāla* renditions. Their *bola-ālāpa* and *bola-bāṇṭa* movements frequently deployed vivacious passages typical of the *ṭappā* genre. Faiyyaz Khan's Gwalior contemporary, Krishnarao Pandit, also adopted such expressions, probably inspired by him. Those who consider this feature to be Bade Ghulam Ali's innovation, are probably misplacing the credit.

There are a total of 14 *druta khayāla*s in the sample. The rendition of these *khayāla*s is dominated by the *bandiśa* itself. The improvisatory movements open with *bola-bāṇṭa*, and medium density *tāna*s, predominantly using the *gamaka* form of melodic execution. The density is then stepped up to a higher level. However, several of his *druta khayāla*s end with *bola-bāṇṭa*, omitting the *tāna* movement altogether. Faiyyaz Khan's *tāna*s are predominantly broad-span passages of simple melodic construction and immense vigour. He uses *bola* as well as *ākāra* articulation. His *tāna*s are primarily of the *ekaharā* (single intonation per *svara*) variety, with repetitive intonation restricted to *gamaka* execution. Only rarely in this sample does Faiyyaz Khan use the 3-stroke and 4-stroke intonations, for which Agra *tāna*s later became famous. In the present sample, there are very few instances of *tāna*s being rounded off with *tihāī*s, for the effective use of which he was renowned.

The sample has two *dhamāra*s. The presentation format is conventional, with the *bandiśa*, followed by *layakārī*. On these recordings, he renders *dhamāra* at a tempo of 120/130 beats per minute, at least twice the beat-density we have generally heard in mid-20th-century *dhamāra*s. At this tempo, the reluctant rhythmicality of the *tāla* does not appear to get justice. I am reliably informed, however, that this acceleration was a concession to the time constraints on radio. At concerts, Faiyyaz Khan's habitual tempo for *dhamāra* was much slower.

We have four *ṭhumarī*-style renditions in this sample. Unfortunately, all are of the *vilambita* Dīpacaṇḍī variety, with no representation of the *madhya-laya tīnatāla*, which he reportedly sang often. The renditions in this sample are faithful to the protocol of the genre, and handle the melody with tender expressions, intricate phrasing and ornamentation typical of the genre. However, for present-day listeners, exposed to *ṭhumarī* by Siddheshwari Devi and Bade Ghulam Ali Khan, these seem less than convincing manifestations of the aesthetics of the genre. In all likelihood, the problem lies in the forceful vocalisation and staccato intonation, which are fundamental to Faiyyaz Khan's vocalism. These tendencies appear to interfere, though to a lesser extent, also with the rendition of the two *dādarā*s in the sample. They are a little more satisfying because of the more pronounced rhythmicality of the *dādarā tāla* and genre, compared to the subdued rhythmicality of Dīpacaṇḍī.

The two *ghazala* in the sample are interesting for their diversity of treatment. The *ghazala* in Pīlū-Khamāja is treated more like a *bola-banāva ṭhumarī*, along with *ṭappā* style ornamentation of phrases, and even *tāna*s. With such features, the *ghazala*, a genre originally intended to exploit the anticipatory delight of the poetic meaning of rhyming alternate lines, appears to acquire a completely different complexion. This *ghazala* rendition establishes the qualities that inspired film-music composers, and the legendary singer-actor, K.L. Saigal, reportedly an avid follower of Faiyyaz Khan's. The second *ghazala* in Paraj is closer to the *ghazala* form as presently performed.

Amongst 20th-century luminaries of the *khayāla* world — Abdul Kareem brought his audiences to tears, Ameer Khan pulled them into a trance, Kesarbai had their jaws dropping in awe, and Faiyyaz Khan made them dance.

The Faiyyaz Khan Legacy

It is common, and proper, to assess a musician's place in history by the durability of his legacy — his style of music and his recordings. Superficially, the Faiyyaz Khan legacy appears to perform less brilliantly than his stature would lead us to expect. However, in the larger context of the cultural process, the picture is luminous, though complex.

Recordings of about 100 of Faiyyaz Khan's radio broadcasts are believed to exist in private collections, and are reportedly in appalling condition. All India Radio, which owns all the recordings, has been unable to release the Faiyyaz Khan archive. A small part of the AIR archive, perhaps all of four *rāgas*, is available on HMV cassettes. In the grey market for archival music, the circulation of Faiyyaz Khan recordings is negligible. Enquiries with the leading music stores will reveal that digitally remastered 78 RPM compilations of Faiyyaz Khan are moving poorly compared to those of his major contemporaries.

For almost two decades after Faiyyaz Khan's departure, the Agra Gharānā did not produce a front-ranking performer. When his brilliant foster-son and disciple, Sharafat Hussain, appeared on the scene in the late 1960s, he had to struggle for acceptance, and moderate the masculinity of his style substantially to suit contemporary musical values. Today, even Sharafat's subdued masculinity has few admirers. All this raises the suspicion that the Faiyyaz Khan stylistic legacy is at an advanced stage of aesthetic obsolescence. This is not unique, as obsolescence of artistic expressions is an inescapable consequence of socio-cultural change.

Faiyyaz Khan fans have often tried to narrow the issue of obsolescence down to his voice production and delivery, both cultivated for an acoustic environment devoid of electronic amplification. Separating the technique from style smacks of sophistry, because the issue is fundamental. The voice technique conditions the acoustic, articulatory and melodic experience, and these three govern everything else that is covered the meaning of "style" in vocal music. His vocalization technique may be explainable as a response to his acoustic environment. But, in a different environment, this fact cannot protect it against its aesthetic consequences. Though aesthetic obsolescence is inevitable, the speed with which the roar of Faiyyaz Khan has faded away from the music scene is, indeed, one of the unsolved mysteries of modern music history.

The siege of the Agra fortress had begun before Faiyyaz Khan's rise to prominence. In the early 20th century — a more primitive acoustic environment than Faiyyaz Khan's — Ustad Abdul Kareem Khan (1872-1936) and Ustad Alladiya Khan (1855-1946) founded highly influential *gharānā*s. Their Kairana and Jaipur–Atrauli styles threw up a galaxy of outstanding musicians starting from around 1940. Omkarnath Thakur (Gwalior), already a front-ranking vocalist in Faiyyaz Khan's era, continued to perform through the 1950s. In the next generation, Bade Ghulam Ali and Ameer Khan, and D.V. Paluskar — all of rival *gharānā*s — contributed immensely to pushing the Agra style off centre-stage. From a historical perspective, it appears that the aesthetic values of the post-Faiyyaz Khan period disfavoured robust, aggressive music with a strong rhythmic bias.

It is inconceivable that Agra's aggressive, *laya*-biased brand of *khayāla* vocalism could suddenly become an unattractive repository of musical value with Faiyyaz Khan's departure. In the new aesthetic environment, it was probably required to transform itself in order to reclaim audiences. Faiyyaz Khan's foster-son, Sharafat Hussain, and Vilayat Hussain's son, Yunus Hussain, commenced the process, but neither lived long enough to give it sufficient impetus.

However, Faiyyaz Khan did set off numerous currents whose momentum outlives him, even if in a less obvious form. Amongst them, the two most significant deserve special attention. One is a lineage launched by his disciple, S.N. Ratanjankar, who headed the Marris College of Music at Lucknow. The other is a confluence of Gwalior and Agra vocalism, engineered by his Agra kinsman and associate, Vilayat Hussain Khan, and his disciples.

The Ratanjankar stream produced scholar-musicians like K.G. Ginde, S.C.R. Bhat, and Dinkar Kaikini in the second generation (this list is not exhaustive), who have excelled as teachers, but failed to emerge as frontranking performers. It was the Gwalior–Agra confluence, which gave the performing tradition a new direction. Faiyyaz Khan's influence motivated some accomplished Gwalior-trained vocalists to seek the tutelage of two great Agra Gharānā teachers, Vilayat Hussain Khan and his disciple, Jagannath Buwa Purohit. This development produced distinguished musicians like Gajananrao Joshi, Ram Marathe, V.R. Athavale, and Yashwant Buwa Joshi (the list is not exhaustive).

Through this confluence, the Faiyyaz Khan/Agra legacy revitalized Gwalior vocalism, while also transforming itself into a style more acceptable to contemporary audiences. Although Agra stalwarts also trained vocalists from other *gharānās*, it was the Agra-Gwalior confluence that made the distinctive stylistic statement, and turned out to be more durable.

This may seem like a trickle considering the tidal wave that was Faiyyaz Khan. But, it exists, and that makes it significant. Today, Gwalior and Agra stylistics remain visibly in circulation almost entirely through the Agra–Gwalior confluence. This is no small compliment to the vitality of Ustad Faiyyaz Khan's legacy (Written : January 2003).

2.3

Sharafat Hussain Khan
The Modernizer of Agra Vocalism

IF the legacy of the Agra titan Ustad Faiyyaz Khan is receding from the musical culture, it is largely because Sharafat Hussain Khan came too late and departed too early. Over four decades separated his arrival from the heyday of his foster father and *guru*, Faiyyaz Khan (1886-1950). In this interregnum, audience profiles had changed, and the absence of a truly great performer from the Agra tradition had surrendered the stage to rival styles. Sharafat modernized Agra vocalism, and acquired a cult-like following. He succumbed to cancer at the age of 55. Before his exit, he secured his place in the history of 20th-century vocalism as the last of the Agra greats.

Sharafat (1930-85) rose meteorically after his adoption by Faiyyaz Khan at the age of eight. He made a stunning debut in

Bombay at the age of nine, cut his first 78 RPM disc at twelve, and in the same year, topped the prestigious Baroda State Music Competition. Starting from the age of about 35, he enjoyed a continuous run of success until he could perform no more. He was made an Honorary Fellow of the Uttar Pradesh Sangeet Nataka Akademi, and decorated with the Padma Shree by the President of India. In 1985, the apex Sangeet Natak Akademi held a special ceremony at the hospital in Delhi to honour him shortly before he breathed his last.

Despite his stature, Sharafat's legacy of commercial recordings is meagre. During his lifetime, HMV recorded one long-playing disc of his (EGSD-2495). In the 1990s, several years after his demise, the company released another title (STCS-02B-6212) from his concert archives. Sharafat's friends and admirers made a limited edition twin-cassette release of his concert recordings in the mid-1990s. The accustic quality of this effort is indifferent, and availability negligible. The recording industry's neglect cannot, however, cost him his place in history, thanks to the connoisseurs' grey market, where his concert recordings are still traded. The other significant facet of his legacy is the body of over 200 *bandiśes* he composed in popular as well as rare *rāgas*, under the *nom de plume Prema Raṅga*.

Impeccable Pedigree and Explosive Talent

Sharafat Hussain Khan was a scion of the Atrauli clan, and the son of Ustad Liaquat Hussain Khan, a court musician in the erstwhile Jaipur State. After being trained by his father till the age of eight, Sharafat was adopted by Faiyyaz Khan and groomed as his heir.

Of all the disciples of Faiyyaz Khan, Sharafat was the sole recipient of face-to-face tutoring. Others learnt by listening to the Ustad and accompanying him at concerts. Because of his prodigious talent, the great Ustad trained Sharafat with a velvet glove, and gave him the freedom to perform solo at an age when any other disciple would have been on probation. Sharafat was 20 when Faiyyaz Khan died. His training continued in the remaining years with his maternal uncle, Ata Hussain Khan of the Atrauli lineage. When Sharafat got married, he acquired a third guide — his father-in-law, Vilayat Hussain Khan of the Agra lineage.

Sharafat was fond of performing common *rāga*s like Mālkauṅs, Darbārī Kānaḍā and Jaijaivantī. Bharat Jani of Ahmedabad, an avowed admirer of Sharafat's and owner of a substantial archive, provided a list of 50 *rāga*s that he has either heard from the Ustad, or whose concert recordings he owns. Over two-thirds of the *rāga*s can be heard frequently on the concert platform even today. Besides these, Sharafat specialized in *ṭhumarī* — mainly in Bhairavī and Khamāja. These have been the forte of the Agra Gharānā, and most definitively, of Faiyyaz Khan before him.

Sharafat's friend, the musicologist, M.R. Gautam thought he treated music "like a game and actually played with it." Vocalist Purnima Sen, his disciple, does not recall ever seeing him do special riyāẓa for a concert. Before commencing his recital, he would merely meditate for a couple of minutes. Thereafter, simple *rāga*s, complex *rāga*s, common *rāga*s, rare *rāga*s, and even esoteric *rāga*s, came out with equal facility. His musicianship could often extract a great deal of complexity out of simple *rāga*s.

He was a vivacious performer. He had a melodious and bold voice, exceptionally endowed with colour and texture. The feature which most helped him reform Agra vocalism was the absence of the grating quality that characterized orthodox Agra vocalization. His musical expressions could be as effectively virile as they could be seductive. Gautam recalls his brilliant flashes of ornamentation in *rāga* development, interesting rhythmic syncopations, and uncanny twists to the *rāga*, *tāla*, or *bandiśa*.

This profile draws upon a volume published in his memory by his disciples. The volume also reveals the private side of his life — his devotion to his family, his calibre as a teacher, his distaste for metropolitan life, his insistence on residing in his native Atrauli, and his passion for fishing and hunting. When faced with a sudden choice between a fishing trip and a concert, Sharafat Hussain is known to have foregone the concert.

Stylistic Perspectives

For this study, I have reviewed over 11 hours of Sharafat's concert recordings — mostly in good acoustic condition. In the *khayāla* genre, the sample consists of: Jhinjhoṭī (85 mts), Rāgesarī (60 mts), Mālkauṅs (70 mts), Kedāra (15 mts), Nāt Kamoda (5 mts), Bairāgī (30 mts incomplete), Darbārī (55 mts), Rāmakalī (40 mts), Mālatī Basanta (45 mts), Megha and Megha Malhāra (45 mts), and Jaijaivantī (truncated: 40 mts). In the *ṭhumarī* and allied genres, the sample consists of Khamāja *ṭhumarī* (30 mts) and Bhairavī (70 mts). The significant amongst these recordings are reviewed here as an indication of the emerging "Neo-Agra" style shaped by Sharafat Hussain Khan.

The *vilambita khayāla* in Rāmakalī (40 mts) is the best available example of Sharafat's Neo-Agra vocalism. It aligns Agra music with the architecture of the *khayāla* form, as it crystallized in the post-Faiyyaz Khan era. In this Rāmakalī, we find his improvisatory movements liberated from the melodic-rhythmic frame of the *bandiśa*, and partially, even from the poetic frame. He relies substantially on *saragama* and *ākāra* forms of articulation. The *ālāpa* has a leisurely quality not associated with Agra vocalism. Staccato intonation and angularity of Agra-style melodic contours are rare. The *tāna*s are largely of the *ekaharā* variety (running melody, without repetitive iteration of *svara*s) and only occasionally of the multiple-stroke Agra variety. This recording sounds a lot like Ameer Khan, perhaps a predictable direction considering the dominant influences of his times. Despite this, the stamp of Agra vocalism is clear. The *druta khayāla* in Rāmakalī, only partially recorded (*una saṅga lāgī*), is pure Faiyyaz Khan nostalgia. Its rendition verges on the *bandiśa-kī-ṭhumarī* in terms of treatment.

The 85-minute Jhinjhoṭī rendition I studied is also Neo-Agra, though a trifle self-conscious. The structure of the *vilambita khayāla* is very neat. The three movements — *ālāpa*, *laya-bāṇṭa*, and *tāna*s — are distinct and sequential, with no regression. The 50-minute *ālāpa* is repetitive, a risk that cannot be avoided in a *rāga* like Jhinjhoṭī. But, the remaining facets of the rendition are truly deviant considering the Agra legacy of the vocalist. Through its entire duration, the *ālāpa* shows no trace of pulsating melody. The reposeful quality of the rendition matches the best of Ameer Khan. Intonation is smooth, and vocalization close to natural. The improvisations are liberated from the *bandiśa*. The use of *tihāī*s is sparing. The *rāga* does not permit easy *ekaharā* movement for vocalists; so the *tāna*s have some multiple-stroke Agra quality. The *choṭā khayāla* is vintage Agra with a *bandiśa-ṭhumarī* flavour, supported by the lively structure of the *bandiśa* (*morī aṅkhiyāṅ una saṅga lāga rahī*).

Sharafat's rendition in Mālatī Basanta, a rare *rāga*, is almost devoid of reformist signs. The melodic contours are angular, with brisk passages punctuating the flow of the *ālāpa*. By present-day standards, the melodic progression is informal. A subtle pulse begins early in the *ālāpa*. The *tāna*s and the *bola-bāṇṭa* sections overlap. Pulsation and rhythmic dexterity dominate the entire rendition. The piece is colourful, even scintillating music — vintage Agra.

The most interesting recording surveyed is a 70-minute Bhairavī, with a *bola-banāva ṭhumarī* (*bājū-banda khula khula jāye* in Dīpacaṇḍī *tāla*), followed by a *bandiśa ṭhumarī* (*na māro bhara picakārī* in *tīnatāla*). This two-tier format is generally reserved for the major genres — *dhrupada* and *khayāla*. Interestingly, of the concert recordings surveyed, this one ends with the most thunderous applause. The *bola-banāva ṭhumarī* on the recording is an unusually seductive piece of *ṭhumarī* rendition — including an attempt at lowbrow humour. It captures the romanticism of the *bandiśa* and the genre more effectively than any of his seniors in the *gharānā*, or even his contemporaries might have managed.

In a departure from the lyrics of the *ṭhumarī* (*bājūbanda khula khula jāye*), Sharafat inserts a nonsensical phrase "*sāṁvariyā ne kaisā kabūtara pālā*" (what a weird pigeon my beloved has bred!) to replace the original *sāṁvariya ne kaisā jādū ḍālā* (What a powerful spell my beloved has cast!), and has the audience burst into laughter. Sharafat's disciple, Purnima Sen, explained to me how the pigeons entered the *ṭhumarī*. Apparently, the concert took place in a hall along the roof of which pigeons had made their nests. While he was singing, the birds distracted him by starting their own conversation. He looked skywards in hapless indignation, and improvized the ridiculous and immensely amusing deviation from the lyrics.

Improvizations of superior taste occur in his *bandiśa-kī-ṭhumarī* rendition in Khamāja (*nā mānūṅgī*), also an Agra favourite. To enhance the romantic spirit of the *bandiśa*, Sharafat enlarges the lyrics by inserting couplets from popular *ghaẓalas*. He also punctuates the rendering with conversational asides such as *ajī hāṅ* (O yes, of course!), borrowed from an endearing practice common to the courtesans of an earlier era.

From the evidence of the sample studied, some observations can be made about Sharafat Hussain's musical inclinations. Temperamentally, Sharafat was suited for a combination of classicism and romanticism. He acquired this versatility from his first mentor, Faiyyaz Khan, who was probably the first 20th-century vocalist to carry it off with aplomb. Sharafat also had the appropriate amalgam of elitism and populism to give him stature along with success. His repertoire of *khayāla* and *ṭhumarī* broadly followed the strategy of Faiyyaz Khan. However, Sharafat did not retain *dhrupada* — prominent in Faiyyaz Khan's music — probably because of its waning popularity in his times. The frequent informality of his approach to the architecture of the *vilambita khayāla* was consistent with that of Faiyyaz Khan. It is, of course, obvious that he worked hard at conforming to its emerging formalism. Sharafat Hussain's *vilambita khayāla*s drifted quite categorically in the Ameer Khan direction, while his *druta khayāla*s remained cheerful and sprightly in the Faiyyaz Khan mould. In the *ṭhumarī* genre, he apparently enjoyed and performed the lively *bandiśa-ṭhumarī* more than the sentimental *bola-banāva ṭhumarī*, which were Faiyyaz Khan's favourites.

Sharafat had inherited a style highly cultivated in medium and fast tempo renditions and less so in slow tempo renditions. By the time he arrived, this relative weakness had become a handicap in terms of acquiring stature, and perhaps even success. He overcame this handicap by mastering the anarhythmic *vilambita ālāpa*. This was a monumental achievement considering the Agra obsession with pulsation dominated or rhythmically informed melody through all stages of *khayāla* rendition. He did not extend the reform effort to other movements of the *vilambita khayāla*s and to his *druta khayāla*s either because he did not have enough time to do so, or probably because the risk of abandoning the Faiyyaz Khan legacy seemed too high. But, in his *tāna*s, we certainly observe a far more sophisticated sense of design than is evident in the music either of his principal mentor, Faiyyaz Khan, or of his Agra contemporaries, Latafat Hussain and Yunus Hussain.

Sharafat may have suffered some denial of stature because of his approach to the *ṭhumarī* genre. His brand of *ṭhumarī* was beginning to acquire a low-brow image by the time he arrived.

Of course, it gave him considerable popularity, which probably made it unnecessary for him to reconsider its aesthetics.

The context of Sharafat's appearance and achievement is unique in 20th-century Hindustani music. His music does not fall clearly within any of the larger tendencies observed in the post-Independence era. His was a distinctive style, evolved by an extraordinary musician, and aimed at adapting the mature Agra tradition to contemporary values. The brilliance of his presentation made its partial anachronism charming to the ageing Faiyyaz Khan constituency, and irrelevant to younger audiences.

His reform of Agra vocalism remained partial. This was probably inevitable considering the complexities of the cultural process. Reforming a mature style requires isolating its essentials from its peripherals, and shedding obsolete peripherals without disturbing the aesthetic coherence of the whole. Unless a truly epochal musician emerges on the scene, or it happens by accident, such a task takes several generations. Sharafat did not live long enough to prove if he could have done it alone. But, as Deshpande points out,[1] a pioneering musician emerges, almost without exception, from exposure to multiple *gharānās*. Sharafat's grooming with three maestros of a highly in-bred cluster of lineages might not have been diverse enough to permit such efflorescence.

Sharafat's surgery on Agra vocalism gave it a short lease of life. Aficionados of Agra vocalism believe that had he lived longer, he had it in him to spearhead an Agra revival. We will never know (Written : July 2004).

2.4

Purnima Sen
The Feminine Face of Agra Vocalism

PURNIMA Sen (b. 1937) is amongst the very few ladies to have made a mark as exponents of the Agra Gharānā. She holds a first degree in Anthropology from Hunter College, New York, occupies the top grade rating as a performer on All India Radio, enjoys a respected presence on the concert platform, has released four CDs, and divides her time between music, and caring for a family of successful legal and business professionals.

In early youth, Purnima studied Western classical music (the violin) in New York, and left her teachers lamenting when she decided to return to India to pursue Hindustani music. By Indian standards, her grooming started late. She made up for it, however, by acquiring some of the best available *guru*s from the Agra and Atrauli lineages, and pursuing her passion with tenacity. During this tutelage spanning almost three decades, she absorbed every facet of Agra vocalism, internalized the principles of music making enshrined in it, and adapted it to her own voice and disposition.

The Triumph of Pedigree

(Purnima Sen Spoke to the Author on 6 January 2003)

"My father was an Economist, and headed the Economics faculty at the Baroda University from 1939 to 1944. That was towards the end of Ustad Faiyyaz Khan's life. During that period, he heard the great Ustad on several occasions, and no wonder, developed a love for the Agra style. From my childhood, I was very keen on learning music, and my parents were most encouraging. But, when I was very young, my family moved to New York. During our stay abroad, my father made it a point — whenever we came to India — to send me to a music teacher to learn music. When I graduated from Hunter College, New York, I had scholarships to study further. But, instead, I decided to return to India with my parents and study music. That was 1957, and I was 19 then.

"My father took me to Ustad Vilayat Hussain Khan, and requested him to teach me. The Ustad was a towering figure in the music world. He was the seniormost vocalist of the Agra Gharānā, and an adviser to All India Radio. He could boast of a galaxy of distinguished disciples. Teaching a near-beginner could not have been an easy proposition for him. But, my father persisted. Khansaheb auditioned me, and despite his reservations, agreed to teach. My father wanted the best available teacher, but also had apprehensions about the suitability of the masculine Agra style for me. Though the issue was not immediate — I knew so little then! — Khansaheb was sensitive to it. He assured my father that I would learn to sing like myself, and not like him. Thus, I became a *gaṇḍ-bandha śāgirda* (a ceremonially initiated disciple) of Ustad Vilayat Hussain Khan.

"He was very enthusiastic about teaching me. One day he landed up at our house, without notice, at three in the afternoon, and asked me to sing Multānī. I was stumped by the suddenness of this test. But, I sang. He was very pleased, and asked me what I would like to learn next. This was an unusual situation. In those days, a disciple dared not suggest what should be taught next; the Ustad always knows best what to teach at each stage of progress. I had just heard Kesarbai Kerkar's Lalita recording at that time, and loved it. I wanted to learn the *rāga*. So, very hesitantly, I suggested Lalita. He hummed and hawed for a while, and said: "Lalita is very complicated. But, you can manage." So, he taught me Lalita. Thereafter, he also taught me Deśa and Basanta. I learnt six *rāga*s with him in about 18 months, before I got married, and moved to Calcutta in 1958. I did not realize how much he had taught me in so short a time. But, by the time I moved, I could perform a *rāga* passably for 30 to 45 minutes.

"Vilayat Hussain gave me a letter of recommendation to his cousin, Ata Hussain Khan, who lived in Calcutta. Ata Hussain was reserved initially — I was only 21 then. After auditioning me, he accepted me as a disciple. On the very first day, he took up Deśī Toḍī — a *rāga* I did not know — and asked me to follow him — to merely reproduce what he sang. He unleashed his sparkling *tāna*s, which left me stunned. He said: "Never mind; try whatever you can manage." He was testing my grasping power. By the fourth session, I could reproduce his *tāna*s. Thereafter, my training settled down to an even keel. He was a very good teacher, who never lost his temper. He taught me most of the *rāga*s I know. I studied with him for twenty years — from 1960 to 1980.

"While Ata Hussain Khan was teaching me, his nephew (and Vilayat Hussain's son-in-law), Sharafat Hussain started accompanying him to our house, whenever he visited Calcutta. On those occasions, Ata Hussain would ask Sharafat to teach me. Gradually, Ata Hussain encouraged Sharafat to initiate me into the more advanced aspects of Agra vocalism as, by now, his own health had started failing. From 1974-75, Sharafat Hussain started staying with us on his visits, and got more intensely involved with my progress. This association continued for almost ten years — until he succumbed to a cancer. That brought to an end almost 30 years of my apprenticeship with Ustads of Agra-Atrauli Gharānā.

"I have never looked at music as a career. It is as much a part of my life as is my family. I became an empanelled vocalist with All India Radio in 1976, and am now a top-grade artiste. My concert appearances have been limited largely to Calcutta and Delhi, the two cities where we have homes, with an occasional concert in Bangalore. I have not promoted myself actively. I have made four CDs abroad, and they have happened on their own. I do teach music in Calcutta. This, too, is very limited because my husband and I divide our time between two cities. This can make unreasonable demands on my students.

"All my *ustāds*, starting from Vilayat Hussain, were sensitive to the masculinity of the Agra style. This was important because the forcefulness of vocalization and intonation determines everything else. Ata Hussain, who taught me for the longest period, accepted that just as a woman speaks differently, and walks differently, she would also sing differently. If she did otherwise, she would sound ridiculous. So, they allowed me to interpret Agra vocalism in a way that suited my voice and personality. The issue became more pronounced in the *tāna*s department where the typical four-stroke *tāna*s of Agra-Atrauli style exposed me to the risk of harsher expressions. Sharafat Hussain worked very hard with me on this, and made it possible for me to sing them without sounding unmusical.

"The same was true of *dhrupada-dhamāra*. According to the

convention in the Agra Gharānā, the Nom-Tom *ālāpa* and *dhrupada-dhamāra* compositions were an essential part of my training. But, I was instructed not to perform them because they were too aggressive for me. I was fortunate in having this sensitivity amongst my *ustād*s. Without it, I could easily have become a knowledgeable musician, whom nobody wanted to hear."

The Music of Purnima Sen

My observations on Purnima Sen's music are based on a study of one CD recorded by her for India Archive Music, New York, and another for Makar Records, France. The recordings consist of *khayāla* renderings in Jaijaivantī, Bāgesarī, Deśa, Khema Kalyāṇa, and Megha Malhāra and a *ṭhumarī* in Khamāja.

Purnima's voice sets her apart from most contemporary female vocalists. She sings with the tonic at approximately A# — the same level as Sharafat Hussain's, but a notch lower than Ata Hussain, who sang at B. This imparts a mildly granular character to her voice. The voice covers a range of two octaves with effortless ease and exceptional tonal precision without any unintended variations in timbre.

The basic issue in Purnima's style is her technique of vocalization. Faiyyaz Khan, the Agra fountainhead, mastered a low-pitched voice, which was husky — almost gruff — but forceful and resonant. In addition to being *his* voice, it also suited his masculine idiom, and was consistent with the acoustic environment of his era. In the succeeding generations, the Agra vocalization technique underwent a considerable change. Vilayat Hussain Khan possessed an authoritarian voice, tinged with a mild nasality in the upper registers. Ata Hussain's voice had the breadth and sonority to match Faiyyaz Khan, but without his senior's abrasive edges. In the following generation, Yunus Hussain (Vilayat Hussain's son) cultivated a voice that was almost melodious, while Sharafat Hussain cultivated a pleasing baritone that could be melodious as well as robust.

All of them performed music in the Agra mould. But, by the time we come to the last two, we are already looking at a fairly well developed acoustic environment, and the redundancy of forceful vocalization for reaching large audiences. We are also looking at a cultural environment in which *dhrupada* was facing extinction, the rhythm-biased and aggressive Agra style was yielding centrestage to the gentler, melody-biased music of Kairana, Patiala, Gwalior and Jaipur–Atrauli styles. Simultaneously, the rhythm-biased space in the music world was being conquered by a generation of brilliant instrumentalists. In this environment, Agra vocalism was obliged to drift towards less forceful and more melodious voice cultivation and greater melody-orientation in its treatment of music.

These factors helped the emergence of Purnima Sen as a distinguished female vocalist of the hitherto masculine tradition. In addition to the sensitivity of her *gurus* to the demands of feminity, it was her acoustic-aesthetic sensibility that adapted the Agra style to her voice and temperament. We therefore find, in her music, all the melodic-rhythmic-poetic features of Agra vocalism, shorn of their stridency. But, the transformation is more radical than this proposition would suggest. The moment the forcefulness of Agra vocalization is subdued, every detail of the melodic intention sparkles. As a result, her style attains a sculptural elegance, which we do not associate readily with Agra. Having discovered this elegance, Purnima has worked on it, and made it her own. Sharafat Hussain, her last *guru*, was the initiator of what we might call Neo-Agra vocalism, and Purnima spears to have crystallized its stylistic personality. This idiom has shifted Agra vocalism from its traditional poetic-rhythmic axis considerably towards the poetic-melodic axis, without a significant loss of distinctiveness.

In my interview with her, she repeatedly referred to her *gharānā* as "Atrauli," rather than Agra. In these references, she could have been alluding to the long tutelage with two Atrauli vocalists, Ata Hussain and Sharafat Hussain. Whatever be the basis for this allusion, its implications deserve consideration. The perspective is clearer in relation to Sharafat Hussain, whose concert recordings are available in decent numbers, rather than Ata Hussain whose meagre recordings within my reach did not permit confident inferences.

A study of Sharafat's archive reveals that he differed from the Agra norm by specializing in leisurely and elaborate presentations of the *ālāpa* in the *baḍā khayāla*. He also relied more generously on the *ākāra* articulation for the *ālāpa* than other Agra vocalists habitually do. This departure could have been inspired by the Atrauli tradition, or even by the formidable influence that his contemporary, Ameer Khan, wielded over *khayāla* vocalism starting from the 1950s. These tendencies are evident in Purnima's music. We also observe that Sharafat was less deeply involved in the purposive exploitation of poetic meaning than the generalized Agra tendency. Purnima's music also stays away from such exploitation.

Purnima's music is sober, and transparently sincere. It eschews Sharafat's flamboyance — the element of surprise, the occasional recourse to melodic mischief, and playful interaction with the rhythm. This difference is rooted partly in her serious personality. In any event, the gay abandon of Sharafat's singing would be considered unbecoming, even today, of a female vocalist from genteel society.

With a transparent separation between the three movements in the *vilambita khayāla*, Purnima also appears to conform more fastidiously to the widely accepted linear architecture of *khayāla* vocalism than Agra or Atrauli vocalists have done. This separation is less obvious in Agra music than in other *gharānās* because Agra tends to introduce an explicit rhythmicality into the structuring of melody earlier during the course of the *baḍā khayāla* rendition than other *gharānās* do. Purnima, instead, appears to respond to the architectural standards set by models of her generation, who came primarily from Kairana and Neo-Jaipur–Atrauli traditions.

Purnima's re-interpretation of Agra vocalism for contemporary audiences with transparency of melodic intent and feminine grace is a rare achievement. Her musicianship proves that, in Hindustani music, if the pedagogical environment can ensure continuity, change often takes care of itself. And, indeed, it does so in a very orderly manner. From a socio-cultural perspective, Purnima Sen's musicianship also underlines the growing role of amateurs of professional calibre in preserving the integrity of *gharānā*-based stylistics in the Hindustani tradition (Written : January 2003).

2.5

Sugata Marjit
Messiah of Post-Modernism

SUGATA Marjit (b. 1959) is poised to emerge as the messiah of post-modernism in Hindustani vocalism after having made his mark as an economist. Along with his academic pursuits, Sugata studied music under competent *guru*s from several stylistic traditions, and excelled in both. He holds two post-graduate degrees and a Doctorate in Economics. Sugata has taught economics at several universities in the US, Europe, and Australia, and currently occupies a prestigious Chair at a leading social sciences research institute in Calcutta.

He has given over a hundred music concerts for small audiences in the USA, Europe, Australia and Hong Kong, and at music festivals in India. His academic credentials have endeared him especially to university audiences. Sugata also composes music for the theatre and television. In 1995, his maiden effort as a composer in the theatre earned him the prestigious West Bengal State Academy Award for the best musical score.

Sugata's music is unorthodox. It reflects the diversity of his grooming, and the stylistically diffused musical environment of the last quarter of the 20th century. As a generational phenomenon, it also hyperbolizes many of the tendencies evident in *khayāla* vocalism over the last couple of decades. By some strange coincidence, these tendencies echo those associated with post-modernist artistic movements in Europe. The acceptability of these tendencies to cultivated Indian audiences and critics remains largely untested. But, Sugata appears reluctant to dish out repackaged doses of the familiar merely to solicit the approval of the establishment.

Sugata is, by now, a credible musician, who has evolved his personal musical statement. But, considering his professional commitments, and delayed launch on the professional music circuit, his post-modernist manifesto has some distance to travel before it is accepted as a part of the Grand Tradition.

"I am a Restless Kind of Guy"
(Sugata Writes about Economics and Music)

"Within economics, I specialize in international economics, development, and economics of corruption and governance. I am writing a book on trade, labour, and inequality — whether globalization leads to increasing inequality, etc. I think I am a soft-hearted human being, who feels for the poor, in spite of being an ardent supporter of market-based incentives. I am not a Marxist; I believe in God; I have taken my *dīkṣa* (spiritual initiation) at the Ramakrishna Mission. The emotional part of me gets reflected in economics as well as music. My research is to make my points through simple, but elegant, mathematical models. I am a theorist. I believe in simplicity, and simple is beautiful. This is the approach I take in my research and in my music.

"My father had a good voice and was my inspiration. He was a Judge. We lived in several towns in West Bengal, before we finally moved to Calcutta in 1973. He used to find trainers for me (wherever we lived). He died in 1994. I miss him a lot. He told me that anyone can be a good student academically; but to be a good vocalist is something else, and that one day, I would realize that it is a blessing to be able to sing. My uncle learnt the sitar with Balram Pathak and Imrat Khan. He was a good sitar player, but gave it up, and now runs a vocal music college in a town in West Bengal. A great talent, and inspiration for me.

"I learnt with many *gurus*, for a few months here and there, until I came to Calcutta. They were people who had been trained by noted Bengali musicians. One of them had, however, been trained by Vinayakrao Patwardhan (Gwalior Gharānā). They had taught me basic *riyāẓa* (self-improvement exercises) to train my voice, and good compositions. The major *tālīma* (training) I had was with Krishnachandra Bannerjee, for 17 years, starting from 1973. With him, I learnt singing in its totality, the intricacies of *rāgadārī* (treatment of *rāga*s), and the finer techniques of vocal music.

"Bannerjee was a disciple of Bhishmadev Chatterjee, a household name in Bengal, who had studied with Badal Khan. That is my Rangeele Gharānā lineage. He (Krishnachandra Bannerjee) did not have a good voice; but he was a great trainer. I could go to him every day. He had heard top vocalists all over India, and could give me the traits of many *gharānā*s — Kairana, Gwalior, etc. Bannerjee died in 1990. I performed his funeral rites. Then, I went to T.D. Janorikar of the Bhendi Bazar Gharānā, learnt with him for a few years until he left Calcutta for Nagpur.

"I am an off-beat person. I like to create all the time. I don't want to know how many greats were born before me and, frankly speaking, be it economics or music, I get tired of knowing what has been done already, and repenting and repeating it because I am not as talented as others. I listen and try to pick up whatever sounds interesting and has the potential for my voice. I love Bhimsen Ji (Joshi) and Ameer Khan. I like possibly each and every vocalist to the extent that I can draw from them and make people dance with *layakārī*, *bola-tānas*, and little pieces of *vistāra*. I am a restless kind of guy; and so is my music, and I don't regret it, because that's me. I don't like too much of structure. I like to think more about my music than physically practice it.

"I like popular Bengali songs of the 1970s, and Baul (a regional folk genre of Bengal). I often use nuances of these in my music. Often, I also use phrases of a particular *rāga* picked up from advertising music, radio jingles, etc. so long as they fit in properly. I am a performer. My lectures are much better than my writing. My music is much better than my knowledge of it.

"I hear all kinds of music, but don't often get much time. Hindi music, the "old gold" type — I like a lot. Beside Ameer Khan and Bhimsen, I listen to Kishori, Paluskar, Omkarnath, Kesarbai, Kumar Gandharva (I love him!), and Rashid Khan. In instrumental music, Vilayat Khan, Ravi Shankar, Ali Akbar, Nikhil Bannerjee, Bismillah Khan, and Hariprasad Chaurasia are my favourites. Unfortunately, over the last few years, I have got so busy, that listening time is too short. I have to get back to it.

"I had never guessed that I would be so successful in academics that it will tend to take away all my time. I have earned a bit, and can retire now if I wish. But, what militates against my taking up music as a profession is (the community of) musicians. There is too much of networking, hitting below the belt, and an un-intellectual ambience. I cannot accept this. I cannot go down on my knees to get a concert. I can't lead a musician's life. That's the problem. Intellectually, I am happier now. But, I am sure there is a golden mean, and I have to find it.

"I have to be more consistent in my *riyāẓa*. I can maintain my job in economics by doing a bit of research; but (from now on) that should be all. I have also to be in India. I have travelled far too much, and now is the time (to stay at home)."

Stylistic Pedigree

Sugata Marjit's music represents an eclectic cocktail of influences, which he cherishes and continuously seeks to diversify. He had his early training with a teacher groomed in the Gwalior style. He then had a long period of training with a teacher of the Rangeele tradition (allied to the Agra and Atrauli traditions). Thereafter, he studied, for a few years, with a leading musician of the Bhendi Bazaar Gharānā. Sugata loves musicians as diverse as Bhimsen Joshi, Ameer Khan, and Kumar Gandharva. In an era characterized by a high-velocity bombardment of aural images through the electronic media, and low-cost access to all kinds of pre-recorded music, his search for novelty has left him open to the influence of instrumental art music, regional and folk music, popular music, and even advertising music.

Sugata's early training in the Gwalior Gharānā has shaped his approach to the rendition of low-density, rhythmically unstructured melody in *baḍā khayāla* renditions. This appears to have been imparted a dramatic twist under the influence of Kumar Gandharva. Sugata's fondness for Nom-Tom articulation on the *auchara* is a Gwalior as well as an Agra tendency. The raciness of his approach to the Behlava movement, his style of intonation, and his partiality towards melodic action in the *uttaraṅga* (upper tetrachord) are all Gwalior traits. Sugata's possession of a medium-weight voice might also partially explain these affinities.

Badal Khan of the Rangeele Gharānā, from whom Sugata claims fourth-generation descent as a disciple, finds scarce mention in recent works on music history, except as one of the *guru*s of the famous Calcutta vocalist, Girija Shankar Chakravarty (1878-1948). As discussed earlier, for all practical purposes the stylistics of the Rangeele Gharānā are no longer distinguishable from those of Faiyyaz Khan's Agra Gharānā. The stamp of the Agra–Rangeele–Atrauli cluster is evident in Sugata's construction of *tāna*s, and their lively rhythmicality, replete with crisp *tihāī*s.

Sugata's tutelage with T.D. Janorikar of the Bhendi Bazar Gharānā was short. This tradition is best known for the brilliant *bandiśe*s composed by, Ustad Aman Ali Khan, for the popularization of the *saragama* articulation in *khayāla* renditions, and for stunning *tāna*s of kaleidoscopic melodic pattern. Sugata has adopted several *bandiśe*s from the Aman Ali tradition, and also makes generous use of the *Saragama* in low, medium, and high-density melodic execution. Other than these features, the influence of the Bhendi Bazar Gharānā appears to be negligible.

A significant feature of Sugata's music is the calculated carelessness, or feigned rusticity, in his articulation of the lyrics of *bandiśe*s, and the use of timbre and volume manipulations in its articulation to impart a heightened emotionality to the expression. Considering that Sugata has named Kumar Gandharva amongst vocalists he loves, these features in his music might be attributable to this influence.

Beyond this mix of traceable influences, Sugata's music is Sugata himself. It is vibrant and absorbing, verging on the entertaining — a most unlikely product of a mind whose professional output is constantly subjected to scrutiny by the finest intellects in the world.

Sugata, the Musician

I base my observations on a study of two CDs Sugata has recorded for India Archive Music Ltd., New York. The CDs feature *khayāla*s in Bhaṭiyārā, Deśakara, Guṇakarī, Bilāsakhanī Toḍī, Lalita, Bihāga, and Mālkauṅs.

Sugata is a rare musician who articulates his philosophy of music making lucidly, and also delivers music that matches his statement of intent. Charles Jencks describes a post-modern building as — "part modern, and part something else: vernacular, revivalist, local, commercial, metaphorical, or contextual" (Charles Jencks, "What is Postmodernism", quoted in *Key Ideas in Human Thought*, ed. Kenneth McLeish, 1993, Facts on File Inc., New York, pp. 584-85). Sugata's music, and his own articulation of his philosophy, both appear perfectly consistent with this description.

In economics, as well as music, Sugata describes himself as an off-beat person, an emotional person, and a restless person, who does not like too much structure, who wants to create something new all the time irrespective of its conformity with tradition, and aims for simplicity rather than complexity. His purpose, as a musician, is to make people dance.

As Foster points out with reference to post-modern films (Hal Foster, *Postmodernism: A Preface*, ed. Post Modern Culture, Pluto, London, 1985), post-modernism is "a combination of lots of different genres, signs, and cultural elements. The features of post-modern films are hedonism, and decadence — things that are often seen towards the end of a culture's life. . . . A feature of post-modernism is its ability to shock, without linking this device to a message."

India's Independence in 1947 was, indeed, an end of an era, although feudal values continued to dominate the performing arts for a couple of decades thereafter. Post-Independence art has undoubtedly taken a different turn, with discontinuities being more prominent than the strands of continuity. It is, therefore, not surprising that Sugata's music should now appear to magnify tendencies that have been evident in the music of the post-Independence generation of musicians. It is almost expected of his generation that its music will rebel against prevailing modes of expression. And, so it does, especially when it is the response of a mind like Sugata's, stimulated by the ideological turbulence of Calcutta in the 1970s, and trained to analyse the socio-economic reality with brutal objectivity. Even if this reality has nothing in common with the triggers of modern European culture, it is a natural enough trigger for music that rebels against "the system", and flows with the tide of Jaques Derrida's post-structuralism, and the nihilistic hedonism of Milan Kundera.

The most significant facet of Sugata's rebellion against modernism is his contempt for the linear architecture of the *khayāla* form. Superficially, his renditions appear to sequence the three principal movements — low-density *ālāpa / behlāva,* the medium density *bola-laya,* and the high-density *tāna*s — in proper order. However, on closer scrutiny, it is possible to observe the occurrence of low-density, medium-density, and high-density melody in each of the movements. The same holds true for the occurrence of melodic complexities, and rhythmic complexities. This feature in his music recalls Goddard's description of his films as having "a beginning, a middle, and an end, but not in that order."

The second significant aspect of Sugata's music is his notion of the *rāga*. Except in fleeting glimpses of total absorption in the *rāga*-ness, there is little indication of an explicit effort to communicate the distinctive emotional content of the *rāga*, or even the thematic highlights of the lyrics. He tends to handle all *rāga*s with almost the same gay abandon, treating poetry primarily as a textural/phonetic device, the *rāga* largely as a melodic structure, and the *bandiśa* as a phonetic-melodic-rhythmic collage of aural images.

Sugata's musical temperament is entirely consistent with the post-modernist world-view. The world-view rejects the existence of anything called "human nature"(Fayaz Chagani, *Essentialising Posmodernism.* www.geocities.com/Athens/Agora/9095/postmodernism.html). It argues that there is nothing universal — whether in a global context or in a culture-specific context, or even across time — about the manner in which people convert sensory stimuli into meaning. This world-view does not therefore accept any established assumptions regarding the proper, or even the most efficient, means of communicating in any language — whether verbal or otherwise.

In the balance of poetry, melody, rhythm, and acoustic effects (textural variety in articulation, and variations of volume and timbre) Sugata's handling of melody shows a consistent and strong bias in favour of rhythmic manipulation and acoustic effects. Poetry takes a backseat in his music, not as much by default, as by a calculated carelessness in its articulation. This defines music that is vibrant, gripping, and explicitly enjoyable.

It is music that invites an animated, rather than a cerebral or emotional response. It is music that "makes people dance" (Sugata's own words), rather than sit still in their seats with eyes closed. This hedonism in Sugata's music cuts across *rāga*s of different emotional content, and *bandiśe*s of explicitly diverse thematic content. Its roots have, therefore, to be found outside of music. It is fair to interpret it as a musical expression of a world-view which recognizes the sexual act as a "self-defining act" as in existentialist thought, or an escapist response to an oppressive reality, as evident amongst the protagonists of Milan Kundera's novels.

An important issue before the critic is whether Sugata's music crosses the borderline between art and entertainment. In making this assessment, he cannot forget that the borderline is a floating one. What is considered art today, would have been considered entertainment only a quarter of a century ago. Every generation of audiences draws its border afresh, and classifies musicians accordingly. The present author can only observe that Sugata is on the borderline, as drawn by the 50-plus generation of Indian audiences. Younger audiences and critics have yet to deliver their verdict (Written : October 2003).

Section 3
The Gwalior–Agra Legacy

3.1

Perspectives on the Gwalior–Agra Legacy

THIS chapter deals with those aspects of the Gwalior–Agra legacy which are immediately relevant to appreciating the stylistic tendencies of musicians covered in this book.

In the post-Independence period, the Gwalior as well as Agra Gharānās suffered a substantial loss of popularity. Amongst the styles with a balanced approach to music making, Gwalior was overtaken by Jaipur–Atrauli vocalism, with its more oblique and clever engagement of melody with rhythm. At the rhythm-dominated end, Agra had no rival in sight. But, the rhythm-dominant extremity itself appeared to have suffered loss of public acceptance. This is evident from the rise of the melody-dominant Kairana vocalism at the other end of the spectrum to pre-eminence, with several Kairana-trained musicians rising to the top of the profession. This situation prompted Gwalior-trained vocalists to look beyond their boundaries on a substantial scale. The drift of Gwalior towards Agra was triggered by a "push" factor as well as a "pull" factor.

The widespread disenchantment amongst Gwalior vocalists — the push factor — was understandable in the early years of independent India. As Deshpande points out,[1] after Omkarnath Thakur, the Gwalior tradition had produced no front ranking performer. Wade[11] points out some factors that might explain this phenomenon. The reason was Gwalior's loss of a distinctive identity. This happened partly because of the widespread dispersion of Gwalior's musical assets through the various *gharānās* that drew inspiration from it, through documentation, and through institutionalized education. Gwalior vocalism was tending to become generic — a style without a style. The Gwalior exodus to Agra reflected, quite clearly, a search for a distinctive brand of music, in addition to the specific attraction of Agra.

The pull factor towards Agra, operating on a large scale through the 1940s and 1950s, was Ustad Faiyyaz Khan's popularity and stature, and his kinsman, Vilayat Hussain Khan's reputation as a scholar and teacher. The influence he wielded over the music world as artistic advisor to the All India Radio also perhaps served as an attraction to those who sought his mentorship. The tutelage of Vilayat Hussain attracted such accomplished musicians as Gajananrao Joshi, Ram Marathe and V.R. Athavale from Gwalior, Malti Pande from Kairana, and Mogubai Kurdikar from Jaipur–Atrauli.

At a time when Gwalior and Agra styles both seemed headed for extinction, Maharashtra, the great crucible of *khayāla* vocalism in the 20th century, forged the confluence of Gwalior and Agra stylistics and produced fine vocalists for at least two generations.

Gwalior: Gharānā and Stylistics

The Gwalior tradition of *khayāla* vocalism is traced to two brothers, Haddu and Hassu Khan, whose grandfather, Natthan Pir Baksh, an eminent vocalist, migrated from Lucknow to Gwalior in the early 19th century. The young lads studied music under their grandfather, and an elder relative, Natthe Khan. According to some accounts, they also surreptitiously studied the music of Bade Muhammad Khan, an eminent vocalist under Gwalior patronage. With these influences, the two brothers crystallized the Gwalior tradition, and rose to the highest eminence in the Gwalior court. Hassu Khan (d. 1859) had a great voice, and was probably a greater musician, considering the legendary status he enjoys in Hindustani music.

Eminent in the teaching line of Hassu Khan were two vocalists, Ramakrishna Dev and Vasudev Buwa. At different stages, both these musicians trained Balkrishna Buwa Ichalkaranjikar. It is believed that Chhote Muhammad Khan, the son of Haddu Khan, also trained Balkrishna Buwa. With this grounding in the Gwalior style, Balkrishna Buwa returned to his home state, and pioneered Gwalior vocalism in Maharashtra. Amongst his disciples were three giants who triggered off a veritable renaissance in the musical culture of the state, which now dominates *khayāla* vocalism in India — Anant Manohar Joshi (Antu Buwa), Vishnu Digambar Paluskar, and Yashwant Sadashiv Mirashi (Mirashi Buwa). Eminent figures in the teaching line of Haddu Khan, was his son, Chhote Muhammad Khan, and Nissar Hussain Khan (1844-1916), Shankrarao Pandit, Eknath Pandit, and Rajabhaiya Poonchhwale.

Despite the difficulties in identifying the salient features of the Gwalior style, Prof. Bonnie Wade,[11] has outlined a generalized picture of the Hassu Khan and Haddu Khan lineages, along with the minor differences between the lineages.

In the Hassu Khan lineage, musicians cultivate a wide tonal range of over two octaves, and achieve secure intonation in leaps across broad melodic spans. Their *auchara* (prelude to the *bandiśa*) is unlike an *ālāpa*, and closer to a free-flowing image of the *vilambita bandiśa* to follow. In their *vilambita khayāla*s, the *ālāpa* is done in pitch-clusters. In the lower half of the melodic canvas, they tend to use primarily the *ākāra* articulation, shifting to *bola*-articulation in the upper half. With the entry of *bola*-articulation in the *ālāpa*, a mild pulsation enters the melody. The *bandiśa antarā* tends to be presented as an *antarā* of the *ālāpa*. In their *madhya-laya khayāla*s, the *sthāyī* and the *antarā* of the *bandiśa* tend to be rendered upfront, and a systematic *ālāpa* may be dispensed with. *Vilambita* as well as *madhya-laya khayālas* have *bola-laya/bola-bāṇṭa* and *bola-tāna* movements. Their proportion tends to vary considerably, and they tend to be rendered as a single mixed movement, rather than discrete and sequentially separated movements. Except for D.V. Paluskar, musicians of this lineage have not performed *ākāra tānas* in significant measure. *Saragama* articulation is also rare in the music of this lineage. *Dhrupada* style *layakārī* and *tihāīs* are an expected feature of their renditions. A *tarānā* rather than a *druta khayāla* will often follow their *vilambita khayālas*.

Based on an analysis of recordings of the descendants of Shankarrao Pandit (Krishnarao Shankar, and Lakshman Krishnarao), Wade[11] outlines the differences between the two lineages. In the Haddu Khan lineage, the *ālāpa* of the *vilambita khayāla* is rendered only in *bola* articulation. They are more consistent in performing the *antarā* of the *bandiśa* than the other Gwalior lineage. In their *madhya-laya khayālas*, the *antarā* is often rendered late in the rendition rather than upfront. *Dhrupada* stylistics and the *tarānā* appear less frequently in their music than the Hassu Khan lineage. They also tend to make less frequent use of the dynamic expressions than the other stream of Gwalior vocalism.

A conceptual perspective on the Gwalior style emerges from Deshpande's work.[1] He conceptualizes Gwalior as a simple, rather than complex, balance of melodic and rhythmic orientations. Its most significant features are its lucidity and simplicity. Its normal tempo is the medium tempo, slightly quicker than the Jaipur–Atrauli tempo. At this tempo, there is very little scope for melodic or melodic-rhythmic subtleties. Its greatest strength is that it is easy to understand for lay listeners. And, the Gwalior Gharānā has, indeed, made a tremendous contribution to the spread of *khayāla* vocalism in the country, and particularly in the state of Maharashtra.

Understanding the Gwalior–Agra Confluence

The Gwalior–Agra confluence can be understood by examining early orthodox Gwalior, orthodox Agra, and representative products of the confluence itself.

As representatives of orthodox Gwalior, and as a choice guided purely by the availability of recordings, I choose to refer to Vinayakrao Patwardhan (1899-1975) and Krishnarao Pandit (1893-1989). A substantial published archive of 78 RPM records of the Gwalior-trained, but original, musician Ramkrishna Vaze (1871-1945) is also available. One *rāga* rendered by Jagannath Buwa Purohit, the Agra vocalist who trained several Gwalior-trained vocalists, was also available for reference. In addition, one concert recording of Gajananrao Joshi, one of the pioneers of the Gwalior–Agra confluence was available for analysis. The sample is far from representative, and the inferences are merely indicative.

Orthodox Gwalior

Orthodox Gwalior does not appear to have as well-defined a stylistic personality as, say, orthodox Agra or orthodox Jaipur–Atrauli. However, from the available archive, I could acquire two specimens that may be useful reference points: Candrakauṁs rendered by Vinayakrao Patwardhan, and Bhīmapalāsa rendered by Krishnarao Pandit. Though the two belong to different streams of Gwalior, the differences seem more individualistic than generic. Essentially, they both conform to the fluidity and simplicity of Gwalior vocalism, with equal attention to melodic and rhythmic elements. Both have performed *vilambita bandiś*es with a strong *uttarāṅga* bias typical of Gwalior, although Candrakauṁs is an *uttarāṅga*-based *rāga*, while Bhīmapalāsa is anchored in the mid-octave region.

Patwardhan sings to the fundamental tonic at F, while Pandit sings between D and D#. They have both cultivated phenomenal tonal range, with Patwardhan stronger in the upper registers and Krishnarao stronger in the lower. It is interesting that Patwardhan's music leans strongly towards the doleful and plaintive model of Abdul Kareem Khan of Kairana (1872–1936), while Krishnarao Pandit, only a few years younger, appears to lean towards the more aggressive and masculine model of the dominant vocalist of the era, Faiyyaz Khan of Agra (1886–1950).

These biases are also reflected in the tempo for rendering their *vilambita khayālas*. Patwardhan's Candrakauṅs in *ekatāla* begins at a sober 26.2 bpm and closes at 29.7 bpm, well within the accepted values for *vilambita khayālas*. Krishnarao's *vilambita khayāla* in Tilavāḍā begins at a sprightly 49.7 bpm and closes at 63.6 bpm, squarely in the *madhya-laya* range. In Patwardhan's music, melody is seeking to liberate itself from rhythm, while Krishnarao seeks to keep melody bound firmly by rhythm.

Patwardhan's music is simple and sincere. It has an emotionally charged quality in its melodic expressions. Krishnarao's is self-conscious music, which tilts strongly towards the dramatic, even theatrical expression. It is replete with broad-span glissandi, and the element of surprise effected through consecutive juxtaposition of *svaras* and phrases in remote regions of the melodic canvas. Krishnarao's drift towards the Faiyyaz Khan model appears pretty obvious in his occasional resort to staccato intonation and phrasing with angular contours, ornate *ṭhumarī* and *ṭappā* style melodic expressions, and emotive and near-conversational use of the poetic element. It is also evident in the frequency and dramatic quality of the engagement of the rendition with rhythmic manipulations on the *tabalā*.

Ramkrishna Vaze, a musician from a generation before the above two, was trained by Nissar Hussain Khan in the Haddu Khan lineage, the same Gwalior stream as Krishnarao. Although Vaze was an original, his style was compatible with orthodox Gwalior. His favoured tempo was *madhya-laya*, appropriate for a balanced handling of melodic and rhythmic elements. Although the 78 RPM recordings do not provide a reliable measure of his temporal orientations, his *jhapatāla* renditions at 110/120 bpm and *ada cautāla* rendition at 50 bpm suggest approximate parity with Jaipur–Atrauli tendencies.

Vaze exhibited a tendency towards dramatic expression, and attention-grabbing leaps between remote regions of the melodic canvas — features magnified in the later music of Krishnarao. The abruptness and deliberateness in his intonation was physiological rather than stylistic. He sang at an artificially strained fundamental tonic at G#, and was also an asthma patient. His era preceded the full impact of Faiyyaz Khan and Agra pressure on rival styles. But, Vaze's temporal orientation and repertoire of rare and compound *rāga*s appear to suggest probable competitive pressure from the Jaipur–Atrauli doyen, Alladiya Khan (1855–1946), who acquired an elitist aura because of these features of his repertoire.

These observations suggest the propensity of Gwalior vocalism to absorb the dominant aesthetic values of the era, without losing its essential Gwalior-ness. It is this propensity that led it towards Agra in the aftermath of the Faiyyaz Khan era. The relative durability of the Gwalior–Agra confluence may point towards a gap in the spectrum for a style close to the golden mean, but tilting mildly towards the rhythmic end. The credit for shaping such a confluence goes largely to Vilayat Hussain Khan of Agra and his disciples. Amongst them was Jagannath Buwa Purohit.

Orthodox Agra

Amongst Agra stalwarts, I am considering only Jagannath Buwa Purohit in this chapter because orthodox Agra has been dealt with earlier, and because Jagannath Buwa actually taught some of the Gwalior musicians who spearheaded the Gwalior–Agra confluence. The only available *khayāla* from a concert recording of Jagannath Buwa Purohit (a rare compound *rāga* — not identifiable) is rendered in a style entirely faithful to his *guru*, Vilayat Hussain and the orthodox Agra style. Jagannath Buwa sang with the fundamental/tonic at E. The tempo of the *bandiśa* in *ekatāla* (54-68 bpm) is closer to what is today understood as *madhya-laya*. The *bandiśa* is the primary vehicle for, and nucleus of, the improvisatory movements. Melody acquires a pulsation very early in the rendition. The major perceptible difference between Vilayat Hussain's vocalism and that of Jagannath Buwa's — based on this single specimen — appears to be that the latter cultivated a more microphone-friendly voice, which also subdued the frequency of staccato intonation and angularities of melodic contours in his music.

Music of the Gwalior–Agra Confluence

Gajananrao Joshi (d. 1987) was the most outstanding product of the Gwalior–Agra confluence. He was primarily a disciple of his father, Anant Manohar Joshi (Antu Buwa), a Gwalior Gharānā stalwart. He had also trained himself in the Jaipur–Atrauli style of vocalism under Ustad Bhurji Khan (one of the three sons of Alladiya Khan), and in Agra style vocalism under Ustad Vilayat Hussain Khan. Gajananrao also mastered the violin on his own, without a tutor, and virtually pioneered its performance in Hindustani music. As a vocalist, Gajananrao could demonstrate any of the three styles without betraying even a trace of the other two he had studied. His concerts of vocal music were prized for the richness of his idiom, which incorporated features of all the three major traditions in which he had received training.

Commercial recordings of Gajananrao's violin performances were published in good number. However, his vocalism has remained apparently unpublished. One concert recording of his, done during the last few years of his life, with Ulhas Kashalkar providing vocal support was, however, available as an indicator of his style.

The concert has three *rāga*s — Jaitaśrī, Gauḍa Malhāra, and Śuddha Nāta. The choice of these *rāga*s, all fortes of the Jaipur–Atrauli Gharānā, might have imparted a Jaipur–Atrauli-style bias to the entire concert. Despite this, Gajananrao's vocalism displays all the characteristics and features of the three *gharānā*s, of which he achieved a highly absorbing fusion.

Gajananrao sang in a natural voice, which acquired a granular, and even guttural, timbre in the lower registers. His vocalization frequently deployed jaw movements, while his melodic execution had angularities, often verging on staccato expression. These features have been associated with the Agra style of singing. However, they were also evident in the music of some Gwalior maestros, such as Ramakrishna Vaze. These features could, therefore, well reflect a generalized response of male vocalists to the early 20th-century acoustic environment, devoid of modern amplification electronics.

In the basic approach, Gajananrao's music exhibits a certain raciness associated with the Gwalior style of singing, which has often been construed as impatience. I see it is more as the reflection of an integrated or holistic, rather than a building-block, approach to *rāga* presentation. Its architecture is informal, rather than clinical, in its adherence to the linear and cyclical disciplines of *khayāla* vocalism. Its purpose is to create an absorbing and engaging musical experience without the deliberateness of progressive intensification. This obviously makes for music which is less demanding on the audiences. Consistent with this basic purpose, the entirety of the presentation, in all its movements, is dominated by the distinctive melodic phraseology of the *rāga*. The music stays away from the overtly geometric and symmetric relationships between phrases, and concentrates more on rendering them with shifting melodic and rhythmic emphasis, while also seeking their interesting juxtaposition against each other.

The durational balance of Gajananrao's presentations appeared to favour the *baḍā khayālas*, which were comprehensive, stand-alone pieces of music. His *choṭā khayālas* or *tarānā* renditions were rather short, and limited to the rendition of the *bandiśa* with a few *tānas*. Like Jaipur–Atrauli vocalists, he frequently skipped the *choṭā khayāla* altogether. He was known to preface the main *rāga* of the concert with a fairly elaborate *ālāpa* in Nom-Tom articulation. This *ālāpa* had neither the linear progression of the *dhrupada ālāpa*, nor the sketchy quality of the *auchara* often encountered as a prelude to a *baḍā khayāla* rendition. It was akin to a comprehensive melodic map of the *rāga* form, painted with bold brush-strokes, with a simple pulse approximating the *madhya-laya ālāpa* in a *dhrupada* rendition. It succeeded brilliantly in creating the atmosphere of the *rāga* before the launch of the percussion-accompanied *baḍā khayāla*.

In *vilambita* as well as *druta* renditions, Gajananrao's music exhibits an explicit, and heightened rhythmicality comparable to Agra vocalism, and certainly a departure from the Gwalior style. His music is almost always in a play with the beats of the rhythmic cycle, and often engaged in a lively interaction with them, which he highlighted, occasionally, with a clapping of the hands to mark the beats. Consistent with this heightened ryhthmicality, he made a greater use of *tihāīs* than Gwalior musicians did, but less generously than Agra vocalists.

In this, the only recording readily available for analysis, Gajananrao renders all the three *baḍā khayālas* in *vilambita tīnatāla* at a base-tempo of 23-25 beats per minute, a distinctive feature of Jaipur–Atrauli music. We have no way of knowing if this was Gajananrao's general preference, or a choice derived from the *bandiśes* or *rāgas* he chose to perform at the particular concert. In the presentation of his *baḍā khayālas*, no clear demarcation is evident between the *bola-ālāpa* and *bola-laya* movements. Rhythmically structured and unstructured phrases and patterns blend with each other in what Gwalior vocalists describe as *behlāva*. *Behlāva* refers to the interesting arrangement of characteristic *rāga* phrases, within an informal observance of linear and cyclical architectural conventions. The concept of *behlāva* subsumes the architectural notions of *bola-ālāpa* and *bola-laya*. In the medium-density *bola-laya* movement, Gajananrao tends to make a sparing use of *saragama* articulation, until then a Kairana speciality.

Gajananrao's *tāna*s were strong on intricacy of sculpture. With the *rāga*'s phraseology being the primary design element, he relied considerably on *baḍhata*, and *laḍīguthāva* patterns for structuring his bewildering rallies of high-density melodic execution. The Jaipur–Atrauli style of medium density *tāna*s, using pairs of *svara*s as a phrasing unit, was conspicuous in Gajananrao's music. His use of *chūṭa tāna*s, rather popular with several Gwalior vocalists, was limited. The more mechanistic varieties of *tāna*, the pure *sapāṭa* or *alaṁkāra tāna*s, which tend to flatten out the *rāga* form, but are dazzling in their impact, found little favour with Gajananrao. He deviated from the Gwalior preference for *bola-tāna*s by a substantial reliance on *ākāra tāna*s. In either form of articulation, Gajananrao shunned the ultra-high density *tāna*s endemic to contemporary *khayāla* music. This was his way of ensuring that the *rāga* form never drifted out of focus.

The need for a reference point for a stylistic perspective on his disciple, Ulhas Kashalkar occasioned my first experience of listening intently to Gajananrao Joshi. I found the music absorbing, and extraordinarily rich in melodic, rhythmic and textural value. His music also comes through as seamlessly integrative of the various stylistic influences. More significantly, I found myself in tears listening to the *baḍā khayāla* in *Śuddha Nāta*, and dancing to the short Gauḍa Malhāra *tarānā*. This, despite his informal observance of the architectural conventions of *khayāla* vocalism, often regarded as essential for effective musical communication!

In Gajananrao's music — to the extent the sample recordings will permit us to infer — it is difficult to isolate the relative strengths of Gwalior, Agra, and Jaipur–Atrauli philosophies of music-making. It is also difficult to ascertain which facet of his vocalism derived from his substantial commitment to the violin. It is, however, amply evident that, with the infusion of Agra and Jaipur–Atrauli stylistics, he rejuvenated the Gwalior legacy.

Coverage of Vocalists

The Gwalior–Agra legacy is represented in this book by Yashwant Buwa Joshi, a first generation migrant from Gwalior to Agra, and Ulhas Kashalkar, a disciple of Gajananrao Joshi. Both justify their classification by virtue of tutelage as well as the quality of their music.

3.2

Yashwant Buwa Joshi
A Pioneer of the Gwalior–Agra Confluence

YASHWANT Buwa Joshi (b. 1927) is an unusual musician who spent most of his adult life as a teacher far away from the limelight, and gained recognition as a performer only after the age of sixty. In what would be considered the sunset years of life, Yashwant Buwa's ("Buwa" is a suffix commonly used in Maharashtra to signify a respected, elderly gentleman) incredible vitality has earned him nationwide popularity, major honours, and a substantial presence in the commercial recordings market. Yashwant Buwa has performed on All India Radio since 1946, and currently occupies the top grade amongst empanelled musicians.

Joshi studied first with Mirashi Buwa (Yashwant Sadashiv Mirashi) of the Gwalior tradition, and switched thereafter to the Agra style. The switch did not, evidently, quench his thirst for musical ideas. He therefore went on to study with several other vocalists, representing an eclectic mix of styles. Today, he is respected as the last surviving pioneer of the Gwalior–Agra stylistic confluence in *khayāla* vocalism.

Struggle, Struggle, and Struggle, all the Way
Yashwant Buwa Spoke to the Author on 5 June 2003

"I was born and brought up in Pune. My father operated a couple of cabs in the city. He was untrained in music, but had a lovely voice and sang devotional songs very well. That is all I can claim by way of a family background in music. It was my uncle, Govardhan Buwa Naik, who was responsible for pushing me in this direction. He was an alumnus of the first batch (1901) of Vishnu Digambar's Gandharva Mahavidyalaya in Lahore under a nine-year apprenticeship in music.

"The only explanation for his having gone there was that lodging, boarding, and training were free. That was my grandfather's way of ensuring that his family could survive on his income. Govardhan Buwa could not sing, but became a competent player of the harmonium, *tabalā* and *dilrūbā* (a short-necked, fretted, lute of the bowed variety). So, after graduating, he started a music school in Bombay. Because he had no children, he was keen that I should train as a musician and take over its management after him.

"At my sacred thread ceremony, which took place when I was nine, my uncle invited the famous vocalist, Mirashi Buwa. My uncle's *guru*, Vishnu Digambar, and Mirashi Buwa had studied together under Balkrishna Buwa Ichalkaranjikar. My uncle and Mirashi Buwa thus belonged to a close-knit *gharānā* fraternity. Mirashi Buwa had just moved to Pune from Nasik, after serving a leading theatre company for 24 years. Over lunch, my uncle requested the stalwart to teach me, and he agreed. This is how it started. Every single day, after returning from school, I would go to Mirashi Buwa's house and learn music. As luck would have it, my uncle died within a year of my starting music lessons. There was no longer a ready business awaiting me. But, I continued studying music.

"The relationship was in the traditional mould, the only difference being that I continued to live with my parents. I paid no fees, and spent all my time — other than school — with my *guru*. Initially, the teaching was by the direct method — reproducing what the *guru* sings. No questions were to be asked. No logic was to be understood. Despite this, within five years, I found myself so intoxicated with music that I could no longer concentrate on my studies. So, four years short of graduation, I quit school in favour of music.

"My training with Mirashi Buwa continued for 12 years. By this time, I was 21, and had to start making a living. Music was all I knew. Those were difficult days for musicians, particularly in Pune. I spent a whole year contemplating my course of action. My childhood friend, and neighbour from Pune, Ram Marathe, was by now in Bombay, making some headway as a professional singer. So, in 1950, I decided to take on the world with his helping hand. Though I had no experience, the only path open to me was teaching music. Fees were poor in those days. Each student would pay Rs. 10 or 15 per month. With great difficulty, I earned about Rs. 50 a month. But, living was cheap — my monthly food bill was Rs. 30 — I managed.

"Though I did not inherit the music school that my father and uncle had intended, teaching was evidently my destiny. For over 50 years now, I have been teaching. I must have, by now, taught over 125 students. Several have become successful vocalists. Some are just making a living as music teachers. Some pursue other professions and enjoy music as a hobby. And, many have merged into the faceless audience of Hindustani music.

"Moving to Bombay widened my horizons. Soon after I moved, Jagannath Buwa Purohit moved into our locality. I was greatly attracted to his style. So, I studied with him for about six years. In the same spirit, I studied with K.G. Ginde, S.C.R. Bhat, Nivrutti Buwa Sarnaik, Master Krishnarao Phulambrikar, Mallikarjun Mansoor, and the *Nāṭya Saṅgīta* singer, Chota Gandharva. In my childhood, I had heard Ramkrishna Vaze, and his style had made a deep impact on me. So, in my singing, you will find the glimpses of each of these stalwarts.

"I am conservative, but not orthodox. I have a strong foundation laid in the Gwalior style. But, I was never a prisoner of the *gharānā*. I sought out every musician whose style attracted me, and learnt from him what I could. Jagannath Buwa often told me that the basic requirement of music is that magical quality called *Raṅga* (literally: colour). As a quality in music, *Raṅga* transcends considerations of voice quality, grammar and communication of *rāsa* (emotional content). Public appeal is not my yardstick for validating my music. I will not sacrifice the dignity of my art to charm audiences. I will not, for instance, make a *ṭhumarī* out of a *khayāla*, or start singing with my body. But, an artiste cannot be a mere scientist. If he wants to command an audience and also command respect, he has to strike the tricky balance between the sanctity of art and the listening pleasure of audiences. If he cannot do this, he can remain a teacher.

"My recordings have been in the market for several years. I have been performing on the radio since 1946, and also broadcast two National Programmes over All India Radio. And, for a long time, nobody noticed. In the last ten years, people suddenly realized that Yashwant Buwa can also sing. Today, I have admirers not only in our home state of Maharashtra, but also in Calcutta, Delhi and a few other cities. Several institutions have bestowed honours on me for my services as a teacher and performer. At 75, I can still hold an audience for two hours. I have no regrets. But, had recognition come when I was younger, people would have heard better music from me.

"Our times were tough. The status of musicians in society was low. There was no support for music either from government or from private benefactors or institutions. There was no "career" in music, except for the greatest. Audiences were small. The *guru* was the only source of musical inputs for students. There was radio, and there was the gramophone; but not many people could afford either. There were concerts; but mainly for invited audiences.

"To begin with, finding a *guru* was tough. We did not pay fees, but rendered all manner of services in lieu of training. The relationship was totally one-sided, and often exploitative. He taught the way he wanted to, and there was no appeal against it. There was no notation, no possibility of recording training sessions, no grammar, no logic. You could encounter musicians who could sing a *rāga* very well, but go blank if you asked them the scale of the *rāga*. Learning was primarily by reproducing what the *guru* sang. From studying music, to making a career, it was struggle, struggle, and struggle all the way. The positive aspect of this was that, because of the price they had paid for their success, the survivors conducted themselves, and practised their art, with dignity. They treated that passage between the stage and the audiences as sacred.

"The situation today is exactly the reverse. Anyone can learn music if he can afford it. Good *guru*s are, of course, more scarce than they were in our times, and locating them can take a lot of trial and error. Recorded music is so accessible that it is possible to become a reasonable vocalist even without a *guru*. The relationship between the *guru* and his disciple is now a commercial one. A student can demand an explanation of the logic and get it. He can record training sessions for revision. Career opportunities are plenty, and the money is good for the successful. Society, government, and institutions encourage music.

"Most important is the emergence of a market, with audiences willing to pay for music. For creating a substantial class of connoisseurs, we have to thank the educational efforts of the two giants, Bhatkhande and Vishnu Digambar, and their followers. Glamour and money have now made music a rat race that everyone with half a chance wants to join. The journey is still tough. And, it is a struggle, which demands compromises with the artist's dignity. It makes art cross the frontier between the musician and the audience and to delve into the audience's pockets. And, yes, many bright kids now get money and fame ahead of maturity, get bloated heads, stagnate, and fall by the wayside. The demands of success are changing, as they inevitably will. Despite these anxieties, I am optimistic about Hindustani music for several reasons — today's kids are intelligent and talented; studying music is no longer difficult; and there are ample opportunities for building a career in it."

Yashwant Buwa's Music

I base my observations on the study of one CD recorded by the artiste for India Archive Music Ltd. New York, and several concert recordings. The repertoire reviewed here consists of *khayāla* renditions in Darabārī Kanāda, Kedāra, Śivamat Bhairava, Bhairava-Bahāra, Alhaiya Bilāwala, Deśakara, Kamoda, Bagesrī and Adanā. Except for Śivamat Bhairava and Bhairava-Bahāra, Yashwant Buwa's repertoire appears dominated by commonly heard *rāga*s, especially from vocalists of the Gwalior tradition. This pattern is confirmed by his concert presence in the recent past.

Yashwant Buwa sings at a fundamental/tonic at D, below the high-pitched norm of Gwalior, though a notch above the

C# common amongst Indian male voices. His voice has a mildly grating quality, with a slight nasality similar to Vilayat Hussain Khan of Agra. Two factors suggest that his natural pitch could be lower — a tightening of the timbre in the voice delivery, and the absence of the *uttarāṅga* bias commonly found in Gwalior vocalism. The slightly uncomfortable pitch might have been acquired while reproducing his *guru*'s singing during his early years of training. Despite this, the voice has withstood the ravages of time admirably, and maintains its timbre and tonal correctness through a two-octave melodic canvas. The voice is equally comfortable in the forceful vocalization of the Agra variety and the fluidity of smooth melodic contours typical of Gwalior vocalism.

Yashwant Buwa's approach to melodic execution is orthodox Gwalior/Agra, relying entirely on *mīṇḍa, gamaka* and *khaṭkā* methods to define his melodic contours. The ornate *murkī* and *kan* varieties of execution are missing from his style. His melodic contours are a combination of the smooth curves found in Gwalior vocalism, and the angular edges found in Agra. Jaw movement, a common feature in early 20th-century Gwalior vocalism, frequently powers his *Gamaka*s.

Yashwant Buwa appears to have no strong predilections in the choice of articulatory devices. His *auchara*s are presented entirely in *ākāra* articulation rather than the *dhrupada* style Nom-Tom articulation often found in Gwalior and Agra vocalism. They convey the distinct impression of being pre-composed, and could therefore reflect the Gwalior practice of structuring the *auchara* as a roadmap of the *bandiśa* to follow. In the *ālāpa*s, true to the Gwalior tradition, the *ākāra* articulation appears more frequently in the lower half of the melodic canvas, and a mild pulsation enters the melody when *bola*-articulation begins in the upper half. He handles his *bola-laya,* and *tāna*s using *ākāra,* as well as *bola* devices. He occasionally substitutes the HA articulation for the AA vowel (*ākāra*) as a device for achieving a rhythmic emphasis with forceful and staccato intonation. In the articulation of the poetic element, Yashwant Buwa occasionally deploys Agra-style timbre manipulations and conversational utterances to highlight literary meaning and suggest emotional content.

The architecture of his *vilambita khayāla* renditions conforms to the informality of pre-Independence Gwalior and Agra vocalism. His *ālāpa*s often have brisk passages smuggled into them. The *bola-laya/ bola-bāṇṭa* movement and the *bola-tāna*s are often treated as overlapping movements.

A fundamental aspect of Yashwant Buwa's music is its vigour and animated quality. This is most clearly reflected in the floor level tempo of his *khayāla* renditions. The *vilambita khayāla*s in *ekatāla/jhūmara/tilvāḍā* are launched at a tempo of 36-38 bpm, and end at 45-52 bpm. This is a brisk tempo, close to the upper limit for *vilambita khayāla* rendition. This has wider implications. The higher the tempo of the rendition, the greater tends to be the degree of correspondence between the poetic, melodic and rhythmic elements, and the greater the grip of rhythm over melody. The slower the tempo of rendition, the greater is the liberation of melody from the rhythm.

In the temporal dimension, there is clearly an element of populism, too. As the tempo rises, music becomes more intelligible to lay listeners, with the more discerning also getting involved enough with counting of beats. This aspect may relate, though not exclusively, to that magical quality called *Raṅga* that Yashwant Buwa's second *guru*, Jagannath Buwa, advised him to cultivate.

Because of the tremendous diversity of temporal practices, it is not possible to typify the temporal approach of Gwalior vocalism in Yashwant Buwa's generation or even the preceding generation. Yashwant Buwa's own tendencies can, however, be appreciated in comparison with typical approaches of other *khayāla* traditions. In Yashwant Buwa's generation, Kairana vocalists at the melody-dominant polarity could launch their *vilambita khayāla*s at as slow as 14-20 bpm. Where melody is completely homogenized with rhythm, orthodox Jaipur–Atrauli launches *vilambita khayāla*s at 25-33 bpm. At the rhythm-dominant end, Ustad Faiyyaz Khan's *vilambita khayāla*s in Jaijaivantī and Bhūpa, both *ekatāla*, are rendered in the 38-42 bpm range, (HMV: STC-850137). Yashwant Buwa's *vilambita khayāla*s in the 38-52 bpm range appear to come closest to the Agra tendency towards allowing the rhythmic element to drive the melody.

Yashwant Buwa's *ālāpa* follows the narrative, rather than the melodic approach often described as *behlāva* (informal flows). The narrative approach is derived from the *dhrupada* genre of Hindustani music, and sees *rāga*-ness as residing in a string of characteristic phrases. The narrative approach is found in orthodox Gwalior, Agra, and orthodox Jaipur–Atrauli vocalism — though in different forms — while the melodic, geometric, and symmetric approaches to progression feature more prominently in *ālāpa*s of Kairana, and even neo-Jaipur–Atrauli vocalism. These latter approaches view the *rāga* as an abstract melodic entity, with its *rāga*-ness residing in the permitted selection and sequencing of *svara*s. As such, they define a more categorical departure of the *khayāla* genre from the *rāga*-elaboration practices of the mediaeval *dhrupada* genre.

In the lower half of the melodic canvas, Yashwant Buwa's *ālāpa*s are reasonably free from the pulsation that enters Agra *ālāpa*s fairly early on in the rendition. The Agra influence is most evident in Joshi's *bola-laya/bola-bāṇṭa* movement, which is Agra's forte. His *bola-laya* is replete with *dhrupada*-style *layakārī*, *dugunā-tigunā* manipulations, and even *sura-paranas*. These are prominent features of Agra vocalism.

In the rendering of his *druta bandiśes*, an important fact of Agra vocalism called *sthāyī bharaṇa* is in ample evidence. *Sthāyī bharaṇa* (filling up/enriching the *sthāyī*) is a technique of timbre variations and emphasis on specific words to enrich the emotive power of the rendition.

In his *tāna*s movement, the Agra influence is relatively minor. The three-stroke and four-stroke intonation typical of Agra is entirely missing. His *tāna*s are predominantly in 2-stroke *gamaka* and *ekaharā* execution. In his medium density *gamaka*-driven *tāna*s, echoes of Mallikarjun Mansoor's Jaipur–Atrauli bias are faintly audible. As in Gwalior, the patterning follows primarily the *chūṭa* and *sapāṭa* formations, with a bias in favour of descending waves across broad melodic spans. The influence of Agra *tāna*s is visible only in the use of forceful staccato intonation for accentuating the rhythmic facet. Well into his seventies at the time of writing, Joshi unleashes his *sapāṭa tāna*s in *ākāra* articulation with a fluidity, and clarity on par with D.V. Paluskar, another Gwalior maestro, who died when he was less than half Yashwant Buwa's age.

Joshi's *rāga* grammar is impeccable and authoritative. However, his melodic exploration of *rāga*-ness exhibits a degree of predictability. This may have become second nature because of the manner in which he was taught in his youth, and reinforced with decades of teaching a large number of variously motivated and unevenly talented students.

Yashwant Buwa's command over the rhythmic element is awesome. His variants on the *mukhaḍā*, and *tihāī*s in *āmada* as well as *mukhaḍā* placements are masterpieces of spontaneous improvization. Throughout the recordings surveyed here, not a single rhythmic manoeuvre — and there are many — exhibits the slightest clumsiness. Finesse in the simultaneous manipulation of rhythmic and melodic elements is fundamental to *khayāla* vocalism and can, of course, be found in the best of all *gharānās*. In Yashwant Buwa's music, its presence is sober and non-intrusive — unlike Agra, where it tends to get magnified by isolation for special attention and, frequently, for titillating effect.

Yashwant Buwa's style displays a considerable influence of Agra vocalism, and leans towards the rhythm-biased end of the stylistic spectrum. His manner has moved towards Agra; but his matter has remained rooted in Gwalior. He was looking for *raṅga*, which belongs to the territory of manner. He borrowed as much of it from Agra as he could integrate into Gwalior, and did so with coherent results.

Joshi enjoys his stature on the concert platform because of the vintage quality of his music, and the electrifying vivacity of his performances. His music possesses special appeal for the 50+ generation of audiences, who have appreciated orthodox Gwalior and Agra vocalism in their heyday. Although the generational divide in audience preferences is perhaps not as sharp as this observation might suggest, it is fair to acknowledge how much *khayāla* vocalism has changed over the last quarter of a century.

Classicism has given way to a marked romanticism, and the notion of *rāga*-ness has achieved a higher level of abstraction, requiring the performer to explore it with much greater imagination and deliberateness. In such an environment, Joshi's music may not successfully combat the forces of aesthetic obsolescence. Considering that the other pioneers of the Gwalior–Agra confluence remain largely unpublished, the substantial body of Yashwant Buwa's recordings with All India Radio, in the music stores, and with private collectors will remain an important testimony to a fascinating stage in the history of *khayāla* vocalism (Written : June 2003).

3.3

Ulhas Kashalkar
Emerging as a "Musicians' Musician"

OF Ulhas Khashalkar, the senior music critic, Prakash Wadhera, (*The Hindu*, 1 December 2000) wrote:

> To listen to Ulhas is to augment your knowledge. Though one is naturally hesitant to call one, who is without a grey hair on his head, a "musicians' musician", Ulhas Kashalkar bids fair to be one in not too distant a future.

Despite the disadvantage of being brought up in a small town devoid of competent *gurus*, Ulhas (b. 1955) pursued his passion for music through academic as well as the traditional routes to emerge as an eminent vocalist.

Up to the age of 20, Ulhas was trained in vocal music by his father, an Attorney by profession, based in Amarāvatī. Along with this, he took his graduation and postgraduate degrees in Hindustani music. Thereafter, under a scholarship granted to him by the Government of India, Ulhas moved to Bombay for training with vocalists groomed in the traditional system. He trained, for six years, with Pandit Ram Marathe, a vocalist of the Gwalior and Agra traditions, and for another six years, with Pandit Gajananrao Joshi, a Gwalior Gharānā maestro, who had incorporated Agra as well as Jaipur–Atrauli features into his idiom. Ulhas' exceptional mind integrated this grooming into a convincing personal statement.

Ulhas became an empanelled artist of All India Radio in 1982, and now occupies its top grade. His discography begins from 1987, and covers recordings published in India and abroad. He started concert tours outside India in 1993, and is now a respected and popular performer in the USA, Canada, UK, UAE, France, and Switzerland. Currently, Ulhas serves as a resident *guru* at the ITC Sangeet Research Academy, Calcutta, India's first conservatory type institution for music education.

Ulhas is a remarkably aware musician. He has a strong grounding in the theory of music. He has studied the music of the modern greats, and acquired an astute understanding of the different *gharānā*s and their styles. He is alert to the complex interplay of continuity and change in the Hindustani tradition. He understands the makings of a vocalist well enough to guide his juniors. He is perceptive of how connoisseurs and influentials of the music world judge, and determine the fate of, musicians. Inevitably, even if unconsciously, this intricate web of sensitivities influences his approach to his own evolution as a musician. And, yet, he refuses to put his own music under a microscope, lest his observation interfere with the mysterious process by which musicians discover themselves.

The Making of a Vocalist
(Ulhas Spoke to the Author on 1 January 2000)

"I have had a variety of influences on my music. Even my *gurus* brought a multiplicity of influences with them. I like great music from all *gharānās*. As a listener, I am also a student. But, my preferences are with individual musicians rather than *gharānās*. As such, I would be hard put to say which *gharānā*'s style dominates my own singing. I don't consciously try singing in any particular style. I am more concerned that my music should be pleasing, and communicate the mood of the *rāga*. All my training, and the great music I have heard, contributes to this effort; and this happens in ways I do not fully understand. And, yet, it is possible that in a particular *rāga*, you can notice a marked influence of a great vocalist whose rendering of it has made a deep impact on me. With so much recorded music available nowadays, this can happen to anyone.

"*Gharānās* are not cages, and were never intended to be that, either. Consider the background of so many modern giants in *khayāla* music. They had all studied with three or four *gurus*, often from different *gharānās*. Bhaskar Buwa Bakhle is a great example. He had studied the Agra, Jaipur–Atrauli as well as Gwalior styles. So did my *guru*, Gajananrao Joshi. Then, consider Vilayat Hussain Khan, whom we consider an Agra exponent. He listed forty *gurus* of his. Obviously, all forty of them were not Agra vocalists!

"I have heard it said that until a few years ago, my music had a strong Gwalior flavour and that, in recent years, it is acquiring the Agra touch. This is typically superficial trade talk, because this is not quite the way it works. Today, a vocalist, if he is good, is exposed to public scrutiny right in the midst of the most vulnerable stage in his evolution — the stage when he is struggling to break out of the shell of his training, and to make his own original statement. Until then, in most cases, his training has not achieved much more than making him a good replica of his *guru*. But, having been thrown into the professional circuit, he cannot risk sounding like a poor xerox of the *guru*. This builds a great deal of tension in him, making him try out different approaches to shaping his original musical statement. During this period, his music can easily seem like a shifting patchwork of clichés drawn from different styles. Sometimes, he might even be judged as impatient, restless, or confused.

"It takes a musician a long time to abstract, from his training, the principles of music making which have been imparted to him. It is only because this is possible and necessary, that a great *guru* can produce several disciples, all of whom are originals, but also have the stamp of his, or the *gharānā*'s, training in their music. Look at the variety amongst Sawai Gandharva's disciples — Bhimsen Joshi, Gangubai Hangal, Phiroze Dastoor. Each of them is unique and yet in the same mould. I would like to know what connoisseurs thought of these luminaries when they were twenty-five. The chances are that they were not even visible, at that age, on the horizon of professional music!

"Even with the best of training, the process of self-discovery in a vocalist matures only around the age of forty. Until then, a vocalist does not fully understand his own training, the significant features of his own and other *gharānā*s, his own musical temperament, or even the eccentricities of his own voice. This is why I discourage influentials in the music world from jumping to premature conclusions about young vocalists.

"Today, the brightest talent is able to achieve recognition much earlier in life than was possible just two generations ago. The market starts paying you early. So, it demands that a twenty-five-year-old should match up to the maturity of Ameer Khan or Kesarbai Kerkar at the age of fifty. I know this cannot be helped. But, we should not be unfair to budding talent; nor can we succumb to the generalized feeling that contemporary vocalists are pushing *khayāla* music down the drain. To those in a hurry to judge us, my request is to give us time until we are forty — until we get our act together. Our task is made more difficult by having to mature under public gaze. But, we are serious about music, and discovering ourselves through it, exactly as earlier generations have done. But, this cannot happen overnight.

At the ITC Sangeet Research Academy, at the moment, I have ITC four students assigned to me under a personalized apprenticeship programme. They are gifted and they work hard. We have our own internal systems for tracking the progress of students. Outsiders watching our efforts often ask how well my wards are doing, and how they will shape up as musicians. My answer is always the same: Give them ten or fifteen years of struggle on the concert platform before you decide. Until then, neither I, nor they, nor you, will know how well their training at the Academy has worked for them.

Stylistic Perspectives

Ulhas' first *guru* with a *gharānā* pedigree was Ram Marathe. According to Ulhas, Marathe had been trained in the Gwalior and Agra styles of classical music, but had chosen to build a career primary in *nāṭya saṅgīta*. An audition of classical performances by Ram Marathe reveals a stronger influence of the fluid and racy Gwalior style, than the more aggressive Agra style. Marathe was reportedly also greatly influenced by the multiple-*gharānā* stylistic blend evident in the magnetic vocalism of Ulhas' second *guru*, Gajananrao Joshi. It would appear that the foundations of Ulhas' vocalism were laid in this mix of stylistic influences.

Of the various influences on Ulhas' musicianship, his last *guru*, Gajananrao Joshi (d. 1987) would appear to have been the most decisive in shaping his style. Concert recordings of

Gajananrao, accompanied by Ulhas are available to establish that Ulhas has substantially internalized Joshi's concert presence, a legacy also evident in Ulhas' renditions of recent years, as a mature musician. By temperament, of course, the two seem to differ. Ulhas' approach to music would probably be considered more cerebral than that of Gajananrao.

Like his *guru*, Gajananrao, Ulhas sings in a natural voice. His timbre has a certain dryness; but his vocalization lacks his *guru*'s guttural potential in the lower registers, and the sharpness of the angularities in melodic execution. Despite this, there is no mistaking the mild aggressiveness of Agra vocalism in Ulhas' intonation. Like his *guru*, Ulhas tends to resort occasionally to jaw-powered vocalisation, encountered more commonly in Gwalior vocalism than any rival tradition.

Compared to his *guru*, Ulhas' music shows a weaker influence of Jaipur–Atrauli vocalism. In Ulhas' music, the raciness of the Gwalior style and the lively rhythmicality of Agra vocalism have been subdued by the melody-oriented and deliberate music-making approach reminiscent of Kairana vocalism, which was at the forefront of Hindustani music throughout his formative years. The Kairana influence is also evident in his treatment of some *rāga*s, like Multānī.

The architecture of Ulhas' *ḳhayāla* presentations falls in line with the formalistic protocol which became "industry standard" by the third quarter of the twentieth century. His *baḍā khayāla* is prefaced with an *auchara*, a summary delineation of the *rāga* form. Like Gajananrao, and several Gwalior vocalists, Ulhas is wont to use *dhrupada* style Nom-Tom (meaningless consonants) articulation in his *auchara*. His *baḍā khayāla* has three distinct movements: the *bola-ālāpa*, *bola-bāṇṭa*, and *bola-tāna*s. In line, again, with contemporary trends, the durational balance of his *khayāla* presentations is no longer skewed heavily in favour of the *baḍā khayāla.*

Except for this architectural standardization, Ulhas' approach to music remains firmly rooted in the Gajananrao mould, with a strong reliance on the melodic personality of the *rāga*, indeed its characteristic phraseology, as the primary building block for his renditions. In comparison to Gajananrao's music, Ulhas' rendition is more transparent of his designing intentions. His approach to developing the melody — through all the movements — exhibits a story-telling intent. He tends to take up a melodic idea, maybe a phrase, and then weaves melodic sentences, and paragraphs around it to consummate its comprehension. This approach makes for an absorbing musical experience.

The formalism of his architecture does not draw any particular attention to itself in the way architecture of Kairana or neo-Jaipur–Atrauli does. His adoption of it does not, in any way, dilute the sculpture-dominant quality of his music. He treats the melody with respect, without any sign of frivolity or populist intent. The *mīṇḍa*, *gamaka*, and *khaṭkā* are his predominant melodic expressions. His use of the more seductive decorative elements such as *kan* or *murkī* is negligible in his *khayāla*s, as also in his *ṭhumarī* rendiitions.

Ulhas' *tāna*s are far more absorbing than those of most vocalists of the post-Independence generation. This is because Ulhas generally avoids the mechanistic varieties of *tāna* patterns, especially the *alaṁkāra tāna*s. He does not sing *tāna*s to either dazzle or intimidate, but to tell a story, using the melodic framework of the *rāga* as the language. Because of his narrative approach, the sculpting of his *tāna*s has to be understood in clusters of *tāna*s rather than in isolation. Like his *guru*, he makes generous use of the Jaipur–Atrauli style medium density *tāna*s structured with tonal pairs, with a mild *gamaka* vocalization.

Unlike his *guru*, however, Ulhas makes considerable use of *chūṭa tānas*, which have been popular with Gwalior musicians. Unlike many vocalists of his generation, he makes considerable use of short-span *baḍhata* and *laḍīguthāva* patterns, which are a part of his story-telling approach to *tāna* construction.

Prakash Wadhera (*The Hindu*, 1 December 2000) makes incisive comments on Ulhas' style and approach to music:

> "Ulhas Kashalkar's merit lies in the fact that he never goes against the technical injunctions of the *rāga*, as set forth in the preamble of the melody. . . . He seldom exercises or seeks fulfilment of his own desires. . . . As to the style of Ulhas, which presents an intimate blend of Gwalior, Agra and Jaipur-Atrauli styles, on the face of it, it looks too monolithic and compact that the eye does not easily detect the graftings. It is only when he comes to the *tānas* that one perceives clear postures of Agra and a lesser degree of Gwalior in the typical patterns, divisions of *laya* and utterance, its snappings, emphatic and ejaculatory accents and emanations. The trend of Ulhas' slow exposition, in his choice of rhythm and pace approaches to the *mukhaḍā* usher into the exposition, bear out his Jaipur–Atrauli connection. In some double-syllabled (two-by-two) *tānas*. . . and in his tapering approach and perch on the *tāra ṣaḍja*, one is involuntarily reminded of the late Mallikarjun Mansoor.

Ulhas' music is an aesthetically coherent blend of various stylistic influences. It is his original statement, which exhibits a fine musical mind at work. It is, indeed, cerebral in its origins, and can be intellectually demanding on his listeners. It is aloof, but not arrogant. It is art music, well fortified against a drift towards entertainment. It is engaging because of its structural soundness, melodic richness, rhythmic dexterity, and the transparency of communicative intent. There is, indeed, a hint of elitism in his repertoire selection, and his approach to music. But, he does not seem to care if his music gives him more of stature than popularity (Written : October 2001).

Section 4
The Jaipur–Atrauli Legacy

4.1

Perspectives on the Jaipur–Atrauli Legacy

THIS chapter deals with those aspects of the Jaipur–Atrauli legacy which are immediately relevant to appreciating the stylistic tendencies of musicians covered in this book.

The Jaipur–Atrauli legacy consists of two streams: the orthodox and the neo-Jaipur–Atrauli. Amongst recorded musicians, the orthodox stream is represented most significantly by Kesarbai Kerkar, and the neo-Jaipur–Atrauli stream by its fountainhead, Kishori Amonkar, who belongs to the third generation. Neo-Jaipur–Atrauli has also acquired a following far beyond the tutelage relationships of *gharānā* maestros.

The founder of the Jaipur–Atrauli Gharānā, Ustad Alladiya Khan (1855-1946) belonged to a lineage of *dhrupada* vocalists practising the Dagar Bani style. He was trained by his uncles, Daulat Khan and Jehangir Khan. The latter, a scholarly exponent of *dhrupada* as well as *khayāla*, is generally regarded as Alladiya Khan's principal mentor. By his own admission, Alladiya Khan had also absorbed the enigmatic style of Mubarak Ali Khan, a vocalist of the Gwalior Gharānā at the Jaipur court, and regretted not having been able to study with him. Considering that Alladiya Khan is not known to have ever served at the Jaipur court or resided in the city, this inspiration might explain the Jaipur prefix to the *gharānā*'s name.

Alladiya Khan served several princely states as a court musician for short periods before finally moving to Bombay to pursue an independent career as a teacher and performer. When he was about 40, one of his princely patrons demanded services which placed an inordinate strain on Alladiya's voice, depriving it of much of its resonance and attractiveness. During the two years it took him to regain performing competence, he was obliged to develop a style that was less dependent on low-density melody (*ālāpa*). What emerged from this struggle was a unique musical experience, which blended his *dhrupada* training with the Mubarak Ali inspiration. The alchemy attracted an enviable following, and laid the foundations of a new *gharānā*.

The stature of the *gharānā* he founded can be judged by the "Koṭhīwāle" (storehouse) suffix that its name acquired. This suffix was accorded only to *gharānā*s and musicians who commanded a vast inventory of *rāga*s and *bandiśe*s. According to Dhondutai Kulkarni, the last surviving exponent of orthodox Jaipur–Atrauli vocalism, Alladiya Khan's repertoire of *rāga*s spanned 4000 out of a total of 16,000 known melodic entities.

As the fountainhead of a new style, Alladiya Khan had an able ally in his brother, Hyder Khan, who was also trained by their uncles, Daulat Khan and Jehangir Khan. Their progeny were gifted, and played a significant role in propagating the *gharānā*. Alladiya Khan had three sons — Nasruddin Khan (Badeji), Badruddin (Manji) Khan, and Shamsuddin (Bhurji) Khan. Of the three, Manji Khan, trained by Alladiya as well as Hyder Khan, was the musical genius, and a brilliant performer. Bhurji Khan devoted his life to teaching. To him goes the credit for grooming several distinguished heirs to the Alladiya legacy. Hyder Khan had one son, Natthan Khan, who was a competent performer and also a good teacher.

Outside the founding family, the two most distinguished exponents of the Alladiya/Jaipur–Atrauli Gharānā were Kesarbai Kerkar (1892-1977), trained by Alladiya himself, and

Mogubai Kurdikar (1904-2001), trained by Alladiya Khan, and probably also by Hyder Khan. In the same generation was also a great, but low-key, vocalist, Lakshmibai Jadhav, who was trained by Hyder Khan. In the following generation, several disciples of Bhurji Khan distinguished themselves. The most famous amongst them was Mallikarjun Mansoor (1910-92), who was trained partially also by Manji Khan. In the generation thereafter, Mogubai's daughter, Kishori Amonkar (b. 1931), gave a new direction to Jaipur–Atrauli vocalism to emerge as the empress of the concert platform in the last quarter of the 20th century.

Beyond the second generation, kinship and heredity have played virtually no role in perpetuating the Alladiya style. What apparently made Alladiya Khan, and his family, highly sought-after as teachers was the sophistication of their vocalism, and their mastery over rare *rāga*s and rare *bandiśe*s. Because their idiom was difficult to master, it acquired an aura of elitism, and attracted exceptional and mature talent trained in other *gharānā*s. The *gharānā* found a way of preserving the core of Alladiya Khan's stylistic legacy, while permitting a cross-fertilization of musical ideas into its philosophy of evolution. This could explain its comparative resilience in an era that exposes other major *khayāla* traditions to a diminishing delivery of outstanding musicianship.

Jaipur–Atrauli Stylistics

In his conceptual framework for the stylistic classification of *khayāla gharānā*s referred to above, Deshpande[1] has placed the Jaipur–Atrauli style at the Golden Mean, characterized by *svara* (melody) conditioned by *laya* (rhythm), and *laya* conditioned by *svara*. Deodhar[3] described it as a style in which melody had been completely homogenized with rhythm.

According to Deshpande, the principal features of the Jaipur–Atrauli style are subtlety and complexity in all departments. The *gharānā* has perfected the technique of linking *svaras* in such a manner as to enable their individual aesthetic appreciation along with their phrasing significance. The melodic contours are devoid of angularities, and distinctive for their curvilinear form, moving in loops. The tempo is ultra-slow, and the progress of melody is marked by a continuous rhythmic swing, though not a distinct pulsation. The melody plays with rhythm not in tandem with the beats — as in the rhythm-dominant style of Agra — but in fractions of beats. It acquires an enigmatic quality with unexpected accentuations or elongations of *svaras*, or punctuation by silences to heighten the contrast. The internal structure of each movement keeps changing all the time, thus avoiding repetition and monotony. In its totality, Deshpande considers the orthodox Jaipur–Atrauli style highbrow, and akin to a musical bank for musicians.

In the style developed by Alladiya Khan, as described by Deodhar,[3] elaborate slow *ālāpas* had been dispensed with, while the total duration of a *khayāla* presentation was curtailed to about 20 minutes. This probably suited the *ustād*'s damaged vocalization mechanism. His repertoire was vast, and included many rare and compound *rāgas*. He specialized in performing several *rāgas* of the same melodic group/family in the same session, thus posing the challenge of *rāga* differentiation to connoisseurs.

His style was characterized by oblique *ālāpas* and *tānas*, with fresh improvizations emerging from a shifting accentuation of different *svaras* or beats. He wove the *mukhaḍā* so deftly into the improvizations, that the *sama* often came and went unnoticed. On other occasions, the *mukhaḍā* would arrive at the *sama* with stunning impact. His *tānas* were scintillating, leading him frequently to be criticised for being obsessed with technical wizardry.

A unique feature of Jaipur–Atrauli vocalism is the manner in which the *gharānā* treats compound *rāgas*. The classical conventions for combining mature *rāga*s fuse compatible *rāga*s either directionally, or at the scalar midpoint. The directional fusion comes into being with one *rāga* being followed in the ascent, and the other in the descent. The fusiosn at the scalar mid-point delivers one *rāga* in the *pūrvāṅga* and the other in the *uttarāṅga*. Jaipur–Atrauli tends to ignore both these conventions and settles for the third, and more difficult, approach — of constructing the entire compound *rāga* as a string of alternating phrases from the component *rāga*s. This approach has the advantage of being able to structure compounds with more than two component *rāga*s. The Jaipur–Atrauli inventory of compound *rāga*s includes *rāga*s which blend as many as six *rāga*s into an alchemical compound. This approach to the fusion of *rāga*s, coupled with the Jaipur–Atrauli flair for rare and esoteric *rāga*s, has reinforced the elitist image of the *gharānā*'s vocalism.

These features of orthodox Jaipur–Atrauli have remained dominant in the music of the lineage right up to Mallikarjun Mansoor. Revisionist tendencies surfaced with the advent of Kishori Amonkar.

Jaipur–Atrauli and Neo-Jaipur–Atrauli

Kishori deviated from orthodox Jaipur–Atrauli in three major respects. Firstly, she stripped the tradition of its elitism in terms of content. Rare, compound, and esoteric *rāga*s, which were the hallmark of her seniors, lost their dominant place in her repertoire. To make sense to contemporary audiences, Kishori even adopted *rāga*s like Haṁsadhvani, a recent import from the Carnatic tradition, popularized primarily by Kairana vocalists.

Secondly, she bade farewell to the aloofness characteristic of the *khayāla* genre, and to the *dhrupada* style melodic sculpture characteristic of Jaipur–Atrauli vocalism, allowing it to express the emotional intensity with which she feels her music. As a part of this tendency, she admitted into the *khayāla* melodic expressions that were hitherto considered more appropriate in the semi-classical and popular genres. In recognition of these tendencies, Deshpande[2] considers Kishori one of the leaders of the romanticist movement in post-Independence vocalism. Considering the significance of her departure from orthodox Jaipur–Atrauli, and the magnitude of her influence, Kishori Amonkar may be regarded as the progenitor of "neo-Jaipur–Atrauli" vocalism.

Finally, she restored to Jaipur–Atrauli a sophisticated sense of architecture. She reintroduced the elaborate and disciplined *ālāpa* movement, which Alladiya Khan had reportedly to abandon. Although Kesarbai before her had substantially enhanced the *ālāpa* movement, Kesarbai's *ālāpa* still followed the narrative approach derived from *dhrupada*, rather than the more abstract melodic approach that Kairana had, by then, introduced to *khayāla* vocalism. Kishori's melodic approach was closer to Kairana vocalism, which dominated the *khayāla* scene during Kishori's formative years. Kishori's *ālāpa* appears inspired by the neo-Kairana vocalist, Ustad Ameer Khan (1912-74). As a corollary to an elaborate *ālāpa*, Kishori also gave Jaipur–Atrauli vocalism a more fastidious sense of architecture — again probably inspired by Ameer Khan.

The Kishori phenomenon has effectively bifurcated the Jaipur–Atrauli Gharānā into two streams, both rooted in the foundations laid by Alladiya Khan. Orthodox Jaipur–Atrauli survives in the art and tutelage links of stalwarts like Dhondutai Kulkarni and Madhusudan Kanetkar, who were trained by the second generation of the Alladiya family. The neo-Jaipur–Atrauli stream is represented by the music and tutelage links of Kishori Amonkar. Neo-Jaipur–Atrauli, however, also has a superficial following amongst the thousands of Kishori xeroxes, for whom her pre-recorded music is the only gateway to her musical wisdom. An interesting, though inexplicable, facet of the two Jaipur–Atrauli streams is that, neither of them can any longer boast of a significant male vocalist.

The Music of Lakshmibai Jadhav

In addition to Kesarbai Kerkar and Mogubai Kurdikar, the music of Lakshmibai Jadhav is an important triumph of Jaipur–Atrauli vocalism. Lakshmibai belonged to the same generation as the two earlier mentioned, but had studied with Alladiya Khan's brother, Hyder Khan. Though a low-key personality, Lakshmibai enjoyed immense stature as a musician, and spent many years as a court musician to the Maharaja of Baroda. A few of Lakshmibai's recordings were available, enabling a glimpse of a relatively unknown exponent of orthodox Jaipur–Atrauli vocalism

What I was able to access is a small selection of Lakshmibai's radio broadcasts, and base my observations on the sample. The 75 minute archive covers the following pieces: Vihaṅga (*vilambita khayāla*: 25 mts), Hiṇḍola-Bahāra (*madhya-laya khayāla*: 3.5 mts. incomplete), Khat (*vilambita khayāla*: 5 mts incomplete), Nanda (*vilambita* and *druta khayāla*: 22 mts) and Basantī-Kedāra *vilambita* and *druta khayāla*: 20 mts).

Dhondutai Kulkarni, who studied with Lakshmibai, reports that Lakshmibai's early vocalism exhibited considerable authority and power, though not quite comparable to Kesarbai's. In later years, after surgical intervention for a serious throat problem, her vocalism lost much of its punch, and the *tāna*s lost some of their agility. Dhondutai suspects that the sample recordings are from the last few years of her life, and to this extent, of limited use for an assessment of her vocalism. It is impossible to gauge which aspects of her vocalism were affected by her infirmity. Despite the probably unrepresentative sample, and its poor acoustic condition, some inferences may be drawn.

Interestingly, except for Nanda, all the *rāga*s in this archive are either rare or compound *rāga*s constructed in the special Jaipur–Ataruli style. All of them, without exception, are characterized by a convoluted or zigzag phraseology. This is a good reflection of the Jaipur–Atrauli Gharānā's penchant for challenging *rāga*s and melodic complexity. Two of the three *vilambita khayāla*s have a *druta khayāla* appended to them. The melodic structure of the *druta khayāla*s is, however, identical to the *vilambita khayāla*s. Independently composed *druta khayāla*s were, evidently, not a significant component of orthodox Jaipur–Atrauli vocalism in its early days.

Kesarbai's surviving archive of concert recordings reflects a similar pattern, while her Kairana contemporary, Roshanara Begum's legacy of Long Playing records contains no *druta khayāla* at all. This suggests that orthodox Jaipur–Atrauli was amongst *khayāla gharānā*s in that era, which treated the *vilambita khayāla* as the real *khayāla*, largely neglecting *druta khayāla*s. By the middle of the 20th century, the *druta khayāla* apparently entered Jaipur–Atrauli vocalism as a concession to its growing popularity. It was in the latter half of the century that *khayāla* vocalism began assigning distinct roles to the two *khayāla*s in terms of musical content. Even today, however, the genre, considered in its totality, is far from conceptual clarity on this issue.

Lakshmibai's voice is a melodious feminine voice, with its fundamental at G, the common pitch amongst Indian female vocalists. It is a voice cultivated in the Jaipur–Atrauli mould, to deliver a clear AA vowel and uniformity of timbre across two octaves, without a trace of nasality. Its breadth is greater than that of Mogubai's voice, but far short of the virtual masculinity of Kesarbai's voice. The delivery of the voice possesses the no-nonsense aloofness typical of orthodox Jaipur–Atrauli vocalists but without the authoritative stance of Kesarbai.

The architecture of Lakshmibai's *khayāla* presentation appears informal rather than either enigmatic (like Kesarbai's) or fastidious (like Kishori's). After the rendition has moved from the *ālāpa* into the *tāna*s, there are frequent regressions into low-density music, which seem more prolonged than would be justified as mere breathers. The relentlessness of progression evident in Kesarbai's *khayāla*s, despite the fluidity of borders between the movements, is absent from Lakshmibai's available recordings. We do not know whether this feature was habitual or a sequel to the debilitation of her vocalization organs.

Lakshmibai's preferred opening tempo for the *vilambita khayāla* was between 21 and 34 bpm for *Tīnatāla* and *ada cautāla*, and a notch higher at about 38 bpm for *jhapatāla*. Her *madhya-laya tīnatāla khayāla* opened at 52 bpm. The acceleration of the tempo through the rendition was imperceptible, and could vary by 15 per cent to 30 per cent from the opening tempo. The temporal parameters are broadly comparable to Kesarbai's music.

Lakshmibai's *vilambita khayāla*s typically have only two improvisatory movements — the *ālāpa* primarily in *ākāra* articulation with an occasional use of *bola* articulation, and the *tāna*s. The *tāna*s, always in *ākāra* articulation, commence normally with medium density passages, stepping up later to medium-high density. Truly high-density *tāna*s of the Kairana, Agra, or even neo-Jaipur–Atrauli variety, are absent. This could either reflect the melodic complexity inherent in the *rāga*s performed by Lakshmibai, or a philosophy that treats complexity rather than speed as the *gharānā*'s hallmark in the *tāna*s department. One notices, in her *vilambita khayāla*s, an occasional use of *bola-bāṇṭa*. But, this form is used as a tension-building device in the *ālāpa* prior to a return to the *mukhaḍā* of the *bandiśa*, rather than as a discrete medium density movement. Lakshmibai also uses short *tāna*-like passages in the *ālāpa* for similar purposes.

Lakshmibai's melodic execution in low-density music has a strong bias in favour of *mīṇḍa*s with graceful, rounded, contours. The *tāna*s tend to make generous use of a racy *gamaka*, causing ripples. Her *tāna*s have the complexity for which Jaipur–Atrauli vocalism is famous, but they rarely approach either the bewildering quality of Kesarbai, or the dazzling quality of Mogubai. Her *tāna*s are primarily of the multiple-stroke variety also found in Agra vocalism, but without the staccato intonation of Agra. *Chūṭa tāna*s also feature prominently in her singing. *Tāna*s of strictly *ekaharā* execution were prominent in only one of the surveyed recordings. These tendencies are consistent with the convoluted phrasing patterns demanded of the *rāga* repertoire. Lakshmibai's approach to melody is essentially austere, and devoid of the *khaṭkā*, *murkī* and *kan* type of melodic expression, often encountered in mid-20th-century *khayāla* vocalism of some rival *gharānā*s.

A significant aspect of style in *khayāla* vocalism is the handling of the *mukhaḍā* of the *bandiśa* prior to the arrival at the *sama*, and its follow through. Jaipur–Atrauli expertise in handling the *mukhaḍā* with melodic-rhythmic imagination, complexity, and subtlety is best reflected in Kesarbai's renditions. By comparison, Lakshmibai's stylization and individualization of the *mukhaḍā* is subdued.

The totality of Lakshmibai's music bears a close resemblance to the music of Kesarbai Kerkar, also a second-generation Jaipur–Atrauli vocalist, and approximately the same generation. This similarity may also suggest the futility of the debate surrounding the respective styles of their mentors, Alladiya Khan (who taught Kesarbai) and his brother Hyder Khan (who taught Lakshmibai).

Coverage of Vocalists

This section covers five vocalists representing the Jaipur–Atrauli legacy including Kesarbai Kerkar. Dhondutai Kulkarni belongs to the orthodox stream, having studied with four maestros of the *gharānā*, including Kesarbai. Although Vijaya Jadhav-Gatlewar's principal mentor, Nivruttibuwa Sarnaik is controversial as a Jaipur–Atrauli maestro, she is classified as Jaipur–Atrauli on the evidence of her music. Ashwini Bhide-Deshpande is classified amongst heirs to the Jaipur–Atrauli legacy on the evidence of her tutelage, and the quality of her music following the neo-Jaipur–Atrauli exponent, Kishori Amonkar. Arti Anklikar-Tikekar is classified as a member of the Jaipur–Atrauli legacy by virtue of her tutelage, though brief, with Kishori Amonkar, and by virtue of the quality of her music. Manjiri Asnare-Kelkar qualifies for classification by virtue of her tutelage with Madhusudan Kanetkar, and by the evidence of her music.

4.2

Surashri Kesarbai Kerkar
Empress of the Concert Platform

"WHEN we went to hear Kesarbai, we went to learn something." This was the sitar maestro, Ustad Vilayat Khan's observation about Kesarbai. In a male-dominated era, no female vocalist, either before her or after, has obliged her male colleagues to acknowledge her as an Ustad. Kesarbai (1890–1977) was the only contemporary of Ustad Faiyyaz Khan (1886–1950) to command a concert fee on par with his. But, there was a difference. Kesarbai cultivated a small, but fanatical, following largely of connoisseurs. Faiyyaz Khan, on the other hand, accumulated a huge, and equally committed, following cutting across all levels of aesthetic cultivation.

The Arduous Journey to the Top

Kesarbai was born in Keri, a small village in Goa. She showed an aptitude for singing in early childhood. When she was eight years old, her family moved to Kolhapur, where she was placed under the tutelage of the Kairana doyen, Ustad Abdul Kareem Khan. This training ended in ten months when her family moved back to Goa. Three years went by without any training, before she started learning from Ramkrishna Vaze, the Gwalior-trained maestro, who visited Goa periodically. The intermittent grooming under Vaze Buwa ended after eight or ten years, when Kesarbai's family moved to Bombay.

In Bombay, she started training under the famous *bīnakāra* and sitarist, Barkatullah Khan. This was not a satisfactory solution, and lasted for about a year until Barkatulla left Bombay. During that period, she made an attempt at acceptance by the Jaipur–Atrauli doyen, Ustad Alladiya Khan — a short-lived experience which both found frustrating. She returned thereafter to intermittent training with Barkatullah Khan during his trips to Bombay, and even had a short stint with the eclectic genius, Bhaskar Buwa Bakhle. By now, she was almost thirty, and had still not found her feet in terms of intensive grooming. This irked her immensely.

The turning point came when, at a soiree attended by influential patrons, one of them rebuked her publicly for her mediocre performance. She then decided that she would study with Alladiya Khan and no one else. She was convinced that his style had that special something, which won the respect of musicians and connoisseurs. She already knew that his was not an easy idiom to handle. But, she was now determined to succeed. When the Ustad was approached, he was adamant in his refusal. Kesarbai put pressure on him through the most influential patrons of the era. Hoping to dodge the pressure, he imposed draconian conditions of commitment and remuneration. All were accepted. Thus began one of the greatest musical sagas of the 20th century.

Starting in 1921, Kesarbai began her intensive tutelage, which lasted almost 15 years. For the first ten years, she was — other than his sons — the *ustād*'s only disciple. During this period, he taught her for nine hours every day, and demanded an additional two hours of pre-sunrise exercises in the lower octave. She suffered severe strain on her health and survived several breakdowns in an effort to avoid giving her *ustād* even the flimsiest excuse for discontinuing her training. Towards the end of her tutelage, her *ustād* accepted other disciples, and spent only half the day teaching Kesarbai. By this time, Kesarbai was already a name to reckon with, driven as much by her ambition and success as by the *ustād*'s demands.

It is wrongly believed that Kesarbai was forbidden to perform solo during the *ustād*'s lifetime, and permitted only to accompany him. While her *ustād* died in 1946, she had begun to create waves as a solo performer by 1930 (age 38). In the early stages of her career, she rivalled the likes of Faiyyaz Khan, Omkarnath Thakur, Krishnarao Shankar Pandit, and rose to be the highest paid musician of the era. She retained her stature even as D.V. Paluskar, Bade Ghulam Ali Khan and Ameer Khan were acquiring formidable reputations. She remained the single most respected Hindustani vocalist till the age of 75, when her failing voice caused her to announce retirement. Interestingly, she remains the only 20th-century Hindustani vocalist to have retired voluntarily.

By the time the end came, she had been decorated with Padma Bhushan (1952), the President's award for Hindustani music (1953), the Sangeet Natak Akademi Award (1959), the Rājagāyīkā title by the Government of Maharashtra, and the title of "Surashri" by poet-laureate, Rabindranath Tagore.

The Personality

Kesarbai's personality was ideally suited to the features of the stylistic tradition she represented. She was the most distinguished disciple of her *ustād*, and the most widely heard and acknowledged voice of the Jaipur–Atrauli Gharānā after him. If elitism was the foundation of the *gharānā*'s philosophy and stance, she had every good reason to practise it.

Everything about Kesarbai — starting with her music — exuded this stance. In her case, it was magnified several fold by her achievement, and the immense power it conferred on her. She enjoyed the power along with everything it brought. The consolidation and preservation of her power was the defining paradigm of her personality. This meant exercising a tight control over every aspect of her art and her public persona.

The most direct protection was obviously given to her art. Until a few years before her retirement, she did not train anyone. In 1962, in response to criticism of her neglect of social responsibility, she accepted her only disciple, Dhondutai Kulkarni. Even in the concert hall, Kesarbai worked systematically at defending her art-asset against "theft" by other musicians. These attempts could be forthright, or sometimes, clever. Listeners at a concert, rival musicians, or their protégés, could find themselves named publicly by Kesarbai and asked to leave the premises before she started singing.

The cunning side to the protection of her art-asset surfaced in different ways. She is known to have played hide-and-seek with *rāga*s and *bandiśe*s in order to befuddle potential thieves. Recordings exist of a few concerts replete with such mischief, though its intent cannot be conclusively determined. On one occasion, she announced *rāga* Basantī-Kedāra, and rendered a well known *bandiśa* in that *rāga*, but in a different *rāga* — Hiṇḍola-Kedāra. On occasion, she would skip a line or an entire stanza from a *bandiśa*, making it impossible for anyone to memorize and perform it without being publicly embarrassed.

As a part of controlling her art-asset, she exercised considerable control over her accompanists. She performed, almost all the time, with the same accompanists — Abdul Majid Khan on the *sāraṅgī*, and Yashwant Kelkar on the *tabalā*. She kept a hawk's eye on their activities to ensure their loyalty — they were expected to stay away from anyone Kesarbai regarded as a rival. Even their substitutes for the rare emergency belonged to a core group of trusted musicians.

Kesarbai kept tight control over her professional engagements. She performed probably no more than 10 or 12 times a year. Her reputation meant more to her than money. She demanded a certain minimum notice before a concert. Her preparation for every concert was ruthless. The famous archivist, Prof. Sharad Mehta, an admirer of hers, recalled the morning before a concert in Ahmedabad in the 1950s, when Kesarbai landed up unannounced at his house, accompanied by Abdul Majid Khan. She asked Prof. Mehta to play for them a particular record of Begum Akhtar to demonstrate to Abdul Majid the precise manner in which she wanted accompaniment on the *sāraṅgī* for her rendering of it that evening.

She was extremely selective about the audiences she would sing for. Her critics have charged that she sang only in the homes of the rich. The insinuation of greed may be undeservedly harsh because, in her era, connoisseurship was intimately connected with wealth, and because she also sang regularly at the most prestigious music conferences all over India, which attracted substantial audiences but paid poorly in her times. However, it is true that, she was much more discriminating than her contemporaries of comparable stature. All India Radio could not persuade her to broadcast her music. After the early round of recordings, which was never released (1933), she resisted offers from the recording companies until the last years of her performing life. She did not permit anyone to record her concerts.

In her aversion to the radio and the gramophone record, she reflected the widespread suspicion of electronics common amongst vocalists of her times. The resistance was voiced as a desire for control over the identity and profile of the audiences. A "faceless" audience was not acceptable to them. But, it had wider ramifications. Partly, one may also surmise, they wanted the occasional errors or the liberties they took to go unnoticed. Many musicians of those times could afford this stance because they enjoyed the security of aristocratic patronage, and had no need to cultivate a market for their music. In addition, the standards of acoustic fidelity achieved by these media were still unsatisfactory. The fidelity problem also delayed the acceptance of the microphone in the concert hall. Most vocalists of the era had cultivated voices adequate for addressing small audiences 200/300 strong without amplification. Kesarbai was amongst those titans who started with an allergy to the microphone, and accepted it reluctantly as audiences became larger and the technology itself matured.

Kesarbai controlled her presence in the print media with equal zeal. Photographers and journalists found her inaccessible. Even the leading musicologists of her times got through only with difficulty. The learned men who interviewed her portray an exceptional musical mind, with great depth of insight into music. This is probably what she wanted. She arrived on the scene at a time when serious, well-informed, writing on music was rare. She wished to be written about, and read about, only by people of a certain level of discernment. She cared a lot about how the press depicted her. She monitored every bit of writing on her, and dealt suitably with her admirers and critics in the media.

In an era when rumpled informality was the norm in the music world, Kesarbai came across as a picture of stately elegance. There was a daunting aloofness in her presence, as much as there was in her music. She was an exquisite specimen of womanhood who, like royalty in her times, appeared in public dressed always in spotless white, with her *sāṛī* covering her head in traditional modesty, and bedecked tastefully with pearl or diamond jewellery. Little wonder, then, that she was called the Empress of the concert platform.

Kesarbai was a rare case of ambition and achievement unaccompanied by the immortality urge. This is not as paradoxical as it seems, considering that the dominant feature of her personality was the lust for power. She had to disenfranchise the world she could not control — the world outside the concert hall, and the world beyond.

The Music

According to contemporary accounts, Kesarbai's concert repertoire was dominated by rare and esoteric *rāga*s. Those named are: Bihāga, a large number of Kānaḍā variants, Basantī-Kedāra, Lalitā-Gaurī, Śuddha Nāta, Badhans Sāraṅga, Triveṇī, Khat, Sāvanī Kalyāṇa, Hiṇḍola-Bahāra, Khokhar, Jaunpurī-Bahāra, Sampūrṇa Mālkauṅs, Mīrābāi-kī-Malhāra, and Jait. Amongst the common *rāga*s, those named are: Gauḍa Malhāra, Maru Bihāga, Multānī, Bhīmapalāsa, Durgā, Megha. On the basis of available concert recordings, a few more may be added: Nāt-Bilāwala, Bagesrī-Bahāra, Nāt-Kamoda amongst rare *rāga*s, and Tilaka-Kamoda, Lalita, Mālkauṅs, and Śuddha Bhūpāl (Śuddha Kalyāṇa) amongst common *rāga*s. However, it is unanimously accepted that Kesarbai's interpretation of even common *rāga*s was always oblique and full of melodic riddles. Even though she performed in an era more tolerant of diversity in the interpretation of *rāga*s than today, her versions were often controversial.

Kesarbai rarely sang semi-classical genres or *bhajana*s on the concert platform. Her 78 RPM recordings do, however, feature such fare. She probably acquiesced merely to placate a small segment of her audiences. From her recorded responses to public requests for *ṭhumarī*, it appears that she did not particularly enjoy performing semi-classical music. The majority view amongst commentators seems to be that, though there are some fine specimens of her *ṭhumarī* in existence, the semi-classical fare was not her forte.

The most conspicuous feature of Kesarbai's music was the masculine breadth of her voice. This breadth was cultivated through the unmatched mastery of the AA vowel across two and half octaves with no alteration in timbre. The *ākāra* foundation of her vocalism gave her voice better reach, a greater continuity of musical effect, and superior manoeuvrability in all regions of the melodic canvas. The breadth and the volume of her voice gave the impression of it being low-pitched. In fact, she sang with the fundamental/ tonic at G, common amongst Indian female voices.

The other feature that contributed to the authority of her music was the total absence of tentativeness or obscurity in the delivery of her musical vision. Her vision was bold, solid, and precise, and she delivered it with élan. Her renditions were so clean and polished that musicians of rival *gharānā*s often spoke of her as a tape-recorder of her *guru*. For several reasons, this criticism appears to be undeserved. Firstly, amongst audiences who were highly discerning, no xerox of a *guru* could have established the reputation she did. Secondly, the totality of her music bears the stamp of several other influences, and indeed, of originality.[9] And, finally, evidence exists — in the form of concert recordings — to demonstrate how differently she treated the same *rāga* and even the same *bandiśa* on different occasions.

For the satisfactory communication of her musical vision, she habitually rendered her *vilambita khayāla*s in ultra-slow tempo. In response to peer pressure and public demand, she stepped it up by a notch; but her *vilambita khayāla*s remained amongst the slowest in her era. Kesarbai sang *druta khayāla*s only rarely. Kesarbai's *ālāpa*s could be as elaborate as Kairana *ālāpa*s in her era, though different in the approach to melodic progression. *Vilambita khayāla*s in her favourite *tīnatāla* or *ada cautāla* often exceeded twice the duration of the 20-minute average typical of Alladiya Khan. Contrary to popular belief, her *tāna*s were not exceptionally fast. In terms of absolute *svara*-density, the *tāna*s of her contemporaries, Mogubai Kurdikar and Roshanara Begum were probably faster. However, because of the breadth of Kesarbai's voice, the tempo at which she rendered her *khayāla*s, and because of their complexity, her *tāna*s conveyed the impression of dazzling speed. The perception of speed was magnified by the fact that every round of Kesarbai's *tāna*s combined different melodic structures, with a substantial element of surprise in their trajectory.

Ranade[9] had occasion to confront Kesarbai with traces of non-Jaipur–Atrauli influence in her vocalism. She admitted the possibility that, in her elaboration of common *rāga*s, there could be the influence of the Gwalior style. This might be attributed to her intermittent training with Ramkrishna Buwa Vaze. Her occasionally elaborate *ālāpa*, Kesarbai claimed, were traceable to Barkatullah Khan, the *Rudra vīṇā* and *sitāra* exponent, who trained her for several years during her youth. Contrary to popular belief, Kesarbai did not entirely shun *ṭhumarī* and other semi-classical genres of music. In fact, she developed a relationship of mutual tutelage with Siddheshwari Devi, the reigning queen of the *ṭhumarī* genre, and even publicly performed a few semi-classical pieces in the Benares style. These facets of her music do not however detract from Kesarbai's stature as the hallmark of orthodox Jaipur–Atrauli vocalism.

A Stylistic Perspective

This stylistic survey of Kesarbai's music is based on a sample of six hours of her concert recordings of classical *rāga*s. The available semi-classical repertoire was ignored. The surveyed archive consists of Lalita (45 minutes), Nāt Bilāwala (20 mts), Khat (22 mts), Basantī Kedāra (13 mts), Bihāga (15 mts), Nāt Kamoda (14 mts), Lalita Gaurī (45 mts), Tilaka Kamoda (25 mts), Tilaka Kamoda (different recording: 22 mts), Sampūrṇa Mālkauṅs (22 mts), Jaijaivantī (20 mts), Kedāra (55 mts) and Śuddha Bhūpāla/Suddha Kalyāṇa (40 mts). In this archive, only Lalita and Kedāra have *druta khayāla*s appended to them, while Sampūrṇa Mālkauṅs has a Mālkauṅs *druta khayāla* appended to it. The remaining are *vilambita* or *madhya-laya khayāla*s rendered as stand-alone pieces. According to her only disciple, Dhondutai Kulkarni, all these recordings belong to the last few years of Kesarbai's performing life (1957-65).

Kesarbai launched the *khayāla*s in *tīnatāla* and *ada cautāla* at a tempo of 25-33 bpm. They qualify as *vilambita khayāla*s. The exception in this sample is the *Tīnatāla khayāla* in Nāt Kamoda, which is launched at over 60 bpm, and qualifies as a *madhya-laya* (medium tempo) *khayāla*. *Khayāla*s in *rūpaka* and *jhaptāla* are launched at 45 to 50 bpm. Here the exceptions are *Nāt Bilāwala* and Khat, which are launched at 25-30 bpm, and therefore qualify as *vilambita khayāla*s. There is, apparently, no rigid relationship between the *tāla* of the *bandiśa* and the tempo of rendition. The only clear pattern emerges in the acceleration of the tempo during the course of the rendition. *Tīnatāla* and *Ada cautāla bandiś*es undergo a minor escalation of 9 to 12 bpm (average of 37 per cent), while the *rūpaka* and *jhapatāla bandiś*es are accelerated by 20 to 30 bpm (average of 60-70 per cent) over the launch tempo.

The most consistent feature of her surveyed recordings is the audible audience participation at the arrival of her *mukhaḍā* at the *sama*. The build-up of aesthetic tension prior to the *sama* is so tangible, and its release at the *sama* so climactic, that it is frequently greeted with an orgasmic sigh by the audiences. It is impossible to conceptualise the quality of *mukhaḍā* delivery that triggers off such responses. This may be amongst the secrets that the great are unable to share — perhaps even with themselves.

The architecture of Kesarbai's *vilambita* and *madhya-laya khayālas* is enigmatic. It does, indeed, incorporate low-density, medium-density, and high-density melody, and in proper order. It also incorporates a progressive enhancement of melodic complexity along with density. But, the transitions are imperceptible and the borderlines are fluid. Passages representing any level of *svara*-density and rhythmicality may be encountered in any part of her *khayāla* renditions. Kesarbai's architecture does not have the transparent progression we find, say, in Ameer Khan or later, in Kishori Amonkar. And, yet, she was never accused of architectural waywardness as, for instance, Bade Ghulam Ali Khan was just a few years after her.

There are probably two reasons for this. Firstly, the notion of strict linearity in *khayāla* architecture had yet to crystallize as a yardstick cutting across *gharānā* boundaries. The second reason probably lies in the steadiness, though opaque, of the sense of progression in Kesarbai's *khayālas*. Her logic came through at some level of audience consciousness. Her architecture was more akin to that of Frank Lloyd Wright — poetry in three dimensions — than to Le Corbusier, who designed machines to live in.

This oblique/non-direct approach to architecture is extended to the textural and rhythmic aspects of *khayāla* rendition. In the *ālāpa*, she primarily deploys the *ākāra* articulation, but occasionally also deploys *bola* articulation. The same is true of the *tānas*, which combine *ākāra* with occasional *bola*. Her *ālāpas* can be anarhythmic, but can often have a pulsation, so irregular and subtle, that it escapes notice. The homogenization of architectural, melodic, rhythmic, articulatory, and textural facets is so complete that her *khayāla* becomes a seamless piece of music from one end to the other.

In Kesarbai's austerity of melodic execution, I observe a considerable influence of *dhrupada*. This is hardly surprising. *Dhrupada* stylistics were, in her era, still visibly present in vocalism of all the *khayāla gharānā*s — with the probable exception of Kairana. Kesarbai's first *guru* of considerable tenure, Barkatullah Khan, was a *bīnakāra* and exponent of the *dhrupada*-inspired idiom of the *sitāra*. Her most significant *guru*, Alladiya Khan, hailed from a lineage of Ḍāgara Bānī *dhrupada* exponents. Alladiya Khan is reported to have recast many *dhrupada bandiśe*s into *khayāla* form, and was therefore probably the first generation musician in his lineage making the categorical *dhrupada*-to-*khayāla* transition. This combination of influences could have left Kesarbai's music with a significant presence of *dhrupada* stylistics. This is evident in several aspect of her music, in addition to the graceful, rounded, melodic contours that are fundamental to Jaipur–Atrauli music. As in *dhrupada*, her melodic execution relies almost entirely on *mīṇḍa*, *khaṭkā* and *gamaka*. Kesarbai also makes generous use of the *sūta* form of melodic execution, which drags a *svara* to a distant *svara* in slow melodic motion with a perceptible alteration of timbre along the route. This form originates in the *ghasīṭa* (literally: dragging) form of execution on the *bīna*.

The *murkī* and *kan* types of ornamentation, evident in *khayāla* renditions of some other *gharānā*s, occur only occasionally in Kesarbai's singing. In the handling of the *bandiśa*, Kesarbai appears to deploy *bola-bāṇṭa* primarily in the *dhrupada layakārī* style, though not as a distinct movement as done either in *dhrupada* or by Agra and Gwalior vocalists. She also resorts frequently to the *dogunā/tigunā* forms, involving the rendition of *bandiśa* passages at twice or thrice their pre-composed melodic density. These are used primarily for the purposes of contrast and tension building prior to the arrival of the *mukhaḍā*. Although the overall austerity of melodic execution is common to all vocalists of orthodox Jaipur–Atrauli, neither the *sūta/ghasīṭa*, nor the *layakārī* type of *bola-bāṇṭa* are evident in the music either of her *gharānā* contemporaries, Mogubai Kurdikar and Lakshmibai Jadhav or Kesarbai's own disciple, Dhondutai. Kesarbai is also the last known Jaipur–Atrauli vocalist to use the ultra-convex *gamaka* typical of the *dhrupada* genre.

Kesarbai's *tāna*s are to be viewed in clusters rather than in isolation. She weaves a complex web of *tāna*s around different focal points of the *rāga*, with the totality covering the entire melodic canvas. In the coverage of the melodic canvas, I observe a special fondness for the ascending melodic motion, and for action in the higher octave. *Ekaharā tāna* forms, especially the broad-span *sapāṭa* formation are almost entirely missing from her vocalism. Short *ekaharā* passages occur, often woven into a more complex construction, which includes *chūṭa* patterns of varying speed, occasionally even including *ālāpa*-like anarhythmic passages. The most common *tāna* form is the *gamaka*-driven multiple-stroke or two-by-two *tāna*, in leaping waves. However, rarely do we find her *tāna*s seeking symmetry or geometry. Her *tāna*s are full of stunning loops, twists, and turns. The element of surprise is most evident in the Nat Kamoda recording surveyed here.

The Legacy

It is difficult, and perhaps also unfair, to scrutinize the legacy of a musician who had no desire to bequeath her art in any form. History is, however, not obliged to respect the wishes of any mortal, no matter how exalted.

Kesarbai's lineage, through heredity as well as tutelage, reflects her nihilism. She insulated her only child, a daughter, from the music world, and educated her in medicine. Kesarbai's only disciple, Dhondutai Kulkarni was already 40 and a mature musician trained by several other stalwarts of the *gharānā* before Kesarbai took her under her wings. Though Dhondutai (b. 1927) is an heir to the Kesarbai legacy, the exclusivity is debatable.

Kesarbai's commercial recordings have to be viewed in two parts. During her early years in the profession, Kesarbai reportedly recorded twelve 78 RPM discs for a lesser known recording company in Calcutta which went into liquidation immediately thereafter. These recordings have finally been released once again. Her 78 RPM recordings with HMV were done towards her last performing years, and are still available in digitally re-mastered versions. It is interesting that Kesarbai was performing well into the Long Playing record era, and yet no LPs of hers were ever made. The glimpses of greatness are unmistakable on her 3-minute renditions.

Kesarbai never sang on the radio, nor allowed her concerts to be recorded. Unauthorized, and therefore acoustically poor, recordings of her concerts do, however, exist. In the 1980s, the vocalist duo known as Khan Bandhu (sons of Kesarbai's *sāraṅgī* accompanist, Abdul Majid Khan) published a limited edition of audio-cassettes of her concert recordings. Apart from the Khan Bandhu release, a few other concert recordings also exist. Despite their poor acoustic quality, there is a flourishing grey market in these unauthorized recordings. They have become collector's items amongst Kesarbai's admirers, and study material for serious vocalists of the younger generation.

Another substantial archive of Kesarbai's concert recordings was in the possession of her neighbour and admirer, Babubhai (Hargovind Raghunath) Raja. According to Babubhai, (d. 2002), who was the present writer's grand uncle, Kesarbai suspected him of having recorded her without permission, and disapproved of his possession of the recordings. She raided his home several times, always at odd hours, and even during his absence, in the hope of retrieving the tapes. Fortunately, she failed. Babubhai donated this archive in the 1980s to the National Centre for the Performing Arts in Bombay. Apparently, he also entrusted copies of that archive to another aristocratic collector, who has intentions of releasing the archive commercially.

Between the grey market recordings and the Babubhai Raja archive, the aggregate asset amounts to over 20 hours of legendary music. Even if their acoustic obsolescence can be neutralized through modern restoration technologies, their remaining commercial life is an issue. Kesarbai's primary audience would be that generation of music lovers which was at least 20 years old in 1965, when she stopped performing. This generation is fast dwindling in numbers. It would therefore appear that Jaipur–Atrauli vocalism of the Kesarbai-Laxmibai variety may now also be vulnerable to aesthetic obsolescence.

Nothing would have made Kesarbai happier than frustrating a music critic attempting to assess her legacy in the 21st century. So far, she has had her way. But, her unpublished concert recordings might still become commercially available, and Dhondutai's disciples might still achieve sufficient visibility for the Kesarbai legacy to be judged. Until then, Kesarbai can rest peacefully in heaven chuckling with glee (Written : July 2003).

4.3

Dhondutai Kulkarni
The Last Bastion of Jaipur–Atrauli Orthodoxy

THE reigning queen of *khayāla* vocalism, Kishori Amonkar, holds her in the highest esteem. As a musician's musician, she shoulders the mantle of the larger-than-life Kesarbai Kerkar, with no successor in sight. The lady is Dhondutai Kulkarni (b. 1927).

Dhondutai's stature is well earned. Five maestros of the *gharānā*, which includes three members of the founding family, have trained her over three decades of tutelage. She became an A grade artist of All India Radio at the age of 20, and currently occupies the top grade. She has been decorated with several honors, the foremost being the Sangeet Natak Akademi

Award and the Maharashtra Gaurav Award of the State Government, both in 1990. She ran a busy concert schedule up to 1970s, and retreated gracefully into teaching, when classicism began to fall out of favour with audiences.

Elitism and aloofness are fundamental to the orthodox Jaipur–Atrauli doctrine. Dhondutai's public persona conforms to this pattern. In Dhondutai's own generation, however, one stream of the *gharānā* embarked on a revisionist path. Kishori Amonkar (b. 1931), the daughter of the illustrious Mogubai Kurdikar, gave the *gharānā*'s style a romanticist direction, while also refining its architectural formalism. Her immensely influential departure is significant enough to be labeled Neo-Jaipur–Atrauli. This leaves Dhondutai as the last citadel of orthodox Jaipur–Atrauli vocalism.

Homogeniety, Diversity and Individuality
(Dhondutai Spoke to the Author on 4 May 2003)

"My father was a schoolteacher in Kolhapur (southern Maharashtra). He was trained in the Gwalior style of vocal music. His greatest regret was never becoming a credible performer. The Alladiya Khan family was the most respected clan of teachers in those days. So, my father decided to give me — his first surviving child — their training, whatever the cost.

"During my childhood, the morning service at the Mahalakshmi temple in Kolhapur commenced with a musical offering to the Goddess by Alladiya Khan's nephew, Natthan Khan. We met him regularly at the temple. One day, my father made bold to request him to teach me. Initially, Natthan Khan had little interest in teaching a beginner of five. But, finally, by a rather convoluted route, I became his disciple. I learnt fast, and by the age of eight, I was singing on the radio. The Natthan Khan tutelage ended in three years, when he left for Bombay.

"After that, Bhurji Khan, Alladiya's son, took over duties at the temple. When my father made the proposal to him, he quoted a fee we could not afford. So the matter rested there until one day, when I was 13, Bhurji Khan turned up suddenly at our house to announce that he would teach me for whatever my father could afford to pay him. So, it started — a daily routine for several hours after I returned from school. Bhurji Khan also taught me the sunrise exercises for maintaining the voice in perfect condition, and made sure that I did them regularly.

"I dropped out of school two years short of graduation in favour of full-time music. Bhurji Khan then started visiting us twice a day. In the meanwhile, my younger sister also started studying with him. I had received 10 years of intensive training with Bhurji Khan when he died (1950).

"For seven years thereafter, I had no guide. By this time, I was already performing professionally — solo as well as duets with my sister. In 1957, Lakshmibai Jadhav, a distinguished disciple of Hyder Khan, retired from the service of the Baroda State, and returned home to Kolhapur. I received a government scholarship to study with her. She taught me in the mornings, and Bhurji Khan's son, Azizuddin Khan, took evening sessions. This lasted for three years, until we left Kolhapur. Another two years passed before I found my fifth, and last, *guru*.

"In 1962, Kesarbai Kerkar issued an open invitation through a newspaper interview to any vocalist willing to submit to her training. So, I wrote to her, certain that nothing would happen. I was surprised to receive a welcoming reply. After putting me through an acid test, she assured me that though old now, she would do her best for me. And, she did — without ever accepting any remuneration or consideration of any kind.

"My father sold his house in Kolhapur to finance the move, and hired an apartment in Bombay for us to live in. Kesarbai was a stickler for punctuality and regularity. Each training session lasted three to four hours, in which we would cover two or three *rāga*s. In addition, I had to continue workouts with the music I already knew, and with sunrise exercises. It was an exhausting routine.

"Two years after I began training with her, she took me on a month-long retreat where she started my voice cultivation using the Alladiya technique. The training enhanced lungpower, improved stamina, perfected the AA vowel articulation, and sustained the timbre of the voice through two full octaves. Thereafter, back in Bombay, the routine continued. In addition, of course, I accompanied her at concerts. She announced her retirement in 1965, and I continued learning with her until 1971 — she was over 80 then.

"In popular belief, my music is closest to Kesarbai's. This may be true. But, not many people know how Bhurji Khan and Lakshmibai sang. So, the truth is more complicated. I cannot assess the impact of Natthan Khan's initiation. It is Bhurji Khan who shaped the fundamentals of my music — from the age of 13 to 23. He started with *alaṁkāra*s (symmetric practice exercises) and shaped me into an A grade radio artist. Lakshmibai, Azizuddin Khan, and Kesarbai had just to build on the Bhurji Khan foundation.

"All my *guru*s sang and taught the same music; but each had an original way of interpreting it. To begin with, they came from different streams of the *gharānā*. Natthan Khan and Lakshmibai belonged to the Hyder Khan stream, while Bhurji Khan and Kesarbai came from the Alladiya stream. More significant for me was the contrast between the voices and temperaments of Kesarbai and Lakshmibai. Kesarbai was like the Niagara Falls, while Lakshmibai was tranquillity personified. I had to sort out and integrate a wide range of musical attitudes because, in the ultimate analysis, my music had to be mine."

The Music of Dhondutai Kulkarni

The observations here are based on insights acquired over 15 years of interaction with Dhondutai, and attending several of her concerts. For purposive analysis, however, I rely on her CD recorded for India Archive Music Ltd., New York, in 2000 (Bihāga, Shahana and Nāt Kamoda), a CD released by Super Cassette Industries (Mīrā Malhāra, and Kabeeri Bhairava) and live recordings of Lalita Gaurī, Sindhūra, Bhūpa Nāt, Mālavī, Gauḍa Malhāra, and Sampūrṇa Mālkauṅs. The entire sample of recordings was made between 1988 and 2000. As a reference point for comparison, I rely on about twelve hours of Kesarbai's concert recordings, and four hours of Lakshmibai's radio broadcasts and 78 RPM recordings. My inferences relating to Kesarbai's music are based on recordings made between 1959 and 1965. The dates of the Lakshmibai recordings are not possible to determine.

At a felicitation of Dhondutai hosted by Kishori Amonkar (transcript published in the September 2004 issue of *Anubhav*, a Marāṭhī magazine), the neo-Jaipur–Atrauli diva introduced her *gharānā* senior with envious references to her voice. This defines the most significant facet of Dhondutai's musical personality. Her voice with its fundamental at G# (a notch above her two female *gurus*) is slightly narrower in timbre than Lakshmibai's, and far from the masculine breadth of Kesarbai's. Her *ākāra* articulation is as substantial as that of Kesarbai. But, it has a captivating — perhaps even sensuous — quality not possessed by any of her female seniors in the *gharānā*.

In addition to nature's gift, her temperament holds the key to this. Interestingly, since childhood, Dhondutai has unashamedly admired Hirabai Barodekar of the Kairana Gharānā, perhaps the most melodious female vocalist of the 20th century, with a voice soaked in honey. Interestingly again, in her youth, Dhondutai excelled at *ṭhumarī*. She stopped singing them altogether when hosts began to request her for concerts consisting exclusively of *ṭhumarī*. There is evidently a romanticist streak in her personality, which is supported by the seductive propensities of her voice. She has kept this facet firmly subordinated to her classicism. She cannot help the fact that these features do enhance the appeal of her *khayāla*s — only repertoire.

These observations hold good, by and large, even for the last recording surveyed, made in her 73rd year. The only noticeable impact of age is an infrequent warble in low-density execution, a slight tightening of the vocalization aperture in the upper registers, and an occasional hesitation in high-density and higher-octave melodic execution. The clarity with which she communicates her musical ideas, however, still compares well with many present-day singers in their prime.

Dhondutai is an encyclopaedia of the rare and compound *rāga*s. Having studied with five *guru*s of the lineage helped. The accumulation of the asset is evidence of a tenacious musical mind. Aware of the bewilderment her orphic repertoire might create amongst uninitiated audiences, she works hard at reaching out to them. When she sings a rare or complex *rāga*, she explains the *rāga*, and launches it with an elaborate *auchara* to delineate its topography. She also takes care to imprint the melodic map of such *rāga*s on the audience's mind by rendering the *bandiśe*s without any stylization before she launches the *ālāpa*.

Veteran connoisseurs frequently debate which of her two female *guru*s Dhondutai's music resembles — Kesarbai or Lakshmibai. The debate is futile because, after accounting for their respective voice qualities and temperaments, the music of the two is remarkably similar. Dhondutai's music is, without doubt, orthodox Jaipur–Atrauli vocalism, and just about escapes aesthetic obsolescence today. Unlike Kesarbai and Lakshmibai, who occasionally sang lighter genres of music, Dhondutai sticks to *khayāla*s. Within the *khayāla* genre, she appears to be more partial to rare and compound *rāgas*. Conforming to contemporary practice, she sings *druta khayālas* more often than her *gurus* did. Judging by limited evidence, her *druta bandiśes* are also more interesting than those of her mentors.

Dhondutai is as comfortable with the 40-mts elaboration of a *vilambita khayāla*, as with the compact 20-mts *madhya-laya khayālas*, the traditional forte of her *gharānā*. The architecture of her *khayāla* renditions has a neatness, which is in contrast to Lakshmibai's informality and Kesarbai's enigmatic formalism. This feature aligns her music with the transparent structuralism of contemporary *khayāla* music. While she launches her *vilambita* and *madhya-laya khayālas* at the same tempo as her female *gurus*, she — unlike them — adopts no acceleration. In this practice, Dhondutai claims to follow Bhurji Khan's training. In the *druta khayālas*, which are a later induction into the *khayāla* genre, she allows a marginal escalation, much as her female *gurus* did.

Dhondutai's approach to low density melody, relying on the orthodox expressions of *mīṇḍa*, *gamaka* and *khaṭkā*, is austere by contemporary standards of embellishment. Ornate expressions like *kan* and *murkī* occur only occasionally in her music. Her melodic contours have the same graceful, rounded quality that her female *gurus* had, with no trace of angularity. The heavier *dhrupada* idiom of *sūta*, convex *gamakas* and *bola-bāṇṭa layakārī*, which was conspicuous in Kesarbai's music, is absent from Dhondutai's. Her articulation (*bola* and *ākāra*) is free from the occasional severity of Kesarbai, and is closer to Lakshmibai's. Her deployment of poetry along with melody can drift in the direction of *ṭhumarī*-style *bola-banāva*, exposing the traces of romanticism in her musical personality.

Like Kesarbai, Dhondutai frequently dramatises her *mukhaḍā* delivery. She either prefaces them with a dramatic passage, or suffixes them with an unexpected trail-off. These devices rarely achieve the impact that Kesarbai's *mukhaḍās* had. The secret of *mukhaḍā* magic in Kesarbai's music, it seems, died with her.

Dhondutai's *ālāpa* is true to the narrative approach established in orthodox Jaipur–Atrauli vocalism. It is a broad-span and informal approach to melodic progression, which differs from the Kairana-inspired *svara*-by-*svara* progression, towards which Kishori Amonkar tilts. Like the *ālāpa* renditions of her seniors, Dhondutai's *ālāpa* has a subtle swing to it, which is never as explicit as the pulsation found in *ālāpa*s of Agra vocalism.

Like her female *guru*s, Dhondutai performs her *tāna*s primarily in medium and medium-to-high density, generally avoiding high and ultra-high density execution. Dhondutai appears to rely as little on broad-span *ekaharā tāna*s as Kesarbai and Lakshmibai did. These *tāna* features are consistent with her repertoire, biased in favour of rare and compound *rāga*s, which tend to have convoluted phraseologies. Her multiple-intonation *tāna*s deploy primarily two-stroke and three-stroke iteration of *svara*s in rippling *gamaka*s, and avoid the 4-stroke vocalization and staccato intonation found in Agra *tāna*s. The reliance on *chūṭa tāna*s is significant, and features a greater sense of geometry and symmetry in their design than either of her female *guru*s attempted. In this respect, they appear closer to contemporary patterns. While Kesarbai's *tāna*s had a jaw-dropping complexity, Dhondutai achieves the dramatic impact more often through melodic leaps and hops between different regions of the melodic canvas.

There is an important caveat to these comparisons. The *tāna*s, more than any other department of vocalism, reflect a musician's temperament, stage of life, and state of health, at the time of the performance. And, here we are comparing Dhondutai's recordings made after the age of 60, with Kesarbai's after 70, and Lakshmibai's made probably at different stages of her life.

The stance of Dhondutai's music combines Kesarbai's authority, with Lakshmibai's warmth, and Dhondutai's own endearing dispositions. In its totality, her repertoire may be more elitist than either of her female *gurus*. But, she cannot be accused of wilful snobbery. Some features of her music are more orthodox than either Kesarbai or Lakshmibai, while others tend towards modernity, and can occasionally even tilt towards neo-Jaipur–Atrauli. Her music is a unique emanation of her training, voice quality, personality, and the times she lives in — in that order.

Dhondutai's analysis of her own music is supported by available evidence. Bhurji Khan was evidently her basic trainer and coach. Lakshmibai and Kesarbai probably enlarged her repertoire. But, in all likelihood, they acted more as sparring mates, challenging her, and shaping her into a polished performer. In this role, Kesarbai's influence could have been more decisive than Lakshmibai's.

Dhondutai is the sole disciple of Kesarbai, whom she also trained till the end of her active life. On this evidence, there is good reason to regard her as the heiress to the Kesarbai legacy. Because of her grooming with four other *gurus* of the lineage, the entire Jaipur–Atrauli orthodoxy now speaks through her. Her contribution has been that of partially modernizing the legacy, without attempting to re-invent it.

The question mark that hangs over the future of this heritage is substantially common to all of *gharānā*-based music. In this specific case, the situation may be more uncertain. Dhondutai has, indeed, groomed a few accomplished vocalists, none of whom has yet been launched in the profession. In the future, orthodox Jaipur–Atrauli could manifest itself solely through other, and less thoroughly "pedigreed" streams of the *gharānā*. Its distinctive features can therefore be expected to demonstrate a progressive dilution (Written : October 2004).

4.4

Vijaya Jadhav-Gatlewar
A Classicist in a Romanticist World

DOES classicism have a chance in a musical culture swamped by romanticism? This is the question surrounding the musicianship of Vijaya Jadhav-Gatlewar (b. 1955). Vijaya is an orthodox musician steeped in the traditional values of the *khayāla* genre, represented by its architectural formalism as well as aloofness of demeanour.

Her music qualifies her as an exponent of orthodox Jaipur–Atrauli vocalism. But, her grooming bears the mark of other influences, as neither of her two *guru*s could claim exclusive grooming in the *gharānā*. Vijaya was first trained by her father, D.B. Jadhav, and later by Nivrutti Buwa Sarnaik. Her tutelage with Sarnaik included a fifteen-year apprenticeship at the ITC Sangeet Research Academy (SRA) in Calcutta.

Vijaya is an A grade artiste of the All India Radio, and a respected teacher, with a concert presence that is growing slowly, but steadily.

Conservatory Grooming

(Vijaya spoke to the Author on 24 December 2001)

"My father, D.B. Jadhav worked as a clerk in a Bombay textile mill, and was an empanelled vocalist of All India Radio. He had studied primarily with Natthan Khan (d. 1946), the nephew of Alladiya Khan of the Jaipur–Atrauli Gharānā. However, he had also studied with senior musicians of Agra, and Gwalior Gharānās. Despite his diverse training, he performed in the Jaipur–Atrauli style. Once he came home from work, our home had only music, and nothing else. He had two or three disciples who took training with him every evening from 6 to 9. I overheard this training, and unknown to my father, started singing. It was only when I opted for music as a subject for my high school graduation that he discovered my talent. Thereafter, he took my training seriously. I became a permanent fixture of his evening sessions with his disciples.

"To speed up my progress as a performer, he encouraged me to enter music competitions all over the country. I competed in light as well as classical segments, and brought home a string of trophies. Once I had gained confidence, my father stopped my competitive activity, because he believed art should not be pursued like a competitive sport. But, by then — I was 18 — I had decided to pursue music as a profession, and my parents endorsed my decision. In 1977, my father placed me under training with Nivrutti Buwa Sarnaik, whom he greatly admired. At that time, my father was approaching retirement, and feared that he would soon be unable to pay for my tuitions. Dada (Nivrutti Buwa Sarnaik) assured him that he would continue teaching me free of charge if this happened. That very year, I was granted the Kesarbai Kerkar Memorial Scholarship of the National Centre for the Performing Arts, and my *guru* was saved from having to make a financial sacrifice on my account.

"Within a year of my starting training with him, Dada was invited to become a Resident *guru* at the SRA. He wanted me to go with him, and my family readily consented. I trained with Dada at the SRA up to the end of his tenure at the Academy (1978-93), taking only occasional breaks, after 1988, to be with my husband in Bombay.

"In every respect, the SRA is an ideal environment for the serious pursuit of music. It has a beautiful campus in peaceful surroundings, and is equipped with an excellent library of recordings. During my tenure as a scholar, the Academy was also a goldmine of *guru*s. Distinguished musicians from outside also visited the Academy frequently and performed there.

"The training system of the Academy is modelled after the *guru-śiṣya paramparā*. Each *guru* was assigned a maximum of two or three students. We lived on the same premises as our *guru*, and trained under his supervision. Our days began at 4.30 a.m. and rarely ended before midnight.

"The personalized training at the Academy was a priceless experience for me. From the very beginning, Dada considered my early training with my father valuable, and started building upon it. At the Academy, his training became even more fine-tuned to my specific needs. Unlike Bombay, where his monetary compulsions forced him to teach a large class, the Academy allowed him to give personalized attention. He made me work hard on the fundamental refinements of my art, such as intonation and voice-culture. Having excelled in competitions, initially I found these efforts humiliating. But he insisted on perfection, and had all the time and the freedom to pursue it.

"At the Academy, I also got to learn *ṭhumarī* from Girija Devi. She trained me with great affection. But, I did not become a *gaṇḍā-banda* (formally initiated) disciple of hers because it would have been impossible for me to do justice to both the genres.

"In addition to giving me the best of my own *guru*, the SRA also gave me what no individual *guru* could have given me. The general sessions for all students included seminars, guided listening sessions, and group discussions, which helped me to acquire an understanding of different approaches to music, and the different genres. The Academy also promoted my career as a performing musician within India and abroad.

"Dada loved the Academy so much that he wanted to die there. But, his health deteriorated dramatically in 1993, and we packed up when he decided he could no longer fulfil his responsibilities.

"After entering the profession, I wonder whether spending so many years in training, away from the concert platform, was really worthwhile. I am disheartened often by the lukewarm response I get for presenting the rare *rāga*s of the Jaipur–Atrauli tradition. But, gradually, I am getting a response from audiences who realise the rarity and the value of my art. Although I am not impatient for recognition and success, it would be nice to have it while I am still in the prime of physical health and creative energy."

The Legacy of Nivrutti Buwa

Nivrutti Buwa Sarnaik (1912-94) was amongst those respected musicians of his generation who devoted their lives to teaching, and managed only a notional presence on the concert platform. He was inducted into music through his uncle, Shankararao Sarnaik, an eminent singer-actor in regional musical theatre. Shankararao himself was a disciple of the Kairana founder, Abdul Kareem Khan. His theatre company, which young

Nivrutti joined while still in his teens, had retained quite a line-up of distinguished vocalists. Amongst them were Alladiya Khan, the founder of the Jaipur–Atrauli style, Rajab Ali Khan of the Indore Gharānā, and Sawai Gandharva, heir to the mantle of the Kairana founder Abdul Kareem Khan.

In a sense, this entire galaxy of stalwarts could be described as Nivrutti Buwa's *guru*s. But, Sarnaik claimed the closest affinity to the vocalism of Alladiya Khan. The lesser-known *rāga*s, which he inherited from the *ustād,* were his forte. The way he rendered them often baffled even hardcore connoisseurs. His *tāna*s were a unique blend of the individual approach of Alladiya Khan and Rajab Ali Khan.[6]

Nivrutti Buwa was a regular broadcaster over All India Radio for the better part of four decades. But, because of his near-absence from the concert platform, his recordings are available only in private archives. The SRA made available one recording of the maestro, done in December 1979, which may be used to establish the dimensions of continuity and discontinuity from Nivrutti Buwa to Vijaya. The recording contains three *rāga*s: *Śuddha Kalyāṇa* (44 mts), Nāyakī Kānaḍā (33 mts), and Shahana Kānaḍā (15 mts). This is far too limited a sample to permit definitive conclusions. Yet, it can be used as indicative evidence.

In evaluating the stylistic biases of these recordings, I was assisted by the veteran musicologist Prof. R.C. Mehta, who has produced classical music for All India Radio and taught vocal music and music theory for almost 60 years. The identities of the vocalists — Nivrutti Buwa and Vijaya — were not revealed to Prof. Mehta until he had given me all his observations on their stylistic tendencies.

Nivrutti Buwa's slightly guttural voice production and timbre control are reminiscent of Agra vocalism in the post-Faiyyaz Khan period, represented by Vilayat Hussain Khan, and Latafat Hussain. The architecture of Nivrutti Buwa's *baḍā khayāla* presentation in Śuddha Kalyāṇa bearṣ the stamp of Kairana vocalism. The rendition consists of only two movements, the *ālāpa* and the *tāna*s. The medium-density *bola-laya* movement is missing. In the *ālāpa* section, Prof. Mehta notices a discernible influence of Sawai Gandharva (Kairana), and his disciple, Dashrathrao Muley. In the brief section of medium density *tāna*s, Prof. Mehta hears faint echoes of Vilayat Hussain Khan (Agra) and partially of Krishnarao Shankar Pandit (Gwalior). In the high-density *tāna*s, robust rhythmicality and melodic construction strongly suggest Agra vocalism of Vilayat Hussain Khan.

The choice of Nāyakī Kaṇaḍa *khayāla* in *madhya-laya Rūpaka* (*mero piya rasiyā*) did suggest some influence of Jaipur–Atrauli vocalism. However, according to Prof. Mehta, this *khayāla* has also been performed in the Agra tradition — though in *tīnatāla*. It does not therefore constitute weighty evidence of Jaipur–Atrauli influences in the absence of other confirming features. The obvious echoes of Agra vocalism in Nivrutti Buwa's music perhaps acknowledge the towering influence of Faiyyaz Khan over the music of the pre-Independence era, cutting across *gharānā* boundaries.

While accepting the limitations of the evidence, Prof. Mehta, who had heard Nivrutti Buwa in person on a few occasions, expressed surprise that Sarnaik was considered an exponent of the Jaipur–Atrauli style. In comparison, he avers, Vijaya reminds him very distinctly of Mogubai Kurdikar in her prime. Vijaya, according to Prof. Mehta establishes a far more faithful link with the orthodox Jaipur–Atrauli style than her mentor, Nivrutti Buwa did.

From these indications, we might conclude that Vijaya Jadhav's grounding in thoroughbred Jaipur–Atrauli vocalism is primarily her father, D.B. Jadhav's gift to her. This conclusion lends credence to Vijaya's own claim that Nivrutti Buwa actually built upon the foundations of musicality that her father had already laid. It is, however, also possible that Nivrutti Buwa could isolate his Jaipur–Atrauli grooming for the purpose of imparting it to his disciples, but performed his own blend of different styles when he faced the microphone. It is equally possible that he sang each *rāga* in the style of the *gharānā* from which he had learnt the *rāga* as did Gajananrao Joshi of the same generation, and another eminent product of multiple-*gharānā* training.

The Music of Vijaya Jadhav-Gatlewar

For studying Vijaya's music, I had access to one CD recorded by her in 1995 for India Archive Music, New York, and a concert recording from 1990. The surveyed recordings cover *khayālas* in Jaitaśrī, Kedāra, Śivamata Bhairava, Alhaiyā Bilāwala, and Bhaṭiyārā, and a *ṭhumarī* in Khamāja. In addition, I have had several occasions to hear her on the stage. These exposures, collectively, allow me to make observations with a degree of confidence.

Despite the diversity of the tendencies her father, and her *guru*, brought to her grooming, Vijaya's music is an aesthetically coherent and polished product. It belongs broadly to the Alladiya Khan — Jaipur–Atrauli style, as distinct from its revisionist stream launched by Kishori Amonkar. If there are traces of other influences in it, they are either marginal, or such as are now standard features of *khayāla* vocalism.

Her approach to music making is reverential. This is reflected in the discipline and thoroughness with which she handles every department to ensure the comprehensive quality of her *rāga* presentation. Her linear architecture is flawless. She maintains an unrelenting and uninterrupted progression of melodic and rhythmic densities and complexities from the beginning of the *vilambita bandiśa* in *baḍā khayāla* format, right upto the end of the *druta bandiśa* in *choṭā khayāla* format. The dovetailing of low-density, medium-density, and high-density movements is seamless, and rendered almost imperceptible by a steadfast adherence to the tempo at which the *bandiśa* is launched. Her observance of the conventions for cyclical development of movements is meticulous.

Unlike most contemporary vocalists who treat the *antarā* as an afterthought, Vijaya gives the *sthāyī* and the *antarā* equal importance in each movement. Her attention to the directional comprehensiveness of her improvizations, too, is rare. This is especially evident in her *tāna*s movement, where she ensures a substantial presence for descending *tāna*s, ascending *tāna*s, bi-directional *tāna*s, and for *tāna*s that treat the *vāḍi svara* of the *rāga* as a melodic focus or terminal point. If these conventions were designed to ensure the comprehensive expression of a *rāga*'s melodic personality, Vijaya leaves nothing to chance.

Vijaya's approach to melodic execution is faithful to the orthodox Jaipur–Atrauli style. The melodic element in her music maintains a subtle relationship with the rhythmic element, with explicit intonations falling on fractional distances between the beats of the rhythmic cycle. The melodic contours of each phrase are rounded, and without angularities. The intonation is almost entirely through *mīṇḍa* and *gamaka*, with a judicious use of *khaṭkā*s. Despite Vijaya's training in *ṭhumarī*, her *khayāla* vocalism never tilts towards embellishments appropriate to the semi-classical and light forms of vocal music. Such austerity in content and expression is supported, as it indeed needs to be, by her sound understanding of the *rāga*'s melodic personality.

Vijaya has special qualifications in the *tāna*s department. The most significant aspects of her *tāna*s is the near-absence of *alaṁkāra* and *sapāṭa tāna*s. In fact, almost no *tāna* pattern appears in her singing in its isolated form. Vijaya allows her imagination to work instead. Some patterns do occur frequently in Vijaya's *tāna*s; but, rarely in the same configuration. In the present environment of vocal music, with its growing emphasis on slick execution rather than imaginative complexity, Vijaya's delivers a breath of fresh air.

Vijaya does, indeed, perform the hopping two-by-two *tānas* in medium density typical of the Jaipur–Atrauli style. But, in the high-density *tānas*, her vocal agility and melodic imagination deliver surprises reminiscent of her senior of the same *gharānā*, Mogubai Kurdikar. This complexity is believed to have been a legacy of Alladiya Khan, and is also evident in Kesarbai Kerkar's music. In addition to the legacy of complexity, Vijaya's *tānas* have rhythmic jerks, twists and turns, similar to the *tānas* of Agra Gharānā vocalists. But, the rhythmicality of the melody does not engage actively with the beats of the rhythmic cycle. This enigmatic quality would appear to be the legacy of Rajab Ali Khan and of Alladiya Khan.

Despite Girija Devi's encouragement to Vijaya in the pursuit of *ṭhumarī*, the sole example of this genre available to me is less than inspiring. The *ṭhumarī* has, in any event, though for mysterious reasons, found the musical soil of Maharashtra mostly infertile. In Vijaya's case, it appears to be a matter of temperament, more than musical capability. It is fair to conclude that Vijaya's is a classicist musical personality, which is not, in any way, diminished by her discomfort with romanticist genres.

Vijaya's music is an example of disciplined creativity. Despite her stylistic orthodoxy, her music shows no signs of aesthetic obsolescence. She suspects that, in her desire to get the most out of her ageing *guru*, she delayed her own launch beyond prudent limits. While this may be so, the more substantive issue might be — what kind of constituency can a classicist build for herself in the current cultural climate? Another question she might ask herself is — what is so terrible about emerging, possibly, as the best qualified and equipped teacher of Jaipur–Atrauli vocalism? (Written : January 2002).

4.5

Ashwini Bhide-Deshpande
Kishori's Heiress. . . and More

Is Ashwini an elitist or a populist? Is she a classicist or a romanticist? Is she an original or yet another Kishori Amonkar xerox? When questions like this begin to get asked, you know you are looking at a significant musician. It may be some time before these questions can be categorically answered. Until then, it is important that Ashwini's journey so far be acknolwedged for its salient features.

In a career spanning over two decades, Ashwini Bhide-Deshpande (b. 1960) has achieved a rare combination of popularity and stature. Stylistically, she now dons the mantle of Kishori Amonkar, the reigning empress of *khayāla* vocalism.

Ashwini is a top grade artist of All India Radio, has attained an abundant presence on the concert platform as well as on the shelves of music stores, and has made eminently successful concert tours of the US, Europe, Australia and Japan.

Ashwini belongs to a generation in which any girl, who could sing, wanted to sing like Kishori Amonkar (b. 1931). Fortunately for Ashwini, her own mother, Manik Bhide, was a senior student of Kishori Amonkar. With the advantage of being one step removed from the fountainhead of inspiration, Ashwini could access Kishori's vocalism without the risk of a stifled individuality.

Just a Good Musician

(Ashwini Spoke to the Author on 9 September 2000 and 31 August 2001)

"In my family, we studied music just as we studied mathematics, grammar, science, history and geography. Only the schools were different. Ever since I can recall, Narayanrao Datar, a vocalist of the Vishnu Digambar (Gwalior) tradition came home three times a week. Three generations of the family's women would learn with him, one after the other. Over and above this, all family members, my parents included, were enrolled at the Maharashtra Music School where we attended classes thrice a week.

"With this training, I passed the Saṅgīta Viśārada when I was 16. At that stage, I had no idea about the depth of our music, or what "*gharānedāra* music" (music as performed by vocalists of the established stylistic lineages) was, or about the journey upon which I had embarked. Had the world of music not encouraged me as generously as it did in later years, I might never have become a professional musician.

"Around that time, we also shifted to a different part of Bombay. Datar's home tuitions ceased, and my mother, Manik Bhide, started guiding me. By that time, she had been a disciple of Kishori Amonkar for over a decade, and had pursued intensive training with her, with several hours of training every day of the year.

"After I completed my high school at the age of 16, I was encouraged to enter the All India Radio Competition. A few months before the contest, I had a serious illness, and feared not being able to compete. At that stage, my mother took charge of the situation. For the next two months, she hammered my music, and my confidence, into shape for the competition. I topped the competition; but in retrospect, that was a minor pay-off. Those two months transformed me totally — as a person and as a musician. For the first time, I sensed the majesty of stylized vocalism, and realized that what I knew was not even a tip of the iceberg. From then onwards, music became an important direction.

"Until my marriage, my mother trained me with ruthless discipline. Along with this, I was pursuing my academic career, going through postgraduate studies in Microbiology, and working towards my doctorate at the Bhabha Atomic Research Centre. After marriage, I have continued to train with my mother, albeit with a declining frequency as my family and career have begun to claim an increasing proportion of my time.

"In 1995, my mother wanted me to deepen my understanding of *rāga*s as performed in our *gharānā*. She persuaded Ratnakar Pai, a senior musician of the Jaipur–Atrauli tradition, to guide me. Pai Buwa (a term of respect for the elderly) is an exceptional musical mind, with amazing clarity about the melodic contours of *rāga*s and the subtle distinctions between them. Being advanced in years, he cannot provide intensive training. He therefore teaches me compositions in different *rāga*s, and I imbibe their melodic subtleties through them.

"The use of pre-composed material as the main teaching

device is well established (in Hindustani music). It is especially important in our *gharānā* because it is *dhrupada*-based. Its musical wisdom is built into our compositions. But, as I found out after beginning training with Pai Buwa, our view of the composition as a repository of the *rāga* form goes well beyond the *dhrupada* notion. The *dhrupada* view is that a composition is a comprehensive melodic map of the *rāga* form, and of the literary content. In the Jaipur–Atrauli tradition, each composition is treated almost like a *rāga*. Conceptually, we do not perform a *rāga*; we perform a composition. The pre-composed shell of each composition emphasizes a particular facet of the *rāga*. That facet must also dominate the improvizations undertaken in its presentation. This is why different *khayāla*s of our *gharānā* in the same *rāga*, when performed, can create the illusion of being in different *rāga*s.

"This approach to transmitting the tradition also has another advantage. *Khayāla* permits us certain freedoms, which are inconceivable in *dhrupada*. And, Alladiya Khan utilized these freedoms to make the transition from Ḍāgara Bānī *dhrupada* to our style of *khayāla* singing. According to Pai Buwa, our *khayāla*s are not intended, specifically, for performance in any particular *tāla* or even at a particular tempo. They can be sung in any *tāla*, and at any tempo. Mastering the *khayāla*s in their excruciating detail is sufficient training for us to adapt them to different rhythmic formats.

"Considering the present stage in my life, and his, Pai Buwa's training does occasionally throw up unresolved aesthetic conflicts. There are, indeed, several *rāga*s on which Pai Buwa and my mother differ. This is natural because Pai Buwa and my mother were taught by different *guru*s, though from the same *gharānā*. On account of such differences, I have dropped certain *rāga*s from my repertoire. I will let my aesthetic convictions decide when, if ever, I should start performing them again.

"Other influences on my music have been Pandit Ravi Shankar and Kumar Gandharva. As a young girl, I was involved with a couple of projects of Panditji. During that period, his approach to music, with its explicit rhythmicality, made a deep impact on me. Amongst vocalists, Kumarji was a hot favourite in my father's home. Every recording of his was actively discussed by the family. From this influence, I probably acquired a special feel for the poetry as a musical element, and the variations of timbre, which discerning listeners have observed in my singing.

"The overwhelming influence on my singing has undoubtedly been my mother. Contrary to popular belief, I have never studied directly with Kishori Tai (term of respect, meaning elder sister). I have always been my mother's disciple, and have acquired Kishori Amonkar's training through her. The most important value I have acquired from it is the insight into the systematic unfolding of the *rāga*, of revealing every single strand in the warp and weft of its fabric. This, I believe, is Kishori Tai's most significant contribution.

"It does not bother me if my music is compared to Kishori Tai's in minor respects too. For one, I am proud to belong to this distinguished lineage. Secondly, neither originality, nor *gharānā* purity, can possibly have the same meaning today as they did half a century ago. We no longer live in a world where we can insulate ourselves totally from the dominant influences of our times emanating outside our *gharānā*. It is no longer possible to be either your *guru*'s replica, or a totally original musician. We start with something we inherit, keep absorbing other influences, and shape our individuality as we go along. What matters ultimately is how we put it all together.

"I don't know if I am the most successful, or the finest, vocalist of my generation. Success is like the morning dew. It lasts only as long as it lasts. You realize this even more acutely when you are a woman. A woman goes through so many physical and emotional changes through her life, that she can never really take her grip over her voice and her music for granted. Life for us is a constant struggle against these changes. But, there's no reliable method for controlling their impact, and also no way of predicting how each transition will affect our performing capability.

"As a professional musician, in any case, you cannot get attached to success. Competition is a reality and good for us. At least four or five of us (female vocalists in the plus/minus forty age group) have a reasonable following; and none of us is complacent. In today's environment, there is, of course, much more to being a successful musician than just being an excellent musician. But, I am not too concerned about what that "much more" might be, because I don't need success that desperately. I am happy with being just a good musician."

Ashwini's Music

I make my observations on Ashwini's music based on the study of two CDs she recorded for India Archive Music in 2004 and 2005, and several concert recordings. The repertoire covered by the recordings consists of *khayāla*s in Bageśri, Kedāra, Śrī, Bihāga, Yaman, Tilaka Kamoda, Bibhāsa, Jaunpurī, Miyā kī Toḍī, Hinḍola, and Bhūpa. The non-*khayāla* repertoire consists of a Mīrā Bhajana, a *dādarā* and a Hori, in Pūraba (Benares) style. I have also studied the compilation of 82 *khayāla bandiśe*s composed by Ashwini, and released as a book of notations along with a demo CD rendered in her own voice. And, finally, my observations draw upon the substantial exposure I have had to Ashwini's concerts and radio broadcasts over a couple of decades.

Ashwini's repertoire tilts more towards the common *rāga*s than Kishori Amonkar's. Her standard repertoire could well be a sign of the times, and of the need to service a less cultivated audience profile than musicians of Kishori's generation did. Before assemblies of learned musicians, however, Ashwini is known to have unleashed formidable renditions of *rāga*s like Khema Kalyāṇa, which have remained the talk of the music world for years after the event. Ashwini knows her audiences, and caters to them at their level of discernment and sophistication, without pandering obviously to the lowest common denominator.

Significant about Ashwini's repertoire is her recent foray into the romanticist genres of the Pūraba (Benares) tradition. In the recordings I studied, I found two examples of these — a Horī and a *dādarā*. Her handling of the Pūraba repertoire — forte of the Benares courtesans — is so convincing that it is difficult to believe that the singer is a Maharashtrian brāhmaṇa.

In recent years, Ashwini has been enlarging her involvement with *bhajana*s, as a genre independently of their place as tailpieces at her classical concerts. She has now acquired a substantial following for her repertoire of poetry penned by the saint-poets of the *bhakti* movement, and set to music by her. The stylistics of her *bhajana* repertoire are true to the Kishori legacy, while the selection of lyrics reflects Ashwini's own literary tastes. It would appear that this development has added immensely to her popularity.

Ashwini has established an enviable track-record of consistency for her performances. She gives to every rendition everything she has, taking no short-cuts in any department of musicianship. This has contributed greatly to her rise in stature amongst connoisseurs.

Ashwini, the Composer

The vast majority of Ashwini's compositions are in the common *rāga*s, which constitute the mainstay of her repertoire. In the 82 *bandiśe*s she has published, however, one does find a few rare *rāga*s. Interestingly, she has composed *bandiśe*s in several *rāga*s of the Carnatic tradition — Cārukeśī, Haṁsadhvani,

Ārabhi, Vācaspati, and Ābhogī. Not surprisingly, she has composed *bandiśes* also in a few of the patent *rāgas* of the Jaipur–Atrauli tradition. Ashwini's command over the rhythmic element is reflected in the variety of *tālas* in which her *bandiśes* are composed. In addition to the *tālas* common to the Jaipur–Atrauli tradition, her composing mind has also taken her into unfamiliar territory with *bandiśes* in *rudra tāla*, *matta tāla*, and *addhā tīnatāla*.

For all the widening of horizons these patterns suggest, there is an underlying accessibility to her compositions. Her compositions are not necessarily easy to sing. But, from the point of view of audiences, none of them is oblique, daunting or clever in an obvious sort of way. The key to her *bandiśes* is *lālitya*, a term I have found impossible to translate. In addition to being consistent with Ashwini's musical personality, her *bandiśes* carry forward the romanticist flavour Kishori Amonkar, Kumar Gandharva and Jasraj have injected into the melodic character of *bandiśes*.

Ashwini and the Kishori Amonkar Legacy

Ashwini's music reveals its source within the first three minutes of singing. The similarity between the timbre of her voice and Kishori's is uncanny. While largely a gift of nature, its deliberate cultivation is also obvious. It has the same mellow quality in the scale-base region, and goes through a similar tightening as it travels up the scale. But Ashwini seems less likely to drift towards the metallic end in the upper registers than her role model.

Ashwini has also internalized Kishori's style of intonation and timbre manipulation efficiently. She is as sensitive as Kishori is to the literary content of music, and as fastidious about its integrity in rendition. Like Kishori, Ashwini has a rich repertoire of devotional music, which she renders without frivolity in handling the *rāga*-ness of the compositions. Ashwini's *khayāla* architecture is as meticulous as Kishori's. Ashwini's *rāga* grammar can be controversial. But, interestingly, it is controversial in the same *rāga*s, and in the same respect, as Kishori's. Like Kishori again, Ashwini freely adopts melodic ornamentations typical of the semi-classical genres in her rendition of *khayāla*s. Neither Kishori, nor Ashwini, leaves any doubt about the exceptional intellect that supports their musicianship — a *sine qua non* of great music.

Kishori's intellect imbues her music with its oblique quality, while Ashwini's intellect expresses itself in the highly disciplined deployment of musical ideas. The two differ also in the emotional stance of their performances. Kishori adopts a caressing intimacy, which is also, in a strange sort of way, intimidating. Ashwini, on the other hand, exudes a friendly warmth. These comparisons are made with the caveat that Ashwini is two generations removed from Kishori, and the two are at different stages of their careers. These realities could well limit our perceptions of their distinctive musical personalities and temperaments.

The balance of the rhythmic and melodic elements in their music is similar and subtle. Kishori's balance is certainly more oblique than Ashwini's. Kishori uses the *tihāī* form, while Ashwini tends not to use it. Ashwini's bias towards explicit rhythmicality is apparent mainly in the structure and tempo of *khayāla* renditions, the gait of *bandiśe*s composed by her, and her treatment of *bola-bāṇṭa* and *laya-bāṇṭa* in *ākāra* articulation.

Ashwini follows Kishori's and the *gharānā*'s practice of *baḍā khayāla vilambita bandiśa* presentation in *tīnatāla* at a base tempo of 24-27 bpm, with only imperceptible and marginal acceleration during the rendition. In her *madhya-laya bandiśe*s set to *rūpaka* or *jhapatāla*, Ashwini seems comfortable with a base-tempo of 55 to 60 bpm. Ashwini's *choṭā khayāla bandiśa* renderings tend to start at 160 bpm. In *ekatāla*, Ashwini begins at 235 to 245 bpm.

Ashwini's *baḍā khayāla* treatment is much like Kishori's. The *ālāpa* is almost always in *ākāra* articulation. *bola-ālāpa* is the exception, perhaps resorted to when a less demanding expression is desired. Like Kishori, Ashwini tends to perform the *ālāpa* in three sections — *sthāyī, antarā* and *sañcārī*, with the *sañchārī* in *bola-ālāpa* articulation. The elaborate *ālāpa* is followed by the *bola-bāṇṭa* movement. Interestingly, Ashwini occasionally replaces the *bola-bāṇṭa* with a *laya-bāṇṭa* in *ākāra* articulation. In rendition, this is, of course, much more demanding than *bola-bāṇṭa*. But, the musical effect of isolating the melodic-rhythmic pulsation from poetics is a connoisseur's delight. As per Kishori's practice, short *tāna*s are subtly introduced into the *bola-bāṇṭa* for a drift into *bola-tāna*s. *Bola-tāna*s finally give way to *ākāra tāna*s.

Ashwini's *madhya-laya khayāla* protocol is similar to Kishori's. *Madhya-laya bandiśe*s in *rūpaka* or *jhapatāla* are presented in elaborate *baḍā khayāla* protocol. The main difference is that she renders the *sthāyī* and the *antarā* of the *bandiśe*s placed up-front, as against the post-*ālāpa* placement of the *antarā* practised in the *vilambita/baḍā khayāla*. Her *ālāpa*s in *madhya-laya* renditions tend to be more compact than in the *baḍā khayāla* renditions. Greater weightage is accorded to the pulse-driven, medium density *bola-bāṇṭa/laya-bāṇṭa* movement, and the *bola-tāna*s and *ākāra tāna*s to follow.

Ashwini's *choṭā khayāla*s, whether in *ekatāla* or *tīnatāla*, have the same format. The *bandiśa sthāyī* and *antarā* are usually presented upfront. The primary improvisatory movements are *tāna*s. The use of *bola-tāna*s is occasional or negligible. The emphasis is on a display of *ākāra* artistry.

Ashwini's *tāna*s are simple in construction, and exceptionally polished in their execution. The jaw-dropping complexity associated with Jaipur–Atrauli *tāna*s — including those of Kishori Amonkar — is not on Ashwini's agenda. These predilections are not unique to Ashwini's music as much as they are endemic to musicians of her generation. In order to achieve higher standards of technical perfection and stunning impact, contemporary vocalists have progressively diluted the cerebral and imaginative quality of *tāna*s.

Ashwini Today

Ashwini aspires to be "just a good musician." As Kishori's arrow shot into the future from Manik Bhide's bow, Ashwini has already achieved this aim by the age of 45. Having said this, it is fair to note that her evolution so far does not provide conclusive proof of her access to the accumulated musical wisdom of the Jaipur–Atrauli Gharānā.

Here, we are drawing a crucial distinction between Kishori Amonkar, the musical product, and Kishori Amonkar, the ideation process that shapes her product. Kishori's ideation process is shaped by the accumulated wisdom of the Jaipur–Atrauli Gharānā, which has exhibited the ability to produce several originals in the same generation. If Ashwini's training has given her the keys to this wisdom, the time has come for her to unlock its potential through an original musical statement broadly within the stylistic and ideological framework of the *gharānā*.

Amongst the thousands of followers Kishori has aquired over the last quarter of a century through various processes of stylistic absorption, Ashwini is the only vocalist to have achieved significant stature. This is a reflection of the fact that, from a musician of such formidable training, talent and intellect, our musicial culture has reason to expect an attempt at greatness (Written : December 2005).

4.6

Arti Anklikar-Tikekar
Stepping out of a towering shadow

ARTI Anklikar-Tikekar (b. 1963) has the unique experience of shaping her music in the mould of Kishori Amonkar, fulfilling her dream of training with her role model, and then discovering that the universe of musical ideas has much more to offer. For Arti, one of the more visible vocalists in Hindustani music for almost two decades, the journey in search of her musical self has been a tricky one.

She was groomed initially in the Gwalior style, and succumbed thereafter to the hypnotic influence of the neo-Jaipur–Atrauli diva, Kishori Amonkar. Arti's tutelage with Kishori lasted two years after which she moved on in search of music which made more sense to herself.

Arti holds a degree in commerce, is an artiste of the All India Radio in the semi-classical as well as classical categories since 1983, has over twenty commercial recordings to her credit in the classical, light and regional music segments of the music market, and enjoys a considerable following in India, the US, UK, Canada and the UAE.

It is the Mind that Sings, not the Voice
(Arti Spoke to the Author on 20 December 2003)

"In the last few years, I find that my definition of the beautiful in music is changing. When I look back on my youth — 20 years ago, when I entered the profession — I realize that I had very strong ideas about what good music is. Everything that did not fit this notion did not seem to qualify as even music. I went through several years of believing that Kishori Amonkar's music was the only music that qualified as music. As I started getting exposed to other leading musicians, I started seeing the beautiful facets of their music too. Then started a phase in which I wanted to sing the *ālāpa* like one vocalist, *bola-aṅga* like another, and *tāna*s like yet another. Gradually, this too faded away, and I started seeing the beauty and integrity of every approach in its completeness. Once I reached this stage, I realized the futility of following models of vocalism, and began relating the universe of musical ideas to my own musical personality — who I am, what my voice can deliver, what I enjoy singing.

"The stages through which I have passed are necessary stages of evolution. The world of music is so vast that it is impossible to enter it — in the early stages — without wearing the blinkers of the *gharānā*s or individual models. It is only when we have absorbed one model well that we can start looking for our musical selves in a larger universe of musical ideas. The search for our musical selves is a part of our evolution as individuals. At some stage, the reliance on borrowed ideas induces a feeling of hollowness within us. We feel the need to immerse ourselves so totally in our music, that we lose consciousness of our selves. This is a difficult stage for audiences to handle.

"There is a substantial section of the audience that wants to hear Arti singing like Kishori Amonkar. This audience becomes uncomfortable when Arti starts singing what she wants to sing. It is a rough ride for the musician as well as audiences. But, it is nothing new in our tradition. Every musician has had to go through this. As my neural chemistry changes, my music will also change. If Arti dives deep enough into the reservoir of her musicality, she will transmit the joy of the experience to her audiences. And, finally, this is what the audiences should expect from the musical experience.

"I am not belittling the tricky aspects of the transition in terms of audience expectations and their fulfilment. Yes, there is some dissonance amongst some sections of the audience. Yes, my audience profile seems to be changing. I am probably no longer making too much sense to the younger crowd, but drawing the more mature audiences. But, I now have to be honest to myself, sing with conviction and total involvement, and let the audience factor recede from my consciousness.

"For helping me along in this direction, I am indebted to my current *guru*, Dinkar Kaikini. It is not easy to guide a musician at my stage of life. I have been around, and fairly busy, for 20 years now. By objective standards, I have no compelling reason to undertake a major overhaul of my music. But, what I do have is the inner urge — a spiritual urge, if you like — to grow as a musician, and through my music, as a human being. At this stage, my *guru*'s inputs are no longer a matter of imparting knowledge of *rāgas*, or *bandiśes* or techniques of melodic execution. These are incidental.

"Kaikiniji has made me realize that it is the mind that sings and not the voice. He has begun to untangle the cobwebs in my mind so that I might discover my musical self. He has made me sense the emotional charge inherent in every *svara*, and demonstrated to me the means of expressing it. He has set me off on the path to self-discovery. I cannot say that I have got there. But, knowing where you have to go, and being on the path is a good beginning. At least I have a good chance of getting there if I persevere. If the audiences accept the results of this journey, well and good! If they don't, I have to be prepared for the consequences."

Stylistic Pedigree

Between the ages of nine and twelve, Arti was taught by Vijaya Joglekar, until then a disciple of Vasantrao Kulkarni, a product of the Gwalior and Agra traditions. Vijaya taught her mainly *bhāva gīta* (Marāṭhī romantic songs) and *nāṭya saṅgīta*. Thereafter, for serious *khayāla* training, Vijaya placed her under the direct tutelage of her mentor, Vasantrao Kulkarni, a respected teacher, who never became a performing musician. It was with Vasantrao that Arti had the longest period of training during her most formative years.

Arti has also been trained, for short periods, by Ulhas Kashalkar, and Kishori Amonkar. Ulhas has built his edifice of musicianship on the foundations of Gwalior, Jaipur–Atrauli and Agra influences imparted to him by his two mentors. Kishori Amonkar is a highly individualistic interpreter of Jaipur–Atrauli vocalism, having chosen a direction significant and influential enough to be dubbed neo-Jaipur–Atrauli. And, as recently as 1996, Arti commenced training with Dinkar Kaikini, an eclectic scholar-musician known best as an heir to the legacy of the Agra scholar-maestro, S.N. Ratanjankar. Kaikini has, however, also studied with K. Nagesh Rao of the Patiala Gharānā, and Omkarnath Thakur, the maverick genius groomed in the Gwalior tradition.

Outside these formal relationships, Arti admits to the strong influence of Ameer Khan and Bade Ghulam Ali Khan recordings. Ameer Khan was an original, identified with the Indore Gharānā, but with affinities for Bhendi Bazar as well as Kairana stylistics. Bade Ghulam Ali was the principal exponent of the Patiala Gharānā. In an unusual departure from tradition, Arti has established a formal relationship with a *tabalā* maestro, Suresh Talwalkar, also known for his formidable knowledge of *khayāla* vocalism.

Interestingly, Arti is perhaps the only significant *khayāla* vocalist who retains a formal presence in the popular segments of music through her empanelment with All India Radio in the *ṭhumarī* and light music categories, along with her status as a *khayāla* vocalist.

With this variety of influences and tendencies, it becomes impossible to place Arti's music categorically within the framework of any stylistic tradition, as hitherto understood. She is squarely a product of the diffused stylistic environment of post-Independence India. In this environment, *khayāla* music is drawing on a variety of stylistic sources, and attempting to shape a homogeneous musical experience mimicking an eminently successful stylistic model (in this case, Kishori Amonkar), with the objective of servicing a national and international audience. However, homogeneity is the antithesis of artistic achievement. The world of art demands individuality, before it concedes stature to an artiste. This is the context in which Arti's musical journey up to this point has to be understood.

Arti's Music

I base my observations on a purposive study of one CD recorded by Arti for India Archive Music Ltd., New York, and another published by Alurkar Music House, Pune. The repertoire studied covers *khayāla*s in Ahīra Bhairava, Salagavarāli, Bilāsakhanī Toḍī, and Deśakāra, and a Mīrā Bhajana. In addition, the present writer has had considerable exposure to Arti's concert career.

Despite the encyclopaedic repertoire of her mentors, Arti's choice of repertoire has a strong bias in favour of the popular and the accessible. The appearance of a *rāga* like Salagavarāli on a recording suggests her willingness to handle Carnatic (South Indian) *rāga*s in order to enlarge her audience. By her own admission, she sings a few variants of the Kānaḍā family, and a few of the *toḍī* variants, all of which are within the realm of audience familiarity. On the art music platform, her tailpieces are generally *bhajana*s, the standard fare offered by *khayāla* vocalists from her home state of Maharashtra.

A seasoned listener of Hindustani music will instantly detect the distinctive timbre of Arti's voice. It has neither the cultivated sweetness typical of female vocalists like Hirabai Barodekar or Kishori Amonkar, nor the rugged masculinity of vocalists like Kesarbai Kerkar or Gangubai Hangal. Arti's timbre has an earthiness, which drifts towards the nasal as her voice travels up the scale.

Arti is conscious of her unusual timbre, and feels it might need some corrective effort. This feature might have, on the contrary, contributed generously to the distinctive appeal of her music — a feature that sets her apart from the hordes mimicking the style and manner of Kishori Amonkar. It might also have given her comfortable access to some masculine vocal expressions, which melodious female voices might not attempt out of the fear of sounding unfeminine . For the semi-classical and light genres, on the other hand, the timbre of her voice might be eminently suitable because of its seductive potential.

Predictably, Arti's *bandiśe*s in *baḍā khayāla* and *choṭā khayāla* formats are drawn from different sources. On the evidence of recordings surveyed here, and of her concert career, she appears not to be in search of the unusual or fascinating specimens of the composer's art. This fact could well reflect her tendency to keep her music within the realms of the familiar.

The architecture of her *khayāla* presentations is the standardized architecture now accepted in *khayāla* music. Her adherence to the progression of melodic and rhythmic densities is meticulous. Her *vilambita bandiśa* in *baḍā khayāla* format has three distinct movements — the *ālāpa*, the *bola-laya*, and the *tāna*s. Her *ālāpa* articulation is generally in *bola*, following the Gwalior and Agra norm more than the traditional Jaipur–Atrauli norm. Her melodic progression, however, reflects the highly disciplined format of Kishori Amonkar. Also following Kishori Amonkar, Arti installs milestones along the progression path, in the form of melodic variants of the *mukhaḍā* of the *bandiśa*.

In the medium density *bola-laya* movement, Arti has adopted the *saragama* articulation popularized by Ameer Khan, and widely practised in Kairana vocalism, but generally eschewed by Jaipur–Atrauli, Agra and Gwalior lineages. Arti's *saragama* movement does not appear to attempt Ameer Khan's mercurial quality. Instead, it attempts an explicit rhythmicality.

Arti's medium density *tāna*s include passages of hopping construction with a suggestion of a *gamaka* typical of Jaipur–Atrauli vocalism. Arti often seems tempted to unleash *tāna*s of melodic complexity encountered in traditional Jaipur–Atrauli vocalism. But, she seems to hold herself back probably in order to better satisfy contemporary standards of slick, polished execution at high speeds of delivery. The predominant emphasis, consequently, is on long-span *alaṁkāra tāna*s found commonly in contemporary vocalism of all *gharānā*s.

It is the sculptural and ornamentational facets of her music that Arti exhibits the greatest influence of Kishori Amonkar. Here, she permits herself the use of melodic contours and embellishments more suited to the semi-classical and light genres of vocal music. To conservative listeners, Arti might appear to be going farther in this direction than Kishori Amonkar does. Even if such impressions are valid, they would merely affirm Arti's artistic persona, which straddles both, the art and popular, segments of the music world.

Arti Today

Arti's manner of presentation bears the distinctive stamp of Kishori Amonkar. However, the substance of Arti's music cannot escape the blend of Gwalior and Agra influences to which she has been exposed through her various guides and mentors.

The romanticist influence of Kishori Amonkar places Arti amongst the rebels against the traditional aloofness of *khayāla* music. Arti goes beyond this to actually retain a professional presence in the light and semi-classical genres of music. Arti's is a seamless world. It has no need for a Chinese Wall between the various genres of art music, or between art music and popular music — whether as a career strategy, or a stylistic barrier.

In the recordings surveyed, her music is still under the spell of her training under Kishori Amonkar. But, interestingly, after performing for the sample recordings, she acquired a new *guru*, representing an entirely different background. In December 2003, when I last heard her perform, Arti had begun to successfully integrate into her music the bold and clever rhythmic artistry typical of Agra vocalism in medium density rendition. This was probably inspired by Kaikini's mentorship. At the time of writing, Arti's music appears to exhibit the confidence of one who has arrived, along with the anxiety of one still in search of her personal musical statement.

This is not an unusual phenomenon in classical music, and will probably be witnessed routinely as the years go by. As

Ulhas Kashalkar says in his interview, featured elsewhere in this book, musicianship in the Hindustani tradition flowers around the age of forty. If this is true of *gharānā*-groomed thoroughbreds, this must be truer of musicians who have not — for whatever reason — undergone a homogeneous stylistic indoctrination. Their simultaneous struggle for aesthetic coherence and individuality is not made any easier when they have to wage it under public gaze.

Arti's trajectory through the musical firmament establishes her significance in the cultural process. The magnitude of her significance could, however, remain indeterminate for some more time (Written : January 2004).

4.7

Manjiri Asnare-Kelkar
A Modern Interpreter of the Orthodox Idiom

WITH Jaipur–Atrauli vocalism being steered categorically towards romanticism by Kishori Amonkar, only an accidental modernization could have given its orthodox idiom a fresh lease of life. Though her musicianship has yet to deliver to its promise, Manjiri Asnare-Kelkar (b. 1971) might just be the kind of accident the Jaipur–Atrauli legacy needed. Manjiri's music maintains a substantial stylistic distance from the last orthodox stalwart, Dhondutai Kulkarni, as well as the revisionist exponent, Kishori Amonkar. And, yet there is no mistaking the orthodox Jaipur–Atrauli flavour in her music.

Manjiri was selected by the Sangeet Natak Akademi for the first Bismillah Khan Memorial Award for Young Musicians in early 2007. A few years earlier, *India Today*, the influential news magazine, hailed hers as the "voice that spans not merely two octaves, but two centuries." In less than a decade, she has established a significant presence on the Indian concert platform, acquired a following abroad, and released five commercial recordings. She became a broadcaster on All India Radio at the age of 16, after topping its nationwide talent-search, and currently occupies the penultimate A grade. She holds postgraduate degrees in English Literature as well as Music.

Coming to Terms with a Musician's Risks
(Manjiri Spoke to the Author on 3 June, 2003)

"My family is deeply involved with music. My grandfather was an attorney in Amarāvatī (a town in north-eastern Maharashtra State), and an excellent *tabalā* player. He had studied with the best percussionists in Amarāvatī, and belonged to the Gyan Prakash Ghosh lineage. The family home was never without music and musicians. Because of my grandfather's love for music, my father also got involved. He trained as a *tabalā* player and, in his youth, stood first in the All India Radio national talent search competition.

"I was brought up in Sangli (southern Maharashtra), where my father served as a professor. He still performs regularly on All India Radio and, of course, accompanies me whenever he can. He was keen that I should study music. When I was five, I was sent to a music school to learn singing. Simultaneously, I was sent to a dancing school to study Kathak. By the age of eight, I was admitted to the best music school in Sangli run by Chintubuwa Mhaiskar, a Gwalior-trained vocalist.

"I did well in both. By the age of ten, I could hold the dance floor comfortably for up to 90 minutes, and was winning dance competitions all over the state. At the music school, I was identified for personalized attention and guidance from

Chintubuwa. By then, I was also teaching myself a little bit. I had become a fan of Malini Rajurkar, especially her *ṭappā* renderings. So, I bought her cassettes, painstakingly took down the notations, and perfected them by rote. By the time I was fifteen, I could present a decent 30-mts *khayāla,* started winning competitions and being invited to perform. The time had come to choose between music and dance. Quality dance training was available only in Bombay or Pune. Pursuing dance after marriage and children is always a big uncertainty in our society. So, I dropped dance, and stuck to music.

"I hit the crossroads again at the age of 17, when I graduated from high school, and secured admission to engineering college. That would have ruled out any significant achievement in music. But the path to music, too, was uncertain, as there was no top class mentor within reach. Hoping that this problem would get solved, I abandoned engineering in favour of music. The problem did get solved soon when Madhusudan Kanetkar (affectionately called Appā) retired from All India Radio and returned home to Sangli. Like all Jaipur–Atrauli vocalists, he was known to be very selective about accepting students, and had so far accepted none. He heard me and agreed to a trial period of six months. That was 15 years ago. Five years ago he moved to Pune, and, around the same time, I moved to Nasik after my marriage. But, my training continues. While we were in Sangli, I trained with him twice a day for two to three hours in each session. After relocation, either he visits us for a month at a time, or I visit him for three or four days at a time.

"Learning with Appā was a major transition. I had, by then, studied music for almost 13 years. My basics were sound, but I had no clue about stylized singing with a stamp of *gharānā* pedigree. Within a month of starting lessons, I was totally lost. I had unlearnt what I knew earlier, and was struggling for a grip over what I was now being taught. One day, I broke down before Appā. He said that my learning would now begin since I realized I knew nothing. He was right. After that, my music sorted itself out quite fast.

"Appā is an unorthodox teacher. He believes that I have to sing my own music in my own voice. He merely wishes to give me an approach, which must inevitably wither away as my musical vision takes over. He never insists that my music be exactly like his, or even conform to the orthodox Jaipur–Atrauli style. He insists I study the great vocalists of all *gharānā*s, observe their special features, and adopt what I like. He encourages me to sing many *rāga*s, which are not sung in our *gharānā*, but are popular today. He locates good *bandiśe*s in them, sets them to our style, and teaches me how to handle them. He does the same for *rāga*s performed in our *gharānā*, but for which *druta bandiśe*s were not composed in his time. He does not give any importance to a musician being able to sing a hundred *rāga*s. What is important is that a *rāga*'s boundaries, and the frame of a *bandiśa*, be treated as sacred. His training emphasises the spirit of the *rāga*'s, and of *bandiśe*s, so that I may capture their musical potential in rendition.

"Even my semi-classical repertoire has been developed under Appā's guidance. He believes that I should remain actively involved with light music because that will add to the emotional richness of my classical renditions. I was interested in *ṭappā*s. So, he compiled a repertoire for me, and taught me how to handle each *bandiśa*. I loved *Nāṭya-saṅgīta*. So, he studied that genre, and guides me on rendition. He has also studied and taught me *ṭhumarī*. But, I have performed them only on a limited scale because I am not yet entirely comfortable with the genre. Holding audience interest with unstructured melody, without the support of *rāga* grammar, and at ultra slow tempo, is tougher than it seems. But, I am working on it.

"I have never felt that Appā's lack of performing experience is a handicap for me. For one, although he never sings in public, his music in private gatherings is charismatic. Secondly, in his career as a broadcaster, he has interacted closely enough with the greatest musicians of all *gharānā*s to understand the niceties of relating to audiences and building a career. Yes, I do make occasional mistakes in judging audiences, and deciding what to sing. This cannot be blamed on my *guru*. This risk is a part of a musician's life, and each musician has to manage it in his/her own unique way.

"In addition to the obvious aspects of professional risk, there are some inscrutable risks, too. There are some venues where I seem to repeatedly perform well, and others where I feel consistently uninspired. This has nothing to do with the acoustics, or audience profiles, or with anything one can explain. Isn't it the same with temples? Some non-descript temples transport you instantly into a different world, while some magnificent ones leave you cold! Some concert halls seem vibrant with musical energy, while others seem sterile.

"When I observe such patterns, I sympathize with our traditional belief that the performing arts have their own presiding deity (*raṅga-devatā*), which has blessed some concert platforms, and frowned upon others — why this should be so, nobody has ever told me, and I have not asked. The notion of *raṅga-devatā* helps an artist come to terms with every risk to the success of a performance that he cannot understand. Once you are in the profession, you perform wherever you are invited, say your prayers to *raṅga-devatā*, calm your nerves, and begin.

"I am often asked how my training in dance helps my career as a vocalist. The obvious aspect of this is my command over the rhythmic element in music. My music *guru*s have been saved a lot of effort because of this. The less obvious advantage is my understanding of body language, and what it does for my stage presence. It is not knowledge I can consciously use; but it is there, and it is working. Even though we reach more people today through recordings than concerts, the concert is still the real thing."

Manjiri's Repertoire

I base my observations on a study of one CD recorded by Manjiri for India Archive Music, New York, and several concert recordings. The repertoire studied includes *khayāla*s in Lalita Gaurī, Bhinna Ṣaḍja, Basanta Bahāra, Naikī Kānaḍā, Bhaṭiyārā, Jaunpurī, Śuddha Sāraṅga, Bhīmapalāsa, Jaitśrī, Sāvanī Kalyāṇa, Soraṭha, Ahīra Bhairava, Alhaiyā Bilāwala, Ajad Hiṇḍola, Mālkauṅs, Śuddha Kalyāṇa, Basantī Kedāra, Ṭappās in Bhairavī and Kafī, and several renditions of *nāṭya saṅgīta* and *bhajana*s. In addition, I have also attended several of Manjiri's concerts over a period of ten years.

In *khayāla*, she appears to allow an almost equal representation to common *rāga*s and the favourite abstruse *rāga*s of the Jaipur–Atrauli Gharānā. However, the presence of esoteric *rāga*s in her repertoire is considerably larger than recent Jaipur–Atrauli vocalists have adopted. It would therefore appear that she is willing to risk the discomfort of the laity to earn the esteem of connoisseurs. She does not, however, come through as an elitist either by temperament or by strategy. She is the first vocalist in many years to revive a constituency for the lively *ṭappā* genre. She obliges audiences readily with renditions of *nāṭya saṅgīta* and *bhajana*s. In its totality, Manjiri's repertoire strategy ensures the broad-spectrum appeal required to build a career in music, while retaining its orphic end as her "positioning" statement.

Manjiri's Music

Manjiri is gifted with a feminine, though powerful voice, which has been trained for pleasing vocalization and intonation in *ākāra*. The timbre of the voice remains uniform through the entire range she handles. However, her occasional difficulty with forays into the lower octave, and sporadic audibility of her breath through the microphones suggest possible neglect of some important aspects of voice training by her mentors.

Manjiri is a Gwalior-nurtured vocalist and a trained Kathak dancer, groomed in the Jaipur–Atrauli style. Her *guru* during her most formative years, Madhusudan Kanetkar, studied orthodox Jaipur–Atrauli vocalism for six years with Bhurji Khan, perhaps the finest teacher amongst the three sons of Alladiya Khan. In Kanetkar's own words (a private interview with the author), he understood Jaipur–Atrauli vocalism "well enough to teach it, but not well enough to perform it." Thereafter, he spent his entire working life as a producer on All India Radio, during which period he studied a variety of vocal styles, and continued to broadcast as a vocalist, without ever seeking a career on the stage.

No recordings of Kanetkar's music are available as a reference point for Manjiri's music. On the evidence of Manjiri's account of her tutelage, her music, and the context, however, certain observations can be made about her musical inclinations.

Manjiri has been able to resist the contemporary attraction of Kishori Amonkar's neo-Jaipur–Atrauli vocalism, endemic to lady vocalists of her generation. However, if Kesarbai, Lakshmibai, and Dhondutai are the yardsticks for establishing orthodox Jaipur–Atrauli vocalism, Manjiri does not fit clearly into their stylistic category either. Her second *guru*, Kanetkar, probably sang and taught the orthodox Jaipur–Atrauli style. But, considering the context of his musicianship, his approach to grooming Manjiri, and the generational gap between him and Manjiri (almost 60 years), it was inevitable that Manjiri's music should be difficult to classify with reference to familiar models.

Manjiri is not a simple case of a Gwalior style musician migrating to Jaipur–Atrauli. She is a Kathak dancer and a

Gwalior trained musician who migrated to Jaipur–Atrauli. Her route to musicianship is stylistically significant. It tilts the balance of her music in favour of the rhythmic element. As a result, her interpretation of Jaipur–Atrauli vocalism is too unique to be given a label. We must therefore be satisfied with calling it a modern interpretation of orthodox Jaipur–Atrauli vocalism.

Manjiri's handling of melodic contours is faithful to the Jaipur–Atrauli style, with explicit intonations relating to the rhythmic cycle in fractions of beats, rather than synchronous to them. The contours of her phrasing do, however, have a mild angularity, which is dynamic (driven by volume and timbre) rather than melodic. She tends to emphasize the first *svaras* of phrases, creating the suggestion of a pulsation even in slow tempo anarhythmic movements.

From the movements of her hands when she performs on the stage, I infer that this appealing suggestion of rhythmicality could be a choreographic metaphor, transposed from her training as a dancer. As a result, the subtlety of the relationship between melody and rhythm typical of Jaipur–Atrauli has been mildly diluted. Considering that no Jaipur–Atrauli vocalist below 50 has been able to maintain this orthodox subtlety, it could also be a generational issue. In any event, Manjiri's enhanced rhythmic sensibility is not pronounced enough to exclude her totally from the Jaipur–Atrauli legacy.

Manjiri's melodic sculpture is austere and consistent with orthodox Jaipur–Atrauli vocalism. She deploys only *mīṇḍa*, *gamaka* and *khaṭkā* for intervallic transitions. The ornate *kan* and *murkī* type of embellishments are absent from her music. If there is a perceptible vivacity in her music, it comes from the hint of rhythmicality discussed above.

Manjiri's temporal approach is consistent with Jaipur–Atrauli stylistics. Her music is faithful to the linearity of *khayāla* architecture. However, she is prone to rendering *ālāpa*s of 25/30 mts in *baḍā/vilambita khayāla*s of 40/50 mts' duration. Such *ālāpa*s often fail to hold interest after the first 10 mts. After the *sthāyī* and *antarā,* both of which are neat, Manjiri enters a movement (or perhaps a combination of movements) whose aesthetic intent would appear to be those of *sañcārī* and *ābhoga,* but whose structure does not quite deliver to the intent. This phenomenon — not conspicuous in her *madhya-laya khayāla*s, generally of much shorter duration — points towards an uncertain grip over architecture. In view of her youth, the phenomenon could also suggest inadequate involvement in the exploration of the melodic potential of the *rāga*s she performs. These features occasionally deny her *baḍā/ vilambita khayāla*s the satisfying quality that arises from the effortless communication of musical ideas, transparency of architecture and a contemporary compactness.

In tune with contemporary conventions, she routinely performs *choṭā/druta khayāla*s after *vilambita khayāla*s — a recent addition to the *gharānā*'s orthodox stream. Manjiri's *choṭā/druta khayāla bandiśe*s are generally unusual, and often of exceptional compositional quality. Her *guru* was evidently a treasure-trove of *bandiśe*s, and perhaps also a fine composer.

Manjiri's *tāna*s exhibit a fertile imagination. She seems relatively immune to the contemporary epidemic of symmetric and geometric *alaṁkāra tāna*s. She rarely deploys *Chūṭa tāna*s, a Gwalior favourite. Sizzling *sapāṭa tāna*s are also rare in her renderings. She has mastered the hopping *tāna*s of the Jaipur–Atrauli style, and deploys them especially for medium-density execution. A majority of her higher density *tāna*s, delivered in *bola* as well as *ākāra* articulation, are of the *laḍīguthāva* variety — strings of intricate passages constructed over short melodic spans, with variation of pace. In many ways, her *tāna* artistry is comparable to that of Vijaya Jadhav-

Gatlewar. Unlike Vijaya, however, Manjiri leaves something to be desired in the "logical" organization of her material. Architectural issues again!

For her youth, she exhibits a creditable command over her creative processes. It is early yet to speak of her style as a personal musical statement. But, considering her unusual trajectory in musicianship, it seems, she could only have been an original musician. Indeed, she has work to do on several areas of musicianship, before she ascends to the next level of stature amongst connoisseurs. But, she seems to have enough time to deliver to her promise (Written : March 2007).

Section 5
The Kairana Legacy

5.1

Perspectives on the Kairana Legacy

This chapter deals with those aspects of the Kairana legacy which are immediately relevant to appreciating the stylistic tendencies of musicians covered in this book.

As a stylistic legacy, Kairana requires us to understand several angles to its vocalism, over and above its stylistics, because they are germane to the understanding of the variety available within the stylistic spectrum called Kairana.

Firstly, it is important to understand the significance of the relationship between Kairana vocalism and the art of the *sāraṅgī*. This connection has given Kairana some distinguished musicians as well as some distinctive features. Secondly, it is important to recognize the special role the musical culture of northern Karnataka has played in the evolution of Kairana vocalism. Kairana, perhaps more than other major *gharānā*s, has thrown up originals within its basic philosophy of music making. Considering historical and stylistic evidence, it appears convenient to think in terms of Kairana as at least two broad streams — orthodox Kairana and neo-Kairana.

The Origins of Kairana

Kairana is a small town on the Haryana–Uttar Pradesh border. The notion of the *gharānā* named after this town includes a cluster of families pursuing the arts of the *sāraṅgī*, *Rudra vīṇā*, the *sitāra*, as well as vocalism. In the *dhrupada* era, these families followed the Gauhar Bānī style, known for its pathos, and doleful undertones. Its *khayāla* style was propagated in the late 19th/early 20th centuries by two maestros, Ustad Abdul Kareem Khan (1872-1937), and Ustad Abdul Waheed Khan (d. 1949), both of whom settled in Maharashtra, and became intimately connected with its cultural life.

Abdul Kareem Khan is known to have been a competent *rudra vīṇa* and *sāraṅgī*-player, while Abdul Waheed Khan is also believed to have trained on the *sāraṅgī*. The style of vocalism developed by them was greatly inspired by the music of Rehmat Khan, the son of Haddu Khan, one of the founders of the Gwalior tradition.

Abdul Kareem Khan's high-pitched voice enabled him to develop an emotionally charged style of singing. His vocalization was also characterized by a constriction of the wind-pipe, and pointedness of timbre. This approach was accompanied by specializing in slow-tempo rendition, perfection of intonation, and subtle use of micro-*svara*s. Consistent with this emphasis was the avoidance of rhythmic-play (*bola-laya*/*bola-bāṇṭa*) as a medium-density movement. In its place, Abdul Kareem introduced *saragama* articulation, which provided a phonetic texture, a suggestion of pulsation and a transitional stage of *svara*-density, but without explicit rhythmicality.

To enable an elaborate exploration of the *rāga* in the *ālāpa* (slow-tempo, and anarhythmic) movement, Abdul Kareem specialized in common, primarily heptatonic, *rāga*s, and rendered them in *tāla*s meant for ultra-slow rendition — *jhūmara* and *tilvāḍā*. Abdul Kareem enjoyed tremendous stature and popularity with all sections of society because of the moving quality of his renditions, and his repertoire, which included the *ṭhumarī*, devotional songs, and popular songs from the musicals in regional theatre.

Abdul Waheed Khan, his contemporary and kinsman,

shared the Abdul Kareem philosophy of music making, along with the preference for slow-tempo rendition and all its correlates as the fundamentals of the style. He, however, raised Kairana vocalism to a higher level of abstraction by a deeper involvement with the Merukhand approach to *rāga* elaboration (see notes below). The resultant melody was intellectually demanding, and could sound repetitive to the uninitiated. Even by temperament, he had no use for the gallery. His music was regarded as "more educative than entertaining."

Orthodox Kairana, as represented by these founders, was criticized for lacking in dramatic contrast, and characterized by a looseness of structure and soporific stylistics devoid of rhythmic interest. In the second and third generations of Kairana vocalism — Bhimsen Joshi, Gangubai Hangal, Phiroze Dastoor, Hirabai Barodekar, Roshanara Begum — some of these biases were corrected. However, it was Ustad Ameer Khan, a virtual outsider to the *gharānā*, who evolved its most influential and durable reinterpretation, drawing inspiration from Ustad Abdul Waheed Khan.

Kairana Stylistics

The *gharānā* is characterized by its melody-dominant approach to music making. Even within this predominant orientation, *gharānā* musicians are known for their mastery over the delivery of *svara* in all its subtlety and emotive power, tonal precision, and the use of *śruti*s (micro-*svara*s) and *kan* (*svara*-fragments subtler than *śruti*s). The Kairana tradition is biased strongly in favour of a tranquil and uncomplicated, though subliminally ornate, melodic experience. This bias results in a subordinate role for the poetic and rhythmic elements.

Kairana's mastery of melody derives probably from two important aspects of the aesthetic indoctrination prevalent in the tradition — the Merukhand system of improvizational programming, and the chain-link approach to melody building.

The Merukhand system is a quasi-mathematical aid to improvization. It consists of 5040 (7 × 6 × 5 × 4 × 3 × 2 × 1) melodic patterns, exhausting the sequencing potential of seven *svaras*. By memorising these patterns in "logical" sequence, Kairana vocalists were traditionally programmed for a high level of improvizational fertility. Though the Merukhand system has been a part of a musician's training even during the pre-*khayāla* era, Kairana is believed to be the only *khayāla gharānā* which attempted to systematically integrate it into performance strategy.

The chain-link approach is a principle for the sequencing of melodic phrases and passages in all movements. As described by the late Kairana maestro, Ustad Faiyyaz Ahmed Khan (personal communication), it prescribes that every phrase should begin on the same *svara* on which the previous phrase ended. The link-chain approach to melody building, combined with the Merukhand discipline, would explain the melodic richness and the effortless flows in Kairana's music.

Faiyyaz Ahmed Khan conjectured that the link-chain approach to melody building, apparently unique to Kairana, could have been injected into its vocalism by its significant *sāraṅgī* connection (see notes below). A *sāraṅgī* accompanist is expected to support and aid the ideational process of the vocalist, without visibly interfering with the pace or logic of the progression. This requirement is best fulfilled if he observes the rules of link-chain melody building. The link-chain might originally have been a training device for the accompanist. When practised by the vocalist, it has the potential to become repetitive and tiresome. And, indeed, Kairana vocalism in the slow tempo has faced this criticism. The finest musicians, however, follow the link-chain rule creatively rather than mechanistically, and as an adjunct to Merukhand.

These aspects of Kairana indoctrination could explain why, in the finest examples of Kairana music, it is difficult to determine where architecture ends and sculpture begins, and even where sculpture ends and ornamentation begins. The music comes through as an elegantly integrated melodic edifice — the product of a highly cultivated sense of design, which appears to shape, carve, and arrange every phrase in a manner that suggests its own inevitability.

Consistent with this basic approach, Kairana musicians specialize in the systematic and encyclopaedic exploration of the *rāga* in *vilambita* (slow-tempo) *baḍā khayāla*. Melody is protected from all manner of angularities, and executed primarily through *mīṇḍa, kan*, and racy, rather than aggressive, *gamaka*s. The base-tempo of their *baḍā khayāla* renditions is generally slower than most other *gharānā*s, and is stepped up only marginally, if at all, during the rendition. To enable an effortless generation and flow of melodic ideas, Kairana vocalists favour mature *rāga*s with vast scope for improvization (e.g. Darabārī, Multānī, Puriyā, Yamana), and stay away from rare and compound *rāga*s. A similar consideration guides their preference for *tāla*s of subdued rhythmicality, such as Jhūmara and Tilavāḍā, for slow-tempo renditions. They do not, however, entirely eschew the more common *ekatāla* or *jhapatala* or *tinatāla* for *madhya-laya* or *baḍā khayāla* treatment.

Although Kairana musicians have traditionally used the *bola* articulation in the *ālāpa*, they do not perform the *bola-bāṇṭa* movement. Instead, they make an elegant use of *saragama* articulation for medium density melodic execution. The *Saragama* movement in Kairana has an implicit pulsation, but does not engage the melody with the beat pattern of the rhythmic cycle as explicitly as the *bola-bāṇṭa* does. In all movements, the Kairana style discourages an explicit rhythmicality in melodic rendering.

*Tāna*s in the Kairana style reflect the same basic philosophy of music making. They are generally in *ākāra* articulation, with *bola-tāna*s being a rarity. *Tāna*s are short and simple in construction, generally of the *alaṁkāra, chūṭa*, or *sapāṭa* variety. Jaipur–Atrauli style jaw-droppers are rare in Kairana *tāna* patterns. The melodic density of the *tāna*s can range from medium to high. Ultra-high density *tāna*s of the Patiala variety are rare. When they do occur, they have a raciness, and are devoid of the aggressive vocalization or staccato intonation frequently encountered in Agra vocalism.

Though comparatively limited in its choice of *rāga*s, the Kairana repertoire has been rich in the range of genres. In addition to *khayāla*, the mainstay of the *gharānā*, Kairana vocalists have distinguished themselves as presenters of *ṭhumarī, tarānā*s, and several genres of regional, folk, devotional, and even popular music.

Ameer Khan and Neo-Kairana

Ameer Khan was the son of Shahmir Khan, a *sāraṅgī* player in the Indore (Central Provinces) court. Because of the Indore connection, he is often referred to as belonging to the amorphous Indore Gharānā. Ameer Khan had received *sāraṅgī* training, along with training as a vocalist. He grew up under the influence of Rajabali Khan, a towering vocalist from neighbouring Dewas, also associated with the Indore Gharānā. Later, Ameer Khan came under the influence of Aman Ali Khan of the Bhendi Bazar Gharānā, a group of musicians from UP, which had settled in the Bhendi Bazar locality of Bombay. Ameer Khan was finally attracted to the music of Abdul Waheed Khan of the Kairana lineage. Documentation is vague about whether Ameer Khan ever studied formally with Abdul Waheed Khan. It is, however, reliably reported that the Kairana maestro ultimately certified him as a worthy follower.

Ameer Khan retained the intellectualism of Abdul Waheed Khan, as also the soporific quality of orthodox Kairana in slow tempo *ālāpa* renditions. But, as Deshpande observes,[1] he brought a degree of animation, and playfulness to bear on his music. His repertoire had a fair representation of medium-tempo *tāla*s, such as *rūpaka* and *jhapatala*. In medium and fast-tempo renditions, under the influence of Aman Ali Khan of Bhendi Bazar, Ameer Khan's music even exhibited a choreographic vivacity. This quality probably came from Bhendi Bazar, once a part of the entertainment district of Bombay, inhabited by some of the most cultivated courtesans in the country. This observation harks back to an era in which the salons patronized by the aristocratic elite prided themselves in their artistic sophistication, and maintained an active involvement with art-music.

Even in the field of pure melody — Kairana's prime turf — Ameer Khan's imagination permitted him to do more than Kairana had hitherto attempted. He used the Merukhand discipline to develop the medium-density *saragama* as a bewitching, and even bewildering, kaleidoscope of tonal images, without imparting to it an explicit rhythmicality. His *tāna*s, largely influenced by Rajabali Khan, also had the same bewildering quality. Ameer Khan also consolidated Kairana architecture with three distinct movements incorporating a progressive intensification of melodic and rhythmic density and complexity, thus reinforcing the structural distinctiveness of the *khayāla* genre. The neatness and the transparency of his architectural vision were certainly major determinants of the magnitude and durability of his influence.

Ameer Khan sang only *khayāla* and *tarānā*. There is no evidence of his having sung even a *ṭhumarī* in public. He was not a popular musician in the category of Abdul Kareem Khan, nor an esoteric musician in the league of Abdul Waheed Khan. Ameer Khan could be described as a cerebral musician, who could also draw you into a trance. He shared with Abdul Waheed Khan his indifference to audiences, and is considered an epitome of the formal aloofness characteristic of *khayāla* vocalism in his era. However, from the appealing qualities he introduced to Kairana vocalism, and the influence he continues to wield even today, it would appear that his aloofness was far less severe than that of Abdul Waheed Khan even if it was not as endearing as that of Abdul Kareem Khan.

The crystallization of Kairana architecture, the introduction of the choreographic element, and a slight relaxation of aloofness, is a clear enough landmark in the evolution of Kairana vocalism for Ameer Khan to be considered the initiator of neo-Kairana. These directions may well have ensured the survival of Kairana essentials in the post-Independence era, which saw the decline of both stylistic extremes — the rhythm-dominated Agra, and the melody-dominated Kairana.

Extrovert Manifestations of Neo-Kairana

Once Ameer Khan had introduced Venus to the saturnine world of Kairana vocalism, a drift towards extroversion was perhaps a predictable direction. This appeared from within the *gharānā* — most prominently in the style of Faiyyaz Ahmed, and Niyaz Ahmed Khan. Their music gave Kairana two new features — the extension of the *saragama* to high density and ultra high-density *tāna*s, and the rendition of ultra-high density *tāna*s in *ākāra* articulation. Both these features are post-Ameer Khan and, conceptually, an extension of the neo-Kairana tendency.

The neo-Kairana directions of Ameer Khan and, later, of the Faiyyaz-Niyaz duo are both relevant to understanding contemporary Kairana vocalism. The Ameer Khan influence is evident as a generalized tendency in all contemporary *khayāla* vocalism, but more prominently in Kairana vocalism. The Faiyyaz-Niyaz influence, though minor as compared to the Ameer Khan influence, also has a presence through the music of Mashkoor Ali Khan, the son of the *sāraṅgī* maestro, Shakoor Khan.

The Sāraṅgī Connection

Originating as a folk instrument for accompanying vocal music, the *sāraṅgī* became the standard accompaniment to the semi-classical *ṭhumarī* by the 19th century, and to the *khayāla*, by the early 20th century. The *sāraṅgī* achieved an intimate relationship with vocalism bcause of its ability to mimic every conceivable expression of the human voice with the minimum loss of acoustic compatibility, this being its *raison d'être*. *Sāraṅgī* players are, therefore, trained in the vocal art, its reproduction on the instrument, and in the art of accompaniment. As a result, the finest *sāraṅgī* accompanists also perform an imperceptible role — that of guiding the ideational process of the vocalist during the performance.

Not surprisingly, some of the most venerable names in 20th-century *khayāla* vocalism either belonged to *sāraṅgī*-playing families, or were trained *sāraṅgī* players themselves, or made a living as *sāraṅgī* accompanists in their early years. The list, according to various accounts, includes Abdul Kareem Khan, Abdul Waheed Khan, Bade Ghulam Ali Khan, and Ameer Khan. Significantly, all of them were masters of melody, and exponents of melody-dominant styles of music. This fact highlights the role of *sāraṅgī* playing families as custodians of the vocalist's art, while also being its most competent companions.

Northern Karnataka, the Nursery of Kairana Music

The three neighbouring towns of Hubli, Dharwad, and Belgaum in Karnataka, adjoining the state of Maharashtra, have given Hindustani vocalism, but more specially Kairana vocalism, some of its finest exponents during the 20th century.

The key to the cultural vibrancy of this region might be the bilingual facility of its populace (Marāṭhī of Maharashtra and Kannaḍa of Karnataka) and the confluence of Draviḍian (southern) and Aryan (northern) musical cultures. Nature having generously endowed its populace with musical talent, the multi-culturalism of this region drove it towards an eclecticism which has led, nevertheless, to the emergence of a distinctive northern Karnataka flavour in *khayāla* vocalism. This flavour sets it apart from the vocalism of Maharashtra and northern India, the other two dominant crucibles of post-*dhrupada* vocalism. The significant components of this flavour may be inferred from the profiles of some of the most distinguished musicians to emerge from this region — notably, Bhimsen Joshi, Gangubai Hangal, Mallikarjun Mansoor, Basavraj Rajguru, Kumar Gandharva, and Sangameshwar Gurava.

Vocalists from the Dharwad-Hubli-Belgaum region tend to exhibit traces of south Indian stylistics, defy the orthodoxy of the major Hindustani *gharānā*s with varying degrees of individualism, and adopt lively, vigorous, and even a theatrical stance in their presentation of music. This observation has to be read along with the caveat that all these features need not be evident amongst all products of this region. Gangubai Hangal is, for instance, a thoroughbred Kairana stylist, though an individualistic one. At the other extreme, Kumar Gandharva's music liberated itself from all identifiable streams of south Indian (Carnatic tradition) as well as Hindustani stylistics.

The powerhouse of Kairana vocalism in the Dharwad-Hubli-Belgaum region was Sawai Gandharva, the most faithful follower of the style of the Kairana fountainhead, Abdul Kareem Khan. He belonged to this region, and trained two eminent and original locals: Bhimsen Joshi and Gangubai Hangal. The other stream of Kairana influence, emanating from the two Kairana founders — Abdul Kareem Khan and Abdul Waheed Khan — was coloured by the fact that several of their disciples in the region were originally south Indian (Carnatic tradition) musicians who had also studied non-Kairana styles of

Hindustani vocalism. This manifestation of Kairana vocalism, being typical of the region, is often also called "Dharwad-Kairana." Basavraj Rajguru and Sangameshwar Gurava are important representatives of this stylistic stream.

The Music of Basavraj Rajguru

Recordings of Rajguru, the Kairana maestro from Dharwad, were not easy to acquire in reasonable numbers. I make my observations based on a single recording of a private concert hosted by Maharaja Ranjitsingh Gaekwad of Baroda in the 1980s. The concert features Khayāla Yamana (56 mts), Khayāla Sarasvatī (11.52 mts), Khayāla Sohinī (20.09 mts), *ṭhumarī* in Basanta (15.51 mts), *ṭhumarī* (34.18 mts), Bhairavī (10.01 mts) and *nāṭya saṅgīta* in Kafi (33.50 mts). The repertoire itself exhibits several features of Dharwad–Kairana vocalism. Yamana is a mainstream *rāga* of the Hindustani system. Sarasvatī is a *rāga* from the south Indian (Carnatic) tradition, performed only rarely in Hindustani music. Two *ṭhumarī* in a 3-hour concert could suggest his affinity, and that of his *gharānā*, for the semi-classical genre, or even the preferences of the audience present at the concert. As Marathi was not Rajguru's mother tongue, the *nāṭya saṅgīta* reflects the bi-lingualism of the region and theatre orientation of its musical culture.

Rajguru has a high-pitched, moderately rich voice, suited to the melody-dominant style of Kairana. However, his approach to music imparts a considerably greater role to the rhythmic element than any other significant musician from the Kairana tradition. There is a strong suggestion of pulsation in his rendering of *ālāpa*s. He enters frequently into melodic-rhythmic exchanges with his percussionist, and deploys *tihāyī*s generously. In this respect, the tenor of his rendition is reminiscent of a later-day Agra vocalist like Sharafat Hussain, rather than the moderate rhythmicality of the Gwalior style, which was a part of his legacy. The key to this may lie in

Rajguru's musical temperament. There is an extroverted quality in his music, and a penchant for the dramatic melodic expression generally eschewed by Kairana. His music sets aside the contemplative aloofness of Kairana, and exhibits the obvious desire to entertain — a magnified expression of the vigor and vitality that typifies northern Karnataka's musical culture.

Rajguru's architecture differs from orthodox Kairana. While Kairana generally adopts a two-tier approach to the *vilambita khayāla* (*ālāpa* and *tānas*), Rajguru takes a three-tier approach with an explicitly detailed medium density (*bola-laya*) movement, more typical of Gwalior. In the sculptural aspects of his music, the Kairana legacy is transparent. His exploration of the melodic potential of *rāgas* suggests the Merukhand approach. In the ornamentation of his phrases, however, Rajguru often goes overboard and crosses the borderline between the *khayāla* and the romanticist genres like *ṭhumarī* and *ghazala*. His *tānas* display the elegant sense of sculpture for which Kairana is known.

Rajguru comes through as faithful to the formalism of the *khayāla* genre, though not entirely in accordance with Kairana practice, but short on the aloofness typical of the Kairana tradition.

The Music of Sangameshwar Gurava

Sangameshwar Gurava is yet another distinguished product of the Dharwad-based stream of Kairana vocalism. Only one concert of his, featuring Yamana, Kedāra, Śaṅkara, and a Bhajana (1993), was readily available for analysis.

Gurava is a master of melody in all its facets, from the *ālāpa* to the ultra-high density *tānas*. The contours of every unit of melody are crystal clear, irrespective of the *svara*-density of delivery. Melodic execution relies heavily on *mīṇḍa*, *kan*, and *gamaka*, but also deploys the more ornate *murkī* in reasonable measure. Numerous melodic variants of phrases follow each other in waves without the slightest hint of cerebral effort. The sequencing of phrases traverses melodic, geometric, as well as symmetric paths in an effortless flow of melody. The different movements appear to dovetail themselves seamlessly into each other, creating a logical progression of melodic density and complexity.

True to the Kairana style Gurava's *ālāpa* in the *baḍā khayāla* is rendered in *bola* articulation. In addition to the common *ālāpa* segments — the *sthāyī*, and the *antarā* — his *ālāpa* includes a *sañcārī*, the third phase of the traditional melodic development protocol, which has receded into disuse in recent years. Gurava's sañcārī functions beautifully as a dovetailing device for the low-density, unstructured melody of the *ālāpa* into the pulse-driven medium-density melody of the *bola-bāṇṭa*.

Gurava's medium density *bola-bāṇṭa* movement, coming after a step-up of the base tempo, is perhaps an import from other *gharānā*s. This movement is brief, and subdued enough in its rhythmic suggestions to go virtually unnoticed. The substantive medium-density exposition is through *saragama* articulation. Like Ameer Khan, Gurava deploys the *saragama* in medium, as well as high-density articulation. The use of *tāna*s in the *baḍā khayāla*s is limited to a brief, winding-up *bola-tāna*s section, probably inspired by the Gwalior style. The elaborate artistry of his *tāna*s is reserved for *choṭā khayāla*.

The striking aspect of Gurava's *choṭā khayāla*s is its retention of sculpture as the dominant musical feature. In the rendition of the *bandiśa*, along with its melodic variants, as also in the *tāna*s, his sense of design reigns supreme. *Tāna*s are almost entirely in *ākāra* articulation, with an occasional use of the *saragama*. Like his low and medium-density movements, Gurava's *tāna*s deploy melodic, geometric, and symmetric sequencing of phrases. The patterns are dominated by *alaṁkāra*, *chūṭa* and *sapāṭa* varieties. The *gamaka* form of vocalisation is frequently in use. The timbre of the voice varies moderately in response to the melodic density, tightening as the density increases. The melodic density ranges from medium to ultra-high. But, even at the highest density, well above the peak normally encountered in Kairana vocalism, the flow is effortless, with no tendency towards the staccato expression. His *tāna*s evoke a sense of marvel and delight by the brilliance of their sculpture, clarity, and speed. Their beauty remains uncontaminated either by mechanistic delivery, or by intimidatory intent.

Gurava's music is neither sad like that of Abdul Kareem and Sawai Gandharva, nor robust and authoritative like that of Bhimsen Joshi or Roshanara Begum. It is also unlike that of the other third-generation vocalists of the *gharānā*. And, yet, it might come closest to being a modern-day textbook of Kairana vocalism. At a superficial level, some features of other *gharānā*s have entered Gurava's idiom; but in its essence, his music is Kairana. Gurava has abstracted, from his training, the melody-dominant philosophy of music making, and forged it into an original, and satisfying musical expression.

Coverage of Vocalists

In the Kairana legacy, I include essays on Sumitra Guha (a disciple of A. Kannan and Malavika Kannan), Mashkoor Ali Khan (son and disciple of Ustad Shakoor Khan), Somnath Mardur (a disciple of Basavraj Rajguru), Kaivalya Kumar (son and disciple of Sangameshwar Gurava), and Rashid Khan (a disciple of Nissar Hussain Khan and a product of ITC Sangeet Research Academy).

All classifications except the last are justified by the history of tutelage, as well as the quality of their music. The last, Rashid Khan, is debatable. Through his familial links and formal tutelage, Rashid Khan claims membership of the Rampur-Sahaswan Gharānā. However, by the quality of his music, he belongs to the Ameer Khan–inspired stream of neo-Kairana vocalism. This constitutes justification for the classification.

5.2

Sumitra Guha
A Migrant from Carnatic Vocalism

HINDUSTANI vocalism, especially Kairana vocalism, has an eminently respectable history of migrations from the Carnatic tradition; but only a handful in recent years. Sumitra Guha (b. 1943) is one such phenomenon. Sumitra's migration was inspired by her years as a student at Shantiniketan and two decades of tutelage under Shri A. Kannan, and Smt. Malavika Kannan, both eminent exponents of the Kairana style. She holds a degree in Philosophy from the Vishwa Bharati University.

She became an empanelled artiste of All India Radio as a Hindustani vocalist in 1972, and occupies its top grade since 1995. In addition to pursuing an active career as a performing musician, Sumitra runs an institution in Calcutta devoted to teaching music. Her recordings have been archived by the Sangeet Natak Akademi. Her concert career has spanned South-East Asia, Western Europe, Central Europe, West Asia, Scandinavia as well as North America.

Sumitra's early training in music took place in the Carnatic tradition. Her first teacher was her mother, who taught her vocal music. Thereafter, she studied the violin under Shri Subanna, and vocal music with Shri S.R. Janakiraman. She was already a well-trained Carnatic vocalist by the time she went to Vishwa Bharati University, and encountered Hindustani music and Rabindra Sangeet. She studied Rabindra Sangeet at Santiniketan under Shantideb Ghosh, a close associate of Tagore, and followed it up with 20 years of training with the Kannans of the Kairana tradition of Hindustani music, and three years with Shri Sushil Bose of the Patiala tradition. Outside of these formal influences, Sumitra admits to the influence of Ustad Abdul Kareem Khan, founder of the Kairana Gharānā, and D.V. Paluskar of the Gwalior Gharānā.

Despite her early cultivation in the Carnatic tradition, her delivery of Hindustani music betrays no trace of the linguistic and stylistic barriers that divide India's south from the north. Her intonation of Hindustani melodies is authentic, and her diction in the enunciation of Hindi poetry, immaculate. The core of her music remains anchored to the melody-dominated music-making philosophy of the Kairana tradition, along with its architecture. In superficial aspects, however, her *khayāla*s exhibit the influence of her brief Patiala exposure. Her musical mind has also acquired some tendencies not traceable to obvious influences.

Sumitra has painstakingly absorbed two substantially different traditions of music-making and has mastered the subtleties of the various genres within each tradition. Her music exhibits a conviction that comes from knowing precisely what she is doing and why.

Stylistic Perspectives

Sumitra Guha possesses a powerful, though feminine, voice with a comfortable range of more than two octaves. Hers is a highly cultivated voice — firm yet malleable — whose timbre remains stable across the different regions of the melodic canvas. In her handling of Hindustani music, her respect for the integrity of *bandiśes* comes through as perhaps the only trace — and a laudable trace at that — of Carnatic grooming.

Her evolution as a Hindustani vocalist has, apparently, been shaped predominantly by the melody-oriented Kairana tradition, with the comparatively ornate Patiala tradition playing a smaller role. Her choice of repertoire broadly reflects both these influences. However, since the *bandiśa-ki-ṭhumarī* has not played a significant role either in Kairana or Patiala vocalism, the presence of this form in her repertoire suggests a temperamental affinity requiring no reference point in her formal affiliations.

A valid reference point for her *khayāla* vocalism is available from a token sample of recordings by her two *gurus*, Prof. A. Kannan, and his wife, Malavika Kannan, made during their peak performing years. A. Kannan and Malavika Kannan are respected vocalists, representing the third generation of Kairana vocalism. What I have for reference is one radio recording of Kedāra by A. Kannan, and a radio recording of Māru Bihāga by Malavika Kannan. Listening to the two recordings, it is easy to marvel at how similar two mature musicians can be in their approach to music making.

Both have agile voices with a comfortable two-octave range. The fanatical Kairana dedication to tonal precision is second nature to both of them. Their music remains true to the melody-dominant *gharānā* philosophy, with creative energies concentrated on the task of sculpting the phrases. The use of ornamentation is judicious and restrained. Their phrasing exhibits an occasional aggressiveness or angularity evident in the vocalism of some Kairana stalwarts, mainly Roshanara Begum, Sangameshwar Gurava, and Bhimsen Joshi.

The Kannans are steadfast in their adherence to the Kairana architecture in *khayāla* presentation. The *ālāpa* is leisurely, elaborate, and deliberate, exploring short melodic spans, in organized sequence, for their melodic potential. The *bola-laya* movement is almost absent. In the medium-density transitional movement, the Kannans perform a short *saragama* movement, which escalates briskly into the *tāna*s movement. In *tāna*s, they show a preference for broad-span melodic runs in ascending as well as descending motion. The *tāna*s are primarily of the *sapāṭa* variety, and possess a breathtaking clarity even at the highest *svara*-densities. Both the Kannans are inclined towards the occasional use of *tihāīs*, a feature not commonly encountered in orthodox Kairana vocalism.

The Music of Sumitra Guha

For my observations, I rely on the study of one CD of the vocalist featuring *khayāla*s in Kedāra, Kirvani and Gauḍa Malhāra, recorded for India Archive Music, New York. The Kirvani presentation on this recording consists of two *bandiśe*s; one in *bandiśa-kī-ṭhumarī* format and the other in *choṭā khayāla* format.

Although the presence of Kirvani in her repertoire suggests an affinity for Carnatic *rāga*s, no special significance may be attached to this as Kirvani has, by now, acquired a reasonably stable melodic identity in Hindustani music. Significantly enough, on this recording, her rendition of other *rāga*s is as convincing as of this Carnatic *rāga*.

Sumitra Guha's approach to *khayāla* rendition speaks of rigorous stylistic indoctrination, and dedicated tutelage. The differences between her music and that of her mentors, are minor, and probably generational more than temperamental.

Sumitra delivers her music at moderate tempi, seeking neither the soporific at the lower end, nor the titillating at the higher. Her *vilambita khayāla bandiśe*s are launched at about 20 bpm, quicker than orthodox Kairana (12/14 bpm), and a step below Jaipur–Atrauli (23/25 bpm). Her *madhya-laya bandiśe*s in *tīnatāla* commence at a standard 150/160 bpm. She makes an exception to this with a *madhya-laya tīnatāla bandiśa* launched at 120 bpm, when she wants to treat it virtually like a *baḍā khayāla*. Her *druta ekatāla bandiśe*s begin at a sprightly 245/250 bpm without significant escalation.

The architecture of her *khayāla* and *bandiśa-kī-ṭhumarī* renditions is immaculate. In *khayāla* renditions, her approach to the sculpting and ornamentation of phrases has departed a little from the aloofness of orthodox Kairana vocalism, but stopped short of embracing Patiala's alluring quality. Her *ṭhumarī* renditions extend beyond the orthodox confines of *bandiśa* renditions to include *saragama*s and *tāna*s, thus suggesting a *khayāla* bias similar to that of *ṭhumarī* renditions by Agra Gharānā singers. Her treatment of the genre, however, remains anchored to Kairana's melody-dominant philosophy of music-making, with a judicious dose of ornamentation.

Her *tāna*s are predominantly faithful to her Kairana grooming. She utilizes all forms of articulation — the *Saragama*, *ākāra*, as well as *bola* — for her *tāna*s. Amongst modes of melodic execution, the *gamaka* form is Sumitra's forte. Her *gamaka tāna*s, though totally Hindustani in their style of intonation, possess a combination of tonal precision and musicality, which might well be a Carnatic legacy. Her *saragama tāna*s in high-density articulation remain well within the bounds of musicality — again perhaps a gift of the south.

The melodic patterns in her *tāna*s correspond primarily to the *baḍhata*, *chūṭa*, and *sapāṭa* varieties, without either the explicit rhythmicality of Agra, or the cleverness of Jaipur–Atrauli. She has achieved an unusual command over the ascending *sapāṭa*s and ascending *chūṭa*s. Interestingly, the two-by-two variety of Jaipur–Atrauli *tāna*s also make an occasional appearance in her rendition. In her *tāna*s, she excels in handling micro melodic spans, delivering her *tāna*s with rare precision and elan. Most of this is traditional Kairana territory. The Patiala influence peeps through this in her fondness for *amad*-placement *tihāī*s constructed from descending *sapāṭa tāna*s — a forte of Bade Ghulam Ali Khan.

In an age when the discernible features of *gharānā* stylistics are yielding to a cocktail, and Kairana stylistics have receded from their erstwhile prominence, Sumitra's music, despite its mild non-Kairana leanings, exhibits a nostalgic continuity with the past (Written : May 2002).

5.3

Somnath Mardur
Unassuming Musicianship in Dharwad

SOMNATH Mardur (b. 1944) is a simple musician, whose world has so far been limited to local radio broadcasts received within a small geographical range, and concert appearances in, and around, his native Dharwad. His musicianship may have remained unnoticed by the world outside, had it not been for the fact that his son and disciple, Kumar (b. 1982), is now rated amongst the most promising vocalists of his generation. Somnath is an A grade artiste on All India Radio, and a *khayāla* vocalist of the Kairana Gharānā, having studied under the eminent maestro, Basavraj Rajguru (d. 1991). Beyond his formal tutelage, he also admits to a significant influence of the Gwalior-trained original, Kumar Gandharva.

Somnath's music is, like the man himself, unassuming and refined. It deviates substantially from the extroverted style of his *guru*, Basavraj. He has an astute grasp of the *rāga*'s melodic personality, and how it relates to its emotional content. He has an exceptional command over the rhythmic element, which is known — in the Kairana tradition — only for its unobtrusive presence. His style is a homogenized and mature blend of the various stylistic influences on his evolution as a musician. His music has a riveting quality, which is not easy to explain. Incidentally, this also makes his relative oblivion a riddle worth solving.

"I have Lived Entirely off My Abilities as a Performing Musician"

(Mardur Spoke to the Author on 30 March, 2004)

"I received my initiation in music at the age of eight with Veerappayya Swami, an ascetic musician, who followed the Gwalior style. After three years with him, I started studying with Basavraj Rajguru.

"Basavraj is known as a stalwart of the Kairana Gharānā. But, he was heir to a more complex legacy. He was a disciple of Panchakshari Swami (d. 1944), a mystic-musician, who ran an *āśrama* (a seminary-cum-conservatory) in Gadag (near Dharwad) with a couple of hundred students. Basavraj was trained, for several years, by Swamiji from 4.00 a.m. to 7.00 a.m. everyday. Panchakshari Swami had been trained originally as a south Indian musician. Under the influence of Sawai Gandharva who hailed from our part of the country, Swamiji was attracted to the Kairana style. So, he became a disciple of Ustad Abdul Waheed Khan. Then — I am not sure about the year — Abdul Waheed Khan migrated to that part of India, which later went to Pakistan. So, Panchakshari Swami continued his training in Hindustani music with Neelkanth Buwa Alurmath of the Gwalior Gharānā. My *guru*, Basavraj Rajguru was a product of this background.

"I studied with him starting in my teens, and remained attached to him until his end (d. 1991). But, I was hungry for newer ideas, and got them from wherever I could. For a few years towards the end of his life, Mallikarjun Mansoor (d. 1992), also taught me. From him, I learnt several *rāga*s and *bandiśe*s of the Jaipur–Atrauli Gharānā. Other than my direct *guru*s, Bhimsen Joshi, Bade Ghulam Ali Khan, and Kumar Gandharva have also influenced me. Amongst these, Kumar Gandharva was unique. He was a self-made musician who followed nobody. He founded a one-man *gharānā* with no disciples. The depth and complexity of his music were unfathomable. He was inimitable, and yet he influenced many musicians.

"My performing career began in 1961 (age 17), when I stood first in the All India Radio competition. Thereafter, I have been broad-casting for over 35 years, and occupy the A Grade today. Very few people outside this region have heard of me. But, I have lived entirely off my abilities as a performing musician. In the early years, I taught music in schools and colleges. But, I found it impossible to combine that kind of work with my own pursuits as a musician. In Dharwad, where I live — unlike a big city like Bombay — even private tuitions cannot be a source of livelihood.

"All significant musicians in our region have had secure jobs to keep the home fires burning. I have no agricultural land or property to live off. So, mine was a hard choice to make. I had confidence in my music, and that enabled me to live a life of self-respect, build a small house, and bring up my children. Moving to a bigger city has never seemed either possible or attractive. The Dharwad region is rich in its musical tradition. Life is peaceful and uncomplicated. It is only here that I could give my children the attention they have received. Shaping them into first-class musicians was my highest priority. They are free now to go out into the world, and achieve according to their potential. I am proud that they are receiving recognition and encouragement from the most discerning people."

The Music of Somnath Mardur

I make my observations based on a study of one CD made by Somnath Mardur for India Archive Music, New York, featuring *khayāla*s in Durgā and Cāndanī Kedāra.

A stylistic perspective on Somnath Mardur requires us to take cognizance of several realities that have shaped his music. To begin with, he is a product of the northern Karnataka musical culture, a distinct stylistic stream in Hindustani vocalism. Even within this regional, Mardur belongs to the Kairana-influenced stream. And, within Kairana, his music needs to be related to his immediate *guru*, Basarvraj Rajguru.

I draw on Carl Seashore's conceptual framework[10] for doing justice to the task of interpreting Somnath Mardur's style, going beyond the conceptual framework deployed by Vamanrao Deshpande.[1]

Seashore identifies "four large trunks in the family-tree of musicality, each of which may develop or ramify to a large extent independently of, or out of proportion to, the others." On this basis, he classifies musical styles and tendencies as being predominantly (a) tonal, (b) dynamic, (c) temporal, or (d) qualitative. The tonal category is defined as concerned primarily with pitch, melody and harmony. The dynamic category is defined as concerned primarily with acuity of hearing, and a manipulation of the loudness factor. The temporal category is particularly sensitive to time, tempo and rhythm and its patterns. The qualitative category is concerned primarily with timbre and texture.

Deshpande[1] limits the analytical framework for *khayāla* vocalism to rhythm and melody orientations, and classifies *khayāla gharānā*s on a continuum on the basis of the relative importance of these two elements in the stylistic inclinations of a *gharānā* or a musician. In the present case, however, we have to include consideration of the dynamic and qualitative elements, which concern themselves with predilections relating to volume and timbre.

Somnath Mardur's music is dominated by melodic qualitative and the dynamic elements. Rhythm does very little to his music beyond imparting to it a structure and a sense of linear progression. Perfect intonation, exposition of the melodic character of the *rāga*, and the communication of its emotional content through an astute, though intuitive, engineering of the aural experience, are the cornerstones of his approach to music.

His architectural approach is informal. His sculpture (phrasing) does not invite any special attention to itself for its elegance. His reliance on ornamentation is judicious, and astute in terms of preserving the integrity of the *rāga* form. His music is deeply immersed in the spirit of the *rāga* he performs, which makes for a riveting quality. Somnath's gossamer, high-pitched voice (E#), and emotionally intense delivery, bring him closer to the music-making philosophy of the Kairana fountainhead, Abdul Kareem Khan, than of his *guru*, Basavraj.

Non-Kairana influences are, indeed, evident in his music and the music is, without doubt, an original, coherent, and convincing personal statement. His vocalism has vigour and vitality, which is more clearly Dharwad-Kairana than orthodox Kairana. In terms of architectural conventions, he appears to alternate between the two-tier Kairana practice, and the three-tier Gwalior practice. His choice of articulatory devices reflects a Kairana preference for variety. His approach to phrasing in the *ālāpa*/behlāva is closer to Gwalior than Kairana vocalism. His sculpting of phrases in low-density melody is often reminiscent of Bhimsen Joshi (Gwalior and Kairana), but equally often exhibits a graceful convexity typical of Mallikarjun Mansoor (Gwalior and Jaipur–Atrauli). In his *tāna*s as well as in the totality of his rendition, he relies greatly on variations of volume and timbre, often even conveying the impression — untintended, of course — of two vocalists performing in a duet. This feature might reflect his admiration for Kumar Gandharva (Gwalior trained maverick), the most recent vocalist to impart respectability to a significant dynamic element in *khayāla* vocalism, and one of Somnath's heroes. Interestingly, Somnath's entire pantheon of role models hails from the northern Karnataka region.

The most notable aspect of Somnath's vocalism is the extraordinary psycho-acoustic sensibility evident in his interpretation of *rāga*s. He has a rare insight into the region of the melodic canvas where the *rāga* most vividly releases its emotional charge. His entire rendition is sharply focused within, and around, the *rāga*'s primary region, with little attention to regions outside it. As a result, the impact of his emotionally intense vocalization and intonation is magnified by the psycho-acoustic potential of the *rāga*'s melodic personality. This facet of his vocalism carries with it the risk of repetition. Somnath appears to accept this risk, and controls it partially through non-melodic devices.

The fundamental quality of Somnath's music is the effective communication of the emotional content and mood of the *rāga*. Considering that a *rāga* is, first and last, an emotional statement, he succeeds in achieving the primary function of *rāga* exposition. We are therefore obliged to consider why he has remained unknown outside the northern Karnataka circuit. Partly, and only partly, can we attribute this to limited ambition. The more important clue might lie in the informality of his architecture.

In the last 50 years, say since early 1950s, Hindustani vocalism has undergone a considerable degree of formalization and standardization of its architectural conventions. It is, of course, true that Kumar Gandharva acquired immense stature while rebelling against the formalism of the *khayāla*. But, he was Kumar Gandharva. Amongst lesser mortals, non-conformism with respect to architecture still appears to invite neglect, no matter how competent they might be on other dimensions of musicianship and musicality (Written : July 2004).

5.4

Mashkoor Ali Khan
Kairana in Search of a Contemporary Idiom

MASHKOOR Ali Khan (b. 1954) is one of the few significant exponents left in the Kairana tradition of *khayāla* vocalism. He studied primarily with his father, the *sāraṅgī* exponent Ustad Shakoor Khan (1905-75) who was groomed in the art by Ustad Abdul Waheed Khan, one of the founders of the Kairana lineage. Mashkoor serves on the teaching staff of the ITC Sangeet Research Academy and also pursues a performing career.

Mashkoor Ali was initiated into music at a young age, and underwent rigorous training for 15 years under his father until the latter's demise. For a short while thereafter, he was trained by other seniors of the family. That was an era in which the *sāraṅgī* faced a bleak future, and the father thought it safer for Mashkoor to train as a vocalist. By 12, Mashkoor was an empanelled radio artiste. He launched his concert career at the age of 22. In 1981, when he was 27, his erudition, and promise attracted an invitation to join the ITC Sangeet Research Academy as a Musician Scholar. In 1990, at the age of 36, he was made a Resident *guru*.

In his attempt at forging a contemporary idiom, Mashkoor Ali draws upon the stylistic values of orthodox Kairana, the Ameer Khan stream of neo-Kairana, Faiyyaz-Niyaz stream of neo-Kairana, and the Kairana-associated *sāraṅgī* tradition.

Mashkoor's Repertoire

I base my observations on a study of one CD recorded for India Archive Music, New York, and several concert recordings, aggregating eight hours of music, recorded between 1999 and 2006. The *rāga*s covered are Lalita, Miyā-kī-Toḍī, Bageśī, Basanta, Bhairavī, Kedāra, Multānī, and Yamana." I have also heard Mashkoor Ali in concert on several occasions.

Mashkoor's repertoire consists clearly of accessible *rāga*s. This is, by and large, consistent with the Kairana philosophy. Despite being considered a veritable encyclopaedia of *bandiśe*s, Mashkoor appears partial to the legacy of the Kairana tradition. However, he is not averse to flashing glimpses of his non-Kairana treasures, as he does in the Kedāra recording I studied, with a zestful rendering of a *caturaṅga*, a class of compositions now almost extinct.

The Music of Mashkoor Ali Khan

Mashkoor Ali Khan owns one of the finest male voices amongst vocalists of his generation. Though a trifle high-pitched (D#) by Indian standards, and endowed with a mild nasality, it is resonant, warm and agile. The voice has been trained for a comfortable range of two octaves in his natural voice.

Mashkoor's command over *rāga* grammar is formidable.

His soundness is obvious from the immense resourcefulness with which he explores the melodic personalities of the *rāgas*. Mashkoor's handling of the poetic element is also exemplary — not surprising, considering his insatiable appetite for learning *bandiśes* from all *gharānās*. His involvement with the pre-composed element is a rare phenomenon in Kairana vocalism, which has traditionally treated poetry as no more than a mix of vowels and consonants for encasing the melody. This quality sets him apart from Kairana vocalists and, of course, also enhances his value as a teacher.

His music exhibits four predominant influences. Firstly, he is an identifiable product of orthodox as well as neo-Kairana vocalism. Secondly, there are discernible strains in his music of the *sāraṅgī* factor, absorbed probably from his father, Shakoor Khan, but also associated with the larger Kairana legacy. There are also traces of Bade Ghulam Ali Khan in his style. And finally, his stance as a performer exhibits the temperament of a teacher, probably reinforced by his long stint in the conservatory environment.

His melodic execution relies heavily on *mīṇḍa, gamaka* and *kan* modes of execution, with only a sparing use of *gītakīrī, murkī* and *khaṭkā*. The most prominent facet of his style is the deployment of *kan*. He does not use the device as ornamentation, as much as a means of imparting meaning to each explicit intonation in the context of the *rāga*'s melodic personality. To this extent, the generous use of this device does no damage to the aloofness characteristic of Kairana vocalism, or to the stylistic divide between *khayāla* and the romanticist *ṭhumarī*. This skill, combined with the sensitivity in its use, probably derives from the *sāraṅgī*, which specializes in the *kan* device in melodic execution. *Kan*-based melodic execution also had a significant place in Ameer Khan's music, but featured there far less prominently than in the style of Mashkoor's father-in-law, Niyaz Ahmed Khan.

Mashkoor's strategy of melodic exploration is clearly inspired by the Merukhand system of indoctrination. By the manner in which Abdul Waheed Khan deployed it, the approach invited criticism as being clinical, repetitive, and boring. When Ameer Khan gave it an aesthetic interpretation, he raised it to the level of high art. Mashkoor, it appears, has the tendency to revert to the academism of Abdul Waheed Khan. As a result, it is possible to encounter, in his concerts, a *baḍā/vilambita khayāla* which lasts 40 mts, and struggles to hold interest beyond the first 15 mts.

The architecture of Mashkoor's *khayāla* presentations is neat, even academic. It conforms to neo-Kairana tendencies, but more particularly to Ameer Khan who, along with Kishori Amonkar, was amongst the most fastidious structuralists in recent history. In accordance with orthodox as well as neo-Kairana practice, Mashkoor's *vilambita khayāla ālāpa* is rendered in *bola* articulation. The medium density *bola-laya* movement in the *vilambita khayāla* is generally omitted, but brief when included. This has been replaced by the medium density *saragama*.

In higher density melodic execution, Mashkoor differs from Kairana as well as Neo-Kairana by relying very substantially on *saragama* articulation. Mashkoor's father-in-law, Niyaz Ahmed, deployed the high-density and even ultra-high density *saragama*, but judiciously. Mashkoor appears to have adopted this technique from him, and ended up relying much more heavily on it than anyone else so far.

Mashkoor's *ākāra tāna*s are fluid and often stunning. Many of them are similar to the serpentine, wriggling sensations we have heard from Bade Ghulam Ali Khan — derived either from the Tanras Khan legacy of Patiala, or from the *sāraṅgī* connection. Their *svara*-density often goes well beyond anything you have heard, except on the *sāraṅgī*. In ultra-high density execution, his *tāna*s can occasionally falter on pitch-precision because of the melodic complexity he attempts.

With respect to his *saragama* articulation in high and ultra-high-density execution, we are obliged to consider issues of aesthetic prudence. The higher the *svara*-density, the greater is the need for vowels for imparting fluidity to the melody. Being a consonant-dominated articulation, the *saragama* forces staccato intonation in high-density deployment, and limits the melodic patterning that can be delivered intelligibly. It has also been observed that, in high-density articulation, the *Saragama* compromises intonation more frequently than other forms of articulation. And, Mashkoor's music is not exactly immune to this risk.

The heavy dependence on *saragama* for high and ultra-high-density melody must also contend with the aesthetics of phonetic density. The bombardment of consonants at the rate of 500 per minute (twice the beat density at 250 bpm) can constitute an aural overload verging on the unmusical. The solfa symbols in the *saragama* do, of course, have vowels. But, high-density articulation does not permit variable elongation.

The issue is also ergonomic. When a choice of three articulatory devices is available, along with combinations thereof, near-total reliance on a single device for high density articulation would seem to be an unwarranted strain on the vocalization organs. There is, no doubt, a trace of exhibitionism in this facet of his music. But, we are also probably seeing here an extreme manifestation of the *sāraṅgī* factor. The human voice is trying to match the competence of a mechanical device in musical territory which it cannot handle without testing the limits of musicality.

One also observes — in Mashkoor's music — more obvious traces of exhibitionism. He is wont to attempt very difficult melodic manoeuvres, resort to dramatic expressions such as chords sung in staccato intonation, and variations of volume and timbre not always placed with aesthetic purpose. It is not uncommon to also find him including classroom-style demonstrations of passages in his performances, first singing them in *saragama*, and repeating them in *ākāra*. Such attention-grabbing features, combined with academism, make for an awkward cocktail, often falling short of emotionally satisfying music.

The Bhairavī recording in the sample I studied almost came through a refreshing change. On that recording, Mashkoor performs *jamunā ke tīra*, a *ṭhumarī* immortalized by Ustad Abdul Kareem Khan on a 78 RPM disc. By and large, this rendering is restrained, and reverential to the memory of the legendary founder of the *gharānā*. However, even on this recording, Mashkoor capitulates, though only briefly, to the lure of exhibitionism.

When a musician of mature age, formidable pedigree, talent, erudition and accomplishments, starts performing to the gallery, the phenomenon deserves sympathetic scrutiny. In Mashkoor's specific instance, these tendencies may represent Kairana's struggle against aesthetic obsolescence. They may be the attempts of a musician, not content with enviable stature as a teacher, eager to build a presence on the concert platform. There could also be something about a career in teaching which militates against the flowering of performing musicianship. All these are plausible explanations. The more worrisome issue, however, is whether contemporary audiences are blameless for such trends. It is they who applaud exhibitionism, while being lukewarm towards soulful music (Written : April 2007).

5.5

Kaivalya Kumar
A Kairana Original — Almost by Accident

KAIVALYA Kumar (b. 1963), the son of the Kairana stalwart, Sangameshwar Gurava (b. 1932) tried very hard to avoid a career in music. Discouraged by his father's moderate success in the profession, Kaivalya educated himself for a career in business, and engineering, achieving academic distinctions in both. When none of these gave him a professional opening, he turned to music. He took a degree in music, surrendered himself to rigorous training under his father, and launched himself into the ancestral profession. Finally, destiny smiled.

As a student in Dharwad, his home-town, Kaivalya became popular as an amateur singer of film music, and *nāṭya-saṅgīta*. Until the age of 22, his training in Hindustani music was casual. Once he dug his teeth into it, he took off, being directly admitted to the A grade of All India Radio — a rare distinction. Since then, Kaivalya has established a respectable presence on the concert platform, released several commercial recordings, and received prestigious honours from cultural organizations all over the country.

Kaivalya Kumar belongs to a lineage of distinguished musicians from the Dharwar-Belgaum-Hubli region of Karnataka. Kaivalya's ancestors were vocalists in the Carnatic tradition. His grandfather, Ganpatrao Gurava, groomed originally in Carnatic music, decided to switch. He studied with Bhaskar Buwa Bakhle (1869-1922), a versatile vocalist of legendary stature, and thereafter, with Ustad Abdul Kareem Khan, the founder of the Kairana Gharānā. Kaivalya's father and *guru*, Sangameshwar Gurava, has retained a strong affinity for Kairana vocalism, but is also heir to the multiple-*gharānā* legacy of Bhaskarbuwa. This amalgam of influences has shaped young Kaivalya's musical vision.

Endowed with a light, high-pitched voice, Kaivalya has found it tempting to model the aural experience of his music after that of the *gharānā* founder, Abdul Kareem Khan. This feature of his music has special appeal for senior audiences who grew up with 78 RPM discs of the founding fathers of the Kairana tradition. Other than this bit of Kairana nostalgia, Kaivalya's music is free from the obvious influence of recent Kairana maestros. Kaivalya's legacy has interacted freely with the contemporary musical environment to give him the material with which to express his musicality.

His search for a personal musical statement has, he claims, been aided by the eclectic legacy of Bhaskarbuwa Bakhle, who introduced Agra, Jaipur–Atrauli as well as Gwalior influences into his family's musical armoury. In addition, Kaivalya has, by his own admission, imbibed some elements from the style of Kumar Gandharva (1925-92). The result is an original musical experience that retains the melody-orientation and emotional appeal of vintage Kairana music, while permitting it to exhibit a more explicit presence of the poetic and rhythmic elements.

Towards an Audience-friendly Music
(Kaivalya Spoke to the Author on 4 June 2001)

"My training with my father has the strong Kairana Gharānā bias of his own music. But, I have also been taught some *rāga*s and *bandiśe*s, which my grandfather, Ganpatrao, had learnt from Bhaskarbuwa, and documented with detailed notations. A good part of the Bhaskarbuwa legacy came from other *gharānā*s — Gwalior, Jaipur–Atrauli and Agra. Our family archive has over 250 *rāga*s, with several *bandiśe*s in each of them. My father had chosen not to master some of these *rāga*s or *bandiśe*s because they either did not suit his musical temperament, or were too demanding considering the manner in which his voice had been trained. He found me capable of handling some of them, and trained me in their exposition.

"Beyond the family's musical legacy, I have been influenced a lot by Kumar Gandharva's music. My father and he were close friends; he visited us often. He was an exceedingly creative musician, with a passion for tonal precision, inspired by our own Kairana Gharānā fountainhead, Abdul Kareem Khan. I liked Kumarji's short *tāna*s, and his use of the poetic form as a musical element. I have tried to incorporate these into my singing.

"I try to think about the content of my music from the angle of compensating for its weaknesses. Our Kairana tradition is very strong on the communication of a *rāga*'s emotional content. But, do we utilize all the elements of music to achieve the desired result? We tend not to give due respect to the poetic form of the *bandiśe*s. And, especially in *vilambita laya* (slow tempo) rendition, we are inclined to make the rhythm almost irrelevant. Without disturbing the essential melodic fluidity of Kairana vocalism, I try to allow the poetry and the rhythm a bigger role in the communication of the emotionality of the *rāga*.

"As a performer, I am concerned that my music should be as satisfying an emotional experience for the audiences as for me. When I am practising, I sing to an imaginary audience and try to anticipate its responses to my music. Fortunately, our audiences have a tradition of responding overtly to music. In the performing situation, I hear exclamatory remarks, such as *wāha*, or *ahāhaha* or *āaaah*, or I suddenly find people listening with their eyes closed. Each of these is a different category of response. Over the years, I have begun to understand what each of them means, even if I cannot describe their precise connotation. The understanding is important because I should know which of these makes more sense to me than the others.

"It is important for musicians to think, all the time, about enriching the content of their music. In many ways, *khayāla* music has become much richer in the last few decades. But, in many ways, it has also been impoverished. Unfortunately, in today's world, there is very little dialogue between scholars and connoisseurs on the one hand and musicians on the other. Musicians themselves, too, are no longer interested in discussing and thinking together about the content of music. You rarely find musicians even attending concerts of other musicians, especially those of comparable stature. Each one is so involved with his own little world, that the sharing of musical ideas is negligible; and that too is taking place by imitation, rather than by an interactive process. From the accounts of our elders, this was not so in earlier days. There was a healthy exchange of ideas even between rivals. Great musicians attended each other's concerts with great respect. The music of our generation is missing out on something valuable because we are not willing to make such efforts."

The Music of Kaivalya Kumar

I base my observations on a study of Kaivalya's recording of one CD for India Archive Music, New York, and several concert recordings. The repertoire studied covers *khayāla*s in Rāgeśrī, Khambavatī, Adanā, Śaṅkara, Sohinī, Gawoti, Sāvanī Kalyāṇa, Kalāvatī, Gorakha Kalyāṇa, *ṭhumarī* in Ghara, and Khamāja, a *bhajana* and a *nāṭya saṅgīta* rendition.

In comparison with traditional Kairana vocalism, Kaivalya's *khayāla* renditions are short, hardly ever exceeding 30 mts per *rāga*. As befits the quality of his voice, his repertoire is partial to *rāga*s which have their melodic focus in the *madhyāṅga* or *uttarāṅga*. His selection of *bandiśe*s is biased towards compositions in *madhya-laya* and *druta-laya*. In the studied sample of recordings, I did not come across a single *bandiśa* in Jhūmara, the traditional favourite of Kairana vocalists. This bias towards the brisk tempi probably reflects an awareness of his limitations in handling the *vilambita khayāla*, and also perhaps the desire to keep his music lively for audiences.

From father to son, the music exhibits elements of continuity as well as change, blended with elements of revivalism which leapfrog several generations. The revivalist facet of Kaivalya's music arises from his high-pitched voice, which enables him to thrill middle-aged and senior audiences with emotionally charged expressions reminiscent of Ustad Abdul Kareem Khan, and Sawai Gandharva. The element of continuity is defined by his steadfast pursuit of melody as the cornerstone of his music, while sharpening his father's tendency towards the ornamentation of its sculpture. The element of change is defined by a marked drift of the music towards the rhythm and poetry-oriented idiom of semi-classical genres, such as *ṭhumarī* and *nāṭya-saṅgīta*, both of which originated in the theatrical arts — dance and drama.

Kaivalya's voice is shorter in range than his father's, which comfortably covered two-and-a-half octaves. Unlike his father's, the timbre of Kaivalya's voice tends to tighten in the upper registers, and in high-density melodic execution. Despite this feature, or probably because of it, Kaivalya is able to imbue his music, at will, with an overt emotional intensity, which his father did not attempt.

Kaivalya's vocal technique exhibits another feature, which marks a departure from his father's music. In the low-density melodic execution of the *ālāpa*, he tends to use his tongue to, almost imperceptibly, articulate the *ay* expression as a replacement for the *ā* vowel. This substitution obviously makes vocalization physically less demanding. Amongst Kairana vocalists, this feature has been characteristic of Gangubai Hangal. But, unlike Gangubai, Kaivalya uses it to impart a subtle pulsation to the movement, which is intended to be explicitly anarhythmic.

As in his father's case, the architecture of Kaivalya's renditions is sound, though neither formal, nor elaborate enough to invite attention. The linear progression of melodic and rhythmic densities and complexities is maintained. Following the Kairana practice, the intermediate *bola-laya* movement is skipped. Kaivalya's approach to melody, though as dedicated to melodic precision as his father's, takes a different direction. It does not have the elegance of design that is his father's hallmark. Instead, it is characterized by a drift towards ornamentation intended to seduce. Such a drift is not uncommon amongst vocalists of Kaivalya's generation, who are responding to diluted audience profiles with blurred stylistic distinctions between art-music and genres on its periphery.

Kaivalya departs from the Kairana tradition by adopting a reverential approach to the *bandiśa*. He commands a substantial reservoir of *bandiśes*. Many of them are rare, and almost all are of outstanding compositional value. Kaivalya's own grip over them is exceptional. He relies greatly on the *bandiśa* to guide his entire presentation. This automatically elevates the role of the poetic and the rhythmic elements to a level not usually found in Kairana vocalism. This makes his music a more balanced musical statement than traditional Kairana, which has relied largely on melody and only marginally on the poetry and rhythm. Kaivalya's handling of *bandiśes* is most remarkable for the melodic precision with which he renders each line of a *bandiśa*, identical in every detail each time.

In comparison with his father's inventory of *tāna* patterns, or even that of other Kairana maestros of the earlier generation, Kaivalya's armoury is limited. This observation is generally valid for post-Independence vocalists of all *gharānā*s. The noteworthy aspect of Kaivalya's *tāna*s is the appearance of staccato *tāna*s in ultra-high melodic execution, which are more typical of Agra vocalism than of Kairana.

Kaivalya's music is aesthetically coherent, technically well endowed in all departments, and emotionally appealing. He has, however, yet to acquire the introspective quality, which qualifies a musician for stature. He may have done well enough for one who started late. But, time will tell if he missed the bus to distinction while he was busy knocking at the doors of commerce and engineering as career options but his father had the energy to teach him (Written : November 2001).

5.6

Rashid Khan
The Prince of Modernism

No vocalist in post-Independence era has had as meteoric a rise as Rashid Khan (b. 1966). Some have attributed this to the long famine of male vocalists that Hindustani music experienced at the time of his arrival. This is probably unfair to his prodigious talent, and also to the discernment of the music community. Rashid made a stunning debut at the age of 11, and became a darling of music lovers and critics before 25. Before he was 30, Pandit Bhimsen Joshi (b. 1922), the reigning monarch of *khayāla* vocalism, had pronounced him the "Great Hope" of Hindustani music. And, at 35, he is reportedly the busiest Hindustani vocalist.

In early childhood, Rashid was trained at his ancestral home by his grand-uncle, Ustad Nissar Hussain Khan (1909-93) of the Rampur-Sahaswan Gharānā. When the stalwart was invited to join the teaching faculty of ITC Sangeet Research Academy (SRA), Calcutta, Rashid moved with him, and stayed for twenty years. During this period, he absorbed the diverse stylistic resources made accessible by a catholic pedagogical environment, along with his study of Rampur-Sahaswan stylistics. The result is a vocalist who poses a challenge to the critic attempting to place him in the cultural process. Even though tentatively, I am inclined to place him in the Ameer Khan-inspired region of neo-Kairana vocalism.

Rashid Khan is a scion of a distinguished lineage of vocalists known as the Rampur-Sahaswan Gharānā. The Rampur prefix links it to the patronage of Nawab Hamid Ali of Rampur (ascended 1896), himself a competent exponent of vocal music as well as Kathak dance. Aspiring to make his principality the cultural capital of northern India, he made his court host to some of the most celebrated performing artistes of his time. Amongst them was a formidable vocalist, Enayet Hussain Khan (1849-1919), who migrated from Sahaswan. Hence the nomenclature for the style he evolved.

Enayet Hussain Khan married the daughter of Haddu Khan, one of the co-founders of the Gwalior Gharānā, and also received training with him. Through this connection, Gwalior stylistics came to have a significant presence in the Rampur-Sahaswan style. Enayet Hussain, his brother-in-law, Haider Khan (1857-1927), and Mushtaq Hussain Khan (d. 1964), are credited with forging the Rampur-Sahaswan style of vocalism. The *gharānā* has remained a close network of kinship, producing no distinguished musicians beyond the clan orbit. Rashid's mentor, Nissar Hussain Khan, was the grandson of Enayet Hussain Khan, the founder of this lineage.

Rashid's Repertoire

Rashid's published recordings up to 2002 provide some clues to his inclinations up to the age of 35. An indicative listing provides some insights. Yamana, Śyāma Kalyāṇa, Jhiṅjhoṭī, Bahāra, Bhaṭiyāra Madhuvantī, Marvā, Śuddha Kalyāṇa, Śaṅkara, Māru Bihāga, Kirwani, Kedāra, Shāhānā, Ābhogī, Kauṅsī Kānaḍā, Cārukeśī, Barwā, Deśa, Purīya Dhanaśrī, Nāt Bhairava, Paṭadīpa, Haṁsadhvani, Sohinī (*ṭhumarī*), Mālkauṅs, Sarasvatī, Hamīra, Joga, and Darabārī.

The broadest inference to be drawn from this list is the bias towards common or popular *rāgas*. The rarest *rāgas* in this list are Barwā, Shāhānā and Kauṅsī Kānaḍā, which cannot be considered rare any longer. A majority of them may be considered special favourites of Kairana Gharānā vocalists, though they are performed commonly enough in other *gharānās* too.

The second visible pattern is the substantial presence of *rāgas* (14 out of 28) whose renditions by Ameer Khan have either been published or are accessible in the grey market. These are: Yamana, Bhaṭiyāra, Marvā, Śuddha Kalyāṇa, Kedāra, Shāhānā, Ābhogī, Haṁsadhvani, Kauṅsī Kānaḍā, Cārukeśī, Nāt Bhairava, Mālkauṅs, Joga, and Darabārī. Overlapping partially with this list is a group of *rāgas* adopted by the Hindustani tradition from the Carnatic tradition — Cārukeśī, Haṁsadhvani, Sarasvatī and Ābhogī.

The pattern suggests that Rashid prefers the mature and widely recognized *rāgas*, especially those performed frequently by Kairana vocalists, but more specifically, Ameer Khan's favourites. His interest in Carnatic *rāgas* does not go beyond Ameer Khan's published repertoire. Broadly, Rashid's repertoire is familiar, accessible music.

Stylistic Tendencies

I have had occasion to hear Rashid Khan in concert several

times over 15 years, and also on commercial recordings. For purposive analysis, I rely on two CDs he recorded in 1995 for India Archive Music (IAM), New York, and a published release of a concert he gave in England (NRCC:0015). The IAM recordings feature *khayāla*s in Megha Malhāra, Marvā, and Kamoda, and a *bandiśa-kī-ṭhumarī* in Bhairavī. The concert recording under review is of *rāga deśa* from a Navarasa release of an appearance at Wolverhampton (England) in March 1993. The entire sample consists of recordings made before Rashid reached 30.

Rashid provides proof of a serious musical temperament in his renditions of Marvā and Megha Malhāra. Having been recorded by Ameer Khan, Rashid's renditions of both these *rāga*s have a strong Ameer Khan flavour. However, despite the profundity of these *rāga*s, and overriding the profound Ameer Khan influence, Rashid's sculpting of phrases — in the Marvā more than the Megha Malhāra — drifts towards a *ṭhumarī*-esque eagerness to please. This tendency, reminiscent of Jasraj, is subdued in the *vilambita khayāla*, but comes through conspicuously in the *druta khayāla*s. In his vocalization and intonation patterns, occasional echoes of Bade Ghulam Ali Khan are also in evidence.

Rashid's renditions of Kamoda and Deśa — neither known to have been recorded by Ameer Khan — appear to formalize this blurring of genre distinctions more obviously. In his voice, the immortal Kamoda Khayāla composition of Sadaraṅg *erī janenā dūṅgi* acquires a vivacity, which could qualify it as a *bandiśa-ki-ṭhumarī* until it comes to the *tāna*s phase. Stylistically, the Deśa rendition goes farther into *ṭhumarī* territory. The rendition consists of a *madhya-laya khayāla*, followed by a *tarānā*, both in *tīnatāla*. In this 50-mts rendering, the *rāga* itself is allowed to drift sporadically into Malhāra and Soraṭha, and occasionally exhibits suggestions of Jaijaivantī. Though both *bandiśa* forms belong to the *khayāla* genre, the renditions feature a laxity of architecture and exuberant ornamentation of phrasing characteristic of the *ṭhumarī* genre.

The *bandiśa-kī-ṭhumarī* in Bhairavī is rendered in its orthodox format, without any improvisatory movements other than melodic variations to the pre-composed form. Rashid shows the fullest respect to the orthodox form. This is noteworthy considering that, by his time, Agra and Patiala vocalists had made an expansive treatment of the genre — replete with *tāna*s and *saragama* passages — acceptable. The restrained classicism in Rashid's handling of an explicitly romanticist genre is truly remarkable for a technically well-endowed musician below 30.

From limited evidence, one observes that Rashid's tendency is to treat *khayāla* renditions with a romanticist tilt, while his *ṭhumarī* renditions can exhibit a generous dose of classicist formalism. In terms of architecture as well as overall demeanour and stance, Rashid's music blurs the distinction between the major mainstream genres — the classicist *khayāla* and the romanticist *ṭhumarī*. This, as Ashok Ranade points out,[9] is a major feature of modernism, as understood in the theory of art criticism.

Modernism, as a phenomenon in 19th and 20th-century art, has larger connotations. It is characterized by a rejection of tradition, a self-conscious determination to re-invent the purposes and techniques of art, and an exploration of the self-validating image (*Modernism: Key Ideas in Human Thought*, Kenneth McLeish, ed., Facts on File Inc., New York, 1993). With respect to the blurring of the distinctions between genres, as Ranade observes,[9] modernism is a well established phenomenon in Hindustani music, going back to the Kairana doyen, Abdul Karim Khan (1872-1937). In the last quarter of the 20th century, the three major romanticists — Kumar Gandharva, Jasraj and Kishori Amonkar — have also contributed significantly to this movement, each in a different way.

Rashid's music has achieved widespread acceptance cutting across generations of music lovers primarily because his is a moderate departure from tradition, without any of the anarchic tendencies typical of post-modernism. And, because his is a moderate departure, it lends itself to a reasonably adequate identification of its antecedents.

The Nissar Hussain Legacy

It is neither possible, nor necessary to attempt an exhaustive analysis of Nissar Hussain Khan's music here. However, a sample of his mentor's music may provide a reference point for Rashid's style. The review is based on three readily available recordings. *Rāga Kalyāṇa kā Prakāra* (A variant of *Kalyāṇa*) was recorded in 1960, and published later (EMI/HMV STC:048:7407). *Rāga*s Khema Kalyāṇa and Jaijaivantī were broadcast posthumously on All India Radio, on 24 July 1993.

Nissar Hussain's music was characterized by aggressive intonation and a tendency towards angular melodic contours. Being probably a response to the acoustic environment of the era, it shared this feature with contemporary vocalists of several other *gharānā*s. As is to be expected of a vocalist almost three generations removed from that era, Rashid's music exhibits no such signs. Today's sophisticated acoustic environment permits him to pursue a relaxed style of vocalization and intonation along with an ornate approach to the sculpting of melody.

The notion of strict linearity is absent from the architecture of Rashid's *khayāla*s, as it was in Nissar Hussain's. Rashid's *vilambita khayāla* is informally structured with respect to the widespread three-tier structure in practice today. In this, he differs from Nissar Hussain, who virtually sang to a two-tier structure. The medium-density movement, in which Rashid comes closest to Ameer Khan and consumes a significant duration in Rashid's renditions, is relatively insignificant in

Nissar Hussain's music. But, like Nissar Hussain, Rashid makes the transitions through overlapping rounds of improvizations rather than clean-cut separations more commonly encountered in contemporary vocalism. Nissar Hussain maintained a steady tempo in the *vilambita khayāla*s from beginning to end. Rashid, on the other hand, conveys the progressive intensification in musical activity more categorically than Nissar Hussain because he steps up the tempo in several discrete stages during his renditions.

Like Nissar Hussain, Rashid renders his *ālāpa* in *bola* articulation, with no use of *ākāra*. However, the *saragama* articulation, which was a negligible feature in Nissar Hussain's music, appears in Rashid's *ālāpa*, dominates his medium density movement, and also features in his *tāna*s. In his *tāna*s, Nissar Hussain used a combination of *baḍhata*, *laḍī-guthāva* and *chūṭa* patterns. Rashid's *tāna*s, in comparison, exhibit a bias in favour of broad span melodic runs of the *alaṁkāra* and *sapāṭa* variety. For rounding off his *tāna*s, Rashid follows his mentor's practice of frequently deploying amad *tihāī*s.

In the very high-density phase, Nissar Hussain's *tāna*s could be as racy and fluid as those of D.V. Paluskar (Gwalior), or as sharp and staccato as Agra vocalists like Vilayat Hussain or Sharafat Hussain. The last five minutes of Nissar Hussain's *Kalyāṇa kā eka Prakāra* recording (1960) could, for instance, well have been the last five minutes of a rendition by Sharafat Hussain. Rashid, on the other hand, maintains a high level of fluidity through his *tāna*s up to a high level of *svara*-density. In ultra-high density *tāna*s, running at above 480 intonations per minute, however, the staccato sharpness of the Agra variety does surface occasionally.

Rashid relies almost equally on *bola* and *ākāra* articulation for his *tāna*s. Interestingly, however, he also uses *saragama* for *tāna* articulation in the early stages of the *tāna*s phase of his *vilambita khayāla*s. Being of medium-to-high *svara* density, these may also be construed as an enhanced medium density form as much as they are a transitional high-density form. *Tāna*s of intermediate *svara* density are in *bola* articulation, while the ultra-high density are in *ākāra*.

As a general tendency, Rashid's *tāna*s favour broad span melodic motion, ending largely either at the bottom of the scale or close to the top. Short span *tāna*s, and *tāna*s with melodic action concentrated in the mid-octave region are infrequent in his music. Considering Rashid's musicianship, it is interesting that *tāna*s of truly stunning construction performed by Nissar Hussain in his prime do not find a place in his presentation. This, as we have observed earlier, is a generational malaise. The imaginative artistry of *tāna*s has yielded to lightening speed and stunning impact.

These observations on Rashid's *tāna* patterns are based on recordings done up to the age of 35. They can therefore only be provisional. The *tāna* patterns, perhaps more than any other facet of a vocalist's art, tend to change over time, reflecting his emotional and physical health and his temperament.

The nuts-and-bolts apart, just listening to a Nissar Hussain recording, followed by a Rashid recording is sufficient to prove that the Rampur-Sahaswan senior's music is not a significant explanation for the junior's musical tendencies. This is hardly surprising considering the other factors that make him what he is.

Other Influences

To begin with, we need to understand the environment in which Rashid Khan's musicianship has evolved. By the time he came on the scene, the "self-validating image" had already become the driving force of Hindustani music. Eclecticism had become eminently respectable by the emergence of formidable vocalists who had broken *gharānā* boundaries in search of their musical selves. During Rashid's formative years, the 1980s, a host of socio-economic forces exposed *gharānā*-based stylistic continuity to the annals of history. Within what was left of it, Kairana was still the dominant force on the *khayāla* scene, especially male vocalism.

The reformist-modernist-romanticist offshoots of some mainstream styles had been launched by Jasraj, Kumar Gandharva and Kishori Amonkar, and were fast challenging *gharānā*-based orthodoxy. Amongst male vocalists, Bhimsen Joshi was still, however, the most popular, and Ameer Khan (neo-Kairana), the most influential model of *khayāla* vocalism. Jasraj, who had started close to the Ameer Khan idiom, was ascending the rating charts by driving *khayāla* towards a *ṭhumarī*-esque musical experience. It was neither possible, nor evidently intended, that Rashid's evolution should be insulated from these forces active in the musical culture.

Though placed under the tutelage of Nissar Hussain at the Academy, Rashid was exposed to a liberal environment, which allowed him ample access to alternative stylistic directions, guided largely by his own musical temperament. It also seems reasonable to believe that, aware of the huge generation gap (57 years) between himself and his ward, Nissar Hussain would not have stifled Rashid's individuality. Instead, the ageing maestro apparently worked on the aesthetic coherence of Rashid's music, in preference to demanding compliance with the Rampur-Sahaswan model. This combination of enabling and regulatory forces drove Rashid towards a unique blend of Rampur-Sahaswan, Bhimsen Joshi (Gwalior-turned-Kairana) and Ameer Khan (Bhendi Bazar/neo-Kairana), but tilting towards Jasraj. Within this configuration of influences, Ameer Khan apparently dominates the musical experience, with the Jasraj influence coming a close second.

Rashid's asset of Nissar Hussain Khan's musical wisdom apparently lies in a state of relative disuse, as he attempts to build a more modern musical edifice by harnessing the other influences he has absorbed over the years. Rashid's voice does not possess either the authoritative quality of Bhimsen Joshi or the richness of Ameer Khan's timbre. Nor does his musical mind exhibit the academism of the Kairana and neo-Kairana legends. But, it has an aloofness, which makes it suitable for Kairana stylistics. And, it has a sensuous quality which enables him to tilt towards Jasraj's seductive manner. He also has a composure that makes his music hospitable to the Ameer Khan idiom. His voice production and intonation, his leisurely approach to unfolding the *rāga* in the *ālāpa*, his limited use of timbre and volume variations in the delivery of music, the generous use of *saragama*s of kaleidoscopic pattern, and his bias in favour of broad-span *tāna*s — all these have an element of Ameer Khan nostalgia. His sculpting of phrases, however, tends towards *ṭhumarī*-like ornamentation characteristic of the recent Jasraj.

It is perhaps fair to observe that the real Rashid Khan has yet to emerge from the shadows of Nissar Hussain, Ameer Khan, Bhimsen Joshi and Jasraj, His prodigious talent has enabled him so far — up to the age of 35 — to integrate a diverse set of influences into an eminently saleable package. The world of music now awaits the emergence of his personal musical statement. When such a statement starts taking shape what has been said of him so far will need to be revisited (Written : November 2004).

Section 6
The Patiala Legecy

6.1

Perspectives on the Patiala Legacy

THIS chapter deals with those aspects of the Patiala legacy which are immediately relevant to appreciating the stylistic tendencies of musicians covered in this book.

The Patiala lineage of musicians owes its name to the patronage of the Princely State of Patiala in Punjab, on the north-western border between India and Pakistan. The state was recognized as an independent political entity ruled by Sikh rulers in 1762. Inspired partly by the centrality of *rāga*-based music to the ecclesiastical tradition of the Sikh religion, music became a dominant part of the Patiala patronage system. The Patiala Gharānā of vocal music, as understood today, was founded in 1857, when British mercenaries quashed the First Indian War of Independence. This manoeuvre wiped the Mughal Court in Delhi out of business, drove the last Emperor and celebrated poet Bahadur Shah II into exile, and dismantled the entire edifice of Mogul patronage.

During the upheaval, Tanras Khan, amongst the formidable *khayāla* vocalists at the Mogul court, fled to Patiala in search of shelter, accompanied by his disciple, Bhai Kalu Rababi. The Patiala Gharānā, as a stylistic lineage, is traceable to the musicianship of Kalu Rababi's son, Ali Baksh, and his distant cousin, Fateh Ali. The team, commonly referred to as "Aliya-Fattu," had the benefit of immense prestige at the Patiala court, and continue to enjoy near legendary stature in Hindustani music.

Aliya-Fattu were groomed in *dhrupada* by Behram Khan Dagar, and in *khayāla* under Mubarak Ali Khan of the Gwalior Gharānā, both at the Jaipur court. The team was also trained at Gwalior by Haddu Khan, one of the founders of the Gwalior Gharānā of *khayāla* vocalism, and by Tanras Khan of Delhi. Thus, the Patiala style received four distinct stylistic inputs in an era that supported distinguishable styles of vocalism.

According to published sources, the Patiala Gharānā gets bifurcated from this point. After Ali Baksh (Aliya of Aliya-Fattu fame), his son, Akhtar Hussain, continued to enjoy the patronage of the Patiala court. He, along with his two sons, Amanat Ali Khan and Fateh Ali Khan, migrated to Pakistan soon after the partition of the country in 1947.

The Patiala Gharānā spawned another stream with Fateh Ali (Fattu of Aliya-Fattu fame) having groomed two brothers from the Kasur Gharānā — Mir Baksh (Kale Khan) and Ali Baksh associated with the court of Kashmir (not to be confused with Ali Baksh, "Aliya" of Aliya-Fattu fame).

The Kasur Gharānā is variously described as one of *dhrupada* singers, and of *mirāsīs*. The most successful Kasur-Patiala vocalists, Bade Ghulam Ali Khan, and his brother, Barkat Ali Khan, were sons of Ali Baksh, and nephews and disciples of Mir Baksh (Kale Khan). They were originally residents of Lahore, which became a part of Pakistan after partition. Barkat Ali settled in Pakistan, while Bade Ghulam Ali obtained Indian nationality in 1957.

In the latter half of the 20th century, thus, the Patiala lineage came to be represented by the Amanat Ali-Fateh Ali duo and Barkat Ali Khan in Pakistan, and Bade Ghulam Ali Khan and his son, Munawwar Ali Khan in India. Musicians of both streams have enjoyed immense stature and popularity on both sides of the Indo-Pakistan border, and become household names.

Deshpande[1] has conceptualized the Patiala style based entirely on the vocalism of Bade Ghulam Ali, totally ignoring the Patiala stream in Pakistan. History has accepted this probably because none of Bade Ghulam Ali's Patiala contemporaries achieved sufficient significance to merit consideration. Interestingly, however, the music of the Amanat Ali-Fateh Ali duo, directly descended from the Patiala lineage (Bade Ghulam Ali's juniors by 30 years), bears a close resemblance to that of Bade Ghulam Ali, and justifies the Deshpande conceptualization.

Coverage of Vocalists

The Patiala legacy is represented in this book by Ustad Bade Ghulam Ali Khan, and Ustad Bade Fateh Ali Khan from Pakistan (the survivor of the Amanat Ali-Fateh Ali duo), both established exponents of Patiala vocalism by virtue of their pedigree as well as quality of music.

6.2

Ustad Bade Ghulam Ali Khan
The Sorcerer of Hindustani Vocalism

THE majestic, though short and dark, figure of Ustad Bade Ghulam Ali Khan, with his cherubic smile, black cap, formidable handlebar moustaches, and the distinctive *svara-maṇḍala* in his lap, is amongst the most powerful and durable images of 20th-century Hindustani music. And, for good reason. Since Faiyyaz Khan, no vocalist has enthralled his audiences, and held them in abject surrender, like he did. Ghulam Ali Khan (d. 1968) was easily the most popular vocalist of his times. Arriving on the scene towards the end of the Faiyyaz Khan era, he achieved this status while sharing the concert platform with the likes of Kesarbai Kerkar, Omkarnath Thakur, D.V. Paluskar, and Ameer Khan. After more than four decades since his departure, his music shows no sign of aesthetic obsolescence, or loss of popular appeal.

He was the first and the last, after Faiyyaz Khan, to straddle the two worlds of *khayāla* and *ṭhumarī* with distinction. While Faiyyaz Khan performed both varieties of *ṭhumarī*, Ghulam Ali Khan concentrated his musical energies on the sentimental *bola-banāva ṭhumarī*, born in Benares. He is credited, along with his brother Barkat Ali Khan, Abdul Kareem Khan and Siddheshwari Devi, with bringing the *bola-banāva ṭhumarī* to a higher level of maturity in the 20th century.[4]

For the durability of his legacy, Bade Ghulam Ali has only one rival from his era — Ameer Khan. Every posthumous release of their concert recordings has sold effortlessly and in large numbers. Beyond this, the comparison with Ameer Khan ceases to hold. Ameer Khan (1912-74) remains, to this day, a model of exemplary *khayāla* rendition, while Bade Ghulam Ali's model is controversial. The question mark relates to the liberties he often took with the architecture of the *khayāla*. His *khayāla* renditions often lacked order. He felt free to throw in a *tāna* (high density) into his *ālāpa* (low density) or *bola-bāṇṭa* (medium density), or to even revert to the *ālāpa* after the *bola-bāṇṭa* or *tāna* movements. This tendency, according to his critics, made the soundness of his *tālīma* suspect, and made his *khayāla*s "too much icing and too little cake" — incapable of making a lasting impression.[1,9]

This tendency did not diminish his stature — for two reasons. Firstly, he was not a habitual defaulter. Prof. Deodhar[3] cites several concerts, in which his rendition was as disciplined as that of Ameer Khan or any other orthodox singer. Several of his published and unpublished recordings support the Deodhar documentation. Secondly, he was not a wilful defaulter. He confessed his weakness, and was honest about his motivations. He argued that audiences no longer had the patience to sit through the systematic unfolding of the *baḍā khayāla*, and became fidgety if he did not give them a few fireworks on the way. He had the notion that, being a Punjabi, he must either cater to the image of Punjabis as frivolous people, or risk losing his audiences. The truth probably is that, he lacked self-control, and rationalized it by an assumed set of expectations amongst his audiences. He bound his audiences in a chain of expectations that suited his temperament, ultimately to find himself its prisoner.[1,3]

Deshpande, perhaps his severest critic, went far enough to say that Bade Ghulam Ali's indiscipline could encourage a form of musical jaywalking amongst succeeding generations of musicians.[1] These fears have been largely belied because the quality control mechanism of Hindustani music, though considerably corroded, has so far functioned pretty efficiently — at least with respect to the architecture of *khayāla* vocalism. Although the tradition permits towering musicianship to break a few rules while giving music a new direction, it has been zealous enough in preserving the essentials. If there is a widespread breach of the *khayāla*'s architectural form in the future, Bade Ghulam Ali Khan will need to share the blame for it with several other luminaries.

For all his greatness, Bade Ghulam Ali Khan has not spawned as many xeroxes amongst later vocalists as Ameer Khan has. Attempts at imitating him have yielded only laughable caricatures. This is probably not because of his controversial architecture, as much as his sorcery — the matchless pliability and musicality of his voice, the enigma of his music, and the mercurial quality of his musical mind. This fact does not make Bade Ghulam Ali either greater than the saturnine Ameer Khan or inferior to him. It just makes a comparison between the two absurd. During their lifetimes, neither of them devoted much attention to grooming the next generation, dedicating themselves entirely to a performing career. In addition to being a great performing musician, Ameer Khan, so it turned out, had the makings of a posthumous *guru*, while Ghulam Ali Khan did not. To present-day music lovers, both deliver aesthetically coherent music, which also answers to the description of great music. In an environment starved of such music, connoisseurs and the laity alike hungrily devour every recording they can acquire of Bade Ghulam Ali as well as Ameer Khan, valuing each of them for what the other cannot deliver.

The Makings of a Legend

Ustad Bade Ghulam Ali Khan's name has often intrigued and amused people — especially because his was, indeed, a *baḍe* (massive/huge) personality. In northern India, the prefix *baḍe* (meaning "the elder") is used for avoiding a confusion of identities when, within the same circle, there is a younger contemporary of the same name, who will have the prefix *choṭe* (the younger). Even though we may not have heard of the Chhote Ghulam Ali, this is almost certainly how Ghulam Ali Khan acquired the Bade prefix. It remained with him throughout life because he also answered to the other two connotations of the word — big-built, and great.

Ghulam Ali Khan was born in 1903 at Kasur, near Lahore, now in Pakistan. There is, indeed, some difference of opinion about his birthdate. The various accounts span a period of four years from 1901 to 1904. But, his was an era in which vagueness on such matters was common, while today, the truth is elusive as well as irrelevant. Ghulam Ali Khan's father Ali Baksh and his brother Mir Baksh (better known as Kale Khan), had studied *khayāla* under Fateh Ali (of Aliya-Fattu fame) in the patronage of the princely state of Patiala. Ali Baksh was a court musician in Kashmir. His brother, Kale Khan (Mir Baksh), remained an independent musician, and was the formal *guru* of nephew, Ghulam Ali.

Ghulam Ali's *gaṇḍā-bandhana* (ritual initiation) with Kale Khan took place when he was five. Some of the most eminent musicians of the era were present at the ceremony. At the age of 12, Ghulam Ali was invited to perform for the visiting Prince of Wales in Lahore. He continued his studies with Kale Khan till the age of 17, when the latter died. According to one account, Ghulam Ali also received training from his father, who was an expert singer of the *ṭhumarī*, having spent a good deal of his time in the Purab region (eastern part of Uttar Pradesh, around Varanasi), where the *ṭhumarī* genre dominated the musical culture.[4] According to another account, in his teens, Ghulam Ali was also coached by one Inayeti Bai of Bombay, a pupil of his father's.[11] No corroboration is available of this phase of his tutelage. Reportedly, in his early twenties, he went to Bombay to study with Baba Shinde Khan of the Gwalior Gharānā.[11] From these accounts, it would appear that, like several other 20th-century greats, Ghulam Ali Khan was a product of a fragmented and eclectic grooming process.

When Kale Khan died, the elders of the clan lamented that the glorious era of Patiala vocalism had come to an end. This remark stung Ghulam Ali. He started practising round the clock to prove them wrong. And the rest, as they say, is history.

It is well known that Ghulam Ali was trained in vocalism as well as on the *sāraṅgī*. In his early youth, he made a living as a *sāraṅgī* accompanist in Bombay as well as Lahore. However, he gave it up as soon as his career as a vocalist took off. His early years as a vocalist — sometimes supporting his father — were limited to engagements in Punjab and Kashmir, and very few people outside the region had heard of him. His big break came when he was almost 40 — at the Vikramaditya Music Conference in Bombay (1944). He stole the show with brilliant renditions of *khayāla*, *ṭhumarī* and *bhajana*. The news of this conquest spread all over the country. Overnight, he became Ustad Bade Ghulam Ali Khan, and thereafter, for over two decades, no major music festival in non-peninsular India was conceived without his participation.

In 1953, the celebrated Carnatic vocalist, G.N. Balasubramaniam (GNB), organized, for him, a concert tour of south Indian cities — in those days, almost alien territory for Hindustani musicians. At first, the stark contrast between the ascetic culture of Carnatic *vidvān*s and Bade Ghulam Ali's majestic personality, raised considerable scepticism. South Indian connoisseurs needed just one concert to change their mind about Bade Ghulam Ali Khan, and to hail him as a "bhāgavatar," the highest honorific conferred on singers in the Carnatic tradition.[11]

Bade Ghulam Ali became an important pillar of Hindustani music so speedily that few know of his having been a Pakistani national for over a decade after Independence. His home was in Lahore, while his audiences were in India, which he could visit for only limited periods each year. Neither government obstructed his movements across the border; but neither formally acknowledged his stature. During that period, even the mention of his name was prohibited on All India Radio.[6] His application for Indian citizenship was pending when, in 1957, the Chief Minister of the erstwhile Bombay State, Morarji Desai, was charmed by his music and took up his case with Delhi. Desai not only got his nationality papers through, but also gave him a comfortable residence in Bombay, along with ancillary facilities. The *ustād* remained a resident of Bombay though, in later years, he developed a substantial presence also in Calcutta.

Once India became his stable home, Bade Ghulam Ali attained a combination of popularity and stature attained only by Faiyyaz Khan before him. Several of his *khayāla* compositions (e.g. *re navelī nāra* in *druta ekatāla*/Kedāra), penned under the pseudonym *Saba Raṅga*, became immensely popular amongst vocalists of all *gharānā*s and are still in circulation. The number of Bade Ghulam Ali titles that has appeared on the shelves of the music stores — during his lifetime and thereafter — could well be a 20th-century record. With his speedy rise to legendary status, the honours could not have been far behind. He was honoured with the Sangeet Natak Akademi Award, and decorated with the Padma Bhushan by the President of India.

At the age of 58, he suffered a paralytic attack. Governments, friends, and admirers pooled resources to see him through the difficult period. Though immobilized for life, he worked hard on his music, and began to perform again, relying increasingly on the support of his son, Munawwar Ali Khan. Because of the arduous *riyāẓa* he had put in throughout life, his voice stood him in good stead till the end. The chastity of his intonation remained unimpeachable though, in the last few years, his *tāna*s were losing their vigour. His health suffered a serious setback in December 1967, and the end came on 23 April 1968.[3]

His contribution as a *guru* was meagre. His elder son, who lived in Pakistan, died in 1973, and not much is known about him. His exceptionally talented younger son, Munawwar Ali Khan (1933-89), did not have enough time to outgrow his father's towering shadow. The *ustād*'s tutelage links with other "disciples" were tenuous, and the results, questionable for stylistic conformity.

Musicianship

Bade Ghulam Ali's voice was "deliciously sweet, bright, silk-soft, and with the pleasantness of the moonlit sky."[2] It was at home at any tempo and across three octaves. By modern standards of voice culture, his manner of voice production was almost ideal. In the perfection of his intonation and the chastity of his *svara*, he stood next only to Abdul Kareem Khan. But, his voice had a nimbleness and manoeuvrability not matched by any 20th-century male vocalist. It was a voice that obeyed every command of its master with effortless ease. Not surprisingly, even his severest critic described him as a sorcerer.[2]

In his incisive assessment of the maestro, Ashok Ranade credits his music with exceptional and unmatched lucidity.[9] This quality, explains Ranade, enables us to have an unobstructed experience of the art-work. The voice was so transparent that the musical design came through as originally conceived. The veil of faulty voice-production was totally absent in his musical endeavours.

In addition to nature's generosity, the quality of his voice was shaped by the pedagogical techniques of his *guru*, Kale Khan. Ghulam Ali was made to practise the scales for hours against the wall of a dilapidated mosque on the outskirts of the city, and to listen carefully to the echo. His *guru* demonstrated the quality that the echo should have; Ghulam Ali had to achieve that quality, and make it his own. Then, there was his *riyāẓa* technique, which could maintain his voice in perfect condition even with very little investment of time. Prof. Deodhar[3] provides a detailed account of the technique, which the *ustād* demonstrated to him.[3]

The perfection of his intonation is attributed, with considerable validity, to his training on the *sāraṅgi*. It cannot be a coincidence that the king of intonation, Abdul Kareem Khan, had also started life as a *sāraṅgi* player. The process of perfecting intonation on a mechanical device, especially a fretless instrument, makes the musician ultra-sensitive to deviations from the desired pitch.[2] For a *sāraṅgī* player, intonation is not merely aural, but tangible. In addition, as an accompanist, a *sāraṅgī* player is directly and immediately accountable to the principal performer, the vocalist, for his technical command over the instrument. His subordinate status in the musical culture and the possibility of a public reprimand constitute powerful deterrents to clumsiness.

Ghulam Ali Khan's obsession with *riyāẓa* is legendary.

Anyone visiting him, at any time of the day found him doing his *riyāẓa* with *svara-maṇḍala* in his lap. All his free time was devoted to *riyāẓa*. He was also a believer in the value of "mental *riyāẓa*." He advised Prof. B.R. Deodhar to contemplate the *bandiśe*s, and the difficult *tāna*s — while in the bath, while on a train or a bus, while taking a walk, anywhere, anytime — in order to have them flow effortlessly in concert.[3] He believed that there was no such thing as free time for a musician.

His concert strategy was highly sensitive to audience profiles. If he found a serious audience, he would give them a delectable feast of *khayāla* music with a little bit of light music at the end. But, if he found an indifferent audience, he would start with a *khayāla*, but shift early to *ṭhumarī* and *dādarā*s and *bhajana*s.[3] Indeed, there exist concert recordings, on which he has either sung only *ṭhumarī*, or presented a *bola-banāva ṭhumarī* followed by a *bandiśa-ṭhumarī* in the same *rāga* simulating *khayāla* presentation format of a *baḍā khayāla* and a *choṭā khayāla*.

Notwithstanding the populism of his concert strategy, he was an immensely conscientious artiste. His consistency rating was enviable. Whenever he had an unsatisfactory concert — mostly because of substandard accompanists or indifferent audiences — he would give connoisseurs a free "make-good" immediately after the paid concert. In 1945, he gave a night long make-good on the veranda of his lodgings after an indifferent concert at the Deval Club in Kolhapur. He repeated such a gesture on a railway platform between 3.00 and 5.00 a.m. in Belgaum, while he waited for his train back to Bombay![3]

Bade Ghulam Ali as a Khayāla Singer

In the *khayāla* genre, Ghulam Ali Khan concentrated on common *rāga*s. Indeed, his most memorable recordings and radio broadcasts were of *rāga*s like Kedāra, Bhūpa, Jaunpurī, Deśa, Guṇakalī, Mālkauṅs, and Darabārī. There are reports of his having performed rare *rāga*s like Guñjī-Kānaḍā and Khat,[9] but these were strictly not his territory. He felt it was improper to sing *rāgas* whose melodic potential had not been fully explored, or whose grammar had not been widely accepted.[3] This objection was rooted in his approach to *khayāla* development, which was expansive, and rich in musical imagination. Rare *rāgas*, being inherently limited in their improvizational potential, had no appeal for him. Likewise, his inventory of traditional *bandiśes* was limited. This might explain why he composed original *bandiśes* in the *rāgas* he performed often, and why he tended to repeat *bandiśes* from concert to concert. This limited repertoire of *rāgas* and *bandiśes* might have aided his popularity, considering the progressive dilution of audience profiles in post-Independence India.[9]

His command over *rāga* grammar was impeccable. At the Vikramaditya Conference (1944), he performed Marvā and Puriyā in succession, and brilliantly — a feat considering that the two *rāgas* have identical *svaras* and are differentiated by several very subtle parameters of *rāga* grammar.[3] At another concert, he performed Kedāra, Chāyānāta, Kamoda and Hamīra in succession — four *rāgas* with identical *svaras* — and differentiated them astutely in rendition, along with explanations.

It was not unusual for him to drift suddenly into a *saragama* rendition with a *mūrchana* (scale shift) in the middle of a *rāga*. In the middle of Bhūpa, for instance, he would suddenly replace SRGPDS articulation with DNrGM^D to suggest Marvā, momentarily shifting *sa* to lower-octave *dha*. This kind of melodic punning achieved two effects — it titillated the uninitiated with an element of surprise, while it delighted connoisseurs with a rare insight into the tonal geometry of the *rāga*. Even in the *ṭhumarī* genre, which is less demanding on *rāga* grammar, Bade Ghulam Ali found it unnecessary to breach the boundaries of the *rāgas*. When, on rare occasion, he breached the melodic boundaries, he did so astutely, and with stunning effect.[4]

Bade Ghulam Ali Khan had an exceptional competence in the rendition of *tarānās*, and was a composer of unusual *tarānā bandiśes*. Like the Jaipur–Atrauli Gharānā vocalist, Moghubai Kurdikar, he had a special liking for *tarānās* in *madhya-laya*, and excelled in their presentation. Memories of his *madhya-laya tarānās* in Bageśrī/*jhapatāla* and in Kedāra/*ekatāla*, both unpublished, still send his admirers into raptures.

On the *laya-svara* continuum on which Deshpande classifies the different *gharānā* styles, Deshpande has placed Ghulam Ali Khan's Patiala style towards the *svara* (melody) orientation end, half way between Kairana at the extremity and Gwalior and Jaipur–Atrauli in the middle.[1] However, he himself admits to the simplistic nature of this classification. While Ghulam Ali did achieve a balance between *laya* and *svara*, and cared a great deal more about *laya* than Abdul Kareem Khan, he was a sorcerer and also a riddle.

As a stylistic innovator,[9] Ghulam Ali Khan imbued his *khayāla* renditions with a marked influence of the mischievous *ṭappā* genre. Along with Faiyyaz Khan, he was thus amongst the early significant vocalists of the 20th century to introduce ornamentation characteristic of semi-classical genres into mainstream art music. This was not a part of any populist design as much as a natural expression of his North Punjab/NW Frontier ethnicity.

In later years, a similar phenomenon surfaced in other parts of the country — the influence of melodic expressions typical of *nāṭya saṅgīta* on *khayāla* vocalists from Maharashtra, and the influence of folk and other regional genres on the instrumentalists from Bengal. In the latter half of the 20th century, these expressions of ethnicity pluralized the notion of the mainstream, which was, until then, homogenized under the ethnicity of the Hindi-speaking belt.

Bade Ghulam Ali in Semi-Classical Music

When the music director, Naushad Ali wanted a voice to sing for Miya Tansen in K. Asif's historical epic, "Mughal-e-Āẓam," his choice inevitably fell on Bade Ghulam Ali Khan. That decision gave us *prema jogana bana ke,* hummed even today by people who have never heard of either Bade Ghulam Ali Khan or of *rāga* Sohinī. Amongst aficionados of classical music, Bade Ghulam Ali is remembered for several other renditions of *ṭhumarī* and *dādarā*.

In the semi-classical genres he was, indeed, a pioneer. His repertoire of *ṭhumarī* and allied forms substantially enlarged the melodic and rhythmic vision of the *bola-banāva* (*artha-bhāva*) *ṭhumarī* as it was performed in his time. He is credited with popularizing *ṭhumarī* in *tāla*s other than the traditional Dīpacaṇḍī, by adding *dādarā, kehervā,* and *mughlai tāla*s. His contribution to their melodic evolution was even greater. He introduced, into them, melodic elements from the folk melodies of Punjab, Sindh, Kashmir and Rajasthan, and the *ṭappā,* a genre derived from songs of camel drivers in the North-West Frontier. In addition, he sang his *ṭhumarī* in folk-based *rāga*s like Pahāḍī and Sindh Bhairavī, Śivarañjanī and Manda. It is believed that he tuned in regularly to radio broadcasts of Persian and Arabic music for melodic ideas.[2] These made his *ṭhumarī* lighter, more playful, and less sober[4] compared to the more classical Benares *ṭhumarī*.

From these elements, Ghulam Ali Khan is said to have forged the "Punjab *aṅga*" *ṭhumarī,* though he himself denied the existence of any such thing. His contention was that Pūraba (the region around Benares) was the birthplace of the *bola-banāva ṭhumarī,* and he was merely blending suitable folk idioms from other regions with the orthodox *ṭhumarī*. He even asked why there should not be a Carnatic *ṭhumarī*.[6] The important thing, for him, was its artistic and emotional depiction.

In Historical Perspective

By temperament, Ghulam Ali Khan was a romanticist. He was ideally suited for playing a pioneering role in the maturation of the semi-classical genres and raising their stature in art-music. This very temperament also made him — by inclination though not by habit, and certainly not by intention — a reluctant observer of formalism in *khayāla* music. The same temperament also inclined him towards a more ornate sense of melodic design than the *khayāla* form had accepted until his time. Admittedly, Abdul Kareem Khan before him had performed a pioneering role in both the genres without a controversial presence in either. But, Bade Ghulam Ali was not Abdul Kareem. In his case, the *ṭhumarī* temperament did affect his approach to *khayāla* performance. To this extent, Ghulam Ali Khan could be considered the forerunner of the romanticist brigade, which redefined *khayāla* vocalism in later years.

After him, Kumar Gandharva crystallized the rebellion comprehensively — through a libertarian approach to *khayāla* architecture, as well as an intense emotionalization of its sculpture and ornamentation, drawing freely on the folk idiom for inspiration. Kishori Amonkar stuck fastidiously to the formalism of *khayāla*, but deviated from its aloofness — moving categorically towards sentimentalism in sculpture and ornamentation. Jasraj moved, though not radically, in the romanticist direction on all fronts — architecture, sculpture, and ornamentation, often blurring the dividing line between the *khayāla* and the *ṭhumarī* genres.

When the distance of time permits the Kishori-Jasraj-Kumar directions to be fully understood, Bade Ghulam Ali may be seen as the titan who paved the way for them (Written : July 2003).

6.3

Bade Fateh Ali Khan

Patiala Across the Western Border

AFTER Partition, Patiala, the Princely State, remained in India. But, Patiala, the *gharānā* of vocalists, got divided. The part of the *gharānā*, that migrated to Lahore, produced Bade Fateh Ali Khan (b. 1935), now the last significant *khayāla* vocalist of the lineage. He is the younger of the singing duo Amanat Ali-Fateh Ali, who enjoyed immense prestige and success in Pakistan as well as India, until the demise of Amanat Ali (1932-74). Amanat Ali-Fateh Ali became celebrities while still in their childhood in undivided India, and achieved their highest official recognition in Pakistan, when the President conferred on them the Pride of Performance Medal (1969). The Baḍe (elder) prefix got attached to Fateh Ali's name after younger Pakistani musicians with similar names started making waves with an entirely different genre of music.

Fateh Ali and his late brother were trained by their father, Akhtar Hussain, a distinguished vocalist in the patronage of the Princely State of Patiala in undivided India. Their grandfather, Ali Baksh, also served the same court, and was a co-founder of the Patiala Gharānā. The prodigious talent of Amanat Ali-Fateh Ali received early encouragement at the Patiala court. They had a glorious debut in 1945 at Lahore, sponsored by the influential connoisseur and patron, Jeevanlal Mattoo. Life changed dramatically for the budding stars when India was partitioned in 1947, and their family migrated to Pakistan, to grapple with destitution. While still in their teens, Amanat Ali-Fateh Ali returned to thunderous applause at the All-Bengal Music Conference in Calcutta in 1949, never to look back. They toured the major Indian cities several times thereafter and performed together for over two decades to claim their rightful place amongst the foremost vocalists of the subcontinent.

After the demise of Amanat Ali, Fateh Ali resumed performing first with his son, Amjad Fateh Ali, to later replace him with either of his nephews Amjad Amanat Ali or Asad Amanat Ali. Though trained also in the mediaeval *dhrupada* genre, the uncle-nephew duo restricts its repertoire to the modern mainstream genre, *khayāla*, and the romanticist genres, *ṭhumarī*, *dādarā*, and *ghaẓala*. With a nephew in a supporting role, Fateh Ali Khan has performed widely in Europe, North America, the Middle East, and South Asia, and released several recordings.

The evolution of Fateh Ali Khan, a soloist since 1974, coincides with a period of general decline in the stylistic continuity of all *gharānā*-based music in response to socio-cultural changes on both sides of the India-Pakistan border. Interpreting his style is, therefore, a threefold task. The first reference point has to be the vocalism of Bade Ghulam Ali Khan as a familiar experience to Indian connoisseurs. The second reference point has to be the music of Amanat Ali-Fateh Ali as duet artists. Finally, considering the complexities of the cultural process, we also need to account for musical influences from outside the Patiala Gharānā, and extra-musical realities.

The Music of Amanat Ali-Fateh Ali Duo

Considering the many factors that could have militated against similarity, available recordings suggest that the music of the Amanat Ali-Fateh Ali duo was surprisingly similar to that of Bade Ghulam Ali. We cannot, of course, discount the possibility that Amanat Ali and Fateh Ali studied and even consciously followed the style of Bade Ghulam Ali Khan, who was their senior by almost 30 years. But, even this would have been possible only if they shared the same stylistic legacy and quality of training.

I could obtain, for study, four recordings of Amanat Ali and Fateh Ali Khan in duet performance. The sample consists of *madhya-laya tarānā*s in Jaijaivantī (*tīnatāla*) and Śaṅkara (*jhapatāla*) and *khayāla* renditions in Bilāsakhanī Toḍī and Hem Kalyāṇa. The age and acoustic condition of the available recordings do not permit me to separately decipher the musical inclinations of the two brothers.

Though on limited evidence, the two streams of Patiala exhibit major similarities and only minor differences. The preference for *madhya-laya tarānā*s in different *tāla*s appears to be common to both streams. The Pakistani duo's handling of Bilāsakhanī Toḍī is controversial. Bade Ghulam Ali is not known to have performed this *rāga*. The appearance of a rare *rāga* like Hema Kalyāṇa in the Amanat Ali-Fateh Ali sample suggests their training could have given them a larger *rāga* repertoire. Aficionados of Pakistani music confirm this view.

It appears that Amanat Ali and Fateh Ali were submitted

to the same kind of voice training as was Bade Ghulam Ali. This voice culture aims to produce a pyramidal voice quality, broad and heavy in the lower registers and narrow and lithe in the upper. The melodic strategies of Bade Ghulam Ali and Amanat Ali-Fateh Ali are also very similar. Their *bola-ālāpa* has the same Gwalior-style melodic progression, with moderate ornamentation. They deploy *saragama* in the *bola-ālāpa*, as well as in medium-density relievers inserted into the *tāna*s movement. Their *tāna* patterns also tend to be similar, generously laced with strings of delicate ultra-high density wriggling phrases in *ākāra* articulation. Based on Fateh Ali Khan's description in a recorded interview, it would appear that these *tāna*s were the speciality of Tanras Khan. Though musicians of other *gharānā*s have tried, only Bade Ghulam Ali — besides Amanat Ali-Fateh Ali — has vocalized these *tāna*s musically. Amongst instruments, only the *sāraṅgī* can deliver them effectively. The Patiala duo also deploys such *tāna*s in *tihāī* formation, much as Bade Ghulam Ali did.

Like their Patiala senior, again, the Ali Brothers use *tihāī*s sparingly and in an unobtrusive manner. Mischievous *ṭappā*-style phrases, evident in Bade Ghulam Ali's music, are absent from the sample recordings I have of Amanat Ali-Fateh Ali. Their melodic strategy, with frequent use of broad melodic sweeps and congruent phrases juxtaposed in different regions of the melodic canvas, has a dramatic element similar to that of Bade Ghulam Ali.

The representatives of the two Patiala streams differ primarily in their compliance with the architectural conventions of the *khayāla* genre, and the handling of high-density melody (*tāna*s). Amanat Ali-Fateh Ali tend to organize their material formally, though imaginatively, in linear progression of density and complexity. Bade Ghulam Ali, as everyone knows, was a frequent defaulter on architectural norms.

In the handling of high-density melody, Amanat Ali-Fateh

Ali exhibit a penchant for forceful vocalization of *tāna*s combined with near-staccato intonation in multiple stroke patterns of the Agra Gharānā variety. Bade Ghulam Ali did use them occasionally, but always with rippling *gamaka*s rather than staccato intonation. Compared to the sparkling fluidity of Bade Ghulam Ali's *tāna*s, these forcefully intoned, multiple-stroke *tāna*s come through as displays of vocal acrobatics. According to Fateh Ali Khan, these *tāna*s were acquired by his *gharānā* from Haddu Khan of Gwalior.

It is interesting that both streams of Patiala have had an intimate involvement with light and semi-classical (romanticist) genres. Amanat Ali (more than Fateh Ali) became popular as a film playback and *ghaẓala* singer in Pakistan. In these genres, Amanat Ali is known to have recorded some songs that made him a household name in his country. Bade Ghulam Ali, on the other hand, carved a place in the history of the *ṭhumarī* genre, and also rendered a few memorable film songs. Despite these involvements, their *khayāla* vocalism appears to have preserved the overall aloofness of the traditional *khayāla*. In this department, Amanat Ali-Fateh Ali may have been marginally more consistent and successful than Bade Ghulam Ali.

The differences between the Pakistani Patiala duo and Bade Ghulam Ali styles with respect to *khayāla* vocalism can easily be explained by the different qualities and capabilities of their voices, their respective musical temperaments, and by the aesthetic values of the constituencies they addressed. Fundamentally, the music of the two Patiala streams, even when separated by a distance of almost two generations, is similar enough to have been the product of training under the same *guru*.

Fateh Ali Khan — Significant Influences

Surprisingly, the music of Fateh Ali Khan, performing solo towards the end of the 20th century, bears only a remote resemblance to the combined music of the duo. This observation requires exploration of probable causes, although we may never be able to ascertain their relative significance in the evolution of Fateh Ali Khan, the soloist.

The most obvious change is in the context. According to knowledgeable sources, Amanat Ali and Fateh Ali were approximately 50/50 contributors to their combined music. Even if this is so, each partner contributes to a duet according to his distinctive competence and temperament. In the solo context, Fateh Ali Khan's music is without the lead/supporting inputs of Amanat Ali Khan. The totality of his musicianship has been on display for over two decades. What we hear today is the product of the interaction beween his own musical inclinations, and the social, political and cultural environment of Pakistan.

Undivided India had several centers of Hindustani music, each with its own stylistic bias, coloured partially by the regional-ethnic musical culture. When India was divided, Lahore in Punjab was the only major centre of classical music to go to Pakistan. Geographically and historically, Punjab has borne the brunt of a large number of invasions from the north-west, and hence evolved a uniquely martial culture. This culture is manifested in the immense vigour, and heightened rhythmicality of its musical and choreographic expressions. Hindustani music in Pakistan acquired these features from the regional culture.

West Punjab, which went to Pakistan, also had a high concentration of the populace well versed in Urdu. Being denied stable access to a market of subcontinental dimensions, Pakistan's classical vocalists found it possible and attractive to diversify their repertoire to cover *ghaẓala*s. This apparently had stylistic implications for *khayāla* vocalism in Pakistan.

The various styles of *khayāla* in Pakistan also interacted

inevitably between themselves, and also with the *khayāla* mainstream across the Indo-Pak border. Within Pakistan, the most prominent and influential *khayāla* vocalists shaping public tastes in Fateh Ali's youth were Roshanara Begum, and the singing duo, Salamat Ali-Nazakat Ali.

Rohanara Begum was the niece and disciple of Abdul Kareem Khan, founder of the Kairana Gharānā. Subsequent to India's Partition, her family opted for Pakistani nationality. Until her demise in 1982, she remained, by far, the tallest Pakistani *khayāla* vocalist, and is regarded amongst the 20th-century legends of Hindustani vocalism. Salamat Ali-Nazakat Ali were descendents of the Punjab-based Shyam Chaurasia *gharānā*, a lesser known lineage of *dhrupada* singers. Drawing from various stylistic sources, including Patiala vocalism, the Salamat-Nazakat duo created a tremendous impact with an athletic *khayāla* style.

Across the border, in India, the dominant styles of *khayāla* vocalism through the 1960s and early 1970s were orthodox Kairana, Patiala represented by Bade Ghulam Ali, and a blend of Kairana and Bhendi Bazaar (effectively neo-Kairana) represented by Ameer Khan. Although the towering presence of Faiyyaz Khan of Agra Gharānā had departed by this time, aggressive Agra stylistics remained in circulation through the influence of Yunus Hussain, Latafat Hussain and Sharafat Hussain. Once recordings of near-concert length duration were available on long-playing records and later audio-cassettes, the musical border between the two countries — never as zealously guarded as the cartographic border — became even more porous. This subcontinental reality evidently influenced Amanat Ali and Fateh Ali, as it certainly influenced other musicians from Pakistan.

Another significant factor was the timing of Fateh Ali Khan's emergence as a soloist. It coincides with the emergence of post-Independence generation as a significant proportion of Pakistani audiences. The cultural gap between the pre-Independence and post-Independence generations has been wide in both countries. It could have been wider in Pakistan because of a much greater disruption of life suffered by its people during Partition, and continuous political instability thereafter. The cumulative impact of the socio-political experience could have shaped a more confused post-Independence Pakistani generation than India's, driving the classical arts in Pakistan more categorically towards exhibitionism and populism than they have done across its eastern border.

Such tendencies could only be magnified by the fact that, for most of its history, Pakistan has been under military dictatorships, struggling to evolve as a democratic country, while contending with intermittent interference from a retrogressive clergy. This would expectedly result in a confused cultural environment. India, on the other hand, has been a stable democracy with a pluralistic political-social-economic-cultural structure, and a state that has maintained a broadly pro-culture stance. Indian artistes, addressing a much larger and diverse audience, have had the choice between elitism, populism, and some optimization in between — a luxury probably not available to artistes in Pakistan.

Collectively, these factors might explain the ascent of Fateh Ali Khan, a musician of formidable calibre, to towering stature in contemporary Pakistan, accompanied by a substantial following outside.

Fateh Ali Khan — The Soloist

I make my observations based on a study of one CD recorded by Fateh Ali Khan for India Archive Music, New York, at the age of 65 featuring *khayāla*s in Śaba Kalyāṇa (an Islamized name for the Carnatic *rāga* Janasammohinī), and Bairāgī Bhairava. I have also had the benefit of listening to an interview he gave to the producer of the above CD in which he discusses his stylistic legacy and its sources.

If Bade Ghulam Ali Khan's music made Deshpande hesitant about classifying it in his conceptual framework, Fateh Ali Khan poses almost as great a challenge to the critic. His music shows a far greater presence of the rhythmic element than did that of Bade Ghulam Ali Khan, but far less prominent than in Agra. On the other hand, his music exhibits a melodic sensibility almost of the Kairana variety. He thus emerges stronger on rhythm than Bạde Ghulam Ali, while also veering towards Kairana on melody. His music probably represents a third variety of balance between melodic and rhythmic orientations. It is not a simple blend of the Gwalior variety, nor a subtle and oblique blend of the Jaipur–Atrauli variety. It is, in some ways, a mechanistic weld, with the seams prominently exposed.

Bade Ghulam Ali Khan breached the formalism of *khayāla* without quite abandoning its aloofness. Fateh Ali Khan is also a deviant, but with the opposite bias. He has retained the formalism of the *khayāla* genre, but bid farewell to its aloofness.

There is a tendency in his music to combine vocalization, intonation, and articulation approaches from different genres of Hindustani music. His prefatory *auchara* relies considerably on the profound stylistics of Dagar style *dhrupada*, which is a part of the Aliya-Fattu/Patiala legacy. The architecture of his presentation is an imaginative, rather than fastidious, interpretation of the *khayāla* as practised in the Patiala and Kairana Gharānās, characterized by the absence of a distinct medium-density (*bola-laya*) movement. His approach to sculpture is greatly inspired by *khayāla* vocalism of the Kairana Gharānā. His approach to ornamentation goes beyond the ornate quality achieved by latter-day Kairana vocalists and virtually merges with stylistics of the *ghaẓala* genre.

Ghaẓala stylistics exhibit a prominent presence in his vocalism primarily due to the autonomous status he imparts to the poetic element, and the tender as well as dramatic manner in which he deploys it to shape the melodic element. This *ghaẓala*-inspired flavour communicates the earnest passion of a lover, rather than the self-seeking seductiveness and artifice of a courtesan characteristic of the *ṭhumarī* genre.

The aesthetic experience of the *ghaẓala* so totally pervades Fateh Ali Khan's *khayāla* renditions in low density movements that even when he uses a potentially intrusive device like a *mukhaḍā-tihāī*, it comes through with a caressing gentleness. In addition to the vocal genres, Fateh Ali brings to his music — especially in the handling of *saragama* in rhythmic play — what Deshpande[1] has described as a choreographic quality evident in the style of the Bhendi Bazaar maestro, Aman Ali Khan.

Fateh Ali Khan's *ālāpa* in the *vilambita khayāla* has a strong Kairana flavour. He tends to take up short melodic spans for improvisation, playing around with various permutations and combinations of the *svaras*, while also varying their durational and acoustic weightage. This approach is derived from the traditional Merukhaṇḍa (Meru = mountain + Khaṇḍa = fragment) pedagogical system in Hindustani music. In recent times, Roshanara Begum, and Ameer Khan, both of whom wielded great influence during Fateh Ali Khan's youth, achieved the most successful aesthetic interpretation of this cerebral device. For the first time, Fateh Ali Khan drives this abstract melodic experience into an explicitly romanticist, and *ghaẓala*-like, poetic-melodic communication.

It is ironic that Fateh Ali Khan, who treats the poetry in *khayāla* with as much respect as in a *ghaẓala*, does not appear to enunciate the entire lyrics of the *bandiśa* in his renditions. In his *vilambita* and *druta khayālas*, as well as in the *tarānā*, Fateh Ali

Khan skips the *antarā* totally. Even the melodic form of the *antarā*, with a categorical ascent to the upper-*sa* is rendered incidentally, rather than with its conventional deliberateness. Treating the *antarā* as a redundant poetic-melodic movement, and the truncation of the *bandiśa*, are recent tendencies in Indian *khayāla* vocalism, which Fateh Ali Khan also appears to find attractive.

The *saragama* form is another significant feature of Fateh Ali Khan's vocalism. Like Bade Ghulam Alam Ali Khan and Kairana vocalists, he uses it sparingly in the *ālāpa*. But, like Ameer Khan and Faiyyaz Ahmed-Niyaz Ahmed, he deploys it predominantly in medium and medium-to-high density *tāna*s. Unlike the others, he imparts a distinct rhythmicality to this deployment, often using it to stunning effect. His *saragama tihāī*s ending one beat before the *sama*, but in a melodic region far away from the *sama*, are typical examples of this usage. These dramatic effects with a choreographic suggestion were reportedly characteristic of Aman Ali Khan of the Bhendi Bazaar Gharānā.

The melodic structuring of Fateh Ali's *tāna*s exhibits a rich imagination. The patent Patiala/Bade Ghulam Ali *tāna*s of wriggling high density melody (Tanras Khan variety, according to Fateh Ali Khan) are now missing from his inventory. Some traces of familiar Patiala patterns are still evident — cascading series of descending phrases, each starting from a different point in the melodic canvas, but culminating at the same *svara*. But, the charming quality of these *tāna* clusters has been overshadowed by complex and forcefully vocalized *laḍī-guthāva* patterns in short melodic spans woven into chains (a legacy of Mubarak Ali Khan, as reported by Fateh Ali Khan), and multiple-stroke *tāna*s with staccato intonation (reportedly a legacy of Haddu Khan of Gwalior).

These features were already evident during his days as a duet performer with Amanat Ali. They now dominate his *tāna*s movement. In their aural impact, Fateh Ali Khan's *tāna*s now communicate a combination of formidable virtuosity and awesome power, accompanied by some loss of musicality. In the last 50 years, only the Pakistani singing duo, Salamat Ali and Nazakat Ali of Shyam Chaurasia Gharānā have unleashed so cyclonic a *tāna* experience upon their audiences. The phenomenon can probably be attributed to the uniqueness of the West Punjab aesthetic sensibility, and to the brazen exhibitionism and populism towards which Pakistani musicians have drifted in the post-independence era.

Conceptually, the *ghazala*-like deliberateness and caressing quality of Fateh Ali Khan's *vilambita ālāpa* is difficult to reconcile with the harsher-than-Agra virtuosity of his *tāna*. For the cultivated Indian listener, it is equally difficult to conceive of satisfying music arising from a blend of Patiala, Kairana, Bhendi Bazaar, Shyam Chaurasia, and Agra stylistics. Yet, it is all there in Fateh Ali Khan's music. And, it holds together by the force of exceptional musicianship (Written : November 2003).

Annexure

An Introduction to Khayāla

THE *khayāla* is the dominant genre of mainstream vocal music today, and has been so for over two centuries. Because of the primacy of vocal music in the Hindustani tradition, it has also had a considerable influence on the evolution of instrumental music. The word *khayāla* is of Perso-Arabic origin, and has been variously translated as idea, imagination, subjectivity, individuality, and impression. All these connotations are consistent with the character of the genre. Bhatkhande suggests that the term may have originally denoted licentiousness. (*Bhatkhande Saṅgīta Śāstra*, vol. I, 5th edn., 1981). This suggestion has some merit considering the vast creative freedom accorded to the musician by the *khayāla*, compared to the highly disciplined formalism of its medieval predecessor, *dhrupada*/ *dhamāra*.

> Among all Hindustani vocal genres, the *khayāla* provides its performers the greatest opportunity and challenge to display the depth and breadth of musical knowledge and skills. Its essence lies in the manner in which artistes take the characteristics that distinguish *khayāla* as a genre, make those choices that lie within their group traditions, summon their own creative individuality, and create a unique *khayāla* at each performance. (Bonnie C. Wade, 1st edn., 1984).

The *khayāla* genre is distinguished from other major genres of Hindustani vocal music — *dhrupada* and *ṭhumarī* — by a linear (progressive) intensification of melodic and rhythmic densities and complexities, and a cyclical treatment of melodic and rhythmic elements within the central linearity of rendition.

The Plastic Arts Metaphor Applied to Khayāla Music

Every artefact can be seen to have an architectural element, a sculptural element, and an ornamentational element. The architectural element relates to the structural and functional relationship between the parts. The sculptural element deals with the contours it defines from a reasonable distance. The ornamentational element concerns itself with features that endear the artefact to the viewer from close quarters. Architecture deals with the manner in which an artefact functions; sculpture, with the way it looks; and ornamentation, with the way it pleases.

In general, one might say that all music has elements of architecture, sculpture and ornamentation, with their relative weight varying between the different genres, and even between the different styles/*gharānā*s within the same genre. Using this framework for understanding the principal genres in Hindustani music, *dhrupada* can be described as architecture-dominant; *khayāla* can be described as sculpture-dominant; and *ṭhumarī* can be described as ornamentation-dominant.

Interestingly, however, what differentiates the *khayāla* genre from *dhrupada* and *ṭhumarī* most conclusively is its architecture. The architecture of *khayāla* vocalism is characterized by an end-to-end linearity, shaped by a progressive intensification of tonal and beat densities and complexities in its rendition. It is probably this unidirectional flow of musical energies that enables the artistic effort to focus itself sharply on the melodic effort, and thus to define *khayāla* as a sculpture-dominant genre.

This linearity of architecture distinguishes *khayāla* from both *dhrupada* and *ṭhumarī*. But, the difference between sculpture and ornamentation being one only of perspective, the sculpture-dominant character of *khayāla* still needed protection from a drift towards the ornamentation characteristic of the *ṭhumarī* genre. It is by this logic of differentiation between the genres that *khayāla* evolved as a genre unidirectional in its architecture, elaborate in its approach to sculpture, and judicious in its deployment of ornamentation.

History and Evolution

The legendary thirteenth-century poet-musician Amir Khusrau is popularly credited with the invention of the *khayāla* form. This belief is conceptually fallacious because no individual can be credited with the creation of a genre. This attribution of even an initiating role to Amir Khusrau is contentious. The architecture and stylistics of the *khayāla* form apparently pre-date Khusrau by several centuries. Thakur Jaydeva Singh traces the *khayāla* form to the *rūpakālāpti* form within the *sādhāraṇī śailī* of vocal music in practice in the 8th/9th centuries. He credits Amir Khusrau, however, with giving it a Perso-Arabic name, introducing it to the patronage of Muslim rulers, and encouraging its practice amongst singers of *qawwālī*, a form of Sūfī religious music. (*Nibandha Saṅgīta*, ed. L.N. Garg, 2nd edn., 1989).

The *khayāla* represents a fusion of older Indian musical traditions with Perso-Arabic influences starting from the 12th/13th centuries. The genre acquired some stature under the patronage of the Sharqui dynasty of Jaunpur (15th century), and attained maturity and sophistication under the patronage of Emperor Mohammad Shah of Delhi (18th century). Since then, the *khayāla* has eclipsed the medieval *dhrupada/dhamāra* genre, and replaced it as the predominant genre of mainstream vocal music.

Sultan Hussain Sharqui (r. 1458-99) of Jaunpur encouraged the evolution of a *kalāvantī khayāla* based on musical forms prevalent in his region as distinct from the *khayāla* inspired by the *qawwālī* encouraged by Amir Khusrau (1253-1325). The immortal composer Niamat Khan "Sadarang" in the employ of Emperor Muhammad Shah, reportedly composed *khayālas* as a challenge to the supremacy of *dhrupada/dhamāra*, by recasting poetic and melodic material drawn from the medieval genre.

The medieval *dhrupada/dhamāra*, which dominated the mainstream between the 13th and the 18th centuries, and the modern *khayāla* genre, which overtook it in later years, have thus been contemporary rivals for almost the entire period of *dhrupada/dhamāra* dominance. Ashok Ranade, the eminent musicologist, has argued that, neither of the two can be described as having been derived from the other, though both would have influenced each other to some degree. *Dhrupada/ Dhamāra* evolved as a highly formal and disciplined art form with a tendency towards being a predominantly pre-composed genre of music. In a parallel development, the *khayāla* evolved as a predominantly improvized form, and a vehicle for individual creativity. (*Journal of the Indian Musicological Society*, 1999).

The Gharānās of Khayāla Music

The century preceding India's Independence, which witnessed the flowering of the *khayāla* genre in various hues and fragrances, is often described as the Golden Age of Hindustani music (V.H. Deshpande, *Indian Musical Traditions*, 2nd edn., 1987). Its foundations were laid in the sunset years of the Mogul Empire (mid-eighteenth century), when a vast resource of musicianship emigrated from Delhi and its environs towards smaller principalities in search of patronage. Several of these feudal principalities, protected by India's new British rulers, became patrons to lineages of musicians (*gharānā*s), which cultivated distinctive musical styles within the broad framework of the *khayāla* genre.

For a variety of reasons, *gharānā*s of *khayāla* music have come to acquire their names either from the principalities where they were cultivated, or from the name of a towering vocalist, who is recognized as the founder of the distinctive style of *khayāla* music.

Vamanrao Deshpande recognizes six distinct *gharānās* as stylistic lineages: Agra, Gwalior, Jaipur–Atrauli, Patiala, Indore, and Kairana. (V.H. Deshpande, ibid.). Prof. Bonnie Wade recognizes six significant *gharānās* of *khayāla* music. They are Gwalior, Agra, Sahaswan/Rampur, Alladiya Khan (also known as Jaipur–Atrauli), Kairana, and Patiala. She considers the Indore/Bhendi Bazar *gharānā* too close to Kairana to qualify as an independent *gharānā*. She, however, acknowledges its principal exponent, Ustad Ameer Khan, as being amongst the towering individuals whose music she does not identify with any of the major *gharānās*. (Bonnie C. Wade, 1984).

Deshpande (ibid.) cautions enlightened opinion against glorifying the *gharānā* system and placing an undue premium on stylistic conformity amongst its followers. He reminds us that the greatest vocalists in recent memory, almost without exception, acquired their art from more than one *gharānā* or *guru*, and openly credited their accomplishments to the multiplicity of influences.

Deshpande (ibid.) offers a conceptual framework for the aesthetic classification of the *gharānās* of *khayāla* music. He classifies *gharānā* styles on a continuum defined by rhythmic orientation and melodic orientation as the two polarities. Amongst the *gharānās* considered by him, he places Agra at the rhythmic orientation polarity, and Kairana at the melodic orientation polarity. Placing them at the exact mid-point of the continuum, he regards Alladiya (Jaipur–Atrauli) as a complex fusion, and Gwalior as a simple fusion of the two orientations. Patiala is placed towards the melodic orientation pole, but considerably short of Kairana. The Indore/Bhendi Bazar Gharānā of Ameer Khan falls between Patiala and Kairana, close to the melodic orientation pole.

With specific reference to the two polarities, Agra at the

rhythm-oriented end, and Kairana at the melody-oriented end, Deshpande (ibid.) observes that rhythm is the principle of motion, while melody is the principle of repose. The bias towards the rhythm end indicates animation, playfulness, and dynamism, while a bias towards the melody end is soothing, tranquillizing, and even depressing.

Prof. Wade (ibid. 1984) adopts a more elaborate framework for comparing *gharānā* stylistics. The dimensions she lists are:

(a) Voice-vocal technique, voice quality, range, ornamentation.

(b) Preferences with respect to *rāga*s.

(c) Preferences with respect to *tāla*s.

(d) Preferences with respect to compositions.

(e) Preferences with respect to performance tempo, and its acceleration.

(f) Balance between rhythmic and melodic elements.

(g) Structure of slow tempo *khayāla* presentation.

(h) Preferences with respect to improvisatory movements and types of articulation.

(i) Strategies with respect to slow tempo and medium/fast tempo *khayāla* presentations.

Although these dimensions have been proposed as a differentiator between the musical styles of the different *gharānā*s, they are equally applicable as a framework for analysing *khayāla* music at an individual level.

The Ensemble for Khayāla Performance

The minimum ensemble for a *khayāla* performance consists of a drone (*tānapūrā*) and a percussion accompaniment (*tabalā*). A majority of concert performers today use two *tānapūrā*s, along with a melodic accompaniment provided either by a *sāraṅgī* or a harmonium player. In addition to this standard ensemble, some vocalists accompany themselves on a *svara-maṇḍala*, a harp belonging to the box-polychord family. Ustad Bade Ghulam Ali Khan was the first significant vocalist to use the *svara-maṇḍala*. Several eminent vocalists, notably, Kishori Amonkar and Jasraj, have followed his example.

The *tānapūrā*, *svara-maṇḍala*, and the melodic accompaniment — *sāraṅgī* or harmonium — perform a very significant and complex role in *khayāla* music. Their role relates as much to aiding the music-making processes of the vocalist, as to enriching the totality of the musical experience for audiences.

The Format of Khayāla Presentation

The *khayāla* genre subsumes three categories of compositional format: the slow tempo *baḍā khayāla* (major *khayāla*) and the medium-to-fast tempo *choṭā khayāla* (minor *khayāla*), both based on a piece of poetry, and *tarānā*, a medium-to-fast tempo compositional form structured around meaningless sound syllables borrowed mainly from the stroke patterns of the plucked instruments (e.g. *da, ra, dir*) and beat patterns of percussion (e.g. *dha, tirkit, dhin*).

The *khayāla* genre permits the musician considerable freedom in structuring his presentation. Different *gharānā*s, and even individual musicians, have their own predilections in terms of the presentation format. Contemporary *khayāla* presentation does, however, tend to follow one of the two principal presentation formats.

The most common format in *khayāla* presentation is a *baḍā khayāla* in *ekatāla* (12 beats), or *jhūmara* (14 beats) or *tilvāḍā* (16 beats) or *tīnatāla* (16 beats) followed by a *choṭā khayāla* in *tīnatāla* (16 beats) or *ekatāla* (12 beats). In such a presentation, the rendition almost always begins with either an *auchara*, a brief free-flowing introduction of the *rāga*'s melodic personality, or merely a *rāga-vākya*, a couple of phrases seeking to achieve no more than identification of the *rāga*. An *auchara-baḍā khayāla-choṭā khayāla* presentation can last 35-45 mts. In rare cases, the vocalist might add a third composition, a *tarānā* in the same *rāga*. This extension could consume an additional 10 to 15 mts, bringing the total duration to about an hour.

In a less common format, deployed mainly by Agra and Gwalior vocalists, the slow tempo *baḍā khayāla* is omitted. In its place, the vocalist presents an elaborate, three/four tiered, *dhrupada*-style *ālāpa* without percussion accompaniment, followed by a *choṭā khayāla*. In such cases, the *khayāla* rendition generally begins at a medium tempo, and accelerates gradually to reach the normal, brisk, *choṭā khayāla* tempo. It is rare for such presentations to end with a *tarānā*.

An even less common format in contemporary *khayāla* presentation is a single medium tempo composition, normally without an elaborate *ālāpa*. The composition is generally in *rūpaka tāla* (7 beats) or *jhapatāla* (10 beats), and sometimes *tīnatāla* (16 beats). The rendition is generally maintained at the same tempo throughout, with only marginal acceleration, if at all. This format is generally avoided for the first or main *khayāla* rendition in a concert. This type of medium tempo *khayāla* presentation rarely lasts more than 20 minutes.

Melodic Expressions in the Khayāla Genre

Melodic execution in Hindustani music, essentially, avoids abruptness in intervallic transitions. This feature has been described as "conjunct" melody, as distinct from the "disjunct" melody found in Western music. In medium and high *svara*-density expressions, as also for the expression of explicit rhythmicality, staccato expressions are, however, frequently encountered.

The theory of music performance describes at least ten

forms of melodic execution/intervallic transitions (*Saṅgīta Kalādhara*, Dahyalal Shivram, 2nd edn., 1938). Other texts have larger inventories. The definitions from the texts are imprecise, and vary from text to text. The categories of melodic contours encountered in contemporary *khayāla* rendition would, however, outnumber all inventories considered together.

The principal categories of intervallic transition/phrasing/melodic expressions are:

(1) ***Mīṇḍa***: The *mīṇḍa* is the basic form of intervallic transition in *khayāla* music. It involves a melodically continuous dragging of one *svara* to another, touching all the microtones along the path without allowing any of them to be perceived as having been explicitly intoned.

(2) ***Kan***: The words means "fraction." When an intervallic transition between *svara*s involves a fractional use of the first *svara*, it is called a *kan*. A generous use of the *kan* is considered more proper in the semi-classical *ṭhumarī* renditions than in *khayāla*.

(3) ***Murkī***: Like the *kan*, the *murkī*, too, is used more generously in the *ṭhumarī* genre. The *murkī* involves the execution of a phrase normally using at least three *svara*s in brisk, wrap-around, jerky expression, as in *pā-mā^-dhā-pā*. The *khayāla* generally deploys single-loop *murkī*s. Multiple-loop *murkī*s are used in the *ṭhumarī* genre.

(4) ***Gītakīrī***: The brisk and explicit intonation of three or more adjacent *svara*s, whether in ascent or descent, without a jerk or wrap-around melodic motion, is called a *gītakīrī*.

(5) ***Khaṭkā***: The word means "a jerk." This melodic expression is generally used for a transition between *svara*s at least two/three *svara*s apart, and in descending transition. The expression drops from the higher *svara*

to the lower *svara*, with a jerk. This is specially useful in *rāga*s such as Gaud Sarang (Descent: *sā'-pā-mā-gā/re-gā-re-mā-gā-pā-re-sā.* The *sā-pā* and *pā-re* transitions in Gaud Sarang require the *khaṭakā* expression almost as mandatory for *rāga* identification.

(6). ***Gamaka***: The *gamaka* expression arises from a repetition of the same *svara* at a medium-to-high *svara* density. Taking the support of the lower *svara* without its explicit intonation, the musician repeatedly hammers the target *svara* to create the *gamaka* expression.

(7). ***Jamajama***: This expression also uses two adjacent *svara*s with one being emphasized by repetition, and differs from the *gamaka* in that the *jamajama* explicitly intones both the adjacent *svara*s, as in *gā-mā-mā/gā-mā-mā/gā-pā-pā/mā-pā-pā.*

These categories of melodic expression define the sculptural and ornamentational facets of a vocal recital. *Gharānā*s and individual musicians differ in their preferences in this regard. These preferences, collectively, constitute a major part of the "stylistics" of *khayāla* music.

The Poetic Element in Khayāla Vocalism

The role of the poetic element in *khayāla* has been a subject of some bewilderment as well as debate. The song texts of *khayāla bandiśe*s are primarily in Braj *bhāṣā*, a dialect of Hindı spoken in and around Mathura. *Khayāla*s are, however, sung by musicians and heard by audiences from all parts of the country, most of whom do not understand the literal meaning of the poetry. Despite this, *khayāla* lyrics in other languages have not been as popular, and Braj *bhāṣā* verses have not been translated into either mainstream or regional languages. Moreover, a large number of vocalists, including the greatest, have been casual about the articulation of the poetic element, treating it almost on par with the meaningless consonants of a *tarānā*. And, yet, there is no general revolt in the music world against the apparent assault on the integrity of the *bandiśa*, or on the listener's rights. These facts do not reflect a blind adherence to tradition as much as they acknowledge the role of the poetic element in *khayāla* vocalism.

Deshpande (ibid., 1987) has argued, persuasively, that the art of singing could achieve its highest level of perfection in *khayāla* because, in this genre, the poetic element surrendered its literary function to its musical function. This musical function has several dimensions. The phonetic and syntactical structure of the poetry imparts concrete form to the *bandiśa*, independently of its semantic significance. It enhances the musical value of the *bandiśa* by adding a psycho-phonetic dimension to the psycho-acoustics of the melodic-rhythmic shell. The semantic significance of the poetry activates the auto-suggestive process of the musician, helping the music to explore the emotional content of the *rāga*.

Deshpande's argument is supported by the fact that the twentieth century has witnessed equally great *khayāla* music from vocalists who treated *khayāla* verses rather casually, and those who systematically exploited its semantic significance. *Khayāla* gives the individual musician the choice. No wonder *khayāla* lyrics are written by musicians rather than poets, and rarely command respect as poetry.

Articulation in Khayāla Music

The *khayāla* genre deploys three categories of articulation:

(a) ***Bola***: The poetic form, representing a vast range of themes, which holds together the melodic and rhythmic elements in the composition (*bandiśa / cīẓa*).

(b) ***Saragama***: The use of solfa symbols as textural consonants in the improvisatory movements.

(c) ***Ākāra***: The vowel *ā*, used in the improvisatory

movements.

The *tarānā* does not use the poetic form in the main body of the *bandiśa/cīẓa*. However, there exists a tradition of inserting Persian and Urdu *rubāīs* (verses) into the *tarānā* as a relief from the otherwise meaningless consonants constituting the phonetic element of the form. In the improvisatory movements, the *tarānā* form is permitted the use of *saragamas* as well as *ākāra*.

These three forms of articulation have collective, as well as individual, roles in the rendition of *khayāla* compositions. At the purely phonetic level, they provide the musician with three distinct textural devices. The poetic form is a balanced and unpredictable mix of vowel and consonant articulations, generally with a bias towards the softer consonants. The *saragama* device uses only consonants, and the range is limited to seven. The *ākāra* has only one vowel, though individual styles can occasionally vary the articulation slightly. Collectively, the three devices contribute to the textural richness of the phonetic component of *khayāla* music.

The three forms of articulation also represent three different levels of abstraction in terms of meaning. The poetic form represents explicit meaning, which interacts, potentially, with the melodic element of the phrasing in the expression of its emotional content. The *saragama* represents musical meaning, by virtue of direct correspondence between the intonation and the articulation. The *ākāra*, being a vowel phonetic, is totally abstract, with the meaning being provided only by the melodic contours of the intonation.

The deployment of the three forms of articulation is guided by aesthetic considerations, and by the stylistic predilections of individual *gharānās* and vocalists. The poetic form is, for instance, used predominantly in slow and medium *svara* density movements. This is because high-density melodic expressions can jeopardize the integrity of the poetic form and the intelligibility of explicit meaning.

The *saragama* is used predominantly in medium density movements. In such movements, it provides a textural option for the poetic form, and greater freedom for melodic-rhythmic improvization than the poetic form will permit. It tends not to be used in very high density melodic movements because consonants militate against high-frequency articulation, in addition to being less pleasing than vowels.

The *ākāra* articulation is the most versatile, but is also the most demanding in terms of lung-power, and is therefore used selectively. Being a vowel form, it is most useful in movements where the melody is not required to express an explicit rhythmicality. Such movements are the low *svara* density *ālāpa*, which is free from explicit rhythmicality, and the high density *tāna*s where the rhythmicality is built into the fixed ratio between the *svara* density of the melody and the tempo (beat density) of the rhythmic cycle at the particular stage of rendition.

The Structure of Compositions

Baḍā and *choṭā khayāla* compositions, and also *tarānā* compositions, have two stanzas, represented by two melodic sections: the *sthāyī*, and the *antarā*. The *sthāyī* is, as a rule, centred in the lower half of the melodic canvas, except when the melodic centre of gravity of the *rāga* falls in the *uttarāṅga*. The *antarā* is identifiable by a deliberate ascent to the upper tonic, with its follow-through centred in the upper half of the melodic canvas. The *antarā*, however, ends with a descent to base *sā*. The two parts together represent a comprehensive map of the *rāga*'s melodic personality. The *sthāyī* also functions as the nucleus of the *khayāla* presentation — the basic theme or refrain to which the rendition returns, repeatedly, after each round of improvizations.

Khayāla Presentation Protocol

The *baḍā khayāla* rendition begins with the presentation of the *sthāyī* and *antarā* of the *bandiśa*, and is followed by improvisatory movements, woven around the *sthāyī*. It is not uncommon, however, for the *antarā* to be introduced after the first improvisatory movement.

The *baḍā khayāla* uses three improvisatory movements, each distinct in the melodic-rhythmic structure. The sequencing of these movements is in consonance with the convention of progressive enhancement of melodic and rhythmic density and complexity. In recent times, it has become customary to match this progression, at each transition, with a perceptible stepping up of the basic tempo of the *tāla* performed by the percussionist.

(a) ***Ālāpa***: The *ālāpa* is a free-flowing, rhythmically unstructured improvization of low melodic density, in which the melodic lines attempt no correspondence with the beats of the *tāla*. The *ālāpa* acknowledges the rhythmic cycle only at the end of each round of improvizations, when it has to rejoin the *sthāyī*. For the purposes of articulation, an *ālāpa* can either use the poetic element of the song (*bola-ālāpa*), or the abstract *ākāra* (the vowel form *ā*), or a combination of the two. In rare cases, solfa symbols (*saragama*) are also found in the *ālāpa*.

(b) ***Bola-laya (articulation in correspondence with rhythm)***: The *bola-laya* movement is also referred to as *bola-bāṇṭa* (emphasis shifts on the poetic element). *Bola-laya/bola-bāṇṭa* is a pulse-driven movement of medium melodic density, which introduces a moderate degree of correspondence, and even playful interaction, between the articulation, the melodic contours, and the beats of the rhythmic cycle. For articulation, a vocalist can use either the poetic form, or *saragama* (solfa symbols), or a combination of the two. Only in rare cases is the *ākāra* articulation encountered in the *bola-laya* movement.

(c) ***Tānas***: *Tāna*s are highly structured melodic runs of medium-to-wide melodic span, and high *svara*-density. They achieve a strong correspondence between their melodic contours and beats of the rhythmic cycle, and can exhibit a lively interaction with them. The melodic structure of *tāna*s is derived from a typology that has matured over centuries of evolution. For articulation of *tāna*s, a vocalist can use either the poetic element of the *bandiśa*, *saragama* (solfa symbols), or *ākāra*, or a combination of the three.

For those familiar with the medieval *dhrupada* genre, it is easy to see that the improvisatory movements of the *baḍā khayāla* correspond to the *vilaṁbita*, *madhyalaya*, and *druta ālāpa* of a *dhrupada* presentation. Structurally, though not historically, the *baḍā khayāla* inserts the *ālāpa* of a *dhrupada* rendition into the rendition of the pre-composed *bandiśa* as a chain of improvisatory movements. With this structural departure from the *dhrupada* format, the *baḍā khayāla* permits the simultaneous manipulation of the melodic and rhythmic elements, and creates a presentation format with an end-to-end linearity of melodic-rhythmic progression. This structural alignment is accompanied by a substantial enlargement of freedom in the choice of textural, sculptural as well as ornamentational devices to establish the *khayāla* as a distinctive genre of vocal music.

The *bandiśa ṭhumarī*, a lively vocal form, originally evolved as an accompaniment to footwork-dominant sub-forms of *kathaka* dance, inspires the second *bandiśa*, the *choṭā khayāla*. The *bandiśa ṭhumarī* is characterized by a one-to-one correspondence between the poetic, the melodic, and the rhythmic elements. This makes the form ideal for rendition in the faster tempi.

A *choṭā khayāla* presentation begins with the rendition of

the *sthāyī* and the *antarā* and is followed by the improvisatory movements. Here again, it is common for the *antarā* to be introduced after a few rounds of improvization rather than immediately after the *sthāyī*. In rare cases, one may encounter elements of *ālāpa* and *bola-laya* in the *choṭā khayāla* too. However, in consonance with the tempo and the aural flavour of the *choṭā khayāla*, the improvizations are dominated by *tāna*s, generally rendered at a *svara* density at least twice the beat density of the rhythmic cycle. In the *tāna*s, the vocalist has the same choice of articulation as in the *baḍā khayāla*. *Tarānā* renditions follow the same format as the *choṭā khayāla*, except that the absence of poetry, and the availability of meaningless consonants for articulation might encourage a greater display of rhythmic dexterity and virtuosity.

The Typology of Tānas

The melodic patterns in *tāna*s are constructed from five basic patterns: (i) *baḍhata* (ii) *laḍī-guṭhāva* (iii) *sapāṭa* (iv) *chūṭa*, and (v) *hopping tāna*s.

(i) ***Baḍhata (progressive) Tānas***: There are two concepts of *baḍhata* or progression in *tāna* construction. The first is to construct them in progressively ascending melodic waves, each wave ascending further upwards than the previous one. The first wave ascends from a certain base, mostly base *sā*, ascends upwards up to a point, returns to base, ascends again, this time a little farther, returns again to base, and so on. The second approach to *baḍhata tāna*s is patterned as a series of short *tāna*s woven around one melodic focus after another in ascending order, without returning to base *sā* after each ascent, but instead reverting to the *sthāyī*. The phraseology of *baḍhata tāna*s can either be flat-out or zigzag. Their identifying feature is the progressive unfurling of the melodic canvas. *Baḍhata tāna*s are, by their nature, appropriate for the ascent.

(ii) ***Laḍī-guthāva* (chain-knitting) *Tānas***: *Laḍī-guthāva* is a special category of *baḍhata tāna* in which the melodic development moves progressively upwards, but continuously without returning to a base, using a very complex web of inter-locked patterns woven around each *svara* along the path. Their identifying feature is the complexity of the melodic web in progressive ascending or descending motion. *Laḍī-guthāva* is perhaps the most demanding *tāna* pattern because of short spans of improvizations and their seamless knitting into an ascending chain. This requires a total mastery over the melodic features of the *rāga*.

(iii) ***Sapāṭa* (flat-out) *Tānas***: *Sapāṭa tāna*s ascend or descend in a cascading motion, with straightforward runs on the *rāga* scale without any twists and turns, with a single intonation supporting the execution of every *svara* on the intended melodic path. They have the desired impact when their melodic span covers at least one full octave. *Sapāṭa*s are rendered in ascending as well as descending movements.

(iv) ***Chūṭa* (leaping) *Tānas***: *Chūta tāna*s are constructed by establishing a geometric (generally first-fifth or first-fourth) tonal relationship between phrases of short melodic spans, delivered in different regions of the melodic canvas. Their structure appears to leap from *svara* to distant *svara* in the process of generating waves of corresponding phrases. The *chūta* pattern can be descending or ascending; but a set of *chūta-tāna* waves will generally be rounded off by a descending *sapāṭa*.

(v) ***Hopping Tānas***: These *tāna*s, generally found in ascending formation, hop across alternate *svara*s, often repetitively. For example, *sā-gā-sā-gā, re-mā-re-mā, gā-pā-gā-pā, mā-dhā-mā-dhā,* Depending on the grammar of the *rāga*, these *tāna*s may skip more than one *svara* in each hop. For obvious reasons, they are sometimes referred to as two-by-two *tāna*s. The hopping/two-by-two *tāna* is also inspired by one of the *alaṁkāra*s. It acquired the status of a *tāna* variety primarily as a speciality of the Jaipur–Atrauli Gharānā vocalists, particularly, Kesarbai Kerkar.

Amongst other *tāna* structures, a significant feature, but simplistic in construction, is the *alaṁkāra tāna*. *Alaṁkāra*s (lit: ornamentation) are a large group of practice exercises of varying complexity given to students with the dual purpose of training them in the precise delivery of *svara*s irrespective of the order in which they are arranged, and preparing them for the techniques of improvization fundamental to Hindustani music. *Alaṁkāra tāna*s are recognizable by their symmetric progression such as: *sā-re-gā-gā, re-gā-mā-mā, gā-mā-pā-pā, mā-pā-dhā-dhā.*

The Aesthetics of Tānas

In the architecture of the *khayāla* genre, the *tāna*s represent a culmination of melodic density and complexity. The advanced level of melodic density automatically makes the *tāna*s a display of virtuosity, and in the advanced level of complexity, the musician has the opportunity of demonstrating his virtuosity, imagination, as well as aesthetic sensibility. But, the issue of aesthetics in *tāna*s is much larger than complexity.

At every level, melodic density has a different psycho-acoustic implication. Omkarnath Thakur (1897–1967), for instance, refused to sing *tāna*s in Nīlāmbarī, because they would militate against the *rasa* of the *rāga*. Swimming against the tide of generalized expectations of *khayāla* presentation protocol, he established Nīlāmbarī as one of his most memorable and popular *rāga*s.

The character of the *rāga* is also an issue in the selection of *tāna* patterns. The melodic personality of every *rāga*, and also its emotional charge, are residents of its *calana*. The *calana* of each *rāga* limits the musician's options in terms of patterning strategies for *tāna*s. *Rāga*s with a zigzag *calana* cannot, for instance, support the *alaṁkāra* or *sapāṭa tāna* patterns. Such *rāga*s could, on the other hand, be ideally suited for the hopping or *laḍī-guthāva* pattern.

Another major issue of aesthetics in *tāna*s is the level of melodic density (intonations per second). Above a certain level of *svara* density, some *tāna* patterns will tend towards an unmusical aural experience. And, there is a threshold of *svara* density beyond which all *tāna* patterns will sound unmusical. The frontiers of musicality are, of course, fluid. But, they demand respect from each generation of musicians.

The issue of aesthetics in *tāna*s stands at the borderline between artistic expression and titillation. If taken seriously by musicians, it can often restrain the demonstration of virtuosity. The greatest of musicians have been guilty of opting for virtuosity at the cost of aesthetics, and the most highly cultivated amongst connoisseurs have been guilty of forgiving them.

Trends in Khayāla Vocalism

The *khayāla* genre has been defined by its "formal aloofness." However, the history of the genre in the 20th century is replete with vocalists — all of formidable stature — who have deviated either from its formalism or its aloofness, or both. Of the two deviationist tendencies, the revolt against aloofness shows a greater resemblance to a movement. Deshpande (ibid.) describes it as a romanticist movement, comparable to a similar movement in Western classical music. The movement argues in favour of explicit emotional stimuli in art music, in addition to the architectural and sculptural variables of the aural experience. The phenomenon is particularly relevant to *khayāla* vocalism because of the freedom it gives the musician, and the premium it accords to his role as a composer over that of a performer.

Stylistically, the recent history of the *khayāla* can be viewed in three phases. The first phase covers the pre-Independence era, dominated by Ustad Faiyyaz Khan. The second phase covers the quarter of a century thereafter, with several giants straddling the *khayāla* platform, approximately ending with the demise of Ustad Ameer Khan in 1974. The third phase begins with the trailblazing emergence of Kumar Gandharva and Kishori Amonkar.

At the dawn of the last century, Ustad Abdul Kareem Khan (1872-1937) had already paved the way for a combination of classicism with romanticism. In the next generation, Ustad Faiyyaz Khan (1886-1950) took the process farther, though with an entirely different style. On a partial review of his radio broadcasts, it appears that he adopted a mildly informal approach to *khayāla* architecture, in addition to introducing elements, which were explicitly solicitous of an emotional response. Expressions typical of the *ṭappā* genre, derived from the songs of camel drivers in north-west India, entered *khayāla* music for the first time in Faiyyaz Khan's renditions. On the evidence of 78-RPM records, the same appears to be broadly true of Ramkrishna Vaze (1871-1945). Omkarnath Thakur (1897-1967), partially their contemporary, was a fastidious formalist, but a diehard romanticist.

In the second phase, Pt. D.V. Paluskar (1921-55), Kesarbai Kerkar (1890-1977), and Ustad Ameer Khan (1912-74) were exemplary models of formalism as well as aloofness. This phase witnessed a solitary deviant, Ustad Bade Ghulam Ali Khan (1903-68). He was, broadly, in the Faiyyaz Khan mould, with an informal approach to architecture, and an inclination towards seductive ornamentation, and emotionally potent musical communication.

Amongst significant vocalists of the third phase, Bhimsen Joshi (b. 1922) stands alone as the bulwark of the *khayāla*'s formalism and aloofness. In this phase, Kumar Gandharva (1925-92) rebelled against both, aloofness as well as formalism. His junior by a few years, Kishori Amonkar (b. 1931) has remained steadfast in her respect for *khayāla* architecture, while rebelling against its aloofness. Their approximate contemporary, Jasraj started as a follower of the fastidious classicist, Ustad Ameer Khan, but has drifted steadily away from the formalism as well as aloofness of *khayāla* vocalism.

The significant aspect of romanticism in the third phase was the consolidation of the infusion of melodic expressions characteristic of the semi-classical, folk, regional, and popular genres of music into *khayāla* vocalism. As a result, *khayāla* was faced with a blurring of the stylistic divide between genres of vocal music.

In all probability, these tendencies had their socio-cultural logic. By this time, several leading performers of the semi-classical and romantic *ṭhumarī* and allied genres — Siddheshwari Devi, Rasoolan Bai, Begum Akhtar, Bade Ghulam Ali Khan, Barkat Ali Khan — had departed from the scene, leaving the genres starved of quality musicianship. Simultaneously, *khayāla* singers with *ṭhumarī* training had also faded away. Emotionally satisfying genres were beginning to disappear from the art-music platform. Around the same time, Jagjit Singh, an outstanding singer of the *ghazala*, a poetry-dominated genre, was enhancing its melodic content to corner a part of this vacant space. The *khayāla*, at that stage, attempted to fill the vacuum with a dual strategy — allowing *khayāla* itself to drift towards a more explicit and ornate emotionalism, and adopting the highly stylised *bhajana* as a tail-piece replacement for the *ṭhumarī*. Little wonder, then, that by the dawn of the 21st century, the *ṭhumarī* is all but extinct, and the distinctiveness of the *khayāla* is sustained almost entirely by its architecture.

The resilience of *khayāla* architecture cannot be taken for granted considering that it has been breached by some of the most formidable vocalists of the 20th century. For the moment, the opinion-makers of the art-music world are committed to its structuralism. However, a more permissive music establishment is likely to emerge out of the cultural discontinuities imposed by Independence. As a result, a more complete expression of post-modern tendencies can now be considered imminent in *khayāla* music.

Glossary

Ābhoga : The term derives from the Sanskrit *bhoga* = satiation/contentment. The *ā* vowel prefix in Sanskrit connotes "in the direction of/towards." The *ābhoga* is the fourth and valedictory phase of *rāga* exposition in any movement. Like the *sañcārī*, it has now been dropped from *dhrupada* and post-*dhrupada bandiśe*s. Its relevance is now limited to the prefatory *ālāpa* and the improvisatory movements of *bandiśa* rendition. The melodic-aesthetic function of this phase is to fold back the melodic canvas which was fully unfolded in the first two phases, and on which, in the third phase, the *rāga*'s distinctive melodic personality is detailed. Though a few musicians do still render a distinct *ābhoga*, especially in the *ālāpa*, musicians differ a great deal in their respective approaches to winding up this improvisatory movement with a distinct valedictory phase of exposition.

Addhā Tīnatāla: *Addhā tīnatāla* is a dented version of the 16-beat *tīnatāla*, used primarily in *ṭhumarī* and other romanticist genres. By silencing some of the beats of the rhythmic cycle in percussion accompaniment, the *addhā tīnatāla* changes the cadences of the cycle to approximate that of the 14-beat Dīpacaṇḍī, the primary *tāla* of the *ṭhumarī* genre. At a certain tempo, the rhythmic experience of *addhā tīnatāla* can even lose all similarity to either the regular *tīnatāla*, or Dīpacaṇḍī, and virtually define an independent *tāla*.

Akademi: The word is an Indianized adaptation of the English word "Academy."

Ada Cautāla : *Ada cautāla* is a *tāla* (rhythmic cycle) of fourteen beats in seven equal sub-divisions of two beats each. Though not very popular in contemporary music, it is amenable to rendering across a wide range of tempi — from slow to moderately fast. It is encountered more frequently in vocal music of the *khayāla* genre than in any other vocal genre or in instrumental music.

Ākāra : *Ākāra* is derived from *ā* = the uttered vowel *ā* + *kāra* = process. It is an important articulatory device deployed in *khayāla* performance. It is found most suited for the delivery of low density and high or even ultra-high density melody. Of the three articulatory devices used in Hindustani (north Indian) art music, the full-throated *ākāra*, arising from the navel, is regarded as having the greatest psycho-phonetic impact, and also the greatest personality-transforming potential. These qualities relate to the neuro-acoustic triggers of this form of vocalization, and the demands this form of articulation makes on the deployment of lung-power. These facets of vocalization are well understood in the Indian mystical tradition, and yogic practice of *prāṇāyāma.*

Alaṁkāra : The strictest meaning of the Sanskrit *alaṁkāra*, derived from its semantic meaning, is adornment, embellishment, decoration. In this sense, all modes of intonation and intervallic transition in Hindustani music, other than staccato, would fall under the category of *alaṁkāra*. In contemporary usage, however, the term has emerged as a generic description of the host of symmetric practice exercises that are given to music students with the aim of cultivating their technical excellence in the handling of melody.

Alaṁkāra Tānas : The word *alaṁkāra* stands for the perfectly symmetrical practice exercises that are given to students of music for cultivating their technical competence in handling melody. These patterns, when deployed as *tānas* — an improvisatory movement — require little melodic imagination. They do, however, appear conspicuously, and often unimaginatively, in contemporary music because of their ability to dazzle with their speed and clarity.

Ālāpa : The word derives from Sanskrit *ālāpa* = dialogue/conversation. The aesthetic implications of this word are appropriately translated in the *ālāpa* movement in Hindustani (north Indian) art music. The *ālāpa* is a leisurely, deliberate, almost conversational, exposition of the *rāga*'s melodic form aimed at achieving, for it, the highest possible level of intelligibility. This intelligibility is achieved by conformity with traditional principles of melodic progression. Within this general definition, the word describes different categories of movements in different genres of vocal music, and on the different instruments.

Ālāpā in khayāla and on wind and bow instruments : The prefatory low density *ālāpa* movement is identical in *khayāla* vocalism and on the wind and bow instruments because, being instruments capable of melodic continuity, these instruments have traditionally presented music in the *khayāla* format. The *khayāla* format presents the *ālāpa* as a percussion-accompanied movement. It is the first improvisatory movement in the *vilambita* (slow tempo) *khayāla* rendition. The *ālāpa* in the *khayāla* format consists of rounds of low-density anarhythmic melodic improvization, in the prescribed progression, woven around intermittent returns to the pre-composed form of the *bandiśa*. In the vocal manifestation, the *ālāpa* of the *khayāla* format may deploy either the poetic form, or vowel forms as articulatory devices.

Āmada : The word is probably colloquial for the Sanskrit verb *āgamana* = to arrive. The *āmada* in a *bandiśa* is the last phase of either the *sthāyī* or the *antarā*, which terminates just before the rendition can return to a rendition of the *mukhaḍā* of the *sthāyī*.

Antarā : The term is an abbreviation of the Sanskrit *antarā-dhātu* = "intermediate material." In the *bandiśa*, *antarā* is centred in the upper half of the melodic canvas. It ascends categorically from the mid-octave region of the middle octave to the upper-tonic, provides a climactic and reposeful pause at the upper-tonic, ascends into the higher octave, and then descends in deliberate steps to base *sā* (the tonic/fundamental). The *antarā* of the improvisatory movements is identical in its progression logic to the pre-composed *antarā* of a *bandiśa*. Collectively, the *sthāyī* and the *antarā* provide a complete coverage of the melodic canvas.

Auchara : The term refers to an anarhythmic prelude, rendered without percussion accompaniment, preceding a *khayāla* presentation. The *auchara* has no clearly defined melodic movements, though it does follow an ascending-descending progression. It remains generally in the lower half of the melodic canvas, does considerably more than merely identifying the *rāga* and aims at creating its atmosphere.

Artha-Bhāva : The term derives from Sanskrit *artha* = semantic meaning + *bhāva* = emotional meaning. The *bola-banāva ṭhumarī* is also called the *artha-bhāva ṭhumarī*, because it uses song-texts as a platform for luxuriant and leisurely melodic ornamentation, with the purpose of making the words come to life.

Baḍā Khayāla : The word derives its meaning from the Hindi *baḍā* = major/big/large/expansive + *khayāla* = vision/imagination. The term denotes the slow-tempo rendition of vocal music in the *khayāla* genre of Hindustani (north Indian) art music. In one context, it represents the pre-composed element (the poetic-melodic-rhythmic shell of the rendition, called the *bandiśa*). In a different context, the term can refer to the entire rendition of the slow-tempo *khayāla*, inclusive of the improvisatory movements.

Baḍhata : The word is Hindi for evolution/progression/growth, and is derived from the Sanskrit *vṛddhi*, an abstract noun of identical meaning. In Hindustani (north Indian) music, it refers to the melodic progression prescribed for the improvisatory movements.

Baḍhata Tānas : The word *baḍhata* stands for a sense of melodic progression. *Baḍhata tānas* are clusters of high density melodic runs, which correspond to a notion of deliberateness and disciplined sequencing of ascending and descending melody in the coverage of the melodic canvas.

Bandiśa (also called Cīẓa) : The word derives from the Sanskrit verb *bandhana* = to bind. A *bandiśa* is that which is bound, encased, pre-composed. The word refers to the pre-composed element in Hindustani (north Indian) vocal or instrumental music. In vocal music, it refers to the pre-composed poetic-melodic-rhythmic shell, which constitutes the nucleus around which the improvizations revolve.

Bandiśa-kī-ṭhumarī : The *bandiśa-kī-ṭhumarī* is the older of the two sub-genres of the *ṭhumarī* genre of semi-classical vocal music. The word *bandiśa* in this context signifies its reliance on the pre-composed poetic-melodic-rhythmic form. The word *ṭhumarī* signifies its origins as accompaniment to Kathaka dance, and its continued association with it. Having evolved from older traditions of dance-related musical forms, the *bandiśa-kī-ṭhumarī* achieved a mature form by the 18th century, touched its zenith by mid-19th century, and had become near-extinct as an independent musical genre by late 20th century. Its evolution into a sophisticated genre was synchronous with the emergence of the princely state of Awadh (Lucknow) as the cultural capital of northern India. Stylistically, the *bandiśa-kī-ṭhumarī* is a lively piece of music, performed primarily in medium tempo, and composed in the popular *tīnatāla*, along with its stylized variants.

Bānī: *Bānī* is colloquial for Sanskrit *vāṇī*= speech/language. The reference is to the various styles of performing *dhrupada* that existed in mediaeval times, which were originally also associated with the different dialects in which their lyrics were written. During the period of Miyā Tānsen's influence over *dhrupada* vocalism (16th century), the different *bānī*s merged their identities into the Seniya tradition.

Baul: Baul is a genre of urban folk music from West Bengal. The genre expresses the anti-materialistic philosophy of a multi-religious cult which uses music as an aid to religious practice, and whose members are also referred to as bauls. Baul songs are also called *dehatattva gānā* (songs about the essence of material existence in the human body). The word *baula* is derived, severally, from the Hindi word *bāwalā* (mad) and the Arabic *aulia*, a word of similar connotation, used to describe a mystic with a non-conformist lifestyle. *Bauls* are, typically, homeless wanderers, dressed in yellow robes signifying the renunciation of organized social life and material values.

Behlāva : The word is Hindi, and has connotations of a leisurely quality, informality and indulgence. It is used to describe the anarhythmic *ālāpa* of certain stylistic lineages of *khayāla* vocalism. The *behlāva* form is characterized by the use of the poetic form as the articulatory device, and its relative informality of progression.

Bhajana : The word derives from the Sanskrit verb *bhaja* = to serve/to worship. A *bhajana* is a song based on devotional poetry. These songs were originally performed in the temples, and moved from there into people's homes as solo or choral expressions. They are composed typically in folk tunes, or based on a handful of classical *rāgas*. The advent of the gramophone record gave a tremendous boost to their popularity and standardization in rendering. The infusion of classicism into their rendition, and their adoption as repertoire for the concert platform is a 20th-century phenomenon. In the latter context, the *bhajana* has steadily replaced, and displaced, the *ṭhumarī* and *ṭappā* genres.

Bola : The word is Hindi for "articulated sound/speech." In the context of Hindustani (north Indian) art music, it refers to the use of the poetic form as the vehicle for the delivery of music. As a vehicle for the communication of musical meaning, the poetic form enjoys the highest premium in the *bola-banāva ṭhumarī* genre, followed by *dhrupada*, and finally by *khayāla*. Being a device equipped with vowels, consonants, as well as semantic and syntactical meaning, the poetic form lends itself to any combination of poetic, melodic and rhythmic manipulation. As such, it is the most versatile articulatory device across a wide range of *svara* densities. Moreover, it is far less demanding than pure vowel devices, to which the vocalist perforce resorts for delivery of ultra-high density melody. These considerations make the poetic form (*bola*) the most popular articulatory device in contemporary art music.

Bola-ālāpa : When the *ālāpa* of the *khayāla* genre is presented using the poetic form as the articulatory material, it is called *bola-ālāpa*.

Bola-banāva : *Bola-banāva* is the leisurely process of using musical expression to convert the semantic meaning of a song-text into emotional meaning. This mode of musical communication is considered appropriate only in the romanticist *ṭhumarī* genre of semi-classical music. The aesthetics of *Bola-banāva* aided the erotic allurement of a courtesan. The process is artistic, takes place in public and fulfils the requirements of decorum worthy of genteel society. Within these constraints, it has to achieve an intimacy not available to the classicist genres, because it is aimed at obtaining the highest price for the courtesan's favours. *Bola-banāva* represents vocal expression of explicitly manipulative intent, traditionally rendered to the accompaniment of mime and gesture. The mode of musical communication relies heavily on ornate melodic embellishments and seductive manipulations of volume and timbre considered inappropriate in the classicist genres — *dhrupada* and *Khayāla*.

Bola-banāva ṭhumarī : The *bola-banāva ṭhumarī* is the more recent of the two sub-genres of the *ṭhumarī* genre of semi-classical vocal music. The prefix *bola-banāva* describes the leisurely process by which the sub-genre uses musical expression to convert semantic meaning into emotional meaning. The suffix *ṭhumarī* refers to its origins as accompaniment to Kathaka dance, and its continued association with it. The *bola-banāva ṭhumarī* evolved and flourished primarily in the city of Benares, and reflects a considerable influence of folk traditions of the neighbouring districts. This *ṭhumarī* sub-genre reached its zenith during the 19th century, and began to loose ground in the early 20th century when it moved out of the salons of the courtesans and into the concert halls. At the time of writing (June 2008), the genre claims only a couple of specialist performers. A few *khayāla* vocalists do, however, still perform the *bola-banāva ṭhumarī* as a tailpiece. The genre now faces extinction as an independent musical genre.

Bola-Bāṇṭa/Laya-Bāṇṭa : The terms are derived from *bola* = poetic form (or *laya* = tempo) + *bāṇṭa* = distribution. They are forms of improvization in the vocal genres of Hindustani music, the distinctions between them being ill-defined with respect to vocal renditions. *Bola-bāṇṭa* alters the relationship between the poetic and rhythmic elements in the pre-composed form of the *bandiśa* without substantially disturbing the melodic element. *Laya-bāṇṭa* (temporal redistribution) is a similar improvization, but may also encompass the melodic component. The term *laya-bāṇṭa* may also be used for comparable improvizations in instrumental music, which do not have the poetic form for manipulation. Both forms are generally practiced in medium melodic density.

Bola-laya : The term is derived from *bola* = the poetic form + *laya* = tempo. *Bol-laya* is the name given to the medium density movement, sequentially the second improvisatory movement, in contemporary *khayāla* rendition. It involves improvizations utilizing the poetic form as the articulatory device, with melody adopting an explicit rhythmicality or pulsation in the rendition. This movement may include elements of *bola-bāṇṭa / laya-bāṇṭa*. Some musicians may, however, choose to replace — either partially or entirely — the poetic form with the *saragama* (solfa symbols) as the articulatory material for this second, medium density movement.

Bola-Tāna : The term derives from *bola* = the poetic form + *tāna* = high-density melodic runs. When *tāna*s are rendered in *khayāla* vocalism with words and phrases from the song-text as the primary articulatory device, rather than the alternatives available, the *tāna* form is called a *bola-tāna*. This form of *tāna* may also be occasionally encountered in *bandiśa-kī-ṭhumarī* rendition, and is routinely adopted in *ṭappā* singing.

Braj Bhāṣa: Braj Bhāṣā is a dialect of Hindi, the mainstream language of northern India. It derives its name from the "Braj" region, a group of towns and villages around the city of Mathura. The culture of this region is intimately connected with the legend of Lord Kṛṣṇa. Supported by its religious significance, and later by the region's proximity to the seat of Mogul power during the middle ages, Braj Bhāṣā remained the primary vehicle for the literary flowering in northern India until the decline of the Mogul Empire.

Carnatic/Hindustani music : The word derives from the name of the "Karnāṭa" region of India, approximately covering all of peninsular India south of the Vindhyachal range of mountains. A unified Indian tradition of art music underwent a bifurcation starting in the early part of the second millennium. The north of the country came under increasing middle eastern (mainly Perso-Arabic) cultural influence consequent to a series of invasions, while south India remained relatively insulated from such influences. This bifurcation was probably magnified by art-music responding more explicitly to the regional musical cultures of the north and south, and to the differing predilections of its patrons. These forces gave rise to two parallel art music traditions — the north Indian tradition, called Hindustani music, and the south Indian tradition, called Carnatic music. The two systems have similarities as well as dissimilarities, and follow their independent evolutionary paths. However, there is evidence of growing cross-fertilization of musical ideas and practices between the two traditions after Independence (1947).

Caitī: The word is derived from the name of the Caitra month of the Hindu calendar (spring). The *caitī* is a genre of folk songs from the eastern part of Uttar Pradesh (northern provinces) and its adjacent districts. Its signatory feature is verse in which poetic lines end with *ho rāma*. The songs are generally of two stanzas each, and of standard melodic construction, which does not correspond to the art music definition of *sthāyī-antarā* progression. The thematic content of the poetry is primarily romantic, and deals with the pangs of separation from the beloved, as narrated by a female protagonist. It is a poetry-dominant genre, possessing limited scope for melodic elaboration and improvization, and set to a 7-beat or 14-beat rhythmic cycle common in *ṭhumarī*-related folk genres. The courtesans of Benares and neighbouring Gayā elevated the *caitī* songs to the status of a semi-classical art form. The genre is regarded as one of the allied genres of the *bola-banāva ṭhumarī*.

Calana : The word derives from the Sanskrit *cala* = to walk or Hindi *cāla* = gait/demeanour. A *rāga*'s distinctive melodic personality is outlined by a set of characteristic phrases, which incorporate a substantial part of its grammar. This set of phrases — generally not more than eight or ten in number — are collectively called the *calana* of the *rāga*.

Caturaṅga: The word *caturaṅga* is derived from *catura* = four + *raṅga* = colour. The *caturaṅga* is an old, but now rare, compositional form, which deploys four different categories of articulatory devices drawn from the Hindustani vocal genres — the poetic form, sound symbols drawn from the language of percussion, the names of plectrum strokes deployed for sound activation on the plucked lute family of instruments, and the meaningless consonants, characteristic of the *tarānā* form. *Caturaṅga*s are generally performed in medium tempo *tīnatāla*, and rendered much like *tarānā*s.

Cauguṇā : The word derives from *cau* = four + *guṇā* = multiple. When any melody is performed at a melodic (*svara*) density four times the beat density (tempo) of accompanying percussion or the base-tempo of the *bandiśa*, the expression is called *cauguṇā*. The highest ratio of *svara* density to beat density practiced in Hindustani music is eight times.

Cautāla (loosely also called Dhrupada) : *Cautala* is a *tāla* (rhythmic cycle) of twelve beats in six equal sub-divisions of two beats each. It is the primary *tāla* of the *dhrupada* genre of mediaeval art music, and is generally performed in medium tempo.

Chūṭa Tānas : The word derives probably from *chūṭa* in Hindi = "abandon/ release." When a melodic motif, once defined, is abandoned or released, it escapes/flees/leaps. The *chūṭa tāna* conveys such an impression by leaping to different regions of the melodic canvas, while retaining the tonal geometry of the basic motif. The totality of the aural image is a collage of similar patterns strewn across the melodic canvas, generally in ascending and/or descending sequence, though not necessarily so.

Choṭā Khayāla : The word derives from the Hindi *choṭā* = minor/small + *khayāla* = vision/imagination. The term denotes the fast-tempo rendition of vocal music in the *khayāla* genre of Hindustani (north Indian) art music. In such meaning, it encompasses the pre-composed element (the poetic-melodic-rhythmic shell of the rendition) as well as the conventional architecture of the rendition with respect to the improvisatory movements. Compared to the *baḍā khayāla*, the architecture of a *choṭā khayāla* presentation is informal.

Dādarā : Dādarā is a *tāla* (rhythmic cycle) of six beats in 3+3 sub-division. The *tāla* is generally used in medium and fast tempi. However, the term also refers to a genre of folk-based semi-classical genre of vocal music allied to the *bola-banāva ṭhumarī*. This genre, originating in the musical traditions of the districts around the city of Benares, is performed not only in the *dādarā tāla*, but also in a couple of other *tāla*s. The dividing line between the *dādarā* and *bola-banāva ṭhumarī* is blurred. The significant feature of the *dādarā* vocal genre is the heightened rhythmicality of rendition, relative to the subdued rhythmicality of the *bola-banāva ṭhumarī*.

Dīpacaṇḍī : Dīpacaṇḍī is a *tāla* (rhythmic cycle) of fourteen beats in 3+4+3+4 sub-division. It is associated with the *ṭhumarī* genre of semi-classical vocal music. Dīpacaṇḍī is encountered almost exclusively in the *bola-banāva ṭhumarī* genre. Like the *dhamāra tāla* (also of 14 beats) the Dīpacaṇḍī *tāla* is also associated with songs celebrating the spirit of *Holī*, the spring festival of colours.

Dhamāra : *Dhamāra* is a *tāla* (rhythmic cycle) of fourteen beats with an irregular/asymmetrical 5+2+3+4 sub-division. It is an integral part of the repertoire of the *dhrupada/dhamāra* genre of art music, and is ideally suited for medium tempo rendition. *Dhamāra* is one of the very few *tāla*s, which does not begin on an accentuated beat. For this reason, and also because of its irregular sub-division of beats, *dhamāra* is considered an enigmatic *tāla* of reluctant rhythmicality.

In the *dhrupada/dhamāra* genre, poetry composed to the *dhamāra tāla*, irrespective of the *rāga* in which it is composed, is related predominantly to the *Holī* (also called *Horī*) the spring festival of colours. This makes the *dhamāra tāla*, along with its associated poetic element connected with *Holī/Horī*, a distinct sub-genre of the *dhrupada* genre.

Dhrupada (Also called *dhrupada-dhamāra*) : The word derives from Sanskrit *dhruva* = fixed/immutable + *pada* = verse. It refers to a genre of *rāga*-based music, which dominated the Hindustani (north Indian) tradition between the 15th and 18th centuries. The genre evolved as an art form consequent to the transportation of the devotional music of the Vaiṣṇava temples to the secular environment of feudal courts. The genre places a high premium on the integrity of its poetic element in rendition and is, therefore, predominantly a genre of vocal music. Its primary instrumental manifestation is the *Rudra vīṇā* (also called *bīna*). After the decline of its strongest patron, the Mogul Empire, in the early

19th century, *dhrupada* progressively surrendered the mainstream platform to the modern *khayāla* genre, taking the *Rudra vīṇā* along with it on the downhill path. *Dhrupada* was near extinct by mid-20th century, but experienced a minor revival in the last quarter of the century, primarily supported by audiences and scholars in Europe and the US.

Dogunā : The word derives from *dvi* or *do* = two + *gunā* = multiple. When any melody is performed at a melodic (*svara*) density twice the beat density (tempo) of accompanying percussion, or the base-tempo of the *bandiśa*, the expression is called *dogunā*. The highest ratio of *svara* density to beat density practised in Hindustani music is eight times.

Druta (or *druta laya*) : An adjectival phrase derived from the Sanskrit *druta* = running/galloping + *laya* = tempo. It describes a rendition in fast tempo. The notion of tempo (slow/medium/fast) is relative and dynamic. It differs between generations, between stylistic lineages, between different genres of vocal music, and between vocal and instrumental music.

Ekaharā: The term describes high-density melodic execution — primarily *tāna*s — deploying a single explicit intonation per *svara*/tone.

Ekatāla : *Ekatāla* is a *tāla* (rhythmic cycle) of twelve beats in six equal sub-divisions of two beats each. The *tāla* is immensely popular for slow as well as fast tempo renditions in the *khayāla* genre of vocal music. It is amenable to rendition in a wide range of tempi, from below 20 bpm to over 240 bpm. Its use in medium tempo *khayāla* rendition is rare.

Fāguna : *Fāguna* is a genre of folk songs, which derives its name from the month of Fālguna in the Hindu calendar (early spring). The genre belongs to the eastern districts of Uttar Pradesh (northern provinces), and evolved as an ally of the *bola-banāva ṭhumarī* performed by courtesans of Benares. In the Indian literary and musical tradition, spring is most clearly associated with man's romantic urges. Hence, the lyrics of *fāguna* songs are dominated by romance. The explicit reference to the month of Fālguna is generally found in *fāguna* songs. The songs are normally rendered with emotive embellishment of the poetic element, but without substantive melodic improvization.

Gamaka : The term derives from the Sanskrit verb: *gam* = to go. In the strictest musicological sense, the word is generic to all intervallic transitions in Indian music, classified according to the melodic contours they respectively define. In contemporary Hindustani usage, however, the word has come to denote one specific category of *gamaka* — the *tribhinna gamaka* — which creates a vibratory melodic contour. It is a contextual intonation of a tone/*svara*, conveying the impression of being repeatedly attacked from an adjacent tone/*svara*. The effect may be compared with a magnified *vibrato* in Western music. The *gamaka* is practised in vocal as well as instrumental music.

Gharānā : The word derives its meaning from the Hindi *ghara* (Sanskrit *gṛha* = house). *Gharānā* is a collective noun meaning a group, which shares the same homestead. In the era of hereditary musicianship, the term came to represent a lineage, which cultivated a distinctive style of rendering music over successive generations. Once kinship ceased to be the primary criterion for entry into the music profession, the term was redefined to denote a stylistic lineage. As a stylistic lineage, a *gharānā* is characterized by three critical features — (a) a long period of rigorous training and aesthetic indoctrination of each aspirant under an authorized *guru* of the lineage, (b) acquisition of the art through aural transmission, and (c) a sworn loyalty of each member to the music-making philosophy and style of his mentor/lineage. The decay of the *gharānā* phenomenon began in the second quarter of 20th century and is now almost complete. The *gharānā* model of continuity and change has been replaced by alternative models, yet to be conceptualized.

Gharānedāra : The word is derived from *gharānā* = clan + *dāra* = in possession of. The etymology is self-explanatory. A musician representing a well-defined stylistic lineage (*gharānā*), and delivering music that corresponds to the distinguishing features of the style, is called a *gharānedāra* musician.

Ghasīṭa/Sūta : The word derives from the Hindi *Ghasīṭa* = to drag, and Sanskrit *gharṣaṇa* = friction/abrasion. The explicit reference here is to an intervallic transition achieved on the plucked string instruments, by dragging a finger of the left hand over a large melodic span under the impact of a single right hand stroke. This process defines a linear, rather than curvilinear melodic contour. Such a transition, when executed in vocal music, is called a *sūta* or *syūta*.

Ghazala : The word is Persian for "addressing a lover in poetic form." The term defines a poetry-dominant genre of music imbued with the romantic sentiment. Its poetic structure derives probably from a corresponding form in Persian literature. The Islamic Sūfī sects from the Middle East adopted the *ghazala* form early during their presence in India, making the love of God an important thematic element. *Ghazala*s were originally written in Persian. When the form was adopted in Urdu literature, its thematic content was substantially enlarged, to encompass *iśq* (love), *aśq* (tears) and *mauta* (death). *Ghazala*s were originally sung in a very simple, repetitive, melodic structure, with no melodic improvization. In the 19th and 20th centuries, its melodic approach began to drift towards that of the *bola-banāva ṭhumarī*. The genre, however, continues to accord an autonomous status to the poetic element, far more categorically than the *ṭhumarī* genre does.

Gītakīrī : The word is colloquial and partially onomatopoeic. There is no consensus on its definition. It is frequently used to signify a short, crisp, brisk melodic passage, across adjacent tones/*svara*s, without loops or angularities. It warrants a nomenclature when inserted, for dramatic effec' into either low density or convoluted/zigzag melodic movements. The presence of this expression is most prominent in the *ṭappā* genre of semi-classical music, though it is also deployed by some lineages of *khayāla* vocalism.

Harmonium : A member of the keyboard-based family of free-reed aerophones. Although such instruments have existed in India and other parts of Asia for centuries, Christian missionaries probably introduced the harmonium to India from Britain in the 18th century, as accompaniment for choirs in Churches. The original import was a platform mounted pedal-primed version, which was later replaced with a portable hand-pumped variant with 37 keys. Despite the incompatibility of its tempered scale with Indian intonation practices, the instrument is now the most widely used melodic accompaniment to all genres of vocal music — other than *dhrupada/dhamāra* — and has replaced the *sāraṅgī* in this role. Attempts to establish it as a solo instrument have met with only limited success.

Hopping Tānas : These are, as the name suggests, melodic patterns that hop across alternating tones/*svara*s, often repeating each hop, and most commonly in ascending formation. They are ocaasionally also described as 2 × 2 tānas, because their hopping movement seems to connect two non-adjacent *svara*s at a time. Only a few stylistic lineages of *khayāla* vocalism practise this form of *tāna*s.

Jamajama/Zamzama : The word is colloquial and partially onomatopoeic. There is no consensus on its definition. It appears to signify a repetitive and deliberate intonation of pairs of tones/*svara*s in quick succession. Though used in the context of instrumental as well as vocal music, it appears to be more applicable to the idiom of the plucked instruments.

Jhapatāla : *Jhapatāla* is a *tāla* (rhythmic cycle) of ten beats in 2 + 3 + 2 + 3 sub-division. This *tāla* is suited for slow to medium tempo rendition.

Jhūmara : *Jhūmara* is a *tāla* (rhythmic cycle) of fourteen beats in 3 + 4 + 3 + 4 sub-division. It is ideally suited for slow and ultra-slow rendition in the *khayāla* genre of vocal music. The *jhūmara* tempo rarely exceeds 20 beats per minute.

Kajarī : The word is derived from Hindi *kājala* = kohl, representing the black colour, darkness. The name of this genre of poetry-dominant vocal music probably alludes to the cloudy skies and the ambient darkness associated with the rainy season (July to September) in which this genre is performed. It is performed by women and accompanied by circular dance. Like the *caitī* genre of seasonal songs, this genre belongs to the folk tradition of Uttar Pradesh (northern provinces) and was elevated to the status of a semi-classical art form by the courtesans of Benares. The genre is regarded as one of the allied genres of the *bola-banāva ṭhumarī*.

Kāna-Sparśa/Kāna Svara : The word is Sanskrit for "grain/microscopic particle." When a tone/*svara* is intoned after, but almost simultaneously with, the fractional intonation of an adjacent tone/*svara*, the incidental tone/*svara* is called a *kāna svara*. This embellishment of intonation is used in vocal as well as instrumental music. In instrumental music, this form of embellishment is executed generally by the consecutive, though near simultaneous, use of two fingers. It involves no more than a summary touch of the incidental tone/*svara*. This is why, it is also called *sparśa*, Sanskrit for "touch."

Kathaka : Kathaka is the name of the principal genre of classical dance in the north Indian performing arts tradition, closely linked to its musical and poetic traditions. The word derives from Sanskrit *kathā* = story + *kāra* = narrator. Kathaka is also the name of an ancient community of story-tellers, who specialized in the narration of episodes from the major Hindu epics through mime and vocal-instrumental accompaniment. By religious orientation, the *kathakas* were devotees of Lord Kṛṣṇa, an incarnation of Lord Viṣṇu. Members of this community, and their religious and artistic traditions, have shaped the modern *kathaka* genre of dance, as well as the modern *ṭhumarī* genre of semi-classical music, both of which revolve around the legend of Lord Kṛṣṇa.

Kehervā : *Kehervā* is a rhythmic cycle of eight beats in 4 + 4 sub-division. It is generally performed in medium tempo.

Khaṭkā : The word is colloquial and partially onomatopoeic. Its definitions vary considerably. The word has two connotations — of a jolting quality, and of a forceful, audible impact. A generally acceptable definition would be the intonation of two neighbouring, though not necessarily adjacent, tones/*svaras* in quick succession, generally staccato, in which the first tone/*svara* is intoned with considerably greater force and impact than the second. The *khaṭkā* description is also appropriate for melodic expressions involving sudden drops across a distance of three or four tones/*svaras* specifically required by the grammar of some *rāgas*.

Khayāla : The term derives its meaning from the Perso-Arabic word *khayāla*, meaning idea, imagination, subjectivity, individuality, or impression. It represents a confluence of *rūpakālāpti*, an ancient genre of Indian art music (8th/9th centuries), and Perso-Arabic music, encouraged by the landmark poet-musician, Ameer Khusrau (13th century). *Khayāla* is the modern genre of vocal music, which replaced *dhrupada* as the mainstream genre starting in the early 19th century. *Khayāla* is an improvization-dominant genre, compared to its predecessor, *dhrupada*, which had a strong tendency towards being a pre-composed genre. The *khayāla* is characterized by its linear architecture, involving a progressive intensification of melodic and rhythmic density and complexity.

Laḍī-guthāva Tānas : The term is a compound of two words: *laḍī* = chain + *guthāva* = knitting. This pattern progressively weaves an intricate web of interlocked patterns along its melodic path.

Laya : *Laya*, Sanskrit for tempo, is the time interval between the equidistant beats of a *tāla*, when rendered. It represents a linear calibration of the flow of time, while the *tāla* is a cyclical calibration of it. *Laya* may be expressed as a number of beats per minute, while the *tāla* is defined, amongst other criteria, by the number of beats within a cycle. In performance, a *tāla*, rendered in a particular *laya*, may be defined by number of seconds or minutes per cycle.

Laya-Bāṇṭa : See *Bola-Bāṇṭa*.

Layakārī : The word derives from Sanskrit *laya* = tempo + *kārī* = expertise/ craftsmanship. When a musician, either a percussionist or a lead-musician, indulges in a display of rhythmic craftsmanship or artistry, deviating from the standard or pre-composed melodic, rhythmic, or melodic-rhythmic form, the resultant musical experience is called *layakari*.

Madhya-laya : An adjective derived from the Sanskrit *madhya* = medium + *laya* = tempo. The notion of tempo (slow/medium/fast) is relative and dynamic. It differs between generations, between stylistic lineages, between different genres of vocal music, and between vocal and instrumental music.

Madhyāṅga: The term derives its meaning from Sanskrit *madhya* = middle + *aṅga* = limb. While the Western tradition divides the octave into two equal halves, the Indian tradition views it as consisting of three overlapping tetrachords (*aṅga*s or limbs). The lower tetrachord (*sā, re, gā, mā*) is called the *pūrvāṅga* (*pūrva* = early + *aṅga* = limb/region). The mid-octave region (*gā, mā, pā, dha*) is called the *madhyāṅga* (*madhya* = middle + *aṅga* = limb/region). The upper tetrachord (*pā, dha, nī, sā*) is called *uttarānga* (*uttara* = north + *aṅga* = limb/region).

Mahārājā/Nawāb/Zamīṅdāra/Sultāna : Mahārājā (*mahā* = great – *rājā* = king), Nawāb (Feudal Lord or Nobleman, generally Moslem), and *zamīṅdāra* (*zamīṅ* = land + *dāra* = owner of), Sultāna (Persian for Mahārājā). These terms denote different levels/categories of power and influence in feudal-agrarian India. Under colonial rule, the *mahārājā*s, *nawāb*s, *zamīṅdāra*s, *sultāna*s were guaranteed military protection of British armies in return for a share of land revenue. This aristocracy became a significant patron of the fine and performing arts. Its support was largely responsible for the emergence of the *gharānā*s in Hindustani (north Indian) art music, and for ushering in the Golden Age of Hindustani music.

Matta Tāla : *Matta tāla* is a *tāla* (rhythmic cycle) of eighteen beats, in nine subdivisions of two beats each. It is a minor *tāla* of the *dhrupada/dhamāra* genre. When performed, it is generally performed in medium to fast tempo.

Mīṇḍa : *Mīṇḍa* is the primary mode of intervallic transition in Hindustani music — vocal as well as instrumental. It describes a transition, akin to a traction, which literally "stretches" a tone/*svara* in order to reach another tone/*svara*, defining a curvilinear path. It is the opposite of a staccato transition.

Mirāsī : *Mirāsī* is the name of a community of Moslem musicians who accompany courtesans on various musical instruments, mainly the *sāraṅgī* or *tabalā*, and teach them music. Being a professional classification, the term also came to be used, though rarely, for Hindu musicians in similar professions. Hereditary musicians residing in Punjab have also been called *mirāsī*s. Traditionally, members of this profession claimed a share of the income of the salons to which they were attached. The profession has been viewed with some reservations in art music circles. A career in the courtesan districts had "second grade" connotations in an era when feudal patronage was the most coveted certification of musicianship. Secondly, accompaniment is/was seen as a compromise forced upon those who are/were not good enough to become lead performers. Thirdly, accompanists are/were not expected to be able to retain/cultivate a clear musical vision. And, finally, the music of the courtesan districts is/was not viewed as "pure" art music. These factors led to an image of *mirāsī*s as unreliable teachers for "pure" music. On the other hand, it cannot be denied that some very respected names in 20th-century *khayāla* vocalism came from *mirāsī* backgrounds. Most of these issues have lost their relevance in contemporary music.

Miyā Tānsen : The word derives from Persian "Miyā" = Honourable/Lord + "Tānsen" = the 16th-century musician who served the court of the third Mogul emperor, Jalaluddin Mohammad Akbar. He was invited to the Mogul court after he had acquired a formidable reputation as a musician in the court of Mahārājā of Rewā in the Central Provinces. A Hindu brāhmaṇa by birth, his original name was Ramtanu Mishra, which became Tānsen upon his conversion to Islam and entry into Mogul service. In addition to his legendary musicianship, Tānsen's significance to music also rests on his contribution as manager of the patronage function at the imperial court, and perpetuation of vocal as well as instrumental musical traditions through his direct descendants.

Mughlai: Mughlai is a *tāla* (rhythmic cycle) of seven beats. It is of folk origin, and has long been out of circulation even in semi-classical music.

Mukhaḍā : The word derives its meaning from Sanskrit *mukha* = face. The word describes the first phrase (but, occasionally a string of phrases) of the *Sthāyī* in a *bandiśa* — literally its face — which culminates at the *sama,* the first beat of the rhythmic cycle. By implication, the term is not relevant for the many *bandiśe*s which commence on the first beat of the rhythmic cycle. By virtue of being the launch phrase of the *bandiśa,* and by also being its most frequently iterated phrase right through the rendition, it qualifies for its nomenclature. The *mukhaḍā* is the signature of the *bandiśa,* and often contains the *pakada* (the catch-phrase or signature) of the *rāga*. The best-composed *mukhaḍā*s are able to build and release aesthetic tension within a very short span of time. For this reason, the composition and rendition of the *mukhaḍā*s is accorded great importance in the musical arts.

Murkī : The term is colloquial, though probably related to the Hindi verb *maroḍana* = to twist. The *murkī* is a special type of *mīṇḍa,* where the phrase involves a twisted/wrap-around execution with a jerky motion. This melodic expression is encountered in vocal music as well as instrumental music.

Nāṭaka: The word is derived from the Sanskrit *nāṭya* = theatre, and describes a theatrical production.

Nāṭya Saṅgīta : The term derives from Sanskrit *nāṭya* = theatre + *saṅgīta* = music. The term refers to a modern genre of *rāga*-based music from regional theatre, which dominated the entertainment of bourgeois society in the western state of Maharashtra during the 19th and early 20th centuries.

The music in Marāṭhī theatre was presented in monologue, conversational as well as choreographic contexts, and is almost always based on classical *rāgas*, though also occasionally on folk melodies. In its balance between poetic, melodic and rhythmic elements, and in the relative weightage to pre-composed and improvized elements, the predominant *rāga*-based segment of *nāṭya saṅgīta* falls between the *choṭā khayāla* and *bandiśa-kī-ṭhumarī* genres of art music. It therefore demands a high level of musicianship.

The theatre movement maintained close links with the stalwarts of the Hindustani art music tradition, enlisting many of them as composers, teachers, singer-actors, and accompanists on the instruments. Very successful and prosperous theatrical companies toured the length and breadth of the large Marāṭhī-speaking region of India. Their activity created the most solid regional constituency for the modern *khayāla* genre of Hindustani (north Indian) vocal music, and supported the cultivation of a massive resource-base of musicianship. Since Independence, the touring theatre company, and the musical theatrical production have both succumbed to the onslaught of the feature film and television as the dominant entertainment media. The accumulated asset of *nāṭya saṅgīta* is, however, still a formidable force in the musical culture of Maharashtra.

Nawāb : See Mahārājā/Zamīṁdāra/Sultāna.

Nom Tom : The term refers to the meaningless consonants used as articulatory material in the *ālāpa* of the *dhrupada* genre of art music, though some *gharānās* of *khayāla* vocalism also deploy this device in their preludes to the *baḍā khayāla*. The practice has its origins in the chanting of the names of Lord Viṣṇu — Oṁ, Hari, Ananta, Nārāyaṇa etc., which later gave way to meaningless consonants (*nom, tom, ta, na, ri,* etc.) encouraged partially by a religious barrier when performed by Moslem musicians, and guided partially by greater articulatory convenience in high-density melody. As a result, the *dhrupada ālāpa* is often also referred to as *nom tom ālāpa*.

Pada : The word derives its meaning from Sanskrit *padya* = verse/poetic form. The word has, however, come to be more closely associated with devotional poetry. In contemporary music, the term is used to denote not merely the poetic element but the entire poetic-melodic-rhythmic shell of compositions in the *dhrupada* genre of art music. A substantial proportion of *dhrupada* verse is no longer of devotional character. However, because of the origins of the *dhrupada* genre in the music of the Vaiṣṇavite temples, the word *pada* has been retained. In the *dhrupada* genre, the word *pada* has the same meaning as *bandiśa* in the post-*dhrupada* genres.

Padma Bhushan: Padma Bhushan is the third highest level of the "Padma" awards conferred on distinguished Indian civilians by the President of India on the occasion of the Republic Day. The Padma awards are broadly comparable to the Queen's Birthday Awards conferred by the British Sovereign on distinguished Englishmen every year.

Padma Shree: Padma Shree is the junior-most level of the "Padma" awards conferred on distinguished Indian civilians by the President of India on the occasion of the Republic Day. The Padma awards are broadly comparable to the Queen's Birthday Awards conferred by the British Sovereign on distinguished Englishmen every year.

Padma Vibhushan: Padma Vibhushan is the second highest level of the "Padma" awards conferred on distinguished Indian civilians by the President of India on the occasion of the Republic Day. The Padma awards are broadly comparable to the Queen's Birthday Awards conferred by the British Sovereign on distinguished Englishmen every year.

Paṇḍita : The word in Sanskrit for a person who commands respect in society by virtue of his knowledge of theory in his chosen field. In the music world, however, the honorific is accorded to any Hindu musician of exceptional attainments as a performer, the knowledge of theory being implicit in his musicianship. A Moslem of comparable attainments is called an *ustād*. No formalized framework exists for conferring such honorifics on musicians. They emerge through an informal process of consensus building within the community of musicians.

Parāṇa/Sura Parāṇa/Tāra Parāṇa : The *parāṇa* (etymology speculative) is the major compositional form typical of the *pakhāwaja*, the prime percussion instrument of the *dhrupada* genre. A *parāṇa* usually spans across at least two cycles of the *tāla*, and may, or may not, end in a *tihāī*. Unlike post-*dhrupada* music, the *dhrupada* genre allows the principal musician and his percussion accompanist to take-off simultaneously into improvizations/variations on the pre-composed form. The percussionist's primary deviations from the *ṭhekā* are pre-composed *parāṇa*s. They are mirrored/mimicked by the principal musician (vocalist/instrumentalist), who matches them with his own improvizations to ensure that melody and rhythm arrive synchronously at the *sama*. The matching *parāṇa* pattern performed by a vocalist is called a *sura* (melodic) *parāṇa*, while the one performed on the *Rudra vīṇā*, or any other plucked instrument is called a *tāra* (string) *parāṇa*.

Pūrvāṅga: The term derives its meaning from Sanskrit *pūrva* = early/lower + *aṅga* = limb. While the Western tradition divides the octave into two equal halves, the Indian tradition views it as consisting of three overlapping tetrachords (*aṅgas* or limbs). The lower tetrachord (*sā, re, gā, mā*) is called the *pūrvāṅga* (*pūrva* = early + *aṅga* = limb/region). The mid-octave region (*gā, mā, pā, dha*) is called the *madhyāṅga* (*madhya* = middle + *aṅga* = limb/region). The upper tetrachord (*pā, dh, nī, sā*) is called *uttarānga* (*uttara* = north + *aṅga* = limb/region).

Rabindra Sangeet : This is a modern (20th century) genre of vocal music named after the Nobel laureate poet-composer, Rabindranath Tagore. His poetry was written in his mother tongue, Bengali. Because of his calibre as a composer, his songs have attained autonomous stature independently of their poetry, and are prized also as pieces for rendition on the instruments. Tagore was well versed in *dhrupada, ṭhumarī* and *ṭappā* genres, had studied the art music tradition of south India, as also the music of the Vaiṣṇava temples. He was conversant with the folk music of his native Bengal, several parts of India, and of many Asian and European countries. His compositions represent a mix of melodic and rhythmic ideas from Indian art music traditions, along with all genres of music from various parts of the world. A lot of his music is *rāga*-based, though not categorically bound by *rāga* grammar. Despite the catholicity of his approach to composition, Tagore's compositions bear the unmistakable and inimitable imprint of his musical vision. In its vocal as well instrumental manifestations, Rabindra Sangeet is performed strictly in its pre-composed form, without any melodic or rhythmic improvization. Although Rabindra Sangeet enjoys a substantial following outside Bengal, it is primarily a regional genre of modern music.

Rāga : The word, generally used as a suffix, is Sanskrit for "attitude/quality of response/emotional content of a relationship." In music, it has come to denote a melodic idea or framework, associated with a specific quality of emotional response. The notion of *rāga*-ness is, therefore, inseparable from the concept of *rasa* in Indian aesthetics. A *rāga* is a psycho-acoustic hypothesis, which states that melody, created and rendered in accordance with a certain set of rules, has a high probability of eliciting a certain quality of emotional response. The set of rules for the creation and rendition of the melody constitute the grammar of a *rāga*. An awareness of the target response enables a musician to transcend grammar and enter the realm of literature.

As a melodic entity, a *rāga* is neither a pre-composed melody nor a mode or scale. It is represented by a set of rules governing the selection, sequencing and treatment of tones/*svaras*. These rules define a framework, which is tight enough to ensure aesthetic coherence, while also providing sufficient freedom for individual creativity. This approach to guiding the melodic content of music was necessary for a tradition, which combines the role of the composer and performer in the same individual. As a cultural choice, this approach harmonizes the competing demands of continuity within change, and unity within diversity. This enables each performed piece of music to retain a familiarity while giving audiences a substantial access to a novelty and freshness of the musical experience. Every *rāga* is a plausible psycho-acoustic hypothesis because of the accumulated experience of society, and continues to remain plausible by every musician being allowed to test it, and even revise it, at every performance. The hypothesis is perennial and ever-changing, never intending to attain the finality of a theory.

Rāga Svarūpa : The term derives from *rāga* = melodic framework + *svarūpa* = form/image. *Rāga svarūpa* is a notion of a *rāga*'s distinctive melodic personality enshrined in strings of characteristic melodic phrases — virtually melodic sentences. This approach, espoused primarily by certain lineages of *dhrupada* vocalism, is more rigid than the *calana* approach, which permits the musician greater freedom in the sequencing of phrases.

Rasa/Navarasa : The Indian aesthetic tradition views the sensory experience as a pathway to the emotional, and the emotional as a pathway to the spiritual. This reflects the fundamental transcendentalism of Hindu thought. All art is, therefore, validated by a single dominant criterion — its ability to elicit an emotional response. This criterion acknowledges that, at its most intense, the experience of beauty evokes a response that transcends its qualitative aspect, and acquires a mystical quality. This defines the potential of the artistic endeavour, and its reception, for personality transformation and spiritual evolution. At the intermediate aesthetic level, however, the tradition allows for the classification of works of art on the basis of the quality of the emotional response. The name given to these qualities is *rasa*, a metaphorical expression derived from the Sanskrit *rasa* = extract/essence/juice.

Rīyāẓa: The word is of Persian origin, and refers to the toil and penances undertaken by a musician (or any other seeker of perfection) in the pursuit of his skill/art. The cultural connotation of the term goes far beyond the number of hours of practice in a day, and extends to the personality transformation and self-discovery which result from the total immersion of the seeker in his pursuit.

Rudra Vīṇa (Also called Bīna). A member of the fretted stick-zither family of plucked instruments. A revered instrument with strong mythological and mystical associations. Evolved around the 13th century when frets were added to a fretless predecessor. The instrument is associated with the mediaeval *dhrupada/dhamāra* genre of music. It was originally used as accompaniment to vocal performances, but later acquired its independent performing domain. As *dhrupada* receded from centre-stage of art music, the *Rudra vīṇā* surrendered its place to later instruments which were ergonomically more efficient, and could adapt themselves to the contemporary environment — acoustic and stylistic.

Rūpaka Tāla : *Rūpaka* is a *tāla* (rhythmic cycle) of seven beats in 3 + 2 + 2 subdivision. Like the *dhamāra tāla*, *rūpaka* also begins on a subdued beat, and has an irregular cadential structure. For this reason, it is considered ideal for slow and medium tempo rendition in art music. Folk traditions do, however, deploy variants of the *tāla*, which are performed at a brisk tempo, though with a dented beat pattern. *Rūpaka* is generally encountered in the *khayāla* genre of vocal music and in instrumental music. A few *ṭhumarī* compositions are also composed in this *tāla*. Contemporary musicians have frequently rendered traditional compositions set to *dhamāra* of 14 beats in *rūpaka* of 7 beats.

Sama : The word is an abbreviation of the Sanskrit *samāvasthā*, a compound of two words *sama* = equilibrium + *avasthā* = state. It defines the first beat of the rhythmic cycle, at which it releases the aesthetic tension built up by its internal arrangement of beat sub-divisions and cadences. The *sama* is also the point at which the *mukhaḍā* of the *bandiśa* culminates, releasing the aesthetic tension built by its melodic design, and its interaction with the rhythmic cycle. Because it is the focal point for the synchronous release of aesthetic tension by the rhythmic as well as the melodic elements, the *sama* has a magnified cathartic value, and is critical to the aesthetics of Hindustani (north Indian) art music.

Sañcārī : The term derives its meaning from Sanskrit *sañcāra* = dispersion/diffusion. This is the third and penultimate phase in the *rāga* presentation protocol. Having been dropped as a distinct stanza in *bandiśes*, this phase of *rāga* exposition protocol now pertains only to the improvisatory movements. As the term suggests, the logic of this phase is freed from ascending-descending progression of the *sthāyī-antarā* phases, which are designed to jointly and systematically unfold the *rāga* across the entire melodic canvas. The melodic-aesthetic function of the *sañcārī* is, instead, to summarize the first two phases, while highlighting the most significant facets of the *rāga*'s melodic personality. It is, in its very character, a free-flowing phase of improvization.

Saṅgīta : The word derives its meaning from Sanskrit *saṅg* = company + *gīta* = song. The term originally referred to the totality of a song, accompanied by instrumental music as well as dance. Gradually, dance was separated from the meaning of the term, which now describes, collectively or individually, the vocal and the instrumental musical arts.

Sapāṭa Tānas : *Sapāṭa* is Hindi for "flat-out," a straight melodic run pattern with no loops or angularities. *Sapāṭa tāna*s can be descending or ascending, and of varying melodic spans.

Sāraṅgī : A member of the short-necked lute family of bowed instruments. An instrument of considerable antiquity and almost certainly of Indian origin. For centuries, the instrument, known by several names, and encountered in several forms, has been used by bards and roving minstrels for accompanying themselves. It entered art music around the 17th century, and has been an accompaniment to the modern genres of vocal music — *ṭhumarī, ṭappā* and *khayāla*. In recent years, it has begun to emerge also as a solo instrument. It is, however, threatened with extinction since the emergence of the *harmonium* as the more popular accompaniment to vocal music.

Saragama : The *saragama* derives its name from the first four solmization/ solfa symbols (*sā, re, gā, mā*) of the Hindustani scale. The use of solfa symbols as an articulatory device in vocal performance is called *saragama*. Such use is well established in the Carnatic (south Indian) tradition. Ustad Abdul Kareem Khan is credited with initiating its use in *khayāla* performance in the early 20th century. Having been only a pedagogical device until recently, it was frowned upon, by some stylistic lineages of *khayāla* vocalism, as childish. The other major genres of vocal art music — *dhrupada* and *ṭhumarī* — do not deploy this device at all. The *saragama* has proven its aesthetic potential primarily as a vehicle for medium density melody in the *baḍā* (slow-tempo) *khayāla*. Its use in low density and high density melody is limited and acceptable. Its occasional use in ultra-high density melody is pregnant with unmusical results.

Śruti: The word is a noun derived from the Sanskrit verb *śravaṇa* = hearing. A *śruti* is, therefore, a pitch that can be heard and, by implication, that which is distinguishable from others, and that which can be reproduced accurately. With twelve primary *svara*s/tones (natural, flat, and sharp), the Indian scale recognizes twenty-two *śruti*s.

Sthāyī in bandiśa : The word is Sanskrit for "stable/immoveable." The *sthāyī* in a *bandiśa* functions as the core of the *bandiśa* as well as the entire rendition, including the improvisatory movements. It is the nucleus around which the presentation revolves, and is the refrain to which the musician returns intermittently between rounds of improvization. The *sthāyī* is generally anchored either in the lower half of the melodic canvas, or in that region of it, in which falls the *rāga*'s melodic centre of gravity. As the core of the pre-composed *bandiśa*, the *sthāyī* generally identifies the *rāga* beyond reasonable doubt, though some *sthāyī*s are deliberately oblique in this respect.

Sthāyī in improvisatory movements: Improvisatory movements have a minimum of two distinct melodic sections — the *sthāyī* and *antarā*. In this context, the *sthāyī* performs a similar, though not identical, melodic-aesthetic function, as in the *bandiśa*. The improvisatory movements follow a linear rather than cyclical logic. Therefore, the *sthāyī* does not function as a refrain for intermittent repetition. The improvisatory movements are, instead, subjected to a discipline of progression. The *sthāyī* of an improvisatory movement is centred categorically in the lower half of the melodic canvas. It is required to commence with improvizations around base *sa* (the tonic/fundamental), to descend first into the lower octave, and then ascend to the scalar midpoint in deliberate steps, before returning to bases *sa*.

Sthāyī, Antarā, Sañcārī, Ābhoga : These are names of distinct phases in the *rāga* exposition protocol prescribed for sequential rendition aimed at the satisfactory communication of a *rāga*'s melodic and emotional personality in Hindustani music. In the 16th century, the legendary Miyā Tānsen enunciated them as rules of composition for *dhrupada padas* (*bandiśes*) consisting of four stanzas of verse each. The soundness of their aesthetic logic caused them to be accepted as guiding principles also for the melodic structuring and sequencing of the improvisatory component of art music. These principles are respected, to this day, in the *dhrupada* as well as post-*dhrupada* genres, though with some telescoping of protocol. The last two movements — the *sañcārī* and *ābhoga* — have been dropped from music in the post-*dhrupada* genres. In the *ālāpa* movement in vocal as well as instrumental music, the four-part protocol is still respected.

Sulatāla: *Sulatāla* is a *tāla* of ten beats with five equal sub-divisions of two beats each. It is ideally suited for fast-tempo rendition. It is an integral part of the repertoire of the *dhrupada/dhamāra* genre of art music. It is rarely, if ever, heard in other vocal genres or in instrumental music.

Svara/Tone : The word derives from Sanskrit *sva* = self + *ra* = illumination. *Svara* is, therefore, an utterance expressing the entirety of the practitioner's being, and has the potential for personality transformation. Though an avowedly subjective expression, it necessarily has certain known and measurable acoustic features. However, the Indian musical tradition also identifies two features, which pose conceptual problems. The Sanskrit texts do not define the terms for them, which are almost impossible to translate. The qualities are *dīpti*, loosely translated as luminosity, and *anuranan*, loosely translated as resonance or haunting quality. Clarity on these dimensions may have to await either an acoustically meaningful translation of these terms, or their recognition as hitherto unknown/unmeasured acoustic dimensions. This brief etymological-acoustic discussion supports the growing realization that *svara* in Hindustani music does not correspond efficiently to the Western notion of tone or a pitch-ratio relative to the tonic.

The Hindustani scale has twelve *svara*s, all of which acquire musical meaning only with reference to the tonic, arbitrarily chosen by the musician. These twelve *svara*s have names. But, the existence of standard frequency ratios for eleven of them, relative to the tonic, is debatable. Nor is it clear that their musical values depend upon the existence of such standardized acoustic relationships. There could, in reality, be stronger evidence to support the opposite argument — that their musical value depends precisely on the freedom the musician has to intone them in accordance with aesthetic, rather than acoustic, principles. This is particularly so since, as a rule, Hindustani music eschews staccato intonation.

This is consistent with the crucial difference between the Hindustani and the Western scales. The Western scale is an octave with eight fixed points, while the Hindustani scale is a *saptaka* with seven intervals covering the same tonal distance. Music-making activity in Hindustani music is focused on the handling of intervals, while Western tradition focuses its attention on handling the tonal points.

The issue here is, in fact, philosophical and cultural more than acoustic. Any cultural manifestation can be held accountable only to its own goals and values. The primary values of the Indian musical tradition are spiritual, with the aesthetic and the sensory being subservient to it. In the hierarchy of music-making goals, the primary place belongs to the generation of *rasa* at the highest possible level of intensity. A musician shapes and re-shapes *rāga*s in order to achieve the *rasa* goal. In the process, he also arranges and re-arranges relationships between the individual units of melodic expression, the *svara*s. The amorphous character of *rāga*s and the floating pitch values in Hindustani music are an essential part of a tradition that gives the musician the combined role of a composer-performer, requiring both these processes to be performed simultaneously. The *rāga* and the *svara* both have only ephemeral validity as the stimuli of an interactive process validated solely by its generation of the target emotional response, the *rasa*.

Svara-maṇḍala : The instrument is a member of the harp family and belongs to the box-polychord variety of plucked instruments. It is used as an accompaniment to vocal renditions of the *khayāla* and *ṭhumarī* genres. Unlike the *sāraṅgī* or the *harmonium*, on which melody is executed, the *svara-maṇḍala* is only strummed intermittently as a filler of silences. The strumming is done bi-directionally with grown finger nails, or guitar-style metallic or plastic picks. The instrument is not a replacement for a *tānapūrā*, and may be used either in addition to a melodic accompaniment, or exclusively. The *svara-maṇḍala* is, however, not as universally used for vocal accompaniment as is the *tānapūrā*. Attempts at establishing the *svara-maṇḍala* as a solo instrument for playing melody have so far been isolated and futile.

Tabalā : Though the name resembles a middle eastern drum called *tabalā*, the *tabalā* is a uniquely Indian instrument. The *tabalā* came into being when the *pakhāwaja*, the ancient tapering barrel drum, was split half-way in order to make the instrument easier to play. Historicity of event remains vague. The bass drum is played by the left hand, while the treble, by the right. Both drums are covered with goat-skin membranes. Both drums have a coating of iron-filings and carbon permanently affixed on the membranes. This coating is affixed in the center of the treble drum and off-centre on the bass drum. The bass drum is made of metal, while the treble drum is made of wood. The *tabalā* is now standard percussion accompaniment to all vocal and instrumental genres of Hindustani (north Indian) music, other than *dhrupada*, folk and some popular genres.

Tāla : The word derives from the Hindi *tāla* = sound of clapping with the hands. It originated in the ancient practice of keeping time with the clapping of hands, or tapping on the thighs to the accompaniment of recitations of Sanskrit hymns. Such a practice was necessary because the hymns were composed to standard metres prescribed by the literary tradition, and their poetic integrity could be preserved only by recitation at a specific tempo. In musical usage, the same function is performed by a rhythmic cycle performed on percussion instruments. Each *tāla* is a rhythmic cycle defined by its distinctive number of beats, sound symbols for percussion impact and beat-subdivisions representing its cadence. Each *tāla* also has a tempo — or a range of tempi — at which it is optimally deployed. The *tāla* also defines the metric structure of the *bandiśa*, and regulates the cyclical component of the improvisatory movements woven around it.

Tālīma: The word is of Perso-Arabic origin, and connotes the training of a musician by his mentor/*guru*/*ustād*. The cultural connotation of the word imparts a sanctity to the relationship between a mentor and his ward, irrespective of the art or craft the latter may wish to acquire from the former, and a mystical quality to the nature of the knowledge/skill being imparted.

Tāna : In contemporary usage, *tāna* refers to high density melodic patterns in the *khayāla* genre and post-*dhrupada* instrumental music. A melodic passage will be generally described as a *tāna* only if its *svara*/tone density is at least twice the beat density (tempo) of the rendition at that particular stage in the presentation of percussion-accompanied music. As a general principle, a melodic run exceeding a *svara*/tone density of four intonations per second can be called a *tāna*. In consonance with the prescribed architecture of the modern genres, *tāna*s are rendered after the rendition has passed through the presentation of low density and medium density improvisatory movements. Even within the high density *tāna*s phase of the rendition, it is considered proper for the musician to observe certain principles of logical sequencing.

Though *tāna*s are essentially a display of technical virtuosity, their melodic construction is subject to the constraints of *rāga*-grammar, and their *svara*/tone density is constrained by the requirements of musicality. It is finally the melodic imagination that goes into the construction of *tāna*s, rather than their speed, that distinguishes the truly great musician from the merely competent. The imagination works —though with varying degrees of success, no doubt — with a few basic melodic patterns which constitute the raw material of *tāna*s.

Tānapūrā : The word derives from Hindi *tāna* = a musical phrase/melodic line + Sanskrit *pūraka* = filler/supplement. This etymology defines its function in Hindustani music. It supplements the aural experience and supports the musician's effort specifically with respect to melodic creation. The instrument is standard accompaniment to vocal music, but optional in instrumental music. The instrument performs primarily a drone function as an accompaniment to music of all genres of vocal as well instrumental Hindustani art music. The instrument is a member of the long-necked family of fretless plucked lutes. In musicological texts, oblique references to it are available from the 13th century, while unambiguous references exist from the 17th century. The instrument has four, five, or six strings tuned to the middle octave and lower-octave tonic chosen by the musician, along with supplementary strings tuned to corresponding/dominant pitches as permitted by *rāga* grammar. Unlike the *svara-maṇḍala*, which is strummed only intermittently, the *tānapūrā* is plucked continuously during a performance. However, like the *svara-maṇḍala*, the *tānapūrā* does not execute melody. Both are designed for a tonally blurred acoustic output, which shapes the acoustic ambience. The *tānapūrā* is, however, valued more for its psycho-acoustic influence on the auto-suggestive and creative processes of the musician, than for the enrichment of the aural experience for listeners.

Ṭappā : The *ṭappā* is a modern semi-classical genre of vocal music. It owes its inspiration to the songs of the camel-drivers of Punjab and India's north-western frontiers. Originally a folk form, later adopted by courtesans, it was accepted in genteel society by the late 17th century. The pioneering role in the refinement of the genre is attributed to Ghulam Nabi, a late 18th-century vocalist from Lucknow, who composed under the pseudonym "Shorie Miya." The genre was enthusiastically adopted thereafter by *khayāla* as well as *ṭhumarī* singers. The identifying feature of the *ṭappā* is a vivacious, even mischievous, treatment of melody. The treatment is not only naughty within itself, but also in relation to the beat patterns of the rhythmic cycle. Like the semi-classical *ṭhumarī* genre, the *ṭappā* is also heading for extinction, though it has a better chance of revival than the former.

Tarānā : The *tarānā* (etymology speculative) is a genre of vocal music, which uses meaningless consonants as articulatory material, instead of the poetic form. Though the contemporary *tarānā* falls broadly within the *khayāla* genre, compositional forms involving the use of meaningless consonants predate the *khayāla* genre. These consonants are drawn primarily from the sound symbols used in the "language" of percussion (*dha, dhin, tirkit,* etc.) and the plucked lute family of instruments (*da, ra, dir,* etc.). The occasional use of *nom-tom* phonemes used in *dhrupada* is also encountered in *tarānā* compositions. *Tarānā*s are composed in all *rāga*s and all *tāla*s, and generally performed in medium and fast tempi. The rendition of *tarānā*s is much like the *choṭā khayāla*, though usually without virtuoso *tāna*s.

Tīnatāla (also called Tritāla) : *Tīnatāla* is a *tāla* (rhythmic cycle) of sixteen beats in four equal subdivisions. It is the single most popular *tāla* of Hindustani (north Indian) art music, more particularly in instrumental music. The primary reason for its popularity is its tested amenability to rendition at virtually any tempo — from 25 bpm to over 500 bpm. Stylized or dented versions of the *tīnatāla* — *addhā ṭhekā*, *qawwālī ṭhekā* and Punjabi *ṭhekā* — are used in the *ṭhumarī* genre.

Ṭhekā: Every *tāla* (rhythmic cycle) played on the *tabalā* or *pakhāwaja* is defined by sound syllables representing the strokes on the two surfaces of the drums. These sound syllables and corresponding stroke patterns represent the internal arrangement of sub-divisions and cadences characteristic of the *tāla*. This standard form of the *tāla*, without any improvization or stylization, is called the *ṭhekā*. Several *tāla*s have *ṭhekā* variants. The immensely popular *tīnatāla*, for instance, has stylized variants variously called *addhā ṭhekā*, Panjabi *ṭhekā* and *qawwāli ṭhekā*.

Ṭhumarī : The word derives from an onomatopoeic expression *ṭhumaka* signifying the sound of anklet bells of a dancer. The *ṭhumarī* is a modern genre of semi-classical music, which originated as an accompaniment to the Kathaka genre of north Indian dance, and evolved into an independent art form. The genre subsumes two sub-genres — a brisk and lively form called *bandiśa-kī-ṭhumarī*, and a leisurely sentimental form called *bola-baṇāva ṭhumarī*. The thematic content of the genre revolves around the mythical romance between Lord Kṛṣṇa, an incarnation of Lord Viṣṇu, and his paramour, Rādhā. In the cult of Rādhā and Kṛṣṇa, the romance is viewed as a metaphor for the intimate relationship between God, representing the male/active principle, and man representing the female/passive principle. The *bandiśa-kī-ṭhumarī* reached its zenith in the mid-19th century and was nearly extinct by the early 20th century. The *bola-banāva ṭhumarī* acquired the status of a mainstream genre in the early 20th century, and is now headed for extinction.

Tigunā/Triguna : The word derives its meaning from *tri* or *ti* = three + *gunā* = multiple. When any melody is performed at a melodic (*svara*) density three times the beat density (tempo) of accompanying percussion, or the base tempo of the *bandiśa*, the expression is called *triguna/tigunā*. The highest ratio of *svara* density to beat density practised in Hindustani music is eight times. (Also see Bandiśa).

Tīhāī : The word derives from the Hindi *tīna* = three. The repetitive iteration of any melodic, rhythmic, melodic-rhythmic, or choreographic pattern exactly three times is called a *tīhāī*. Its purpose is to create rhythmic interest by building up and releasing aesthetic tension within a very short period of time, normally less than a minute. The triplet form which probably originated in the choreographic art, was mimicked by the percussion art which accompanied it and finally found its way into melodic expression. The *tīhāī* is a rhythmic expression which may be interpreted choreographically, rhythmically, or melodically. The number of iterations in a *tīhāī* (three) has a very definite aesthetic significance, which cannot be fulfilled by any other number of iterations of the pattern.

Tilvāḍā : *Tilvāḍā* is a *tāla* (rhythmic cycle) of sixteen beats in four equal sub-divisions. It is suited for slow and ultra slow rendition in the *khayāla* genre of vocal music. The *tilvāḍā* tempo rarely exceeds 20 bpm.

Urdu : A dialect of Hindi, the mainstream north Indian language, with a substantial presence of Persian and Arabic vocabulary, but only minor syntactical influence. The dialect is written in the Persian script. The name derives from the Turkish word "Urd" = the market in a military camp. This suggests its origins amongst settling soldiers from conquering Middle Eastern armies. Unlike Persian, Urdu never became a language of the feudal courts in India. However, the dialect did trigger off a major literary flowering during the colonial era (19th and early 20th centuries) primarily through the *ghaẓala* genre.

Ustād : The word is Persian for a teacher. In the music world, it signifies a Moslem musician of sufficient attainments to qualify as a teacher. A Hindu of comparable attainments is called a *Paṇḍit*. No formalized framework exists for conferring such honorifics on musicians. They emerge through an informal process of consensus building within the community of musicians.

Uttarāṅga: The term derives its meaning from Sanskrit *uttara* = northern/ upper + *aṅga* = limb. While the Western tradition divides the octave into two equal halves, the Indian tradition views it as consisting of three overlapping tetrachords (*aṅga*s or limbs). The lower tetrachord (*sā, re, gā, mā*) is called the *pūrvāṅga* (*pūrva* = early + *aṅga* = limb/region). The mid-octave region (*gā, mā, pā, dha*) is called the *madhyāṅga* (*madhya* = middle + *aṅga* = limb/region). The upper tetrachord (*pā, dha, nī, sā*) is called *uttarāṅga* (*uttara* = north + *aṅga* = limb/region).

Vilambita (or vilambita laya) : Adjective derived from Sanskrit *vilamba* = delay. In music, it is used to describe slow-tempo rendition. For ultra-slow tempo renditions, the term used is *ati-vilambita* (*ati* = extreme). The notion of slowness, or briskness, is relative and dynamic. It differs between generations, between stylistic lineages, between different genres of vocal music, and between vocal and instrumental music.

Zamīṅdāra : See Mahārājā/Nawāb/Sultāna.

Zamzama : See Jamajama.

Index

Ali, Fateh, 230-31, 236, 247

Ali, Naushad, 244

All India Radio, 41, 52-53, 55, 71, 82, 85, 92, 117, 128, 138, 141, 148, 158, 161, 167, 193, 199, 201, 212, 224, 238

Alurmath, Neelkanth Buwa, 200

Amonkar, Kishori, 11, 14, 63, 102, 104, 106, 112, 123, 128-29, 132, 143, 146-148, 157-164, 166, 172, 209, 223, 227, 245

Anklikar-Tikekar, Arti 112, 157-165

Asif, K, 244

Asnare-Kelkar, Manjiri 112, 166-175

Athavle, VR, 43, 71

Bai, Inayeti, 237

Bakhle, Bhaskar Buwa, 95, 114, 213-14

Baksh, Ali, 230-31, 236, 247

Baksh, Mir (Kale Khan), 231, 236, 237, 240

Balasubramaniam, G.N., 238

Bandhu, Khan, 126

Bannerjee, Krishnachandra, 62

Baroda University, 53

Barodekar, Hirabai, 132, 162, 180

Begum, Rosharnara, 109, 121, 180, 191, 196, 252, 255

Bhabha Atomic Research Centre, 148

Bhat, SCR, 43, 85

Bhide, Manik, 147, 156

Bhide-Deshpande, Ashwini, 112, 146-156

Bose, Sushil, 194

Chakravarty, Girijashankar, 64

Chatterjee, Bhishmadev, 62

Chaurasia, Hariprasad, 63

Classicism, 14, 92, 129, 137, 145, 146, 223

Compound ragas, 105-106, 108, 133, 134, 182

Corbusier, Le, 121

Dagar, Behram Khan, 231

Dastur, Phiroze, 96, 180

Datar, Narayanrao, 147

Derrida, Jacques, 67

Desai, Morarji, 238

Dev, Ramkrishna, 72

Devi, Girija, 140

Devi, Siddheshwari, 40, 121, 234
Dey, Manna, 35

Gandharva Mahavidyalaya, 83
Gandharva, Chhota, 85
Gandharva, Kumar, 14, 63-65, 150-153, 187, 199, 204-205, 213-14, 223, 227, 245
Gandharva, Sawai, 96, 187, 191, 216
Gharana, Agra, 5, 18-20, 28-33, 35-36, 39, 41-44, 47-48, 50-53, 55-57, 59, 64, 70-71, 74, 77-79, 81, 89-90, 92, 94-95, 97, 105, 110, 124, 135, 138, 141, 160, 163-64, 183, 185, 188, 197, 213-14, 218, 223, 250, 252, 254
Gharana, Atrauli, 28, 31-32, 45, 52, 55, 58, 90
Gharana, Bhendi Bazar, 18-19, 62, 64-65, 183-84, 252, 255, 257
Gharana, Gwalior, 5, 18-19, 39, 43, 57, 62, 64, 70, 74, 78-81, 83, 88-92, 94-95, 97, 99, 102, 124, 129, 138, 147, 157, 160-61, 163, 164, 172-174, 179, 189, 190, 194, 199-200, 203, 213-14, 220, 237, 250, 254
Gharana, Indore, 18-19, 141, 183
Gharana, Jaipur-Atrauli, 5, 18, 19, 42, 57, 70, 73-74, 76-81, 90, 94-95, 98, 102-109, 111-12, 116, 124-25, 129, 133, 135-137, 140, 142-144, 148-49, 155-56, 160, 163, 166, 168, 171, 173, 183, 197-98, 201, 203, 213-14, 243
Gharana, Kairana, 5, 18-20, 30, 42, 57, 59, 62, 70-71, 75, 80, 90, 98-99, 106-07, 109, 110, 124, 132, 135, 146, 142, 163, 178-192, 193-198, 199, 200, 202, 203, 207-08, 214, 218, 252-254
Gharana, Kasur, 231
Gharana, Patiala, 18-20, 57, 183, 194, 195, 197, 223, 230-232, 246, 248, 252, 254, 257
Gharana, Rampur-Sahaswan, 18, 191-92, 220, 227
Gharana, Rangeele, 28, 31-32, 35-36, 62, 64
Gharana, Shyam Chaurasiya, 252, 257
Ghosh, Gyan Prakash, 167
Ghosh, Shantideb, 194
Ginde, K.G., 43, 85
Goddard, Jean Luc, 67
Government of India, 94
Government of Maharashtra, 115
Guha, Sumitra, 193-198
Gurav, Ganpatrao, 213-14
Gurav, Sangameshwar, 188-91, 196, 212-13
Gwalior-Agra confluence, 20, 43, 70, 74, 76, 82-83, 92
Hangal, Gangubai, 96, 162, 180, 187, 217

Hunter College, New York, 52
Hussain, Akhtar, 231, 247
Ichalkaranjikar, Balkrishna Buwa, 72, 83
Jadhav, D.B., 137-38, 142
Jadhav, Lakshmibai, 108-111, 125, 130-135, 172
Jadhav-Gatlewar, Vijaya, 112, 137-145, 174
Janakiraman, SR, 194
Janorikar, T.D., 62, 65
Jasraj, 14, 153, 222-23, 227-28, 245
Joglekar, Vijaya, 160
Joshi, Anant Manohar, 72, 77
Joshi, Bhimsen, 63-64, 96, 180, 187, 191, 196, 201, 203, 219, 227-28
Joshi, Gajananrao, 43, 71, 74, 77-80, 94-95, 97-98, 143
Joshi, Yashwant Buwa, 43, 81-92
Kaikini, Dinkar, 43, 159, 160, 164
Kanetkar, Madhusudan (Appa), 107, 112, 168-69, 171
Kannan, A., 191, 193, 195
Kannan, Malavika, 191, 193, 195
Kashalkar, Ulhas, 77, 80-81, 93-100, 160, 165
Kelkar, Yashwant, 117
Kerkar, Kesarbai, 40, 54, 63, 96-102-03, 107-109, 111-127, 130, 131, 133-35, 162, 172, 233
Khan, Abdul Kareem, 40, 42, 75, 114, 140, 179, 184-87, 191, 194, 203, 211, 213-14, 216, 223, 234, 239, 240, 252
Khan, Abdul Majid, 117, 126
Khan, Abdul Waheed, 179, 183-187, 200, 206, 209
Khan, Ali Akbar, 63
Khan, Alladiya, 42, 76, 102-105, 107, 111, 114, 121, 124, 129, 131, 138, 143, 149
Khan, Aman Ali, 65, 183-84, 255
Khan, Amanat Ali, 231, 246-249, 251-52
Khan, Ameer, 19, 40, 42, 48, 50, 58, 64, 96, 107, 115, 123, 161, 163, 180, 185-86, 190, 192, 209, 220, 221, 228, 233-35, 255
Khan, Amjad Amanat Ali, 247
Khan, Amjad Fateh Ali, 247
Khan, Asad Amanat Ali, 247
Khan, Ata Hussain 46, 54-56
Khan, Azizuddin (Baba), 130-31
Khan, Baba Shinde, 237
Khan, Badal, 64
Khan, Bade Gulam Ali, 35, 38-40, 42, 115, 123, 161, 186, 198, 201, 208, 209, 222, 231-45, 247-250, 252, 254
Khan, Bade Mohammed, 71
Khan, Barkat Ali, 231, 234
Khan, Barkatullah, 114, 121, 124

Khan, Bhurji (Shamsuddin), 77, 103-04, 130-31, 134, 136, 172
Khan, Bismillah, 63
Khan, Chhote Muhammad, 72
Khan, Daulat, 102-03
Khan, Enayet Hussain, 28, 220
Khan, Faiyyaz, 28-29, 31-32, 34-43, 44-47, 49-50, 53, 56, 71, 76, 90, 113, 115, 141-42, 233-34, 238, 243
Khan, Faiyyaz Ahmed, 181, 207, 256
Khan, Fateh Ali, 231, 246-257
Khan, Fida Hussain, 36
Khan, Gulam Abbas, 36
Khan, Haddu, 71, 179, 220, 231, 250, 256
Khan, Hyder, 103-04, 108, 111, 130, 131, 220
Khan, Hamid Ali Nawab, 220
Khan, Hassu, 71-72, 75
Khan, Imrat, 62
Khan, Janggu, 28
Khan, Jehangir, 102-03
Khan, Kallan, 36
Khan, Khadim Hussain, 39
Khan, Latafat Hussain, 39, 250, 252
Khan, Liaqat Hussain, 45
Khan, Manji (Badruddin), 103-04
Khan, Mashkoor, Ali, 185, 191, 206-211
Khan, Mubarak Ali, 102-03, 231, 256
Khan, Munawwar Ali, 231, 239
Khan, Mushtaq Hussain, 220
Khan, Nasruddin (Badeji), 103
Khan, Natthan, 103, 129, 131, 138
Khan, Natthe, 71
Khan, Nazakat Ali, 252, 257
Khan, Nissar Hussain, 72, 75, 191, 220, 224-26
Khan, Niyaz Ahmed, 185, 207, 209, 256
Khan, Rajab Ali, 141, 183-84
Khan, Ramzan "Rangeele" 28
Khan, Rashid, 191, 219-228
Khan, Rehmat, 179
Khan, Salamat Ali, 252, 257
Khan, Shahmir, 183
Khan, Shakoor, 185, 191, 206, 208
Khan, Sharafat Hussain, 32, 41, 42, 44-51, 54, 56-57, 188, 225, 252
Khan, Tanras, 209, 230-31, 249, 256
Khan, Vilayat Hussain, 42, 46, 54-56, 71, 76-77, 88, 95, 141, 142, 225
Khan, Yunus Hussain, 42, 50, 53, 56, 252
Khudabaksh, Ghaghe, 28
Kulkarni, Dhondutai, 103, 107, 108, 112, 116, 122, 125, 127, 128-136, 166, 172
Kulkarni, Vasantrao, 160

Kumar, Kaivalya, 212-218
Kundera, Milan, 67, 68
Kurdikar, Mogubai, 71, 104, 108-09, 111, 121, 125, 129, 142, 243
Maharashtra Music School, 147
Mangeshkar, Lata, 35
Mansoor, Mallikarjun, 85, 91, 100, 104, 106
Marathe, Ram, 71, 84, 94, 97
Mardur, Kumar, 199
Mardur, Somnath, 191, 199-205
Marjit, Sugata, 32, 60-68
Marris College of Music, 43
Mhaiskar, Chintu Buwa, 167-68
Mirashi, Yashwant Sadashiv, 72, 83-84
Modernism, 219, 223
Muley, Dashrathrao, 142

Naik, Govardhan Buwa, 83
National Centre for the Performing Arts, 126, 139
Neo-Agra, 47, 48, 57
Neo-Jaipur-Atrauli, 59, 90, 99, 110, 112, 129, 132, 136, 157, 160, 172
Neo-Kairana, 107, 178, 183, 185, 192, 207, 209, 220, 227

Pai, Ratnakar, 148, 149
Paluskar, D.V. (Dattatraya Vishnu), 42, 63, 73, 91, 115, 147, 194, 225, 233
Paluskar, Vishnu Digambar, 72, 83, 87
Pande, Malti, 71
Pandit, Eknath, 72
Pandit, Krishnarao Shankar, 39, 73, 75, 76, 115, 142
Pandit, Lakshman Krishnarao, 73
Pandit, Shankararao, 72, 73
Pathak, Balaram, 62
Patwardhan, Vinayakrao, 62, 74, 75
Phulambrikar, Master Krishnarao, 85
Pir Baksh, Natthan, 71
Poonchhwale, Rajabhaiya, 72
Post-modernism, 14, 60, 61, 66
Post-structuralism, 14, 67
Prem Piya, 35
Prem Rang, 45
Purohit, Jaggannath Buwa, 43, 74, 76, 77, 85, 89

Rababi, Bhai Kalu, 230
Raja, Babubhai (Hargovind), 126, 127
Rajguru, Basavraj, 188-89, 191, 194, 200, 202
Rajurkar, Malini, 168
Ramakrishna Mission, 61
Rao, K. Nagesh, 160
Ratanjankar, S.N., 43, 160
Romanticism, 14, 92, 107, 129, 137, 145, 146, 223, 245

Sab Rang, 238

Saigal K.L. (Kundanlal), 35, 40

Sangeet Natak Akademi, 6, 45, 115, 128, 139, 166, 194, 239

Sangeet Research Academy, 94, 97, 138, 191, 206, 220

Sarnaik, Nivrutti Buwa, 85, 112, 137, 140, 141, 142, 143

Sarnaik, Shankararao, 140

Sen, Purnima, 32, 46, 47, 52-59, 138

Shankar, Ravi, 63, 150

Swami, Panchakshari, 200

Swami, Veerappayya, 200

Tagore, Rabindranath, 115

Talwalkar, Suresh, 161

Tansen, Miya, 244

Thakur, Omkarnath, 42, 63, 70, 115, 160, 233

Vasudeo Buwa, 72

Vaze, Ramkrishna Buwa, 74-75, 78, 114, 121

Vishwa Bharati University, 193-94

Wright, Frank Lloyd, 123